PRAISE FOR TAHOE DEATHFALL

"THRILLING, EXTENDED RESCUE/CHASE...
Easygoing, self-confident Owen provides the perfect
counterpoint to the menacing forces arrayed
against his teenaged client...a practiced debut."
- Kirkus Reviews

"HIGHLY LIKABLE CHARACTERS...
It's likely (Borg) will graduate to the hardcover
big leagues before long."
- John Orr, San Jose Mercury News

"THRILLER SCORES...TWISTS AND TURNS...
The writing is crisp and often funny."
- Sam Bauman, Nevada Appeal

"A TREMENDOUS READ from a great writer."
- Shelley Glodowski, Midwest Book Review

"TWO THUMBS UP...NAIL-BITING ACTION...
One of the best I have read for quite some time."
- Timothy Barr, Colfax Area Express

"TAUT MYSTERY...A SCREECHING CLIMAX."
- Karen Dini, Addison Public Library, Addison, IL

"BORG OFFERS A SIMPLY TERRIFIC DOG...Borg has a
warm, easy style...a gift for plot."
- Barbara Peters, The Poisoned Pen

"McKENNA IS BRIGHT AND WITTY...SPOT IS A
wonderfully drawn character."
- Marty Steinberg, Deadly Pleasures

LIBRARIAN'S CHOICE BEST FICTION, 2001
- Cincinnati Public Library

WINNER, BEST THRILLER
- Bay Area Independent Publishers Association

PRAISE FOR TAHOE ICE GRAVE

"BAFFLING CLUES...Owen, a wry courtly sleuth of the old school, consistently entertains."
- Kirkus Reviews

"A CLEVER PLOT AND AN INTRIGUING MIX of Hawaiian, Native American and Western culture... a spectacular setting, a charming Great Dane who likes microwaved treats...Recommend this mystery to readers who like puzzlers set in stunning, exotic country."
- Booklist

"A BIG THUMBS UP...Mr. Borg's plots are super-twisters...(Owen, Spot and Street) make for a winning combination of grit, intelligence, strength, and tenderness."
- Shelley Glodowski, Midwest Book Review

"THIS ACTION-PACKED STORY definitely holds your attention...I find myself eagerly awaiting the next edition in this series." Chosen one of Wedgwood's Top 5 books of 2002.
- Gayle Wedgwood, Mystery News

"GREAT CHARACTERS, LOTS OF ACTION and some clever plot twists...Readers have to figure they are in for a good ride, and Todd Borg does not disappoint."
- John Orr, San Jose Mercury News

"OWEN McKENNA...a forensic-entomologist girl friend and a Great Dane named Spot...a formidable team..."
- Laurie Trimble, Dallas Morning News

"ENTERTAINING AND OFTEN WITTY...a most entertaining read...the climax is bloody and spine-tingling."
- Sam Bauman, Nevada Appeal

"A WELL-WRITTEN STORY about the wonders of nature and the dark corners of some men's minds."
- The Raven, Kate's Mystery Books, Cambridge, MA

"AN ABSORBING WHODUNIT...a dynamite climax."
- *Catherine Abel, Tahoe Mountain News*

"TWISTS AND TURNS...WEALTH OF well-drawn characters...suspenseful and nail-biting conclusion."
- *Joan Walthall, National League of American Pen Women*

"ONCE YOU READ AN OWEN McKENNA NOVEL, YOU'RE HOOKED FOR LIFE!"
- *Karen Dini, Addison Public Library, Addison IL*

"A CLEVER PLOT, A SPINE-TINGLING CLIMAX."
- *Susan DeRyke, Bookshelf Stores*

PRAISE FOR TAHOE KILLSHOT

"A WONDERFUL BOOK containing fascinating characters, hard-hitting action, a fast-paced plot and believable dialog."
- *Gayle Wedgwood, Mystery News*

"A GREAT READ!"
- *Shelley Glodowski, Midwest Book Review*

"BORG BELONGS ON THE BESTSELLER LISTS with Parker, Paretsky and Coben."
- *Merry Cutler, Annie's Book Stop, Sharon, Massachusetts*

"A WINNER"
- *Tom Williams, Placerville Mountain Democrat*

"KEPT ME TURNING PAGE AFTER PAGE. I highly recommend the Owen McKenna mystery series."
- *Donna Clark, Librarian, Odessa College Library, Odessa, Texas*

"SPOT ROCKS!"
- *Nancy Oliver Hayden, Tahoe Daily Tribune*

"KEEP 'EM COMING, BORG. Offers all the pleasure of sitting down with an old friend to hear another good story. And it is a good story."
- *Sam Bauman, Nevada Appeal*

TAHOE SILENCE

Other Titles by Todd Borg:

TAHOE DEATHFALL
TAHOE BLOWUP
TAHOE ICE GRAVE
TAHOE KILLSHOT

TAHOE SILENCE

by

TODD BORG

THRILLER PRESS

First Thriller Press Edition, August 2007

TAHOE SILENCE
Copyright © 2007 by Todd Borg

Library of Congress Control Number: 2006911140

ISBN: 978-1-931296-15-1

Cover design and map by Keith Carlson.

Manufactured in the United States of America

For Kit

AUTHOR'S NOTE

This novel is about a girl with an unusual variation of autism. While I've written about autism as accurately as I could, nothing about autism or about any child with autism should be inferred from this story. Nevertheless, I've tried to show the trials and triumphs that people with autism, and the people who care for them, experience.

ACKNOWLEDGEMENTS

Thanks to Pam Bloedoorn for explaining how the Special Education system works. For those areas of the educational system that I got correct, the credit belongs with her. Any mistakes are all mine.

Thanks to Liz Johnston for great editing. Without her help, this book would be scattershot with mistakes and glitches.

Thanks also to Eric Berglund for editing. He knows English like Strunk and White, and he helped fix many problems.

Thanks to Keith Carlson for a great cover. Ominous and dark, this cover is superb.

As always, special thanks to Kit. She does the first and last read and helps makes the story work. I write it for her, and she makes it all worthwhile.

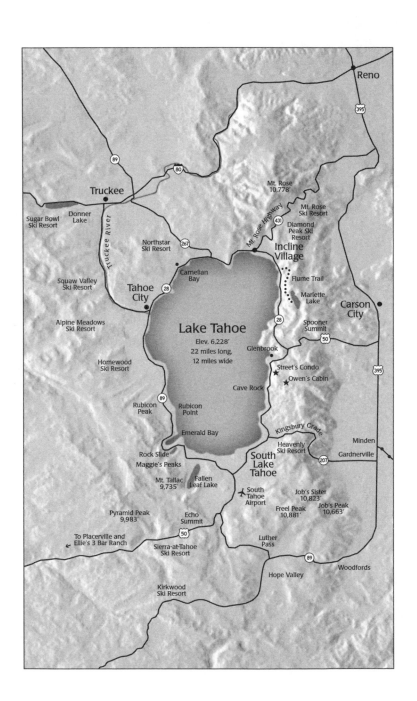

PROLOGUE

At the first roar of the motorcycles on Pioneer Trail, Silence shut her eyes, tucked her sketchbook under her left arm and plugged her ears with her fingers, turning inward, retreating to her safe zone. She took a deep breath and dropped her head toward the ground as if she were meditating. She rotated on the ball of her left foot and propelled herself by pushing off with her right foot.

Her pace began as a leisurely adagio drumbeat. One one-thousand, two one-thousand, three one-thousand...

Each slow push was forceful enough to rotate her body 360 degrees. She pushed off again, her foot landing on the exact same spot each time she came around.

Soon she picked up the pace. Andante.

As the motorcycles grew louder Silence accelerated like a conductor gradually building the tempo. Spinning kept the bikers and their ear-ripping noise at the fringes of her awareness, as if by centrifugal force. She went faster, then faster still until eventually she was spinning in a blur and her foot was slapping the gravel of the driveway. Allegro.

Silence knew the musical terms from the visit to Sacramento a couple weeks before. Not counting Reno and Carson City, it was her first time out of Tahoe. Every detail was still vivid.

One detail came back to her now. The radio was on, tuned to a classical station and a show about music tempo. The announcer was describing musicians playing to different beats. He talked about beats that were stately and classical, worthy of a grand orchestra in a big city concert hall. Some beats were forceful and driven like those of a marching band on the gridiron at a college football game. And some beats hopped and jumped around like a bluegrass fiddler at a country dance in the hills of coal mining country. The announcer's descriptions made pictures of tempo.

It was the same way Silence saw musical time and movement. In pictures. Silence's entire world was made of pictures.

Moderato. Prestissimo. Everything had a beat, and she could see the beats.

Some of the bikers on Pioneer Trail slowed as they approached the street where Silence lived. But Silence didn't notice. She was lost in her spin, in the pictures of rhythm.

Silence didn't know the words of tempo to speak them. Speech, or even sign language, was something inaccessible to her, in the same way that playing improvisations on the tenor sax or piano was inaccessible. But like music and beats, she knew how words sounded and what they meant by the pictures they made.

The radio announcer even talked about some people seeing pictures when they heard sounds. He called it synesthesia.

Silence held those pictures in her mind as she spun.

Other people didn't understand spinning. Especially her mother Marlette, who tried to stop her, tried from the time Silence was a little girl to derail her impulse to spin.

It didn't matter. Spinning shut out a world of far too many inputs that assailed her hyper-sensitive nervous system. If she opened her eyes when spinning – something she almost never did – everything would be comfortably blurred. The crush of detail that overwhelmed her vision would be gone. Spinning pushed away the scouring brightness of the sun and the burning glare that bounced off cars and windows and water. The sharp smells that caused her sinuses to fill were softened on the circular breeze of her own making. The sounds that so often stabbed at her ears and made her cry became jumbled in the Doppler shift of spin, and they lost some of their harshness. Spinning even soothed the constant burning itch of her hot skin, washing her arms and legs in a rush of cool air. And the choking, throat-cracking dryness in her mouth went away, replaced by the soft spiraling wind.

Although the outside world was gone to her now, Silence heard her brother calling. Charlie's was the only voice that could penetrate her spin.

"SalAnne, stop spinning! Come inside. Some of those bikers turned down our road. They're looking at you!"

But Silence knew that if she stopped, the world would close in on her, nothing but sharp edges making her flinch and recoil. Spinning could keep it away. She worked her foot harder. Turned even faster.

Without actually counting, she nevertheless kept track of her revolutions. It was automatic, the same way a musician always knows where she is in a twelve-bar blues or a thirty-two-bar waltz or an eight-bar pop song. If someone had asked, Silence would know she was at twenty-seven revolutions, a moment later, twenty-nine. Though she couldn't have said the words.

"SALANNE!" Charlie yelled.

Whenever Silence didn't respond Charlie yelled louder. Everybody talked way too loud. And because she didn't talk back, they talked louder as if she were deaf. It only made her withdraw more.

"SILENCE!"

That was unusual, coming from Charlie. Everybody else who knew her well called her Silence. But not Charlie. Her brother always called her SalAnne. He thought her nickname was the one thing that was too focused on her way. That was how he phrased it. He always said things like, "I know it ain't your way, Sal, but other people like to touch each other. It's how they show they care. They touch you. I know it makes your skin burn, but you gotta get used to it." Or, "Sal, your way of not looking at someone's eyes when they talk helps you think. I know that. Your way works for you. But other people got different wiring.

They think you should look them right in the eyes. It's hard, but you gotta try."

Charlie was the only one who even knew her way.

Her mother didn't, never had. Marlette was like the video camera she constantly pointed in Silence's face. Her mother was deeply engrossed in a world that she arranged for the camera and she ignored everything that happened outside the picture frame. Marlette wanted to live in a make-believe place, a place like her videos where unhappy moments didn't exist.

But Charlie lived in the real world, and he helped Silence get through the tough times. He was her personal valet, attending to her every need. He was a mind reader. Even though he was three years younger, Charlie knew what helped her to function. Reduce the inputs. Keep it basic. And always, always keep it quiet.

"You call her Silence," he'd say to their mother. "Didn't you ever wonder why she doesn't speak? You know she understands what you say. Maybe not the same way the rest of us hear words, but you know the comprehension is there even if it's jumbled up. Well, maybe she doesn't talk because she likes it quiet. Maybe you could learn to not have the TV blaring all day long. You know how she always goes to her room to draw whenever you turn that thing on. Did you ever think of reading a book? Maybe if you tried things her way, you'd understand her better."

"SILENCE!" Charlie shouted again.

Silence was spinning so fast her name was just a distant voice on the wind. If she slowed, the motorcycle roar would pierce her ears and suck the air out of her lungs and send electricity through her brain.

She kept spinning as the roar intensified, bass rumbles shaking her chest, reaching through the spin barrier and searing her nerves.

She kept her eyes shut as Charlie grabbed her, stopped her spinning and tried to pull her away.

Suddenly, a blast of hot air, thick with odors of gas and exhaust, blew over her.

Charlie yelled something, but not to Silence.

She heard him grunt, but she couldn't open her eyes. The motorcycles were too loud.

Then Charlie grabbed her again. A bear hug. Silence smelled some kind of leathery cologne mixed with sweat and sour body odor.

But Charlie never wore cologne.

Silence tried to pull away, but the bear hug grew tighter and lifted her up. Other hands grabbed her ankles, big hands, rough as tree bark. They lifted her legs off the ground. She kicked and twisted to the left. Jerked her head and body like a hooked fish. Jammed her right elbow back into soft belly flesh.

Everything familiar in her life was suddenly gone. Panic rushed over her like a cold surf holding her under, drowning her. She gasped for air and clutched her sketchbook with all of her strength as they hauled her away.

ONE

"Mr. McKenna! Mr. McKenna!"

The words were tiny against Spot's sudden barking.

"Mr. McKenna!" A yelled whisper. Female.

I turned in bed, pulled at sheets that were twisted around my left leg. Looked at the red numbers on my alarm clock. 4:00 a.m.

"Mr. McKenna!" Rapid pounding on the door.

"Holdonaminit," I called out, my words garbled. I freed my leg from the sheets and sat up. The room tilted.

"Mr. McKenna! Wake up!" Thuds echoed through my cabin, loud enough to suggest bloody knuckles.

"Gimmeeasec," I shouted.

I pulled on a robe and stumbled into my little living room.

Spot was at the front door, reaching his giant head up five feet high, growling and barking.

"Easy," I said, grabbing the loose skin of his neck to let him know he could cool down.

I turned the bolt and pulled the door toward me. Flipped on the switch for the outside light.

A woman stood in the glare of the yellow bulb. A thick serape wrapped her shoulders and torso, covering most of her blue work shirt and part of her faded green khakis. Veins roped her brown hands, which clutched the edges of the woven fabric. Her fingers were long and graceful but callused. She was very thin, thinner even than Street Casey, and she shivered in the cold

October night air.

"Mr. McKenna, you have to help me!" she said. Black eyes scorched the air between us.

I once knew a Washoe Indian woman whose eyes, when angry, had flecks of orange light behind the blackness, like obsidian on fire. This woman had the same eyes.

Spot pushed through the doorway. The woman was tall, but still he could reach up and sniff her chin.

The woman glared at him but didn't recoil.

"My babies are gone! They took them! You have to find them!"

I stared at her, trying to wake up.

"Will you!" She screamed.

"C'mon inside," I mumbled, trying to gain a moment for my brain to come to life, circadian rhythms at the lowest dip on the sleep curve.

We walked into the dark. She hesitated behind me and I realized I should turn on some lights. I hit the kitchen switch. Spot put his nose on her, up and down.

"Got coffee," I said. "Takes a minute." I'd loaded it four hours earlier. I pushed the button.

"You have to help me," she said, her voice high and strident. "I've got nowhere to turn. You have to..."

I held up my hand. "Wait."

The woman stood rigid at the entrance to my kitchen nook. Her eyes were wild, ransacking my homemade butcher block table and Shaker chairs, the old, yellowed plastic coffee maker, the ancient propane stovetop, the chipped kitchen sink. I didn't know who had put her onto me, but I was pretty sure I wasn't measuring up to her expectations.

I didn't struggle to pull Spot away from her. A person who barges into a dog's cabin in the middle of the night has to expect the standard canine inspection, even if the nose of a 170-pound Harlequin Great Dane is six times bigger, wetter, and colder than that of your average dog.

Her eyes narrowed and radiated impatience. Her smooth

redwood skin was strung tight on two sharp cheekbones that were set up high and wide and gave her a warrior's countenance.

Spot was sniffing her feet, long, narrow and sockless in running shoes. Her ankles were like Street's, smooth skin over nothing but bone and sinew. Shaped to intrigue running coaches and seduce artists.

I pointed to one of the chairs. "Sit," I said. "I'm going to change into some clothes."

I went into the bedroom and pulled on jeans and a flannel shirt. I went into the bathroom and splashed cold water on my face. She was still standing when I came back out. Spot had lost olfactory interest and was lying at her feet. The coffee was done. I grabbed two mugs and poured. I put the mugs on the table and sat down. "Black okay?" I said.

She stared at me, wordless with fury at my slow transition to wakefulness.

"Sit," I said again. My brain was still wandering. The coffee would work in a few minutes.

She stepped over Spot, pulled the chair back and lowered herself down to the seat. She didn't bend but kept her back straight like someone with dance training. She crossed her very good ankles under the chair. I remembered the Alvin Ailey dance performance Street had taken me to in Oakland. Put this woman in dance slippers and she'd fit right in.

I gulped coffee. Too bitter and too strong. Perfect.

"I can't wait forever while you drink your coffee," she said, exasperated. "Are you awake, yet? My kids are gone and you look like you're about to order eggs. Are you going to help me or not!"

"You're a dancer," I said.

She flinched, an involuntary look of disgust. Her lip lifted in a little sneer.

"Ankles," I said. "Posture while you sit. And you're too thin."

"Years ago," she finally said.

"What's your name?"

"Marlette Remmick."

"What happened, Marlette?"

"They were kidnapped!"

"Who?"

"I told you! My daughter and son. SalAnne and Charlie."

"When?"

"This afternoon."

"Where?"

"Out of my front yard."

"Did you call the police?"

"Yes, of course. I dialed nine-one-one immediately. They came. Two young men questioned me, then two more after a few minutes. They took notes and talked on their radios. One of them went outside and talked to the neighbors. But they didn't do anything to find my kids. Then a woman cop came. They called her sergeant. But she was as worthless as the others. After an hour an SUV arrived. Plain, without any markings. A middle-aged guy got out. He was a cop, but he didn't wear a uniform. He didn't do anything, either." She squeezed her hands in each other, twisting her fingers as if to wring out her psychic pain. "You have to help me! I've got nowhere else to go."

"How did you get my address?"

"The older cop. He said that if I was unhappy with how the cops were handling it, I could call you, that you used to be a cop and now you were private. He said I could hire you."

"What was his name?"

"Commander Mallory."

"Mallory gave you my address?"

"No, he just said you lived in Tahoe, over on the east side. He only gave me your name and phone number. So I called and called. But you never answered. Why would you do that? Not answer or return my call?"

I pointed to the corner of the kitchen where the answering machine pulsed an incessant red light like a miniature emergency vehicle. "I was working and got home late. I don't usually listen to messages or return calls at midnight. You didn't answer my question about my address."

Marlette looked annoyed. In an obvious effort to calm herself she drank some coffee. "When you didn't answer or call back, I started calling everyone I knew who lives or works on the east side and asked if they knew you or where you lived. I've heard of your name, so I figured other people might've heard of you, too. Finally, an hour ago I thought of Ellis Gordon who works for Webster Tree Service in Zephyr Cove. He goes to my church. I woke him up. It was a wild chance, but it worked. He said he was up here last month cutting out one of your trees that was burned in that forest fire a year ago. He said it took a year to die. Anyway, he didn't know your address number, but he said you lived in a cabin on this road. So I drove up here and, well, it was obvious. All the other people on this little road have big fancy houses."

I drank the last of my coffee, got up and refilled my cup. "Why did Mallory think you were unhappy with what the cops were doing?"

"It was obvious they weren't going to find my kids. They didn't go look. All they did was ask questions!"

"Any idea who took them?"

"A motorcycle gang. They were there one moment, gone the next. There were motorcycles everywhere. They must have taken them."

I thought about the Tahoe Biker Heaven festival I'd read about. It was due to begin on Sunday. Bikers were already pouring into the basin.

I watched Marlette. Her attitude was peculiar. She radiated intense energy. Yet aside from her anger, no other emotion showed. No tears, no quiver of lip. No doubt she was fearful, but that didn't show, either. Her emotions were under lockdown, blocked by the trauma of her missing kids or by something else. But it was obvious that a hot fire burned within. White showed all around the perimeter of her irises. A solar corona during a total eclipse.

"How old is your daughter?"

"She just turned seventeen."

"And your son?"

"Fourteen."

"Your daughter is almost old enough to go where she pleases."

"Not SalAnne. She has autism. She doesn't go out on her own. Never will."

"Did you see the motorcycle gang take your kids?"

"No."

"So you don't know they did."

Her eyes flamed at me. "They were right there. In the street. We searched. Me and my neighbors. Two of the policemen stayed and searched, too. Those bikers had to have taken her. My neighbor even heard Charlie call out."

"Call out how? What did he say?"

"She said his voice was muffled. But she thought he said, 'SalAnne, those bikers are looking at you!'"

"How long were your kids out of your sight?"

"Two, three minutes."

"Maybe they wandered off. Maybe they got lost in the woods. You can go a long way in two or three minutes."

"My kids wouldn't do that. My son, especially. I know them. My son I know better than I know myself."

"But not your daughter?"

"I told you. She has autism. She's different."

"You sound very certain they were kidnapped considering that you didn't see it happen."

"My God, you're just like the cops! You can know something without actually witnessing it."

"Okay, let's assume your kids were kidnapped, and..."

"They were!"

"Right. Let's pretend you hadn't seen any motorcycles. Does anyone you know seem a likely suspect for taking your kids?"

"No. I can't imagine why anyone would kidnap them. It's not like I have money for ransom."

"Are you married?"

"Was. Fifteen years. We've been divorced three years."

"What's his name?"

"Shane Ramirez. I went back to my maiden name of Remmick after our divorce. The kids are still Ramirez."

"Where does Shane live?"

"San Diego. He was here until two years ago. A liftee manager."

"Liftee manager?"

"Liftee managers assign which liftee is stationed on which chairlifts, where and when. They keep the whole mountain running. He was over at Sierra At Tahoe. Started years ago, back when it was called the Sierra Ski Ranch. A great job, but Shane wanted something else."

"Not many ski lifts in San Diego."

"He always wanted to be a rapper and music producer. Latino rap. Even took a rap name. Calls himself NSNG. Stands for No Shane, No Gain."

"Shane doesn't have a motorcycle, does he?"

Marlette's mouth opened, but no sound came out for a moment. "My God. That thought never occurred to me."

"That means he does?"

"Yes. A big Harley."

TWO

"It couldn't be Shane," Marlette said. "He wouldn't kidnap our kids. What would be the point? If he wants to see them or be with them all he has to do is ask."

"Do you have custody of SalAnne and Charlie?"

"Yes. Shane likes Charlie, but they're not real buddies. And he has no interest in SalAnne at all. I can't imagine him wanting her around. They never got along. And anyway, if he wants them in his life he can just ask me. I think children should have a father present. I would make arrangements."

"He didn't fight giving you custody?"

"No. He was grateful."

"He sends child support?"

"Yeah. He's late sometimes. But he sends it. I'm surprised, actually. I thought he'd be less reliable."

"You said you don't have enough money to entice someone into thinking about a kidnapping for ransom."

Marlette shook her head vigorously. "No. Absolutely not. I mean, don't worry, I'll figure out a way to pay you. But ransom? No way."

"What about someone you know? A relative with money?"

Marlette was still shaking her head. "None that I ever knew of. Not that I ever even knew my relatives. My family isn't... I don't keep up with any of them." She clenched her teeth, jaw muscles bulging.

"Any friends of yours who have money? Or someone at

the kids' school?"

"No."

"Neighbors? Someone who cares about your kids?"

More head shaking. Then she stopped. "Well, there's Emerson Baylor. He lives up the street. He's pretty rich. So you're thinking someone could kidnap my kids and send Mr. Baylor a ransom note?"

"It's happened before. How well does he know your kids?"

"Not very. We just say hi when we walk by."

"He doesn't come over, socialize with you?"

"No, nothing like that. He's just a nice neighbor."

"Tell me about your kids. Start with your daughter."

"You're wondering if her autism would make it easy to kidnap her?"

"No, I wanted to know what SalAnne is like."

"Well, she's a nice child, really. But you wouldn't know it meeting her because she is standoffish. That's an autistic thing. Silence doesn't meet people well. She's got walls around her. But the main thing is, she doesn't talk. Never has."

"Silence?"

"Her nickname is Silence. Everyone who knows her calls her Silence."

"Does she have friends?"

"You need to understand that kids with autism..."

"Marlette, the only thing I'm understanding is that you are focused on her autism. I want to know about Silence the person, not about Silence the kid with autism."

Marlette made a dismissive snorting sound. "You don't have a clue what it's like."

"Does she have friends?" I repeated myself.

"Not really. Most of the kids at school either ignore her or make fun of her. There's one girl who used to live in Tahoe. She'd be the only person I might think of as a friend to Silence. But her family moved away to Santa Monica a couple years ago. I even tried calling her yesterday after the cops left. She was out so I talked to her mother. She didn't know anything."

Marlette turned and stared out my window toward the mountains on the west side of the lake. Mt. Tallac was just starting to glimmer a soft pink with the alpenglow of dawn.

"You were telling me about Silence," I said.

Marlette spoke in a soft voice, more toward the distant mountains than toward me. "Silence is a strange child, very removed and distant. Most people would think she's quite retarded, not talking and all. You can't communicate with her. At least, not in any normal way. She's locked into her own frozen world. But in some ways she's pretty smart."

"Does she play games or sports?"

"No. She's not very physical."

"Does she watch TV?"

"Not really. She doesn't have enough focus to stay with TV shows or movies. I think the sound bothers her."

"Listen to music?"

"Sometimes. She doesn't sing along, of course. But I think she likes the rhythm. She moves in a rhythmic fashion. And she likes to spin."

"Spin," I said, not sure I understood.

"Yeah. It's another autistic thing. I know, I know. But autism is such a big part of her."

"What's it like?"

"Spinning? Well, she just turns in place, pushing herself faster and faster. She's very good at it. Never falls down. I don't know why she likes it. I think it helps her escape the world. Something about the way it feels, I guess. Another way she's physical is squeezing. She likes to be squeezed. Maybe it's a womb substitute."

"How does she manifest it?"

"She climbs under her mattress and just lies there letting the weight push down on her. She's gone under the sofa cushions a few times, but the mattress is her favorite. I don't think the sofa cushions weigh enough to give her the feeling. I think she assumes that all creatures like to be squeezed hard, too."

"Why? Does she hug extra hard?"

"Oh, no. Not at all. Silence doesn't like to touch people. But she likes animals. She's fascinated by them. When our neighbor Rachael moved in next door, Silence was fixated on her cat. Always trying to grab it. One day the cat walked onto her lap and Silence squeezed it so hard the cat clawed her and bit her hand. I thought a dog would be tougher. Dogs like to roughhouse and such. So, for a birthday present I went down to the animal shelter and got her a puppy. It was a sturdy little mutt, some kind of Cocker Spaniel mix, cute as can be. Spinner, we called him, because sometimes he turned in circles when he got excited. How perfect is that, Silence having such a dog? And Silence instantly showed that dog more touching than she'd ever touched in her life. But it turned out to be a mistake."

"She hugged it too hard," I said.

"My Lord, that poor dog couldn't take a breath. I tried every way to show Silence how to pet him gently. But she just didn't get it. It was like trying to show a dog how to eat a piece of meat slowly."

"You had to get rid of it?"

"Yes. Either that or come home some time and find it asphyxiated. She even took it under the mattress with her. I thought the poor thing would have broken bones."

Marlette went quiet, remembering. "The rest of the time, Silence is very delicate, very careful. She moves with precision. I suppose that helps her with her art. She's a really good artist."

"Art? That's great. What art is Silence interested in?"

"I don't know. She just does drawings. She can draw anything. Sometimes she does repetitive images. The same thing over and over. Like that famous guy did. What's his name? Warhol. I saw her looking at a magazine article about him, once. I think she likes Warhol."

"I've read that Andy Warhol had a mild form of autism."

"What? I never..." Marlette stared at me for a moment. Suddenly, her personality seemed to shift and the warrior glare was back. "What does this have to do with her kidnapping!"

"I don't know. Anything could be pertinent."

"Mr. McKenna, I don't think that..."

"Owen."

"Owen, I don't think that her art or anything else matters in this case. I think what matters is that..." she stopped.

"What?" I said.

Marlette Remmick studied the table, then turned to study the propane stovetop. "Silence is an unusual-looking girl. She's very thin and she's certainly not beautiful. Her face is all edges and angles. But she's got... Oh, this is ridiculous."

"Nothing you think is ridiculous," I said. "Usually, when a client thinks it's ridiculous, it is in fact relevant."

Marlette held her breath and then sighed. "Silence has, I don't know, a radiance or something. She has pale green eyes and reddish brown skin. The combination kind of glows."

I waited.

Marlette looked at me. "Anyway, Silence doesn't realize what men are like. She is so innocent. I've tried to tell her how she needs to be careful. But she closes down. Shuts her eyes and hugs herself. Or she just disappears into her sketchbook. You will never see that child without her sketchbook. It's like the way some girls are with dolls. And now she and Charlie are..."

Marlette Remmick burst into tears. Not a mere sudden thunderstorm, but a shattered dam. The torrent came through like a river that had been held back for a decade and then suddenly released. She shook and heaved and gasped as tears nearly squirted from her eyes. I handed her a box of tissues. She grabbed a handful and blotted her eyes so hard she could have been trying to blot spilled wine out of the carpet. Marlette sucked at the air and choked and sniffled.

When she calmed a bit she grabbed her coffee mug and drank from it so forcefully I heard her teeth click on the rim.

When the deluge eased, I spoke.

"What about Charlie? What is he like?"

At the mention of his name Marlette brightened. "Oh, Charlie, Charlie," she said, a smile pulling at her sad mouth. She blew her nose, a strong honk that made Spot's ears twitch. "He's the best boy. He's kind and sweet and sensitive. A very good student. He plays football and baseball. And he has a baseball card collection that goes way back. A few months ago I took him to a collector's fair at one of the hotels here in Tahoe. He went to all the tables and talked to the old guys. Know what he said to me after we left? He said that he knew more stats about the ballplayers than the old-timers did. So I asked him if he let them know and he said it was better to be humble than to brag." The memory brought more tears and Marlette mopped them up with another handful of tissue. "Can you imagine a fourteen-year-old boy saying that? That it's good to be humble?"

"Sounds like a good kid," I said.

"And of course he's Silence's lifeline to the world. He looks after her 'round the clock. Every little thing. Charlie is always there for her."

"Do you have pictures of your kids that I could have?"

"Yes, of course. Only I didn't bring any. I'll get them to you. Videos, too. I took a lot of videos over the years. I had them put onto a DVD." She paused and looked around at my little cabin. The dawn was now bright enough that it was easy to see I didn't have a TV. "Oh," she said, looking at the bookcase that sat where most people would put the entertainment center. "Lots of books. You do have a DVD player, don't you? In your bedroom?"

"No, but I can play them on my laptop."

Marlette frowned, no doubt trying to puzzle out what kind of strange creature I was.

THREE

By 8:30 a.m. Marlette was exhausted from talking and crying. She'd explained that she had some savings from her job cleaning houses and said I could have it all. I told her not to worry about it, that we'd work something out, and she left. I got Commander Mallory on the phone a couple minutes past 9:00 a.m.

"You sound groggy, McKenna, like you just got up. Some of us have been up for hours."

"Right," I said. "Had an early morning visitor. Marlette Remmick. Daughter and son went missing yesterday. She said you made an appearance."

"Yeah," Mallory said, exhaling in my ear. "Told her we'd do our best but we couldn't perform miracles. No direct evidence of a crime leaves us a little empty. We put out an Amber Alert. But I may live to regret that." He breathed impatience into the phone. Another phone was ringing in the background.

"But her kids are missing," I said. "That's evidence in some circles."

"Yeah. Kids go missing lots. Were I one of her kids, mom like that, I'd go missing, too."

"You're a harsh man, Mallory."

"Call it like I see it."

"What's your read on the motorcycle thing?" I said.

"I don't know. Could be something there. Word is the Granite Mountain Boys are in town. You familiar with them?"

"No."

"I'm just learning about them myself. Soon as we got the

word they were around we got a file on their leader. He and his first lieutenants all spent time at the Granite Mountain State Prison. Up by the Oregon border. Toughest Super Max in the country. Even the guards gotta prove they're psychotic before they can get a job. They got perps in there, some of them old men, who are running gangs from the inside."

I'd heard about Granite Mountain for years. Now I recalled a report about it on National Public Radio. "Aren't those the guys who do the Aztec thing? Coded messages written micro-small in the Aztec language on items that can be smuggled out by visitors?"

"That's it," Mallory said. "They call 'em Nahuatl supposi-tories."

"Say again?"

"Nahuatl is the ancient Aztec language. The old boys write down the commandments on whatever can be shoved into the visitor's orifice of choice. Of course, most of the boss men are in solitary in the SHU."

"The Security Housing Unit."

"Right. Twenty-three hours alone in the dark and damp and strict supervision in the yard the twenty-fourth. So they've developed a tapping code. The walls are too thick for voices to be understood. But they can tap. Kind of like Morse code, but that would be too easy to break. These Aztec king wannabes tap out the code, the next guy passes it along, and eventually it gets passed on to a nobody who didn't do anything more serious than torture and mutilate a dirtball who couldn't make a drug payment. Because the nobody has such a sweet and pure track record, he's allowed to have visitors. So he listens to the tapping code and then makes a Nahuatl suppository and hands it to a visitor. Next thing you know, a rival drug lord gets aced in South Central L.A."

"How does that translate to the motorcycle gang?"

"The Granite Mountain Boys are run by a man named Antonio Gomez. He spent three years in the Super Max's SHU for ordering a rape and murder. The victim was a twenty-three-year-old kid who screwed up a delivery on some of Southern

Mexico's finest powder. Gomez wanted to set an example, and from what I read in the file it worked very well."

"How'd he get out?"

"Yeah, my question, too. Turns out Tony Go has a lot of dirty money. Lots meaning eight figures. He's also got a lawyer who is a miracle worker. Knows every technicality about DNA tests and testing labs, which were critical in Gomez's conviction. He presented a case that got Gomez's conviction thrown out. The result was that the state opened those big steel gates and let one of the worst cell jockeys in California history walk."

"And now you think he's in Tahoe?"

"According to a tip from an informer who rides with his boys. There's a deputy up in Northern Cal who's made the Granite Mountain Boys his hobby. He's the guy who runs the informer. I'll make a note, have him give you a call.

"Anyway, Tony Go is one of those really charismatic guys, and like a lot of those types he collects followers. He has something like fifty hard core followers, guys who would do whatever he says. Then there's another hundred men who want to be part of the action because they're losers and they like the idea that they belong to something, especially something that makes them look tough. Of course, mostly they're a bunch of wimps. They carry chains and guns and knives and if they were trapped all alone in an alley and Little Red Riding Hood said boo, they'd wet their pants."

"Could Gomez have kidnapped Marlette's kids?" I asked.

"Yeah, sure. He's got the rep. But it's hard to separate reality from bullshit when it comes to Tony Go."

"Give me an example?" I said.

"There's a wacko rumor going round that he performs sacrifices at the full moon."

"Killing people? Like an ancient Aztec thing?"

"So the rumor goes."

"You don't believe it," I said.

"Would you? My BS meter rarely redlines, but it did on that story."

"What's your guess on the Ramirez kids? They get kidnapped? Or did they run away?"

"She tell you about the last time?" Mallory said.

"Last time what," I said.

"Last time the daughter went missing."

"No. What happened?"

"A few years ago. The daughter went missing, ran away and stayed at a friend's house for two days. Ms. Remmick called it into the police."

"A missing persons' report?"

"No. She said her daughter had been kidnapped."

FOUR

After I got off the phone with Mallory, I went back to bed for a few hours, then put Spot into the back of the Jeep and drove into South Lake Tahoe. Marlette Remmick had given me her address. I found her street near the Stateline end of town a couple blocks up the mountain from Pioneer Trail. I turned down the narrow pine needle-covered asphalt, watching the house numbers. Marlette's house was a pale yellow box, one of the early Tahoe cabins built in the '40s or '50s. It squatted down low on concrete block piers with just enough space beneath the house to allow lost cats to hide out of the reach of human hands and to let the cold winter wind freeze the plumbing. The narrow lot was overhung with a heavy pine canopy that dropped a thick mat of needles over the old cedar shake roof. The shallow eaves were not much higher than Spot could reach standing on his hind legs. I'd have to be careful when I stepped through the door.

I parked on the street and as I got out I saw Marlette through the living room window. She was riding an exercise bicycle. Her exertion didn't look so much like exercise as it did a test to gauge the strength of the metal components. She stomped down on the pedals, spinning them into a blur. She gripped the handlebars as if to rip them off, and her head bobbed with ferocious intensity. I realized I was witnessing an exorcism of sorts and I was reluctant to interrupt. Then again, maybe it was imperative I stop her before she self-destructed.

I knocked on the door. Then, realizing she'd never hear over the noise of the bicycle, I pounded on the wood with the meat of my fist.

The whirling subsided and stopped. Marlette opened the door and beckoned me in. She had on the same pants and blue work shirt as she'd worn at my cabin hours earlier, only this time the shirt was dark between her shoulder blades, wet with sweat. She smelled of sweat but also of fear, biting and acrid.

We sat in the kitchen at her dining table, a pine plank affair coated with a thick layer of glossy varnish.

Her chest still heaved with oxygen deficit.

I said, "Mallory says you called in some time back and said that Silence had been kidnapped, that this is the second time."

"That was different," she said between breaths.

"How?"

"It was three years ago. Shane had just left me. I was nervous and afraid. Except for going to school, Silence had been a shut-in up until that point. Then one morning she went to school and didn't come home. I called and the school said she never showed up. She'd never done anything that would have made me think she could disappear or run away. So I assumed the worst."

"She was okay," I said.

Marlette nodded. "Yeah. Instead of going to school, she went to a classmate's house. The girl I mentioned this morning. The one who moved to Santa Monica. I had no clue. Gave me a fright to stop my heart. Silence came home a day and a half later. I wanted to slap her I was so upset. In fact, I would have if I thought it would've made any difference. But with Silence you never know if you're reaching her."

"What was her reason?"

"That's why it's so hard, her not ever talking."

"Doesn't talk, or can't talk?"

"Silence is non-verbal. She's never uttered a word in her life."

"Because she's autistic," I said.

"Yeah. She's what's called verbal receptive, but not verbal expressive. Which means that she doesn't talk even though she can sort of understand what people say. I've studied it. All parents of autistic kids have. It's so frightening to have an autistic child, we've practically started an industry trying to figure it out. Discussion groups and support groups and books and talk shows and Internet sites. I don't know that what we're all learning has made a huge difference, although certainly some kids have gotten much better treatment and done much better than they would have in the past."

"It sounds like you don't think Silence has improved."

Marlette seemed to stare at the air above my head. "The thing is, many autistic kids start off normally and begin to learn to talk. Then they regress at eighteen months or two years and lose their ability to make words and simple sentences. They stop looking at you and stop responding to you. It's like you're not in the room."

"Do they get better?"

"With intense therapy they sometimes do. Some kids eventually learn to talk and communicate. Not like you or me, but they acquire enough words and sentences to get what they need."

"But not Silence?" I said.

"No. With Silence, there never was any communication. She never noticed me, not from the time she was a newborn. Didn't grab my fingers, didn't look at my face. I tried to breast feed her. My God, it was a nightmare. It was like I was a food bottle, nothing more. She didn't turn to look when I came in the room. She didn't notice anybody. And, no, she never learned to talk. Not one word. Not even the word mama."

Marlette winced at the memory.

I didn't speak for a minute. Finally, I said, "What are her capacities? How does she function in other ways?"

"I'm her mother, but I still haven't figured her out. In many ways, she seems retarded even to me. Just like they say."

"What do you mean, 'just like they say?'"

"Most non-verbal autistic kids are quite retarded. Their mental capacity is not enough to allow them to take care of themselves in any way. A lot of them need full-time caregivers."

Marlette looked embarrassed. "Let's face it, I'm poor, so it's not like I can take Silence to every specialist in the books. And, frankly, I haven't been very good at obtaining help from the various social service agencies. But over the years, many people have looked at Silence. The Special Ed teachers at the school have been especially thorough in getting Silence all the tests and doctor evaluations and putting together her IEP and her planner."

"What's the IEP?"

"Individualized Education Plan. I really owe those teachers for how hard they've worked with Silence. But some of the specialists have said that Silence is retarded and will never get any better. They say she'll always need someone to live with her and attend to her needs. Don't get me wrong, she can dress herself and feed herself, things like that. But they say she'll never be able to arrange for her own living situation or manage her finances. Of course, how could it be otherwise? She can't talk."

"How does she communicate? Does she sign? Can she write?"

"No. The school psychologist says that signing or writing is another form of talking. If you can't talk, but you can sign or write, you are verbal in most ways. For example, deaf people who sign are verbal. They just talk with their hands. But Silence is nonverbal. She can only communicate in the most primitive ways. She grunts and points and makes these little chirping sounds. Sometimes she pushes you toward what she wants. It's hard to know what she wants. Very hard." Marlette paused.

"Charlie knows. Charlie and Silence have some other kind of communication. I've never understood it. It's like he understands her sounds as if they were words." Marlette was shaking her head. "I don't know... Sometimes I've thought he is just making up what he thinks she wants. Then he says it like it is absolute fact.

"There's a psychiatrist in town who's done Silence's annual evaluations, and I asked him about it. He said it was possible that Charlie and Silence communicate the way identical twins do when they have their own private language. But he also said it was extremely doubtful. He's a nice man. Thoughtful and caring. But he didn't want to give me false hopes. He doesn't think there is any hope that Silence will get better."

"It sounds like you disagree," I said.

"I don't know. I'm not sure I disagree. It's just that one of her teachers really disagrees."

"You mean she has a teacher who thinks she will be able to learn to talk and communicate?"

"No, I don't think she thinks that. But she has said many times that she's convinced that Silence is very smart. She even said she was brilliant."

"Who is this teacher?"

"Henrietta Johanssen. She's one of the Special Ed teachers over at the high school. She's been working with Silence for quite a few years and has become her advocate. She says that Silence has convinced her of her intelligence in many ways."

"How?"

"Well, there's her drawings. She's always had an amazing ability to draw the things she sees. Henrietta says it's a clear sign of high-level mental functioning."

"May I see them?"

"Of course. Come look in her room."

I followed Marlette down a short hall and into a bedroom. It was like how I imagined any other teen-aged girl's bedroom might look, painted lavender with purple trim. In one corner was a twin bed with a lavender bedspread. A small wooden desk had a lavender top and legs. The drawers were painted purple. In case the room didn't have enough color, the lampshade was hung with a purple scarf.

But where other girls have posters of movie stars and rock bands, Silence's walls were covered in drawings. Wall-to-wall drawings. There seemed to be no theme. The drawings were in pencil on lined notebook paper, and they showed a hundred different subjects from Silence's bedroom to various Tahoe mountains and landmarks and scenes of the lake. There were drawings of the high school and classrooms. There was an entire section of pictures of Spinner, the dog. As rendered in pencil on paper, Spinner was handsome in spite of a large thatch of head fur that stood up straight like a fright wig.

On the dresser were two stacks of sketchbooks. I picked one up. It was filled with drawings, all very detailed, all incredibly accurate.

The only thing that seemed consistent in her drawings was the lack of people. There were just a few drawings that depicted a boy. Young but tall, strong and poised. The drawings were so realistic you could get a sense of his personality. He looked to have that unusual quality of knowing exactly what he wanted out of life. He was the kid you'd pick out of a group and remark that he was going to go places.

I pointed at the drawings. "Charlie?"

"Yes," Marlette's voice was thick.

"What do the doctors think about her artistic ability?"

"They say it's just a talent she has. That it is different than intelligence. They call her a savant. They say it happens with autistic kids. I've always remembered Dr. Power's words. He said it's uncommon, but it's a regular occurrence."

"Henrietta thinks otherwise?"

"Oh, yes. Henrietta says Silence notices things other kids don't notice. She says in many ways Silence is even smarter than most other kids, but that she just can't speak."

"What do you think?"

Marlette shook her head. "I don't know. I just don't know. Sometimes I think Henrietta reads things into what Silence does. Like if Silence picks up a rock and looks at it, I'd probably think she was just picking up a rock. After all these years of taking care of her, day and night, month after month, I'd be pretty convinced that Silence was just, you know, picking up a rock. But Henrietta would say Silence was studying it, wondering about its composition. Things like that. Don't get me wrong, I'd love nothing more in the whole world than to find out that Silence was like Helen Keller, a smart girl who just couldn't communicate. But it's not what I experience day after day. Maybe some people would say I'm heartless and unimaginative." Marlette's eyes watered. "But I'd say I'm practical and realistic. It's what I see."

"When Silence ran away for a couple of days and you thought she'd been kidnapped, where did she go?"

"The girl I mentioned who moved to Santa Monica. Her name is Jersey. Jersey Walker. She's an unusual girl. Almost as strange in her way as Silence is. She's not autistic or anything like that. But she was an outsider at school. And she never really talked to anyone except herself. I sometimes wondered if Jersey and Silence found a connection in their mutual dysfunction. Maybe Silence could tell that even though Jersey can talk, the fact that she mostly doesn't talk makes her a little like Silence. Like they have something in common. I don't know that Jersey really thought she could communicate with Silence. But how do I know what goes on with two kids?"

"Silence ran away to Jersey's house?"

"Yeah. She walked two miles to Jersey's house and stayed in her bedroom for two days. Not even Jersey's parents knew Silence was there. Prior to that she'd practically never left my side in her life. Without any glimmer of such a possibility I assumed the worst and called the cops. It was a mistake."

"But you think this time is different."

"Yes. As different as can be. I heard those motorcycles. My neighbor heard Charlie call out. And if Silence learned anything from the last time she ran away, it was never to do it again."

"What were your kids wearing when they disappeared?"

"Silence had on brown khaki pants and a pink long-sleeved shirt. Charlie had on his usual, jeans and a white T-shirt. He never wears anything else, summer or winter."

"Didn't you say this morning that you called Jersey yesterday after Silence went missing?"

"Yes. Her mother said that Jersey wasn't home from school. So I told her mother that Silence was missing. I didn't say she was kidnapped because of what happened before. Her mother said that she would talk to Jersey and if they heard anything about Silence they'd call me."

"Are there any other kids who are friends with Silence?"

Marlette shook her head. "I don't even think Jersey was a friend in the way we normally use the word. Jersey was just, well, she happened to be there when Silence ran away. She accepted Silence in a way the other kids didn't. But it's not like they did stuff together. Anyway, none of the other kids at school would qualify as friends of Silence. At least, not that I know of."

"I'd like to talk to Jersey. Can you give me her number?"

"Sure, let me get my address book." Marlette went into her bedroom and came out with a small brown notebook. She wrote Jersey's name and number on a Post-it note and handed it to me. "I just remembered. Silence has school pictures." Marlette opened her daughter's desk drawers, searching. "Here. Silence and Charlie and, here we are, Jersey." She handed me three small photos. "The one on top is Jersey. The picture is old, but it gives you an idea of her. She's a little different."

I glanced at the photo. The girl had purple hair and rings in her eyebrows and a tattoo of a sword on her cheek.

I slid it off and looked at the next photo.

Charlie looked just like the pencil drawings on the wall. The photo showed just how accurate the drawings were. The photos made the same powerful impression of the kid who was going places.

The next photo would be Silence.

Unlike Jersey and Charlie, she wasn't facing the camera. Her eyes looked at something on the floor, but the overall impression was that she was staring inward. She'd shut out the camera and the photographer and the commotion around her and retreated to some inner place.

Her face was all corners, from cheekbones to chin to pointed nose. She looked like what a sculptor might create using triangular pieces of red clay. Although she wasn't pretty, she was striking.

I put the photos in my pocket.

"May I see Charlie's room?"

"Yes, it's the next one down."

Marlette walked in, flipped on the light and began straightening things up.

"You don't need to pick anything up. I prefer to see his room in a natural state."

Marlette looked embarrassed, although the room was much neater than I expected. But for a pair of jeans and some socks on the floor and a couple of empty Red Bull cans on the dresser, it was quite orderly.

There were two 49ers posters above the bed. His iPod hung from the desk chair, its cord plugged into a computer below the desk. To the side of the computer monitor was Charlie's football helmet. His closet door stood open and more jeans hung from hooks on the inside of the door.

There was nothing to connect him to any of the outsider groups, no drug paraphernalia, no ashtrays, no posters intended to offend parents. His only stickers seemed to be on his football helmet rather than on the walls where they would be hard to remove.

Next to the door, above the light switch, was a 3x5 color photo in an inexpensive frame. It was from several years earlier before Charlie had started his growth spurt. It showed Charlie holding his older sister on his back, his arms holding her legs. She had her arms around his neck. He was clearly laughing hard, his mouth open, teeth bright. She was looking ahead, no laugh pulling at her mouth, but not unhappy, either.

"Looks like they get along very well," I said as I backed out of the room.

Marlette had a faraway look in her eyes. "He's simply the best brother to her. Sometimes I wonder how he'd be with a sister who wasn't autistic. I think he'd be very nice. But with Silence, Charlie has a special purpose. It's like his calling. I always know that Silence is okay because Charlie looks after her."

"Can you give me the names of a couple of Charlie's best friends?"

"I'd hardly know where to start. Everyone loves Charlie."

"Pick a couple whose phone numbers you have."

FIVE

After Spot and I left Marlette's house, I drove across the state line, turned up Kingsbury Grade and pulled into the little alley behind the building where Street Casey has her lab not far from my office. I told Spot to stay put and left him in the Jeep.

The last time we'd visited, Spot, in his excitement at seeing Street, wagged so hard that his tail swept all the papers off her desk. As we tried to calm him down and get him to sit, he backed up and did the same to her workbench. Six bug containers hit the floor. Five of them popped open and suddenly five armies of orange and green beetles were lifting up their little shell-type wing coverings, spreading vibrating gossamer wings and taking flight, filling the air with a buzz like distant chainsaws.

From now on Spot stays in the Jeep unless Street has Spot-proofed her workspace.

When I walked into Street's lab she was sitting at her microscope, looking through the lenses. It was a double eyepiece affair with a digital camera attached. The cables went to a computer. On the screen was some kind of purple bar graph. Or maybe the bars were touch-screen sliders like on a music mixing board. I couldn't tell.

"What's playing at the microplex?"

"Cockroach Love Story," she said without looking up. "I'm studying some quirks of mating behavior. Properly exploited, it may provide some new chemical-free cockroach population control. Hormones, pheromones, stuff like that."

"Can't we teach them to just say no?"

"Well, it's true that cockroaches have more discipline than your average teenager, but that approach hasn't attracted many proponents."

"Is it exciting?"

"Watching cockroaches perform a mating dance? Very. If you want to know more, I'm giving a paper at an entomologists' conference a week from Saturday at the San Francisco Marriott." Her tone was dry.

"It would be fun. We could do theater and dinner afterward."

Street rotated her head away from the scope and looked at me. "You mean, dinner and theater would be fun."

"Your talk would be, too."

"Tell the truth," she said, turning back toward the slide or petri dish or whatever it was that the probing end of the microscope was jammed against.

"Really. I find bug stuff interesting," I said.

"You've never found it interesting enough to come to any of my talks. I've given maybe a dozen of them now. One of them as close as Reno."

"Well, I've wanted to, but something has always gotten in the way." As I said it I realized that the truth was I had no excuse.

Street looked at me again. "Owen, bugs mean a lot to me. You want to be supportive of my work, and I appreciate that. But if your words about my work are too casual and sound hollow, that's worse than coming right out and saying that you find what I do boring."

"It's not that I don't find your work..." I suddenly stopped as I remembered the proverb that says when you find that you're digging yourself into a hole, stop digging.

I grabbed one of the old mismatched wire chairs that Street has here and there, brought it over and sat next to her. "A week from Saturday at the Marriott?" I said.

Street nodded as she used the computer mouse to adjust something on the screen.

I said, "What time is your talk?"

"The seminar is from nine a.m. to five p.m. You probably wouldn't find the whole schedule worth listening to. I give my paper from two-thirty to three. If you just came to hear me that would make me very happy."

"Okay, count on it. Any preference for dinner and theater?"

"Quiet restaurant and a thoughtful play?"

"Done. Do we ride down together?"

"No, sorry. Do you remember me mentioning a bug colleague named Sandra Barrington at Stanford? I'm meeting with her the evening before down in Burlingame. I'll fly down on the shuttle from Reno and I'll stay with her Friday night. So you and I can meet at the Marriott Saturday afternoon. I'll be all yours after five. Then we can drive home together on Sunday."

"I'll pick a restaurant," I said, "But will you pick the play? You know me and theater."

"You're still thinking about that Greek tragedy that turned out to be a musical in drag?"

"Yeah. The soldiers in feather boas were my favorite."

"I've got last Sunday's Chronicle at home," Street said. "How 'bout kebabs and Sierra Nevada Pale Ale while we read up on the theater? You can go there now if you want. I'll be along in a few minutes."

"Spot and I will be waiting," I said as I kissed her and left.

Dark October clouds swirled ominously around the mountains across the lake as Spot and I drove up the east shore to Street's condo. The clouds hinted at the coming storms of winter and made me think about the two Ramirez kids, possibly yanked from their front yard, possibly held at this moment somewhere in the Tahoe mountains. I didn't know what to think about the Granite Mountain Boys, but I knew that ten thousand or more motorcyclists were coming to Tahoe for the various biker festivities. Some of them, doctors and dentists and veterinarians and insurance salesmen and pilots and art dealers and software engineers and fashion designers and consultants and professors would stay at the luxury hotels, watching the showroom productions and soaking in the hot tubs and ordering champagne sent up to their rooms. Other bikers, perhaps of different socioeconomic strata, would camp out, small and large groups alike huddled around campfires, drinking beer and barbecuing burgers and pulling their leather jacket collars up to ward off the cold high-altitude wind.

Neither group was necessarily more likely to have members who would kidnap a brother and sister, but I had the absurd hope that if Silence and Charlie were being held by bikers, they were kept in a warm hotel room and not huddled in a freezing tent camp at 8000 feet.

As I unlocked Street's door, a gust of wind hit me and the temperature dropped ten degrees in a second. An involuntary shiver shook my shoulders. Like many people, especially those in law enforcement, I'd confronted some of the bleakest things that people can do to other people. At those times I'd learned that you can't survive without pushing it back a little here and there. If you face the darkness 24/7 you wear down and eventually succumb to it. So you periodically go around turning on lights and looking in closet doors to see if there is any room left to stuff a little more inside, way at the back where it won't be so readily seen and heard and smelled.

A little sparkle and crackle and pop in the fireplace seemed appropriate. So I grabbed some kindling and a couple of split logs off the pile next to Street's front door. Spot looked at me with anticipation.

"Sorry, didn't mean to be neglectful of your mastication needs," I said to him. I handed another log to him and he took it the way other dogs grab a stick. His big jowls flopped over the rough wood and he trotted inside with it.

I got the fire going as Spot did his best to splinter his log into twelve thousand Lodgepole pine toothpicks. "What is it with the chewing work ethic?" I said to him as I pulled two Sierra Nevadas from Street's fridge and opened a Kunde cab to catch a little breath. Spot's ears perked toward me and his eyes lifted up against his drooping lids, but he kept his nose down and his teeth focused on the task.

Ten minutes later, he dropped what was left of the log and lay his head down on the wood chips that covered his paws.

"Not working to ability," I said as I lifted his head, scooped up the chips and splinters in my cupped hands and tossed the detritus into the fire. "There's still half a log left." I tossed it on the flames as well. Spot didn't seem to care.

The door opened and Street breezed in, open coat flowing behind her tight jeans.

The cold breeze had gotten stronger, so we skipped the outside barbecue and put beef and onion and green pepper kebabs under the broiler while we drank our beers. We were nearly through with our wine and dinner before I brought up my activities that had started sixteen hours before at four in the morning.

When I was through explaining what I'd learned about Silence and Charlie and the Granite Mountain Boys, Street just sat quietly, shaking her head. Finally, she said, "What is your next move?"

"Tomorrow I'm going to call the girl in Santa Monica. Then I'll drop in on Charlie's friends. Marlette gave me a couple of names."

"Time is a worry, isn't it?" Street said.

"Anytime kids go missing, every hour longer that they're gone, the less likely it is that they turn up alive."

Street winced and her eyes moistened and I thought I should have put it more softly. But it was too late. I'd already opened the closet door.

SIX

I was awake and coffeed-up and showered before dawn, which was arriving later and later each day. At 7:00 a.m. I called the number Marlette had given me for Jersey Walker, quiet friend of quieter Silence.

"Hello," a stern-voiced woman said after the second ring.

"Mrs. Walker?" I said.

"Yes?"

I tried to make it sound official. "Good morning. This is Detective Owen McKenna calling from Lake Tahoe. Apparently, Marlette Remmick explained to you the other day that her son Charlie and her daughter Silence have gone missing. I understand your daughter Jersey knew Silence when you lived in Tahoe. I'd like to talk to Jersey and ask her a few questions about Silence."

"I'm sorry, I don't see what Jersey has to do with them disappearing."

"Nothing, I'm sure," I said, "but Jersey was Silence's closest friend in Tahoe and I'm hoping she can give me some insights into Silence and Charlie."

"That's ridiculous. Silence never had friends. Least of all my daughter. There is nothing she can help you with."

In the background I heard a small voice say, "Who's that?" followed by Mrs. Walker's muffled voice saying, "Never mind, be quiet."

I said, "Mrs. Walker, I won't trouble your daughter for long. I just have a few questions. May I speak to her for a minute?"

"No. As I told Marlette, if we hear anything about Silence

or Charlie, we'll let her know. Although I'm certain that won't happen. Now I must be going." She hung up.

I dialed back and it rang six times before synthetic voice-mail answered and said to leave a message. I hung up, wondering what Jersey's mother was so afraid of.

I decided to put my other ideas on hold and go down to Santa Monica and talk to Jersey in person. If I hurried there was a chance I could catch her as she left school. If she went to school.

It was a reasonable risk.

I called Street, and she said she'd stop in and attend to Spot. I drove over Spooner Summit to Carson City, sharing the highway with several knots of bikers, then headed north on the freeway to the Reno Tahoe Airport.

Inside, I studied the departure board and found that if I hurried I could catch a United flight to L.A.

The flight time was only one hour. I didn't have time to find a rental car, so I grabbed a cab over to Santa Monica and had the driver drop me outside of the high school where I hoped Jersey spent her days. It was nearly 3:00 p.m. I didn't know what time the school let out so I waited across the street.

Fog rolled in off the ocean and pushed up around the buildings, swirled around the high school in tendrils so thick I could almost feel it wrapping around my legs.

The front doors of the school pushed open at 3:30 and a flood of kids surged out.

I walked over, aware that high schools across the country were implementing security procedures, guards and cameras, designed to keep strange men off campus. But I had my license and a reason to be there. Nevertheless, I stayed back and let the kids fan out past me.

Jersey was one of the stragglers at the rear of the pack, unmistakable with her facial metal and tattooed cheek and colored hair, which was now electric pink. She was one of the new segment of teenagers who've embraced the fat stomach, pushing it out and swinging it proudly in front. Her tight elastic shirt came down over small breasts to the bottom of her ribcage, and her jeans hung low on her hips to allow a full display of belly flesh that, in an earlier era, would have indicated a pregnancy eight months along. Now it just indicated pride in what no exercise and a large daily intake of junk food can produce.

Most of the other kids headed for cars, and for a moment I worried I'd lose her to a vehicle. But she came out to the street as if to walk home, and when she drew even with where I stood leaning against a post, I spoke.

"Hi Jersey. I'm glad I found you. My name is Owen McKenna. I called this morning to talk to you about Silence Ramirez, but your mother wouldn't let me speak to you."

Jersey stared at me. Up close, I could now see that the smudges around her eyes were some kind of deep purple eye shadow applied not to enhance beauty, but to look like a Halloween ghoul. A flicker of worry shaded her face, but her natural sullen demeanor wouldn't allow any strong reaction to me, pro or con. After staring for another moment, she looked away and continued walking.

I turned and walked along next to her. "I know you're busy and that's why your mother is being a good executive secretary, screening your calls and all, careful to make certain you don't fire her ass for incompetence."

Without turning my head I looked down at her and saw a tiny grin that disappeared almost immediately.

"So I thought I'd catch you during your commute. 'Course, if you have to tune up the cell, send off some text messages or videos or something, no problem, I can wait. But maybe when you're done I could..."

"I don't have a cell," she said, her voice high and angry. "Don't want one. They're stupid. I don't even want a laptop. Technology's stupid. Why would I want to talk to anyone anyway? People suck."

"Lotta people, lotta the time, I agree. But from what I've heard, Silence doesn't suck. She and her brother are missing and they were maybe kidnapped and you probably don't think so but you were Silence's best friend. So I need to talk to you. I need to pick your brain even if you don't think you can help. I'm trying to find Silence and Charlie and right now, you're all I've got."

Jersey kept walking, staring down at her feet.

We walked a block without talking. "Please help me?" I said.

"So ask," she said. "What. Ever."

"Here's what I'm wondering," I said. "I'm picturing Charlie and Silence are outside of their house. Out on Pioneer Trail a bunch of bikers are going by. There's a big biker gathering in Tahoe in a few days. Some witnesses say they heard motorcycles coming down the street. The prevailing view is that these bikers grabbed both Charlie and Silence and hauled them away."

"Hauled? Like on the back of the bikes? That's stupid. I've been on a bike. You can totally fall off the back if you want."

"My thought exactly. So I'm wondering if Silence and Charlie would do that, try to fall off the backs of the bikes. Or would they be too scared and just hang on?"

Jersey was staring at the fingernail on her left index finger. The nail was torn and bitten far back and had dried blood in the cuticle. She found a little piece left to chew and twisted her arm around, elbow stuck out in front of her, to get at it. She mumbled as she tried to get purchase with her front teeth. "Charlie, no. No friggin way. But Silence. I dunno. Maybe."

"Maybe she'd be too scared to fall off?"

"Maybe. She might just hang on cuz of fear and stuff."

"Okay, she's a maybe," I said. "But Charlie definitely would be difficult to haul off on a bike against his will."

"Totally. He's like a soldier, a tribesman," Jersey said. Her inflection was full of pride.

"He earned your respect," I said.

"What?" she mumbled, cranking her arm around so she could attack the fingernail from a different direction. "Gimme a break. I don't respect him. He's just a kid. He's, like, three years younger then me."

"Sure," I said. "So if they couldn't haul Charlie away on a bike, then they would have to stuff him into a vehicle."

"A van," Jersey said.

I walked a few paces. "Why do you say a van?"

"Obvious." She pulled her hand from her mouth and looked at her finger. There was fresh blood leaking from the back edge of her nail. She dabbed at it with her tongue. "A car has small doors. He could grab onto the edges. Charlie's strong. It'd be hard to get him in. Unless you handcuffed him. But a van's got a big door. You could push him in. And smoked windows."

"Smoked windows?"

"Of course. Lotsa vans have smoked windows. So you couldn't see them once they were inside. Or maybe it was a panel van. Even better."

"If they just wanted to kidnap Silence, would Charlie fight them? Is he brave enough to do that?"

Jersey swung her head up and frowned at me. "Whad' I say. He's a soldier."

"Right. How about Silence? Would she put up a struggle or is she too docile for that?"

"She'd struggle. Kick and scream." Jersey paused, still licking her finger. "But she's skinny. You wouldn't need a van. It wouldn't be hard to stick her in a car. Or maybe, like if you were driving the bike..." Jersey stopped walking and demonstrated a movement with a disturbing ferocity. "You could slam her on the back of the bike, get on and then stick her arms under your arms and clamp down!"

Jersey held the position for a moment then resumed walking. When she spoke she was again calm. "I still think it was a van. It would be the MOC."

"Pardon me?"

"Thing on a cable show. MOC is mode-of-choice."

"Oh," I said. "Did Silence communicate with you much?"

Jersey rolled her eyes so hard her head rolled, too. "They didn't tell you? She doesn't talk."

"They told me that. What I wondered is about other ways of communication. For example, if Silence likes something, does she have a way of letting you know? Or does she always keep it to herself?"

"Oh, she always lets you know."

"How?"

"She pushes you toward it. And there's this sound she made. Like a hmmm, hmmm sound."

"What kinds of things make her do that? Push you toward them?"

"I moved away a long time ago, so I don't really remember."

"Try."

"Just stuff. You know. Food. Like cupcakes. Anything chocolate. And Dylan. He's a musician from way back. I have him on my iPod. Every time I'd scroll down my list, Silence would push me when Dylan came up. And Cal at school in Tahoe. He was, like, the perfect jock. A total jerk. A year older than us. He'd be walking down the hall totally ignoring us and Silence would always give me a big push toward him. I'd yell at her every time. But she was so stoked on him. It didn't matter what I said."

"Do you remember Cal's last name?"

"King. Callif King. They called him King Cal."

"Would he still be in school, or would he have graduated by now?"

"Whad' I say. He's a year older. He'd be a senior by now."

"Jersey, I've been told that some doctors who examined Silence think she is retarded. Do you agree with that?"

Jersey came to an abrupt stop. She turned and gave me an incredulous look. "That's the stupidest thing I ever heard."

"You think she is smart?"

Jersey shook her head back and forth as if amazed by how dense I was. "She's totally smart."

"How does she show it?"

Jersey started walking again. "She just knows stuff. Smart stuff. I could tell. Charlie could tell. It was obvious. Other kids could tell, too. Even the ones who were mean to her."

"What about Cal? If I asked him, would he say she was smart?"

"I told you, Cal's a jerk. Just because he's a jock he thinks he can ignore anybody. I hated him."

I walked a bit farther and then stopped. "Jersey, if I need to talk to you again, how do I reach you?"

She studied my face for a bit, trying to make a decision. Then she pulled out a pen. "Gimmee your palm."

"How about a card instead?"

She rolled her eyes again as I pulled out a business card and handed it to her backside up.

She wrote on it and handed it back to me. "That's my email. You can write. Maybe I'll write back. If it gets through my Spam filter."

"I thought you said technology is stupid."

"It is." She turned and walked away.

SEVEN

When I got back to Tahoe I stopped at Street's condo before heading up to my cabin. Spot met me at the door, nose on overdrive, sniffing out hints of ocean and airplane and Jersey Walker.

Street was spending the evening working on her speech for the upcoming entomology conference, so Spot fetched his tennis ball and we said goodbye and headed home. When we rounded one of the curves on the climb up the private road that I share with my wealthy neighbors, I saw a flickering light out on the mountainside where normally there was only dark forest. My guess was that the light came from a campfire and I wanted to check it out.

But the moment we got out of the Jeep, Spot whirled to face up the road and got down in a half-crouch. From up in the shadows by Mrs. Duchamp's house raced Treasure, the Toy Poodle who weighs possibly four pounds and, uninhibited by the 166-pound difference, is thus a fearless playmate. She charged Spot at full speed, leaped up and gave him a full body block on his shoulder, slamming him back at least a quarter inch. She bounced off him, hit the ground and launched a second time. Again he was pressured back another quarter inch toward the end zone. But he never dropped his ball, which was completely hidden in his mouth. He decided to make a break and he took off down the field. Treasure dogged him like a pilot fish darting around the mouth of a Great White shark. She leaped up at his head and neck, over and over, nipping at his flesh, issuing a torrent of little high-pitched barks, her tail wagging furiously. Spot went around in circles until Mrs. Duchamp's voice ripped a hole in the night like Pavarotti hitting a high C.

"TREASURRRRRRRRRE!" she sang out, her tremolo notes so sheer and potent that, were they the beginning of the national anthem at a Kings game, she'd bring down the roof of the arena.

Treasure disappeared into the Duchamp palace, and Spot charged back to me.

"You didn't drop the ball, did you?"

Spot did a kind of nod he favors and then, from the hidden recesses of his cavernous mouth, out popped the tennis ball, which bounced and rolled, hit my cabin wall and stopped. Spot stared at it, glanced up at me, then looked back to the ball, his tail held high but exhibiting just a hint of wagging motion.

"Sorry, your largeness. I have other exercise in mind." I went inside to get my binoculars and flashlight, then headed down the road.

Although it was quite dark, Spot and I entered one of the trails that threads its way along the mountainside. The sliver of new moon, not yet set over the mountains to the west, provided a tiny bit of light to help see the trail through the forest.

I looked at the moon and thought about the rumor Mallory had told me, that Tony Go and his biker group performed sacrifices at the full moon. Mallory said he thought it sounded ridiculous. I had a hard time imagining such a thing, too. But I had seen sicker stuff in the past.

If it were true, the moon would be full in about ten days.

The trail traverses the slope at a slight upward angle. After a half mile it begins switching back several times as it climbs up to meet the Tahoe Rim Trail not far from Genoa Peak. It was very cold, and I hiked fast to generate some warmth.

My destination was the second switchback, where the trail comes to an opening in the forest. There is a house-sized boulder one can climb up on and get a great view of the surrounding mountains.

Spot ran up the trail as if the moon sliver were the sun, his nose taking up where his eyes left off, eager to catalog every species, plant and animal, on the mountainside and deduce from their odors alone their nocturnal activities.

Fifteen minutes later, I called Spot, then put my hands against the giant boulder, palms on a sloped portion of the rock about six feet above the ground. "Paws here, Spot." I patted the rock.

He raised up on his hind legs and put his paws next to me, his panting, lolling tongue next to my face in the dark. "Okay, remember how I boost you up, rear paws in my hands?"

I did as I said and he almost tipped over, but then he got a good grip with his nails on the lichen-covered granite and he scrambled up to the top. I followed him and sat down on the very top.

The campfire was easily visible about a half mile to the north. I saw movement and heard somebody laughing and Spot did a little growl as I put the binoculars on the scene.

There were three men standing near the fire. Three motorcycles glinted in the dark behind them. They must have found a good trail to brave taking road bikes into the woods. But I knew all of Tahoe to be laced with good trails. Some were recent, carefully constructed to low-erosion standards by conservation groups. And some dated back to the days of Mark Twain, when loggers clear-cut the Tahoe Basin to provide lumber for the mining tunnels of the Comstock Lode in Virginia City.

I watched through the glasses for ten minutes, then sat with Spot for another ten. When I looked through the glasses again, nothing had changed. The bikers were just enjoying a campfire with the world's greatest view for a backdrop, something many bikers were probably doing all over the Tahoe Basin. Nothing about the scene could be connected to missing children except in my imagination.

Spot and I climbed down from the boulder and went home to bed.

EIGHT

When the South Tahoe High School let out the next day, I was there.

I had called the numbers that Marlette gave me for Charlie's friends and visited the mother of one of the boys. She was much more forthcoming than Jersey Walker's mother had been. The woman gave me a description of her son and his friend, class pictures of both, a peanut butter sandwich, corn chips, a glass of milk and a description of her son's friend's car, which they drove to and from school.

I was at the car now, an old Camaro in the process of being restored. The body filler had been sanded smooth. I walked around it and saw a small spray of hot red paint just behind the right front wheel well. Otherwise it was all gray primer. I wasn't leaning against it or even touching it as the boys approached.

"Steve?" I said. "Steve and Jason?"

"Yeah," said Steve, the one who held cars keys in his hand.

"Owen McKenna." I reached out and shook their hands. "Jason, your mother told me where I could find you guys. Said you could answer a question about one of your classmates."

The reaction with all kids is standard and predictable. If you're not a teacher or employer, suspicion shapes all social intercourse. They can be good, honor-role kids and still they assume you're a cop looking to make trouble for one of their own. Steve and Jason had that look.

I tried to ease their tension. "Nice ride," I said. "What is it, a sixty-eight?"

Steve made a little nod.

"You going to customize it, or keep it stock?"

"I dunno. The last owner kinda tricked up the engine, but I might build it back down, go with authentic original parts."

"That's what I'd do," I said. "What color you gonna go with? Black? Or red, maybe. Red would be cool."

Steve raised his eyebrows and gave me a little grin. "Yeah, I was thinking red. Friend of mine works in a body shop. He showed me a color, Ferrari red. Awesome. He put a little sample down on the rocker panel." He pointed.

I nodded. "Hey guys, I won't keep you long. I'm a private detective looking into the disappearance of Charlie and Silence Ramirez. You know them, right?"

Jason went wide-eyed. "They really were kidnapped?"

"We don't know. Maybe. I'm wondering if either of you have heard from either Charlie or Silence."

Steve glanced at Jason then turned to me. It was the kind of glance that could be loaded with meaning, or it could just be that he was looking to see if Jason was going to talk first. "Well, me and Jason, we talk to Charlie lots. He's younger than us, but he's real mature for his age. He mostly hangs out with kids our age. His sister is the same age as us."

"He say anything to you in the days before he disappeared?"

"Not anything that would be like a clue or anything. Just the usual. Same as every day."

"You mean, talk about school, girls, stuff like that?"

Both Steve and Jason grinned.

"Yeah," Steve said. "He always wants to know where I'm at with the rig." Steve looked toward the Camaro. "How many more coats of primer. What am I gonna do with the transmission. Like that."

"Either of you heard anything about Charlie or Silence since they disappeared?"

They both shook their heads.

Jason said, "Just rumors. Whether they ran away. Or could they have really been kidnapped."

"Steve?" I said.

"Yeah, I'd say the same thing. The rumors have been pretty thick at school."

I paused. "One thing came up. It's possible they were taken by bikers. Do you think bikers could do that? Take Charlie and Silence on the back of motorcycles?"

Steve was shaking his head. "If they didn't want to go? No way. Charlie's a fighter. He's only fourteen, but he's gonna be a serious athlete. He can already bench one-eighty. He'll be pumping two-twenty, two-thirty in a year. And he's still just a kid."

Jason was nodding. "They try to put Charlie on the back of a bike against his will, he just wouldn't let it happen. He'd strangle the driver or gouge his eyes out."

"Do either of you think that Charlie and Silence would run away? Or that they would go somewhere for a few days without telling anyone?"

"You mean, not even call their mother?" Steve asked.

"Yeah."

They both shook their heads.

"Charlie would call," Jason said with conviction. "Isn't that right, Steve? Charlie wouldn't leave his mom hanging."

"That's right," Steve said. "Charlie is respectful of his mom. He's respectful of all adults."

"How was Charlie about his sister? Was he protective of her?"

"No kidding," Steve said, making an exaggerated nod. "It'd be real stupid to say something bad about Silence with Charlie around. Even if you could take him, he'd still do his best to remove your head. No fear, that kid. Don't get me wrong, we'd never say anything bad about Silence. I like her. I mean, she's kinda out there, but I like her. Don't you, Jason?"

"She's a sweet kid. Not like I'd ask her out." His giggle was short and nervous. "But she's nice. I think a lot of kids are starting to think that she's not so weird after all. But there's still those who make fun of her, not talking and all. And she never looks at you. That still bugs me a little."

Steve spoke. "Charlie is responsible for changing the way kids see Silence. He is so focused on being good to her that it kinda spreads to other kids. And partly, he's getting big and strong and if you don't do right by her he's going to get in your face."

"What about Callif King?" I said. "Is he around? I have a question for him."

"You want to talk to King Cal?" Jason said, surprise in his voice. "He's right over there." He pointed across the parking lot toward a group of kids. A half-dozen girls surrounded a boy who had blond hair, a letter jacket and a toothy smile.

I thanked Jason and Steve and walked over to where Cal stood at the center of the circle of admiring girls.

Outside of the ring stood four other jocks, smaller, not as handsome, not as confident. They shifted positions as I approached.

It is a carefully studied nonchalance and indifference that popular high school male athletes adopt. The world exists for them alone. Other people are paper cutouts, positioned at appropriate distances to direct attention to those on center stage. If any other male of size or substance comes near, the threat is ascertained, the support troops mustered to intervene, and the collective athletic unconscious draws together to cordon off the royalty, to protect those who are anointed and have the power to dispense favors to the second string.

The mindless girl groupies who pull in tight, jostling for a position close enough that they can bump up against the lettered flesh, seem unappreciative of the fact that they outnumber the varsity boys four to one. Most of their group will be cast off to hook up with the B-squad boys who, like coyotes following grizzlies, are eager for any scrap the big boys leave behind.

The four second-stringers got nervous as I approached. They pulled together to intercept me, but they fidgeted and didn't know whether to look at me or pretend to ignore me.

"Hey, man," one of them said to me. Both a greeting and

a challenge.

"I'm here to talk to Callif King," I said.

One of them glanced over his shoulder, towards Cal, then frowned, thinking up his line, trying to be brave.

"He's busy right now. Would you like to leave a message?"

The other three kids laughed.

"Funny," I said. I walked ahead. They contracted even tighter and contrived to intimidate me. I walked through, bumping one of them. They bounced away.

The girls turned and looked at me. Cal looked up. He was a big kid. Probably outweighed me by twenty pounds. He telegraphed confidence and cockiness. He'd never known a time in his life when he wasn't Numero Uno.

"I'm Detective McKenna. Got a couple questions I'd like to ask you," I said. One of the girls snickered.

"What if I don't want to answer?" he said.

"How 'bout I ask? If you don't want to help, you can tell me to leave. I'll respect your decision."

King Cal looked at me for a moment, trying to figure out if I were bullshitting him. For him it had always been a matter of who was bigger and tougher.

"Silence and Charlie Ramirez have disappeared."

"I didn't have anything to do with that," he said.

"Of course, not. What we need is some background on Silence and Charlie. I've spoken to one of their friends and you were mentioned as the guy to talk to. Charlie of course looked up to you as an extraordinary athlete, and Silence, well, I guess it's no secret she had a crush on you."

The group of girls burst out giggling in unison. "Oh, that's cute," one of them sang out. "The silent girl who spins and stares at the floor wants to get it on with Cal."

"I thought they were kidnapped," Cal said.

"Maybe they were," I said. "But there's no ransom note and no other indication.

"I don't understand what you want from me," Cal said.

"What do you mean about background?"

"We're looking for motive," I said. "Someone with your intelligence and position as a leader in school, you can see things that others would miss. You would see if something about those kids would make them a target. We have nothing specific to go on in looking for them, so we're looking at everything. For example, you would notice if anyone had a grudge against those kids."

Cal glanced over at the girls. "Some kids, I don't know, they have this thing about Silence. Like they take offense that she's mental. Not that I have a problem with that."

"No, of course not."

Cal lowered his voice so that he wouldn't be overheard. "I actually thinks she's kind of nice. She doesn't hurt anyone, even if she's, you know..." he stopped talking.

"Does anything about her come to mind that would make someone do her harm?"

"I can't imagine anybody doing that."

"What about Charlie? Is he a hothead? He ever get somebody real angry at him?"

Cal shook his head.

"What if some bikers came by and said something rude to Silence? Would Charlie blow up at them, give them the finger, get them coming after both him and his sister?"

"The thing is," Cal started, scrunching up his forehead, slowly figuring out how to say it, "Charlie's, like, two kinds of people. On one hand, he's Silence's bodyguard. If anyone threatened Silence, he'd be all over them. He's physically strong, and he's even stronger mentally. So he can go into a situation and call the other guy's bluff and pull it off. Know what I mean? But the other thing is, Charlie's real smart. He can size up a situation. That's why he's going to be a great quarterback some day. If he looked at a situation and saw that the odds were that it would end badly, he'd make a quick retreat. Same as football. If you can see that your big move is gonna get you busted up real bad, you find a way out. You let the easy tackle get you, or you run out of bounds, whatever it takes."

"People like Charlie, don't they," I said.

"Oh, yeah. Charlie's a good kid. No way would anyone want to hurt him. And just knowing he's looking out for his sister, no way would anyone want to hurt her."

"Thanks for your help," I said.

I got Mallory on my cell as I drove away. "Wanted to update you," I said when he answered. "I've talked to Silence's best friend who now lives down in Southern Cal, and Charlie's friends here in Tahoe. Two or three things seem relatively certain.

"One is that the kids wouldn't run away without Charlie calling their mom. Two is that you couldn't kidnap Charlie by forcing him on the back of a motorcycle. He was tough and he would resist. You'd have to have a car at minimum, better yet a van. Three, I don't think anyone has heard from Charlie or Silence. I don't think these high school kids could keep it quiet. So it's looking more and more like a kidnapping."

"For the girl," Mallory said.

"What do you mean?"

"An hour ago an El Dorado Sheriff's Deputy found the boy's body near the chain-up area below Echo Summit."

I took a deep breath.

"Cause of death?" I finally asked.

"Looks like blunt-force trauma to the head."

After a moment I said, "I've learned that Charlie was the girl's guardian and protector and main connection to the world."

"Sorry to hear it," Mallory said. His voice had the fatigue that you can only hear from cops middle-aged or older. "There's more."

"A ransom note?"

"No. Writing on the boy's forehead. Ballpoint pen. Hard to make out because the body is showing major deterioration. But it looked like strange writing. So we asked LAPD about it and they gave us the number of a professor at UCLA. We faxed a photo of it to him. He just called back. He said he's not positive he can make it out, but it looks like a Nahuatl word for an Aztec god."

NINE

Within hours South Lake Tahoe erupted as only a small town can when a much-loved child meets a tragic death. The South Lake Tahoe PD and the El Dorado County Sheriff's Department put on all their available manpower. The CHP ramped up their presence on streets throughout the California side of the basin. Diamond Martinez called from the Douglas County Sheriff's Department on the Nevada side and said they were putting most of their deputies from Carson Valley up at the lake to help patrol any areas where bikers were hanging out, which was everywhere.

From comments made by Mallory and Diamond, it sounded like the counties on the north end of the lake were following suit, making as big a show of law enforcement as any locals had ever seen.

The El Dorado Sheriff had decided that the Nahuatl word on the boy's forehead would be kept quiet so that it could be used as an identifier with anyone who eventually claimed knowledge of the murder.

Since the body had been found, there were no more doubts about the kidnapping, and it was screamed continuously from TV and radio stations from Sacramento to Reno and featured on the national evening news broadcasts of every major news organization from coast to coast. There was a young girl out there presumed kidnapped and alive and held by the same bikers who murdered her brother. Although the media did not know about the Aztec evidence, the presumption was that because

Marlette and her neighbor heard the bikers in the street, the bikers were the ones who took the kids. That the girl was autistic and could not talk captured the attention of listeners nationwide, but the fact that she was Silence, sister of beloved Charlie, threatened to rip the heart out of Tahoe.

After I'd left the high school I inched through exceptionally heavy traffic near the "Y" intersection, the result of a huge influx of law enforcement vehicles. I reached for my cell to call Street.

She answered with as somber a voice as I'd heard from her in memory. I could hear road noise in the background.

"You heard," I said.

"Yes. El Dorado Sheriff's Department called me at my lab. Because the body has been off to the side of the road for awhile, they want me to do a time-of-death analysis and look for general insect evidence. I grabbed my kit and left immediately. I'm heading out Pioneer Trail now. I'll be there in a few minutes."

"Are you all right with that, working on a child?"

"No. But they need me and I can do it. I've done a lot of forensic consults. I can remind myself that this is just one more."

"And you can remind yourself that Silence may benefit, too. Your work could help in some unforeseen way."

"Yes."

"It's been so cold at night. Does that make it difficult?"

"Yes. If someone is killed during a cold night, there won't be any flies to lay their eggs on the body until things warm up the next day. I'll have to make allowances for that in my calculations. Cold also affects which species find the body. But it's been three days since the kidnapping. If he was killed soon after the kidnapping there will be plenty of insect evidence despite the cold nights."

"You are made of stainless steel," I said. "I'm amazed."

"Thanks, but you're wrong. I stain very easily." Her voice wavered. "Very easily. I better call you later," she said, voice catching, and hung up.

My cell rang almost immediately.

"Owen, Glennie. You were my first call. As always." Glenda Gorman was a reporter for the Tahoe Herald, and she wrote incisive articles with the assurance of a big-city reporter. She'd had several offers from the Chronicle and Mercury News in the Bay Area, but she was a skier and hiker and sailor and she always opted to stay at the lake.

I was lost in my thoughts about what Street had to do in the next hour or two. I didn't say anything.

"This is a terribly sad one," Glennie said. "I'm hoping to frame the story in a way that will provide the greatest chance that my words will help someone find the killer. But I will not sensationalize this."

"I know that, Glennie."

"You're working on it, right? A woman I know from Soroptimists goes to the same church as the mother, Mrs. Ramirez."

"Ah," I said. "Only, she went back to her maiden name after she got divorced. Marlette Remmick."

"Good to know. Anything happening at this point? Can you do a summation?"

"Not much to tell. We had no direct evidence of the kidnapping until the boy's body was found this afternoon. At the time of the kidnapping, both mother and a neighbor heard motorcycles in the street. So there is a possibility the kids were taken by motorcyclists. At this point, everything is supposition. There are few facts, but I will let you know if I learn anything useful."

I didn't tell Glennie about the Nahuatl word written on Charlie's forehead, because that was being withheld from the public.

Glennie thanked me and hung up.

I was coming up on Al Tahoe Blvd, so I turned right and drove over to the police department to see if Mallory was in. He was.

"Come in, sit down, drink coffee, enjoy the view from the executive suite," he said, his voice as dark as I'd ever heard it. He gestured at the windowless walls of his small office.

I sat on a hard metal chair, wedged between two four-drawer file cabinets. My knees brushed Mallory's metal desk. Mallory picked up a Coke can and tried to sip something from it, but it was empty. He set it down hard enough to dent it.

"Has Marlette Remmick been informed yet?" I asked.

"Did it myself. Just got back. The El Dorado boys wondered if they should do it. But I felt a little guilty after doubting her story before. I knew she would fall apart big time – not that I blame her – so I called Doc Lee and asked him to come along. He had to finish something at the hospital, so I waited. Doc brought his bag. After I told her he gave her a sedative and smoothed out the shock waves." Mallory paused, revisiting what must have been an excruciating moment.

"Did you know Doc Lee once wanted to be a cop?" Mallory said, obviously trying to find a different subject. "It wouldn't've been an easy career for him, what with being a small and gentle type. Better he became a doctor. But that surprised me, Doc Lee ever wanting to be a cop."

"Yeah," I said. "That is a surprise."

"Anyway, he gave her some pills. He'd followed me over there in his own car. So I left him there. She'll probably get through okay until she has to ID the body. But that can wait a bit."

"How'd she take it when you told her?"

"The way you'd expect a mom like her would. Pretty much an explosion. If her grief was fireworks, the streamers would still be filling the sky. It was loud. There was a lot of movement. I think she loved that kid pretty good." Mallory looked at the wall to his left.

I don't imagine it's possible for Mallory's eyes to get moist without eye drops. But I'd seen him do some squinting in the past when he was having trouble. He was squinting now.

TEN

Mallory told me that I should call Doc Lee before I stopped by to see Marlette. I got him on my cell.

"She's sleeping," Doc Lee said. "She'll come around later this evening. Her neighbor Rachael Clarkson was there and will be checking in on her. I told Rachael to give Marlette some soup and another pill and send her back to bed for the night. Hold on," I heard muffled voices in the background, a soft voice over a loud-speaker, hospital sounds. "Sorry," Doc Lee said. "What was I saying?"

"When can I talk to Marlette?" I said.

"Tomorrow. She'll be sedated, so you will want to adjust your expectations accordingly."

"Thanks, Doc."

The next morning was Sunday, the beginning of the ten-day biker festival. Mallory called to tell me that Marlette's neighbor Rachael took her to ID the body.

"How'd it go?" I said.

"About like when I told her yesterday. The woman doesn't hold back."

"You think she'll be able to talk?"

"Give it a try, I guess," Mallory said.

I knocked on Marlette's door an hour later. The woman who answered was the physical opposite of Marlette. Very rotund and almost albino white, Rachael Clarkson moved ponderously, doing a side-to-side weight shift under a pale yellow tent dress as she stepped from one foot to the other. "You must be the detective. The doctor told me about you. Come in, come in, Marlette's up. I'm sure she wants to talk to you."

Marlette was sitting on one end of the living room couch, sunk deep down into the soft cushions. Her knees were up, her red terry cloth robe wrapped over them.

Blue pajama bottoms protruded a few inches below her robe. She had on fuzzy blue slippers below her strong brown ankles. A cup of coffee sat next to her on the broad wooden arm of the couch. It looked like it had gone cold. Marlette clutched a framed picture to her chest. I could only see the back of the gold frame, but I was certain the picture was of her children.

"Hi, Marlette," I said as I sat on the edge of the nearest chair. I reached out and gently touched her upraised knee. "I'm sorry about Charlie." It is one of those statements that overwhelms with its insufficiency, but nothing is sufficient in such a situation.

Marlette stared over her knees at the carpet. Eventually, she spoke through gritted teeth. "They're never coming back. Silence is probably already dead like Charlie. The police will find her body. Someone will scribble on her forehead, too. They'll both go to their graves with graffiti on their faces!" Marlette slowly turned her head and looked at me. Her eyes were on fire. "Isn't that right, Owen? I'm not going to be deluded about this. I have to face the facts."

Rachael came from the kitchen. "Marlette honey, your coffee's gone so cold it's probably got a layer of ice on it. Let me warm that." She reached out her hand. Marlette didn't respond, so I picked up the cup and handed it to Rachael.

I said to Marlette, "They didn't find Silence. That is a good indication that she is still alive. We can still save her. And you can help."

Marlette continued to look at the carpet, but she was seeing something else, a memory of Charlie perhaps, a private moment that no one else would ever know.

"You can help," I repeated, "by telling me more about your family. Let's start with your ex-husband. When was the last time you saw him?"

Marlette didn't look at me and she didn't answer. She just hugged the picture frame to her chest. "They're never coming back," she said again in the lifeless voice.

Rachael came slowly back, panting with effort, holding out a fresh cup of steaming coffee in one hand and a little plate with a pastry in the other. "Here you go, honey. Hot coffee and coffee cake, too. That's what you need, honey. A girl needs to eat. No dieting at a time like this."

Marlette ignored her.

I took the coffee and cake and set them on the arm of the couch.

"Maybe Marlette needs to rest," Rachael said to both of us. "Isn't that right, honey? You need some quiet time. Mr. Owen should come back later. Am I right, honey?"

Marlette didn't speak.

I thanked her, touched her knee again and left.

ELEVEN

I stopped at Street's lab and again left Spot in the Jeep. He stuck his head out the window and moaned as I walked away. It's a moan you'd think he perfected in acting class. It starts out high, goes down very low and ends with a little hiccup like a yodeler cracking his voice.

I turned around. "What's your problem, large one?"

He wagged.

"A few private minutes with my sweetheart is not too much to ask," I said and pulled open Street's door.

Street had on an apron and white latex gloves. She sat on a stool at a high counter. She held a jar with what looked like little white grains of rice in a liquid. She was making notes in a notebook. "Hi," she said, her voice low and serious.

I walked over and kissed the back of her neck.

"Have you spoken with Marlette?" she asked. "How is she doing?"

"Doc Lee has her sedated. She's awake but depressed and angry and nearly cataleptic with grief. I'll check back this evening." I looked again at the jar in her hand. "Are those the specimens you collected?"

"Some of them. These I put in a solution to preserve them at this stage of growth. The rest I'm growing to maturity to identify the species of fly." She pointed over to a counter where there was a metal box about the size of a countertop refrigerator. It had a temperature dial on it and a timer and could be set to a range of temperatures that would fluctuate in an attempt to mimic the daily temperature swings where the body was found. There was a window in the front of the device. I had no desire to look in.

Street said, "I also found some insect evidence in the boy's hair. Three segments of legs off a beetle that I don't recognize as native to Tahoe. They probably won't tell me about Charlie's death, but if a future suspect has similar insect parts on his clothes or in his home or vehicle, it could help bring a conviction." Street glanced at the incubator. "Either way, eventually, I'll be able to estimate the time of death to a fairly narrow time window."

"Any unofficial guesses at this point?" I said.

She gave me one of those looks that showed how much tolerance was required to accommodate my presumption.

"I know. Scientists do not like to speculate," I said. "But a guess would help. If Charlie's body was left in the ditch shortly after the kidnapping, then the kidnappers could have taken Silence anywhere in the days between then and now. But if he was killed much more recently, say just before his body was found, then they couldn't have gone so far. There would be a greater chance that Silence is nearby. The knowledge would help focus our search."

"Based on these specimens and the cold nighttime temperatures I can pretty much guess that the boy was killed shortly after he and the girl were kidnapped. These maggots simply could not have grown to this point with less time. But I'll have an official opinion in a few weeks."

TWELVE

That evening I left Spot at home and called again on Marlette. Rachael Clarkson met me at the door. She held her finger up to her lips and motioned for us to go back outside. She shut the door behind her and spoke quietly, shaking her head.

"I just wanted to warn you. Those stages of grief we always hear about? Well, I don't know how many there are or what's supposed to happen when, but let me tell you, this woman is all over the scale. Crying, sobbing like you've never heard, then explosions. You have to be ready to duck. She throws things and then kicks at the wall and next thing you know she falls to the floor writhing like a snake. After thirty minutes or so she goes limp like she's in a coma. I've never seen anything like it."

"Okay, thanks for letting me know."

She turned and preceded me into the house.

Marlette was sitting on one of the stiff kitchen chairs, her back rigid. She was staring out the black window toward where Pioneer Trail curved through the darkness.

I pulled out the chair across from her at the table and sat down. "Hi, Marlette."

"Owen," she said in a tiny, airy voice. She didn't look at me, just kept looking out toward the backyard. "Don't worry. I can talk. Whatever you want." Marlette spoke in a monotone voice like a child reading lines in a play. "Tell me what you want. If there is any chance of bringing back Silence, any chance..."

Then she called out to Rachael, her voice so soft and dream-like it was like a sleepwalker talking. I couldn't tell if

Marlette was suffering from some kind of post-traumatic stress or if she was in a trance. She said, "Rachael? I forgot to give Owen one of the videos yesterday. Could you get one of those DVDs?"

I heard Rachael moving in one of the bedrooms.

Marlette said to me, "Last spring I had my videos put on a disc. They made several copies, so you can have one. You'll like it, Owen. My kids are very fun to watch." Then the tears were back.

Rachael appeared and set a disc on the wood. "Honey, I'm just going to pop home for a bit and do some things. You'll be fine with Mr. Owen, here. I'll be back later, okay?"

Marlette didn't answer. Rachael left.

I said, "You gave me those small photos of your kids. Do you have any of the whole family? You and Shane, too?"

Marlette walked over to some shelves in the living room and brought back a picture in a frame. "This is from a few years ago. Our last family shot. Shane left a couple months after that."

It was a portrait with Marlette on the left, Shane on the right and the kids in the middle. All but Silence had big smiles.

"Have the kids changed much since this was taken?" I asked.

"Just like those school photos you got yesterday. Charlie's bigger and his hair is blacker. Silence still looks similar, a little more mature is all."

"May I borrow it?"

"Of course."

"Tell me about your ex-husband Shane," I said.

Marlette wiped her eyes with the backs of her hands, pushed her chair back and stood up from the table, her back straight and her footsteps light and graceful and assured like the dancer she'd obviously once been. She walked across the kitchen, almost gliding. She got out two glasses, filled them out of the faucet and returned, carefully setting one glass directly in front of me and the other in front of her. She took such care in positioning them, it was as if there were an invisible chessboard and the glasses had to go in the right squares or the queen would be lost to the enemy and the king would be in check.

I waited, took a sip of tepid water, waited some more.

"Shane Ramirez," she finally said in a wistful voice as if remembering a sweet dream. "If only he wanted to be a husband and a father. If only he wanted one good woman. If only he could appreciate the God-given beauty that surrounds him instead of always searching for greener grass. If only he could be rooted in a community and go to church with his family."

Maybe I looked judgmental at Marlette's sentimental reverie. Or maybe this was just one of the mood swings Rachael warned me about, for she paused and suddenly gave me a hardened look.

"I gather that you are not married, Mr. McKenna." Her voice was harsh.

"Please call me Owen. No, I'm not."

"So you don't have children?"

Normally, I do not let a client pigeon-hole me with such questions. But I saw no problem with it other than my loss of privacy to a woman who was on the verge of fracturing into pieces.

"No," I said.

"Have you ever been married?"

"No."

She thought about that for a moment. "Do you go to church?"

Again, I would normally ignore such an inquiry and try to redirect the conversation. Instead, irritated, I said, "My church is the piney woods and the moonlit mountains and the impossibly blue and sparkling lake and the night sky thick with stardust and, yes, I am there as often as possible."

Marlette's breathing became labored. For a fraction of a second her eyes flamed. Then she crossed her arms and slid them onto the table and lowered her head onto them, her face turned away from me. Her black hair had just enough loft and heft to shiver a little and drop down like it was melting. I guessed she was one-third Native American, one-third African-American and the rest a mix of Mexican, Caribbean, and Brazilian with seasoning from people who arrived on boats from Polynesia a thousand years before. The result was rich, brown, perfect skin. Maybe her ancestry also produced the mercurial temperament with eyes that could light afire at the tiniest strike of emotional flint.

In time her breathing slowed and she spoke. "I'm sorry I judged you. I've always been too quick to draw conclusions, too quick to find fault. The reason is, I was a heathen child. I never had a father and I ran away from my mother in the barrio in L.A. at the age of fourteen, the same age Silence was when she went to Jersey's house. I suppose that's why I wanted to think she was kidnapped. Because I couldn't bear to think she was like me.

"I ran in a pack for awhile until a sleazy scumbag in a shiny car gave me money and a place to sleep and made me do horrible things to earn my food. Two years I was trapped in that world. One day a customer took me away, kidnapped me, really, and brought me against my will to Santa Barbara. He dragged me to a church and delivered me into the hands of Sister Caroline. Sister Caroline fed me and clothed me in proper respectable clothing and made me go to Bible class and showed me how I could find His grace and forgiveness."

She paused a long time, so I asked. "How did you find it?"

"From working in the kitchen. And from dance. Sister Caroline took me to a dance studio run by the very scary and very focused Madam Descartes. Madam Descartes taught me positions and steps and rhythm and music and physical discipline while Sister Caroline taught me cooking and how to serve others.

"I lived in the convent for two years. I behaved perfectly. I was their model for other girls who came later."

Marlette stood up and walked around the kitchen, then circled again, pacing, almost stomping. "But I failed! I broke! I met a man and came with him to Reno. He said I could be a showgirl, that I had the look and the dance skills. And he was right. I got a job as a chorus girl in a revue. It was scandalous. We wore almost nothing for the ten o'clock shows and then danced naked for the midnight shows. It's disgusting what that attention does to a young woman. The men, the money, the glamour, the famous people wanting to meet you.

"But one night – it was about three in the morning - I called Sister Caroline back in Santa Barbara. I woke her up. I was crying and scared. I knew I was going to hell. She talked to me for hours. She talked about what I could do to come back to a pious life, to a life of meaning.

"So I did what she said. Not all the way. Not back to Santa Barbara. But I quit the dance life and moved to Berkeley because another girl was going there and she said I could stay with her for awhile. I got a job working at a cleaning service. The service had a contract to clean some buildings on the university campus. We also cleaned some houses. It wasn't fun, but it's good honest work. I still clean houses now.

"I met Shane at one of the houses in Berkeley. I was twenty-one. Shane was a friend of the homeowner and they were there one day when our crew showed up. They were funny and gracious and left to get out of our way.

"But the next day a delivery from a florist came to the room where I was living. It was a single pink carnation in a vase. The note said that the cleaning service wouldn't give him my address but they agreed to forward a note and a flower. The note also said he was performing at a club and that he would like to invite me and one of my friends if I so desired. Enclosed were two tickets. So I took my girlfriend. He was a good rapper. After the show he and his drummer came into the audience and asked if they could take us to a late-night coffeehouse. We all had a great time and ended up talking most of the night.

"Shane and I saw each other every night after that, and I fell in love with his flash and humor." Marlette stopped, a vacant look on her face.

I waited.

She said, "I suppose I'm not the first woman to marry someone without ever first wondering if the man would make a good husband. We moved to Tahoe because Shane and I both love the mountains, and we were married just one month later.

"Shane was a great romantic. He read poetry. We hiked a few times and he'd recite a poem at the top of the mountain.

Shane could be a real charmer.

"But he turned out to be continuously distracted by what he didn't have. He didn't have a Mercedes. He didn't own his own house. He didn't have a powerboat. He didn't have a record-ing contract.

"It was that last thing that made the most trouble. Shane wanted to be a rapper. He wrote quite a body of work. He had a style and developed a look. The whole No Shane No Gain thing had a lot of potential. And he was good! But trying to become a famous rapper is like trying to become a movie star or a rock star. The worst odds in the world. There are only a few rappers who can get to the top. But there are millions of young men and women trying to get there. Add to that the fact that he is getting old. He's thirty-nine, now. It's just not going to happen. But tell that to him. Charlie had been born and was the greatest kid ever, but Shane didn't really care. Charlie was eleven when Shane left.

"Shane's been down in Southern Cal since then, still try-ing to put it together. I'll give him that. He tries hard." Marlette looked up at me. "They always say you should follow your dream. Did you ever notice that? Well, so what. Shane has pur-sued his dreams with such focus you wouldn't believe. But it got him nowhere. Dreams are like fairy dust. They look so great in the movies. But they don't come so easy in real life, do they?" She waited, wanting a response.

"No, they don't," I said quietly.

Marlette walked over to the window and looked out at the backyard. "It was eighteen years ago when I married him. He hung in there for fifteen of those years. But the truth was he wasn't a good husband. And he wasn't a good father."

I watched Marlette's head from behind, three-quarter's profile. Her jaw muscles bulged in and out.

"The teacher you mentioned the other day," I said. "The one who thinks Silence is smart. What was her name again?"

"Henrietta Johanssen. I'll write down her number for you." She wrote on a Post-it note and handed it to me.

"Thanks. I'll give her a call and be in touch."

THIRTEEN

When I got home I made a quick sandwich for dinner, then plugged Marlette's DVD into my laptop and sat down in my rocker to watch. It opened with an image of Lake Tahoe as seen from somewhere on the East Shore. It was a long telephoto shot so that Pyramid Peak and the Crystal Range on the west side of the lake filled the background.

Super-imposed on the water portion of the image came a fade-in title and background music started playing, a jazzy version of the piece that Bob Hope had always used as his theme song.

The title said, My Sweet Children, and underneath in smaller type it had the song title, Thanks For The Memories, and underneath that it said, Starring: Silence and Charlie Ramirez; Director: None; Cinematographer: Marlette Remmick.

The writing and the view of Tahoe faded away and were replaced by a shot of a young Charlie blowing out five candles on a tall chocolate birthday cake. Eight-year-old Silence stood off to the side looking absent from the festivities.

Charlie's grin was predictably huge with excitement as he stabbed his right hand into the frosting and then stuck it into his mouth. The video then cut to a close-up of Silence standing rigid, her left hand holding a sketchbook at her side and her right hand delicately holding a fork on which was a small piece of cake. She gracefully ate it without getting any chocolate on her hand or face. She didn't look at the camera. Neither was she particularly focused on the cake. A casual and perhaps crass observation would be that there didn't seem to be anyone behind those averted eyes.

As she turned to reach for another bite her face was vacant, apparently registering nothing. Nobody was home.

A more generous observation would be that she was looking inward, reflecting on some thought that she was unwilling to share with others. But I couldn't make myself believe it.

Then Charlie stuck his head into the picture, mugging for the camera, holding up his hands, palms out, which were brown with chocolate as was his face. He stuck out his tongue, grinning like a crazed monkey clown, then turned back to feast with gusto.

The screen faded to black, new music started, an old Lovin' Spoonful standard called "Summer In The City." The picture that came up showed Silence and Charlie down in Reno during the Hot August Nights celebration. They stood at the side of a crowded street where dozens of spectacular hotrods were parked, doors and hoods open, people crowding around. Charlie again stole the show with his antics and mugging and dancing, while Silence stood to the side, holding her sketchbook in a white-knuckled grip as she reached up to plug her ears.

This time, her face didn't seem vacant. Rather, she appeared to be in pain, as if the noise and lights were an assault on her senses. I couldn't tell what she was looking at because the ambient light was too dim. Then the camera zoomed in and I could see that she had her eyes clamped shut. Suddenly, the young Charlie appeared and wrapped his arms around her. He seemed to squeeze her hard and he held the position for many seconds, rocking her back and forth until the screen went dark.

On it went, Marlette's production displaying the typical subjects of home videos. Holidays, toboggan parties, the arrival of a surprise puppy, the kids in new clothes ready for the first day of school. The pattern in each scene was similar to every other.

There were only a few scenes of perfunctory domestic life. One showed Charlie and Silence brushing their teeth. Charlie clowned around, dabbed toothpaste on the mirror and grinned so the camera could capture just how foamy a mouth could get.

Silence was the opposite. She stood in the corner facing the wall, brushing with her left hand in precise mechanical strokes, her lower arm moving like a machine.

The scene shifted to another birthday party, this one for Silence. She stood rigid most of the time and Charlie opened her presents. She finally became animated when Shane came in carrying the last present, a puppy with a red bow around its neck. Silence immediately reached for the dog, held it tight to her chest, her sketchbook pinched between her and the dog. She rocked her upper body back and forth and the camera jerked as Marlette tried to keep her in the frame. The camera zoomed in and the dog looked terrified. It became apparent that Silence was squeezing the puppy too hard for it to breathe. Shane rushed in and pried the dog from Silence's hands and he set the dog down on the floor. The dog sprinted away. Silence burst into tears and the scene cut off.

In every scene, Charlie was exuberant, bursting with energy, in love with life, overflowing with personality and always protective and guarding of Silence who stayed to the side, looked away, didn't show interest in anything except her sketchbook.

She carried the sketchbook like a security blanket. If I hadn't seen her bedroom walls covered in drawings, I would have wondered if she just liked the feel of it. But then came a scene showing Silence sitting down on the floor in the hallway, facing the open bathroom door. She opened her sketchbook and began a drawing on a blank page. What happened next was astonishing. She held the book open with her right hand and drew with her left. Her hand moved in a blur. She never paused to reflect on her strokes or consider her approach. She just sketched like a machine, very fast, very accurate, and she finished the drawing in less than a minute. The video didn't show the details well, but I paused the picture. Then I zoomed in on the drawing. From what I could see the drawing looked like a grainy photo of the bathroom.

A half hour into the video came another unusual scene.

The kids were a little older, Charlie perhaps seven and Silence ten. They were at a park, on the swing-set. Charlie swung as if to go over the top. Silence sat on a swing, barely moving, sketchbook in one hand while the other hand held one of the swing's chains. Suddenly, there was a loud rumbling noise. The camera swung over to capture a huge cement truck turning into the park, roaring down a dirt road toward a building pad where men standing on foundation forms were waiting for cement. Although the truck was very loud, it was clearly heading past the kids and presenting no danger.

Yet, as the camera swung back it caught Silence as she jumped out of the swing. She plugged her ears and started vibrating with terror. It looked like she was in the beginning moments of a seizure when she stopped, lifted her right foot and pushed it down as if pushing down a bike pedal. Her foot hit the playground sand and turned her partway around as she rotated on her left foot. She lifted the right foot again and pushed off again, rotating a little faster. Her head bowed a bit so that her face was toward the ground, and she went around a little faster, then faster still. Her right foot was pumping in a powerful rhythm, and the tempo accelerated. She didn't fall over, didn't even waver, but continued to speed up until she was spinning like a figure skater.

The camera zoomed in on her so that her spinning form filled the frame.

She had her ears plugged, her sketchbook held at the side of her head, and her eyes were shut. But something unusual happened to her demeanor. Despite spinning so fast that she was almost a blur, she seemed to relax. The tension that had clamped her elbows to her side loosened and went away and her arms began to look like those of a twirling skater, held for esthetic position rather than stiff function. The rigidity of her hands at her ears disappeared and they looked less like claws at her temples and more like a model's hands, thin little fingers floating, middle and ring fingers gently curled into graceful curves. Her right foot continued to pump and her spin seemed to evolve as her body changed its unyielding straightness into a flowing curve.

It was like watching a ballet where the awkward protagonist, hobbled by disability, steps into the mysterious forest and is transformed into a creature of grace.

At the end of the scene Charlie rushed in, bouncing his

palms off her shoulders as she spun, trying to slow her down, but careful not to stick his hands into her whirling form lest he hurt either of them.

When he succeeded in arresting her spin, he hugged her hard and for so long it seemed more like a therapy he'd devised over time rather than the physicality of affection.

The camera stayed on Silence as Charlie released her from his grip. She no longer looked terrified, but she didn't look the picture of grace, either. The flowing form was gone, replaced by the rigid girl's body where it seemed no one was in residence.

I was so struck by the scene that I played it again, studying the transformation that was like a chrysalis metamorphosing into a butterfly and then turning back into a caterpillar.

The video went on to show additional domestic scenes similar to the previous ones, but I was now spoiled by the last bit of drama. So I fast-forwarded through the video, looking for another scene that would catch my eye. Nothing did until the kids were much older. A scene that was possibly shot within the last year began with all of the prosaic qualities of most of the video. The kids were at home and the video showed Charlie pulling a tarnished brass trumpet out of the well-worn red velvet cradle of the instrument case. Silence sat nearby, paying no attention.

But when Charlie began to play a series of loud screeching practice notes, Silence ran from the house. Marlette got up to follow, and the video jumped and jerked with her movement. Then the camera was held steady just inside the front door and the video captured Silence as she started another spin in the driveway.

It was like the spin of several years earlier, head down, ears plugged, sketchbook clutched tightly. She sped up into a blur and the same physical changes took place, a transformation that started with how she held her body and ended with the revelation, at least to my uneducated eye, that there was something of a soul inside the quiet, seemingly empty girl.

I skimmed at fast-forward through the rest of the video and found nothing else of interest except a reprise of the tooth-brushing scene from years earlier. It was eerie how, despite the passage of time, Silence brushed exactly the same as when she'd been a little girl. She stood in the corner, faced the wall and brushed as if her arm movements were controlled by servomechanisms, hydraulics, gears and a timing device.

I turned off the laptop and went to bed and lay in the dark thinking about those kids.

Charlie was easy to quantify. Bright, engaged, eager and resourceful in dealing with his sister. Silence was his opposite. An unusual child, afflicted with a disorder that seems devastating.

It's hard to say what it is that makes a fully-functioning human. On a long list of essential qualities are several that seemed to go missing in Silence. She didn't talk, didn't communicate at all by most measures, didn't exhibit normal human intelligence. She didn't show normal curiosity, didn't watch movies or TV in any focused way. If she could read, which seemed highly doubtful, she didn't pursue books like a typical reader.

But more than that, I thought as I lay staring at the ceiling, was the puzzle of consciousness. Was Silence self-aware? Did she ask herself questions about duty and purpose and meaning? She clearly showed the emotion of fear. But could she experience joy or hope? Did she have any ambition to make something of herself? Did she feel a drive to pursue an interest or a hobby other than her drawings? Was her drawing a passion? If so, did Silence have a passion for anything other than art?

No matter how I looked at it, the facts seemed to suggest that she was a shell of a person, quite retarded, unlikely to ever learn to take pleasure in those most human of activities.

But the sketching and the spinning nagged at me. I saw focus in both activities. And I saw joy in the spinning, maybe passion, too. And I realized that as much as I wanted to save her from her kidnappers because of what they might do to her physically, I wanted to save her to let her find that little bit of joy again.

I concentrated on that spin as my own consciousness wavered and crossed over into a few hours of ragged, fitful, unsatisfying sleep.

FOURTEEN

I was up early, drinking coffee, watching dawn imbue the clouds in the western sky with a reddish brown hue that made me think of blood being diluted by tears. Over the next thirty minutes the tears washed the blood away until there was only a melancholy pink stain, lighter in the sky and slightly darker in the reflection that rosed the lake's surface.

The phone rang and it was Glennie from the paper calling for an update. I explained that I'd made no progress to speak of and that our main focus was watching the various groups of bikers around the lake.

"Have you got the morning paper, yet?" she asked.

"Not yet."

"When it comes, let me know if I'm compromising your work in any way."

"Will do."

We said goodbye.

I appreciated that Glennie tried to report events in a way that would not compromise my investigation. But I also knew that our friendship would never stop her from printing anything that she considered newsworthy. The only reason she was willing to adjust any aspect of her journalism was because I was her best source on this crime, and she wanted to keep me cooperative.

I could anticipate the coming paper delivery by the sound of the old International Harvester four-wheel-drive that the delivery woman drove. It came laboring up our steep road, hesitating and coughing and spitting as if to beg for a transfer from 7200 feet of elevation to a sea-level route where oxygen was thick as soup.

Spot was standing at the door wagging when the paper plopped out on the drive.

"Okay," I said to him, my voice heavy with gravitas as I walked to the door. We'd been working on breaking him of a new destructive habit he'd developed. This time I grabbed his snout to get his attention. "No chewing this time. No slobber. No donating it to Treasure's mom."

Spot ignored me and stood, nose to doorknob, waiting.

I opened the door and he bounded out.

"Spot, bring the paper!" I called out in the commanding voice that a doggie night-school teacher had once claimed would work miracles.

Spot shot out the drive, grabbing the paper the way a center fielder scoops up a grounder on the run. But instead of firing the paper back to first base, Spot kept on running out of the park, gravel flying from his paws as he lit up the road toward Mrs. Duchamp's and disappeared into the still dim morning.

Taking a deep breath, reminding myself that I was still in complete control, I walked out in my robe and stood wondering if I should fetch a deck chair to wait.

Soon he materialized from the grayness up the road. Having reached full speed, Spot bore down on me. I willed myself to be still as Spot came in fast, playing chicken with me, making me guess to which side he would veer at the last moment. Instead, I wondered if in fact he would veer off at all or if, in the excitement of speed, would simply forget and plow into my hips and knees and send us both to the hospital for surgical reconstruction.

It was close, but he went left in the nanosecond before impact. The paper was still in his mouth.

Spot has this playful technique of torturing the item in his mouth as he runs. At each galloping leap he opens his mouth and the object of his affection floats weightless for a moment as it arcs up and down with Spot's motion. As his paws reconnect with terra firma, Spot clamps down on it, sinking his teeth deep.

Most days since he surprised me with this new habit, Spot

has eventually yielded the paper to me, proud that he can out-shred the most expensive paper-shredder and add sufficient moisture to begin the pulping process. I was determined that this day would not be another one.

I waited until he came in on another strafing run and I ran toward him with my arms extended. Seeing my strange behavior, Spot veered away much sooner. I took three running steps and dove through the air toward him. He easily dodged my assault and I went down hard and slid on my side in the dirt, my bathrobe making a loud rip.

But Spot did give the paper a toss into the air and let it go as he ran by, tail held high with pleasure. I got up slowly, stiff and sore and leaking blood from a scrape on my elbow. The paper was wet and punctured, but still readable, so I considered it a victory of sorts, even if of a Pyrrhic flavor.

Back inside I spread out the soggy mess.

The headline was in seventy-two-point type. The story was under Glennie's byline.

KIDNAPPED BOY FOUND DEAD

Charlie Ramirez, who went missing along with his sister SalAnne five days ago, was found dead yesterday. An El Dorado Sheriff's deputy discovered the body near the chain-up area at the bottom of Echo Summit. Although an autopsy has not yet been completed, the cause of death is believed to be a blow to the head.

The discovery of the body confirms suspicions that the children had been kidnapped when they disappeared from their own yard on Wednesday afternoon. The girl is still missing and is presumed alive. No ransom note has been delivered, and no motive for the kidnapping or murder has been revealed.

According to South Lake Tahoe Police Commander Mallory, there were no witnesses to the kidnapping. However, the children's mother Marlette

Remmick and several neighbors heard motorcycles in the neighborhood.

Mrs. Remmick has retained local Private Investigator Owen McKenna to aid in discovering what happened to her children. When asked about whether bikers may have kidnapped the children, McKenna said that it is only speculation at this point. He added that anyone who has information is urged to call Commander Mallory at the Police Department or contact the Secret Witness program.

Law enforcement agencies around the Tahoe Basin have put on extra personnel. Sergeant Diamond Martinez of the Douglas County Sheriff's Department said that the department is sending several officers from Carson Valley up to the basin. When asked if they were focusing on the bikers who have come to the basin for the Tahoe Biker Heaven Festival that began yesterday, he echoed McKenna's words saying that while they weren't ruling out anyone, there was no specific evidence indicating that bikers were responsible. FBI Special Agent Ramos said they are focusing appropriate resources on the kidnapping.

I put down the paper and thought about calling Agent Ramos. I'd dealt with him on past cases and found him to be a condescending jerk. Not only did he pull rank and interfere with local law enforcement, but he refused to divulge pertinent information, claiming that local cops had insufficient need-to-know.

I decided, instead, to call Henrietta Johanssen, the Special Ed teacher Marlette had told me about. The school operator put me on hold, and Henrietta came to the phone in a few minutes. She was gracious and agreed to see me after school let out.

Next, I made a call to Dr. Power, the psychiatrist that Marlette had mentioned. He was the doctor who'd given Silence annual evaluations. His secretary said he would be able to see me late that morning.

FIFTEEN

Dr. Power had his practice in one of the medical buildings across from Barton Hospital. I parked in the lot and left Spot in the Jeep. He had his head out the rear window, pointy ears held forward as he watched a Toyota pickup several spaces over. There was a Golden Retriever lying in the back, its snout resting on the tailgate where a little bit of sun shown through the heavy pine canopy. The Golden paid Spot no attention.

I grabbed Spot's head as I got out. I leaned down close to him and said, "Don't let anything bad happen to anybody anywhere anytime," I said.

He focused his eyes on the Golden and wagged his tail.

I found Power's offices on the third floor. A sign on the door said, Raymond Power M.D., Psychiatry, in gold letters.

The door was whisper quiet as I pushed it in. Some kind of herbal air freshener mixed with the scent of coffee. A huge aquarium took up most of one side of the reception room. A group of bright blue fish chased a single larger orange fish, its scarred, chewed fins barely able to propel it forward.

A young woman came through a door to the side of the reception counter. She wore a red and green plaid skirt, perhaps the only one in all of Tahoe. Her green sweater was snug over a hard, muscled athlete's body. Her bobby socks were carefully folded down below thick calf muscles to just above brown leather shoes with more than the usual number of laces. She had chocolate brown hair cut shoulder-length and set in wavy curls. Either I'd missed a sea change in fashion in the last week or she was auditioning for a movie about a New England prep school, circa 1959.

She said, "Oh, hello, I didn't hear you."

"Just walked in. My name is Owen McKenna. I'm here to talk to Dr. Power."

"Oh, sure, dad is expecting you. Just a minute." She turned and walked through a doorway.

In a moment she was back. "Please come with me."

I followed her down a short hallway and into a corner office. A tall solid man with eyebrows like chipmunk tails stood up from his desk, came around and gave me a strong handshake.

"So you're Owen McKenna," he said. "I've heard of you. I'm Raymond Power." Power had on brown trousers that were rumpled and two inches too short for his six-three frame. His brown socks were scrunched down on ankles as thick as an ox's, and a little ring of crinkly dry white skin showed above them. The polish on his loafers was scuffed. He wore a tweed sport jacket with leather elbow patches.

"Thank you for seeing me on such short notice," I said.

"Certainly. As you may have observed, my reception room is empty. Business is slow. I have only two appointments today, and they are later this afternoon. So it's no trouble at all."

The telephone on his desk rang. "Yes, Sheila," he said when he picked it up. "What? Oh, hold on." He hung up and turned to me. "Sorry, I have to answer a question out front. Make yourself comfortable?"

"Yes, of course."

He left. I wandered around, wondering what it would be like to have an office half the size of my cabin. There were large windows with what realtors call a filtered view of mountains. Which meant, if you got in just the right position, knees bent, head turned, and the wind blew hard against the obstructing branches, you could get a quick glimpse of Heavenly through the trees. Down below was my Jeep. Spot still had his head out the window, still watching the Golden sleep.

Power's desk had a green leather-lined blotter, a gold

pen-and-pencil set, and the phone, nothing else.

Over on a wall of shelves were some community service awards from the Rotary and Soroptimists and the Hospital Auxiliary. There were many hardbound medical books. The only softcovers were on computer technology and a dog-eared book on global positioning systems. One shelf was covered with sailing magazines with pictures of boats at anchor in tropical lagoons.

There was one family photo, Raymond and his daughter Sheila standing in front of a small barn, holding the reins to two beautiful horses. They wore jeans and cowboy hats and boots. In the background on the left was a steep forested slope and to the right was a view of Freel Peak. From the angle it looked like the barn backed up to Heavenly Mountain.

I heard Power come back in behind me.

"I see you ride," I said, pointing at the photo.

"Used to. We had two Arabians. Kept them up here spring through fall, then boarded them down in Carson Valley for the winter. You know how it is. Sheila was a typical girl growing up, stark raving nuts about horses. Then the equine edge wore off and we sold them. Now the barn sits empty."

"Good memories," I said.

"Yes, but sad. I don't miss the expense, though. With the gentrification of Tahoe, it's getting harder for doctors to make it, let alone bear the expense of horses. Local homeowners are being displaced by vacation homeowners. All of my Tahoe colleagues have been forced to open up offices down in the valley. Some have even closed their Tahoe offices. I still keep an office here at the lake. But I also have an office down in Reno and I am there more days than I am here." He paused. "You mentioned the Ramirez girl on the phone."

"Yes."

Power pulled a manila folder out of a desk drawer, came over and sat on a chair. "Have a seat, Owen," he said.

I sat down on a leather couch across from him.

He gave me a somber look. "Where shall I begin?"

"I just came to ask you about her personality, her behaviors, that sort of thing."

Power shook his head back and forth three or four times. "That poor girl getting kidnapped. And her brother murdered. I never met him. I understood that he was younger by a few years."

"Three."

Power shook his head. He was visibly upset. "One of the reasons why Sheila and I moved to Tahoe was to stay away from that kind of crime. I did my residency in New Haven and practiced there for ten years. The crime in New Haven was worse than New York. As bad as Newark. After Mary died it became increasingly clear that New Haven was not the kind of place a single dad should raise his daughter. So Sheila and I got out a map and an encyclopedia – Sheila was five years old then – and we did a little armchair traveling. We developed a scoring system and when we totaled up the columns, Tahoe came out on top. It's been twelve years. Now Sheila is practically grown up. Of course, as the gods of irony would have it, now she plans to apply to a bunch of New England colleges. And wouldn't you know it, her first choice is Yale. Right back in New Haven."

He opened the folder in his lap and flipped through several pages. "Sorry, I digress."

He continued. "I went over my notes on the Ramirez girl before you came in case I've forgotten anything pertinent." He looked up from the folder, his face open and questioning. "Can you give me a little idea of your focus? From what I read in the paper, a motorcycle gang took her. Of course, I want to help. Anything to catch the monsters who did this. But how is learning about her personality going to make a difference in finding her? I would assume the various county sheriff's departments are scouring the basin looking into every possible motorcycle group and campgrounds where the bikers are and so forth. My past evaluation of her probably won't change anything."

"That may be true. But I'm hoping that some aspect of the girl's personality might point toward some aspect of the kidnapper. At this point we have almost nothing to go on. Any additional information is helpful. I'm also considering the possibility that she wasn't a random victim."

Power frowned at me. "I'm not sure I understand."

"The prevailing view in town and among local law enforcement is that Silence was taken by an opportunistic gang looking for nothing more than a young woman. Nearly any young woman would have served their purposes."

"And you think otherwise?

"I don't know. It's possible she may have been kidnapped for reasons that are specific to her, her personality, the people she knows."

"What gives you that idea?

"Partly, a hunch. Partly, an awareness that Silence is very different from 'nearly any young woman,' as I phrased it a moment ago."

"Excuse me," Power said. "You say, 'Silence.' Is that her nickname?"

"Yes. Sorry. Her mother Marlette, and her teacher Henrietta, call her Silence. The kids at school call her that as well."

"Funny," Power said, "I don't recall hearing that before."

"They sometimes stay with SalAnne in public. Anyway, there isn't a delicate way to put this – and I could be very wrong – but I imagine that a biker gang would grab a girl who appeared to advertise her wares, so to speak. I think they would pick up a girl who was hitch-hiking or strutting her stuff in front of one of the town's bars or even just wearing the revealing clothes that are so popular today. Nothing wrong with those girls, but Silence was not one of them. I don't think she would have been noticed by bikers racing by.

I continued, "The house where she lived was two blocks from Pioneer Trail, the road where the bikers were riding. You can see the yard from Pioneer Trail, but it's not easy. And according to her mother, Silence had been out in the yard. But it doesn't make sense to me that anyone on Pioneer would see her at that distance and be enticed."

"All good points," the doctor said.

"For example, what if there hadn't been bikers in the

area? If so, few people, cops included, would think she'd been a victim of convenience, chosen because she was a young woman who could be seen from Pioneer Trail. They would instead look at the location off the highway in a quiet neighborhood and the victim covered up in long sleeves and pants, and they'd think there was another reason for the kidnapping. At the very least, they'd give serious thought to the idea that the kidnapper knew Silence."

Power was frowning. "Interesting. You may be right. I never thought of it that way. Like others, I'm too accepting of what I read in the paper and see on TV. But if your notion is correct, then that places a good deal of importance on what we can glean from our knowledge of the girl." Power sighed.

"Please tell me about her," I urged. "Everything you can think of. Even the smallest details can help a case.

Power nodded. "Right. But first, a disclaimer," he said. "I'm not a pediatric psychiatrist and I'm not an autism specialist. You may want to talk to a pediatric psychiatrist or a pediatric neurologist for more complete information on children with autism.

"Having said that, the school has had me evaluate SalAnne Ramirez once a year for several years. I've always been hesitant because Autism Spectrum Disorder is not my specialty. But I was available.

"SalAnne seemed to me quite typical of autistic children. She is what we call a low-functioning child, IQ around sixty or so, completely non-verbal from birth. She has very limited language receptivity, responding to the spoken word in only the vaguest of ways." He opened the manila folder, pulled glasses out of his shirt pocket, put them on and glanced at his notes. "From what her mother reported when I first saw the child, SalAnne was distant and non-responsive from the day she was born. She didn't turn to the sound of her mother's voice, didn't show interest in human faces, was very slow to acquire even the most rudimentary skills." Power took off the glasses.

"I should point out that some autistic children go through a period of twelve or eighteen months of steady, albeit slow, development. Then they regress, losing the limited nascent speech they had begun to learn, and become non-verbal. But SalAnne displayed all of her limitations from the beginning. The variety of tests I administered failed to reveal much aptitude in any area. She can eat and wash and dress herself, but not much more.

"The most interesting thing about the Ramirez girl is her remarkable ability to draw. I remember observing her here in my office. I found there was little or nothing that I could do to take her out of her private world. But when I gave her some paper and a pen she quite amazed me with her rendering of her surroundings. And she was, I believe, only about seven years old."

"What did she draw?"

"Simple things. The lamp. My desk. The view out the window. It actually was disturbing to watch. Here was a child who acted as if you didn't exist. As if her own mother didn't exist. Yet she could draw like a genius." Power turned and stared out the window. "A long time ago I looked through a monograph on Picasso. We all think of him as the innovative painter, always pushing the limits of spatial understanding and so forth. But what most amazed me in the book were reproductions of drawings he'd done as a young child. They were masterful renditions of his subjects. Accurate right down to the smallest details of the scene, and with perfect perspective. He was clearly a prodigy. A genius."

Power turned back from the window and looked at me. "SalAnne's drawings were like that," he said.

"But you don't think her drawing ability indicates any substantial level of intelligence."

"In this case, no. I think she merely has a remarkable ability to record the three-dimensional world on two-dimensional paper. Like a camera. Nothing more."

His phone rang. He answered it, then covered the mouthpiece and said, "Sorry, I have to take this call. Can we talk again tomorrow? I'll call you when I know what my schedule is."

I nodded, handed him my card and said, "Thank you for your time," then left.

SIXTEEN

Henrietta Johanssen gave me directions over the phone. She lived on Gardner Mountain, one of the older neighborhoods in South Lake Tahoe. I drove west through town, watching roiling gray clouds race over the top of Mt. Tallac. I took a right on Emerald Bay Road. A few blocks down I turned left on 13th, went up the big hill, turned again and found her cabin looking tiny and toy-like under a stand of five or six giant Jeffrey pines. A single Incense cedar, even larger than the pines, rose just behind her house. Its furrowed trunk had the soft sienna-tan glow of a Sequoia and, at four feet in diameter, made Henrietta's cabin look like a doll house.

She answered the door holding two mugs of steaming tea.

"I saw you pull up, and I thought, I bet he drinks tea. You are Owen, correct?"

"Yes to both," I said.

She handed me one of the mugs. It smelled strong. A floral scent.

"Thank you," I said as I followed her into a small cozy living room with knotty pine walls.

A small fire sparked and popped in a cobblestone fireplace. She gestured me to an out-sized upholstered chair with worn leather that looked like it had been made in the Nineteenth Century. Henrietta sat on the stone hearth, her back to the flames. With her long gray hair pulled back into a ponytail and her little wire-rimmed glasses, she too would have fit into the Nineteenth Century milieu had she been wearing a long dress instead of white coverall-style painter pants over heavy hiking boots. Under the coverall straps was a thick red wool shirt.

She reached a plate off the mantle and held it out to me. "Would you like a homemade chocolate-chip cookie?"

"Thank you." I took the plate, lifted a big cookie, gave it a significant chomp and almost choked. It tasted like a combination of bitter chocolate mixed with cilantro and jalapeno peppers. My mouth was electrified. I grabbed the tea and tried to wash the chemicals away.

"Do you like the cookies?" she asked, eager anticipation in her smile. "That recipe is my special secret."

"Yes, very inventive," I said as I set the remaining bit of cookie down on the plate. Stick two paper clips into Henrietta's clay-like chunk of electrolyte and they would spark with measurable voltage.

"You don't like it," she said. "I'm sorry. I misjudged."

Before I could protest, she stood and picked up the plate of cookies. "Henrietta's Secret Herbal cookies," she said. "No wonder I get so many marriage offers."

"Marriage offers aren't a measure of someone's worth."

She looked at me without moving. Then she set the cookies down again and slowly sat down on the hearth. After a moment she looked away and blinked her eyes hard. "I can't believe they killed Charlie and kidnapped Silence," she said suddenly, closing her eyes against the thought.

"I'm hoping you can help."

"Of course. Anything. I'd do anything for her." Her eyes searched mine. Her hands gripped the edge of the hearth.

"I want to know more about them," I explained.

She nodded slowly. "I didn't really know Charlie. I only met him when he would come to fetch Silence."

"Silence, then. Her likes and dislikes, her personality quirks, her special abilities."

Henrietta's hands gripped one another. "You've spoken to her mother?"

"Yes. Marlette told me about Silence, showed me her

drawings, gave me a disc of videos that Marlette took over the years. But a mother has a mother's perspective. A teacher, especially a teacher close to a student, can see another side."

Henrietta nodded. "I understand, but I don't know where to start."

"For example, Marlette told me that you believe Silence is bright. Is that so?"

Henrietta smiled. "Oh, yes. Oh, yes. You can't imagine."

"What makes you think this? I spoke to Dr. Power. He said she is quite retarded."

"No offense, but he is wrong. Very wrong."

"It sounds like he has tested her several times over the years."

Henrietta shook her head. "Let me explain something. You know how tests can miss the obvious? Like the way Edison or Einstein did poorly on tests? Well, Silence has been through them all. Woodcock-Johnson, Brigance, CARS, Kaufman. They all suggest that she is profoundly disabled, and to an extent that is true. They don't reveal her intelligence because they are not designed that way. You've heard of Autism Spectrum Disorder?"

"Yes."

"It's called that because there is such a wide spectrum in how autism presents. Well, Silence is at the very end of the spectrum."

"She's not like other autistic kids?" I said.

"In some ways she is. Her lack of speech, her lack of emotional involvement with other people, her awkward, mechanical movements. But in other ways, she's one in a thousand. One in ten thousand. Tests don't reveal Silence's knowledge or ability. And I think the main reason that doctors and others can't see past the test results is her lack of verbal ability. People are understandably focused on speech. It is the very essence of how most of us function. So when a person doesn't have speech, we have a hard time believing that anything substantial is going on inside. But I've seen it in Silence. There is a lot going on. She just can't express it. It's hard to articulate, but after working with her it becomes obvious."

Henrietta pointed to a small bookcase against one wall. "For example, you see those books? One spring day after class – it was maybe two years ago when Silence was fifteen – I brought her over here. This neighborhood is just down from the high school, so we walked. I wanted to show her my little wildflower garden. The buds were just coming up." Henrietta pointed outside the living room window at several wine barrels that had the remnants of what had been robust flowers in the summer. "Silence loves flowers. But I couldn't get her to even notice the plants. We were outside, but she kept looking in through the window at these books. So I finally asked her, 'Silence, do you want to go inside to see my books?' And she gave me a little push toward the house, meaning yes. I should explain that when she meant no, she'd pull you away instead of pushing.

"So I took her inside and she went and knelt down in front of the books and pulled them out one by one. She ran her hands over them, opened the pages and then put them back on the shelves. I thought it was a tactile thing, like picking up toys. It didn't seem that she noticed what was printed on the pages, just the way the paper felt. But then she stopped on one book. She touched the pages, flipped forward and touched some more, then went back as if searching."

"Which book was it? Do you remember?"

"Of course, I remember," Henrietta said, looking at me as if I were a dim child. She went to the bookcase, pulled out a large volume and brought it to me. "My college math text. Very dry and boring, I must say, even if I am a teacher."

I took the text and opened it. To a mathematician, it would perhaps hold interest. For the rest of us, I agreed with Henrietta. Numbers and formulas and exercises that seemed to have no purpose beyond pursuing a rigorous mind or preparing one for working at NASA or the Jet Propulsion Laboratory.

I closed the book. "Did you get a sense of what interested her about the book? Was there something specific, or did she just seem to connect to pages with numbers on them?"

Henrietta's eyes got wide. "There was definitely something she was interested in. Here, I'll show you." She reached over and took the book from my hands. She sat back down on the hearth and flipped through the book. When she got close, she licked her middle finger and turned the pages one by one. Forward, then back. Here we are." She handed the book back.

"Fibonacci numbers," she said.

I glanced over the introduction to a kind of number series discovered by a Thirteenth Century Italian mathematician named Leonardo Fibonacci.

"I don't really know about it," Henrietta said, "other than you take two numbers and add them to get a third. Then of those three numbers you ignore the first and add the second and third together to get a fourth. You keep on going that way. Apparently, it's an important kind of series that is used in lots of areas of math. You start with one and one, always adding the last two numbers in the series."

"One and one is two," I said. I'd never been very good at numbers, so I had to go slow and visualize. "Then, out of the sequence of one, one and two, you add the last two, correct?" I said.

Henrietta nodded.

"One plus two gives you three. Two plus three equals five. Three plus five equals eight. So the sequence would be one, one, two, three, five, eight, thirteen, twenty-one and so on."

"Yes," Henrietta said. "I couldn't imagine why Silence cared about Fibonacci numbers."

"Is she really good at math?" I said.

"I don't think so, but you know what is really cool?" Henrietta's eyes sparkled. "She carried the book over to the window and looked out at that bush in the corner of the yard."

"The bush?" I leaned forward to look and saw a withered little thing that most people would probably uproot and throw away.

"Come with me, I'll show you." Henrietta's excitement was effervescent.

I left the textbook on the chair and we went outside.

Henrietta walked to the corner of the yard, knelt down and pointed at the bush. "Look at this. The main stem adds its first branch at this point, so then you have two. Then one of the branches divides, so you have three. Then two of the branches divide so you have five. Then, at this point, three of the branches divide so you have eight branches. Now, when I raise my finger one more level you have a total of thirteen branches."

"The Fibonacci sequence," I said.

"Yes! And Silence saw it immediately! But get this, there's more!" Henrietta was doing a little bounce on her toes.

"She found something else with the same sequence?"

"Yes. When she finished looking at this bush, she picked up one of these huge Jeffrey pinecones and turned it around in her hand." Henrietta picked one up and handed it to me. "Careful of the prickers," she said. "I didn't realize how it worked because there are hundreds of prickers on it. After Silence looked at it, she ran to the side yard and picked up one of those little Lodgepole pinecones and turned it over in her hands."

"She saw something in the pattern of both," I said.

"Right, only I couldn't figure it out. So I asked Nelson at the school. He's one of the math teachers. He didn't know either, but he said he'd look it up. The next day he told me it was the whorls. The spirals. Here, look at it this way." She took the big pinecone from my hand and angled it. "See how the pattern spirals to the left at one angle, but also spirals to the right at a different angle? If you count the spirals one way you get eight, if you count the spirals the other way you get five."

I stopped her. "Wait, let me remember. One, one, two, five, eight, thirteen and so forth. So the five and eight relationship is part of the Fibonacci sequence."

"Exactly."

I walked over and picked up one of the little Lodgepole cones and began counting. "I'm not sure this one works."

"Here, let me see." Henrietta almost grabbed it away from me. She counted, frowning. Turned it over and counted again. "Look, it works from the top. Watch." She put a fingernail at one point and counted one direction. "Five spirals." Then she counted the other way. "Eight spirals. You were counting from the bottom."

"It only works from the top?"

"No, you just grabbed a cone with a defect." She pointed. "It gets screwed up at this point. Nature isn't always perfect."

"This is a Fibonaccilly-challenged cone."

"Right. It needs a Special Ed teacher."

"Is it a weird coincidence that your bush and pinecones exhibit the Fibonacci characteristics?"

"No. Since then, I've read about it. It turns out those numbers are all over the place! For example, pineapples have eight spirals one way and thirteen spirals another."

"Fibonacci numbers."

"Right. And if you look at those tiny little bumps in the center of a daisy you can usually count twenty-one clockwise spirals and thirty-four counter-clockwise spirals."

"Thirty-four being the next number in the sequence."

"Right. Eight plus thirteen is twenty-one. Thirteen plus twenty-one is thirty-four."

"Can Silence just spot this stuff, nature patterns that have mathematical significance?" I said.

"Yeah, it's amazing."

"Do you think she was always aware of the mathematical patterns in nature and only later learned that mathematicians wrote about it? Or did she first learn of it in your textbook and was immediately able to recognize it in nature?"

Henrietta shook her head. "I don't know. I've thought about that, but I don't know."

We went back inside and Henrietta talked about Silence Ramirez for a couple more hours.

Henrietta stopped for a time, thinking, and stirred the coals of the fire and put another log on it. "I think much of her interaction with the world was done through Charlie," she continued. "In most ways he was a gift. An absolute gift. But I've also thought at times that he hindered her."

"Because with him she didn't need to learn to communicate with others?"

"Yes. He could tell what she needed, and he automatically provided it for her. Without him she might have come out of her shell a bit."

"You mean, learn to talk?"

"No. I don't think anyone believes that Silence will learn to talk. She hears okay, and she understands what people say. Maybe not in a linear sense the way you or I do, but she gets the gist of anything you say. But I think the nerve connections for talking just aren't there."

Henrietta turned and blew on the coals under the log. The swirl of smoke disappeared in a puff of flame. She sat down on the hearth. "I think the closest that Silence ever comes to direct communication is her drawings."

"I've seen some of them. Marlette told me she is never without her sketchbook."

"That's true even at school. It's like the way some young girls carry dolls. Even when she has no intention of drawing she clutches it to her for reassurance."

"Reassurance that she won't lose her one communication tool?"

"Precisely. Although I might be the only one who sees it that way."

"Who doesn't?" I said.

"The doctors, mostly. And Marlette a little bit, too."

"The doctors don't think she uses drawings to communicate?"

"No." Henrietta said it with a certain disgust in her voice. "They say she is recording, not communicating. They say she is a savant who replicates her surroundings with her sketches. But I've spent hundreds of times as many hours with Silence as they have. In some respects I've even spent more hours with her than her mother has, at least the kind of hours that are focused on learning rather than mealtime hours and such. Don't get me wrong,

Marlette is a good mother. She loves those kids. But mothers have to spend so much of their time taking care of children's physical needs. I have the luxury of focusing on their intellectual needs." Henrietta suddenly stared at me intensely. "I know that child, Owen. Her drawings are a form of communication with others. She shows them to me. She wants my reaction. Why would she do that if she were just recording the world for herself?"

We talked a little longer and then I stood up and said I had to go. Henrietta stopped me as I was going out the door.

I was down on the front steps, which put Henrietta's eyes level with mine.

"You think there's a chance, then?" she said.

"There's always a chance."

Once again she stared at me hard. Her voice was a whisper when she spoke.

"Silence is the closest thing I have to a daughter. I know what her world is like. To have a universe of feelings that you keep to yourself, that no one knows..." Henrietta trailed off.

I reached out and shook her hand.

"Good luck," she said, then turned quickly and went inside, pulling the door closed behind her.

SEVENTEEN

I still hadn't heard back from the deputy who studied the Granite Mountain Boys, so I decided I couldn't wait any longer to probe in the direction of the bikers.

I have an old friend who sells mutual funds. Geoff Lambdon is a small man with red hair and freckles on his cheeks like a kid. He's 39 and looks a virginal 19. He wears a thin gold necklace, shaves a very careful pattern into the stubble on his chin to accentuate a look he calls Hollywood Hot. Geoff puts oil in his hair and combs his eyebrows with a miniature brush. His wife is a beautiful blonde with a huge appreciation for his devotion to their three kids. She's also a sweet woman who'd love him even if he didn't have a quarter-million dollar income. For fun, Geoff likes boating and golf and chess and five-card stud and going to the jazz shows that the Reno NPR station helps sponsor.

And Geoff loves his Harley.

I called Geoff, and he agreed to meet me for a very late lunch.

I walked into the Cantina on Emerald Bay Road at four o'clock. Geoff was at the bar. He had a margarita in front of him.

"McKenna! It's been, what, two, three years? I think the last time was at that Rotary meeting where you came and talked about the quiet life of a detective in Lake Tahoe. I guess your last few cases made a liar out of you! Here, sit down, sit down!" He patted the barstool next to him. I sat, held a finger up toward the bartender and pointed to Geoff's drink.

"Linda and the kids are well?" I said.

"Yes, yes. Thank you."

"And business is good?"

"Oh, ho, ho," he laughed like Santa Claus and slugged my shoulder. "You know, you're about the only one at the lake I haven't put together a plan for. Is that why you called? Are you ready to settle down your savings into a good long-term plan?"

"Maybe next year," I said. "Gotta get some savings first." The bartender brought me my drink. I took a sip, salt off the glass rim mixing into sweet icy fire. "What I wanted to talk to you about was your Harley."

His smile widened. "McKenna, you are a surprise. I got me a new Fat Boy just last year. I knew it would turn heads here, there and everywhere, but I didn't think your head'd be one of 'em. Ready to jump into the game?"

"No. But I'm curious about the game. Where do you ride. Who do you ride with. That sort of thing."

"What's this for?"

"General info," I said.

He nodded. "Sure. Like when my mother said she wanted to check my pockets before I went off to school. General info. Oh, now I remember reading that you were working on that kidnapping. So you think bikers took those kids?"

"We're considering it. The Tahoe Biker Heaven Festival," I said. "Are you part of it?"

Geoff beamed at me. "Certainly am. Baddest mutual fund guy in the basin. I can talk one-year, five-year and ten-year returns right up there with displacement, horsepower, compression ratios and tread patterns." Geoff laughed, picked up his drink and took a sip. Then he leaned over and knocked his elbow against mine. "Know what the coolest accessory is that I've found this year?" He paused, then continued. "Grip fringe."

I raised my eyebrows.

"Really," he said. "They attach to the ends of the handlebar grips. Just like on our bicycles when we were little kids. Only these are real leather. When you're cruising they flap like a flag on an F-Sixteen." He drank more margarita. "To fringe or not to fringe a bike is like to load or not to load a fund. The essential dilemma of the millennium."

"Where do your ride as part of the festival?"

"Some of the rides are organized with cookouts and beer tastings at the finish. Others are impromptu. It's funny. Mostly we ride the same places as always. Us locals can push it harder than the tourist bikers because we know the roads. We cruise the passes and all the tight switchbacks. Kingsbury grade from Dagget Summit down to Carson Valley and back up, of course, is prime. Real prime. Echo Summit doesn't have as many tight curves, but riding on the edge of a thousand-foot cliff for a couple miles is enough to make you trade your beer for a bourbon.

"Riding around the lake is always a must. Counter-clockwise being my favorite. I still love where you come off Emerald Bay and hit that section where the land drops away to the bay on the left and Cascade Lake on the right, and you are on the knife-edge with the whole world below you and Tahoe stretched out in front of you. I call it the Great Wall of China. You take it fast for thrills, then hit those calipers hard because that first switchback is a ten mile-per-hour one-eighty, and if you miss it, well, let's just say it was fun to see your red taillight arc in a free fall toward the big water."

Geoff picked up his margarita and, aided by the daydream, took a big gulp.

"The trip from the Mt. Rose Pass down to Reno is the best of all. Nine thousand feet of elevation down to forty-five hundred in just a few miles of twisty turny asphalt ribbon. Doesn't get better than that. Talk about Biker Heaven." He turned to me. "You done any of those rides?"

"All of them, one time or another. Who else do you know who rides in the festival?"

"Hell, practically everyone. My dentist Bill Massenruud, Reverend Vitale, my stockbroker Arturo Rodriguez..."

I interrupted, "Mutual fund salesmen have stockbrokers? I thought you'd do that all yourself."

"Oh, McKenna, my man, Arturo is the NYSE's offering

to the investment gods. If you're not on board, well, you gotta get on board. Arturo's analyses are what's going to get all of us into financial heaven."

"Who else," I said.

"Well, there's my barber Babe Ruth, the softball phenom of Tahoe, and Smilin' Joe Johnson who owns the snowboard shop by your office on Kingsbury. My lawyer Pierson Giovano- vich and his wife Myra. You should see her in her leathers on her Low Rider. She's perfect. Those hips. Absolutely perfect." Geoff looked at me. "You want me to keep going?"

"What you're saying is that a whole lotta regular guys go out on their Harleys and cruise to these different events."

"What else would anyone do with a Harley in Tahoe's mountains and an entire celebration devoted to it?" Geoff said.

"Do any of these guys know any real bad-ass bikers?"

"You mean, like, gang types? Hell's Angels and such?"

"Yeah. Are your friends all Boy Scouts, or do any of the guys you know flirt with the darker side of biking."

Geoff was shaking his head. "McKenna, I'm surprised you even ask the question. These are all upstanding citizens. They go out for fun. We put on the leather uniform and rev up the machine, cruise around and make a lot of noise. But nothing else. It's a good time, nothing more, nothing less."

"But you and your friends are aware of the wilder side of biking."

"Sure," Geoff said. "That's part of the fun. You know it's out there and so it gives you a little buzz, like playing pretend when you're a kid. Hey, didn't you used to have a bike?"

"Twenty years on my seven-fifty Yamaha. Thing finally wore out. Thought about getting a replacement some day."

"Then you know what it's like. You hit the gas and lean into a curve on a mountain road. There's nothing better. Doing it with friends only adds to the fun. But it's just clean fun. You look around at these festivals. Hell, even the giant ones like Sturgis, South Dakota. Ninety percent of the bikers have regular jobs, probably more white collar than blue collar. Doctors, lawyers, architects and accountants. Of the rest, probably five percent are on the margins, sketchy employment history, maybe some run-ins with the law. It's the last five percent that you're wondering about. The idiots and serious crooks. But the rest of us so out-number them that no one can tell who's who."

"Because except for a few standout dirtballs, you all look the same," I said.

Geoff drank more margarita. "I never thought of it that way, but, yes, you're right. Interesting, now that I think about it. I suppose it's a herd thing. We mostly look alike, ride the same machines, go the same direction and make the same noise."

"I have a request for you and your biker buddies," I said.

"Shoot."

"I'd like to talk with a bunch of them. Here at the Cantina or at my cabin, wherever works. I've got a favor to ask."

That night, we met at Geoff's house in Skyland, the fenced community over on the East Shore just north of Zephyr Cove. Despite the last minute notice, several of Geoff's friends showed up. There was Bill and Arturo and Pierson and Myra and Babe Ruth and a guy Geoff hadn't mentioned, Marven Anderson, a guy with a ruddy face and amazing red hair who looked like a Swedish lumberjack but was actually an industrial designer from Des Moines, Iowa.

Geoff and Linda served beer and chips and salsa and after about fifteen minutes of idle chatter Geoff interrupted and said, "Yo, guys, Myra. My friend Owen McKenna here is a detective working on the murder case of that kid, and he would like to say something. Right, Owen?"

I stood up and faced the group. They were loosely arranged around the table with the chips and salsa. The men quieted down except for Bill and Arturo who were seriously engrossed in a conversation dissecting the pros and cons of various fuel mixtures.

"Arturo, Bill," Myra scolded.

They stopped talking and looked at me.

"Thanks," I said. "Yes, I've got a request for all of you. You've all heard of the Ramirez kidnapping and murder. I can add very little to what you've already read in the paper. Charlie was fourteen. Silence is seventeen. No one saw the kidnappers, but several people heard and saw motorcycles in the neighborhood. One neighbor heard bikers revving their machines in front of the Ramirez house.

"So, while we don't know that bikers were involved, we're looking. There is also some indication that a serious biker gang called the Granite Mountain Boys is in Tahoe for the festival. They have a bad reputation, some of it based on rumor, some on truth. The name comes from the Granite Mountain State Prison, a Super Max facility near the Oregon border.

"The reason I'm here is that if in fact bikers were involved, we need to infiltrate the biker groups all over the basin. I'm asking you to be our eyes and ears."

The man called Babe Ruth said, "Isn't that gang run by some kind of Mexican drug lord?"

"The leader of the group is Antonio Gomez, a felon convicted of rape and murder and released on a technicality. He leads a group of bikers who are drawn to him for all the usual reasons. He's a natural general with a few colonels who also have ties to the Granite Mountain State Prison, and the losers who follow him need some kind of leader to give purpose to their lives." Some of them nodded as if it were old news.

Arturo spoke up. "Do you have specifics on what you'd like from us?"

"Go about your regular activities. Cruise the lake, attend the concerts, camp out with everyone else. Don't do anything you wouldn't normally do. But watch and listen for anything that could suggest involvement with a kidnapping or the location of any child or any talk that might be revealing.

"If you hear of anything at all, no matter how slight and unlikely, please call me." I pulled out my cards and handed them around.

That night Street called me just after I'd fallen asleep.

"I heard glass break," she said in a whisper.

Adrenaline shot through me. I was wide awake in a second. "You're at home?"

"Yes. In the bedroom."

I thought about the layout of her condo. "Go into your bathroom and lock the door. Pop the towel rod out of its mounts. If you're careful you can do it silently. Do you remember how?"

"Yes."

"It's a good weapon. Turn off the bathroom light, stand in the shower and wait. I'll be there in a couple minutes."

EIGHTEEN

I hung up, pulled on my jeans, and Spot and I were out the door in moments.

I raced down the mountain and stopped at the side of the road well before Street's condo complex. I grabbed Spot's collar.

"Quiet," I said, laying my finger across his nose.

We ran through the dark forest to approach her door from the side. I whispered to Spot, "Find the suspect!" as I put my key in the lock. I turned the key and opened the door.

He ran inside, claws scraping the floor. It was dark inside Street's condo, but it doesn't matter with a dog. In less than a second I knew no one was there because Spot hadn't alerted. I went to Street's bedroom and flipped on the light. Spot was standing at the closed bathroom door, tail wagging.

"It's okay," I called out. Street opened the bathroom door. She hugged Spot, then me.

"After you hung up," she said, still holding me, "a couple of motorcycles started up. They were so loud they probably woke everyone in the building. They roared off."

I walked through her condo, checking all the windows and the deck door. Nothing was broken.

"Keep Spot in here with you," I said. "I'll check outside."

I went around to the back side of the condo building. On the ground below Street's bedroom window was a broken beer bottle. I picked up a piece of glass. The beer smell was fresh. Next to her window was a wet mark where the bottle had hit the wall.

It could have been vandalism. A couple guys drinking in

the woods, tossing the last unfinished beer at the condo. But I didn't believe it. It looked like a warning. The warning said, "We know where your girlfriend sleeps."

I stayed at Street's that night. We sat up late in her bed, discussing the possibilities. Street was convinced that it was only a scare tactic. If they really wanted to harm her, they would have kicked in her door.

It was an image that kept me awake long after Street fell asleep.

In the morning I asked Street if she'd like to join Spot and me in some exercise.

"Good idea. You want to do your road?" she asked, referring to our normal course up and down the steep private drive I share with my neighbors.

"I was thinking about going out to Meyers and having a go up the old Meyer's Grade."

"And you want to stop by the Echo Summit chain-up area and look at where the boy's body was," Street said.

"The thought occurred to me. We could have a quick look, then head up the grade. But first I have to buzz up to my cabin and get my running shoes. I'll be back in half an hour."

My phone rang as I walked into my cabin.

Diamond Martinez said, "Surprised you're awake at this hour. White Irish-type boy like you. Thought you'd still be asleep."

"Scottish, mostly, sergeant," I said. "And some Welsh along with the Irish. Either way, I won't take it as a racial slur."

"No slur. It's just that while you Scottish types are sleeping, brown boys like me get up before the sun gets too hot. Pick the food you eat. Wash your car. Clean your hotel room."

"I'm worn out just listening to you and I haven't even started my run-walk," I said.

"You're going out for a jog. Maybe I should come along. I could talk to you then."

"I pick Street up in twenty-five minutes. Going out to

Meyer's Grade."

"On my way," Diamond said and hung up.

I didn't know if he planned to intercept me at my cabin or at Street's condo. I filled my water bottles, put on my running sweats and let Spot out the door just as Diamond pulled into my short drive in his old pickup.

"Your civilian wheels make you look more like a lettuce picker than a sergeant for Douglas County Sheriff's Department."

"I spent a couple summers picking lettuce. Only been a sergeant a couple months. I could show you how to tell the best heads. Maybe I should load up your laundry, too."

"You can strip the bed when we get back."

Diamond climbed into the Jeep and Spot got in back. Spot was excited because Diamond was his favorite person on the planet, the result of several inappropriate gifts of Danish pastries that irreparably destroyed his proper appreciation of chunked-sawdust dog food.

Street was waiting outside her condo, stretching, one leg up on the railroad-tie retaining wall, her body arced forward, fingertips to toes. She'd put on tight periwinkle Spandex shorts that came to mid-thigh and a tight matching shirt with sleeves that came down to just below her elbows. Her running shoes were bright white and she wore those little girl socks that just peek out from her shoes so that her perfect ankles can glow in the sun. Her hair, more black recently than her natural auburn, was pulled back in a tight bun revealing little gold loop earrings. Although Street was very slim, in her case thin meant she had just enough meat in just the right places, but not one ounce of extra in a not-so-right place.

Diamond looked at her, then glanced over at me.

Street straightened up from her stretch, came over and jumped in behind Diamond, crowding Spot over to the side of the small backseat.

"Diamond, what a nice surprise." She leaned forward and kissed his cheek, with Spot sticking his nose in and making it a threesome. "You going to join us on our run?"

"Somebody gotta protect you from this predacious lout."

"Predacious?" I said.

"The look in your eye when the lady came up to the car," he said. "She looks good, sure. Doesn't mean you should salivate like this hound, here, before he eats a filet mignon."

"Wow," Street said. "I've never been compared to a filet mignon."

"You're a beautiful lady. You should find a sophisticated gent. With this guy you're FDA Prime Number One Grade A."

"I'll work on it," Street said.

I headed south down the highway, drove through State-line and turned onto Pioneer Trail, the shortcut out to Meyers and Echo Summit. When we got to the chain-up area in Meyers, Street reached forward from the backseat and pointed.

"Up there. Way off to the side."

I pulled up to where she said and stopped. Diamond and I followed as Street walked off the pavement and stepped around a group of manzanita bushes. "Right there," Street said, pointing to an area of ground that had been disturbed by hundreds of foot-prints. "The body was on its side, one knee up, one arm back. There is general agreement that the boy was already dead before they threw his body out of a vehicle. His head wound had bled copiously prior to death, but there was no blood on the ground. One shoe was missing. Maybe it didn't get tossed out with the body. Or it could have gotten carried away by a dog."

Diamond walked across to look at the patterns in the dirt, patterns that were mostly obscured by the footprints. I stepped next to Street and put my arm around her shoulder. I felt a shiver go through her thin body. Without moving I looked across the area she had indicated. There wasn't much to see. Despite our proximity to the Sierra Crest and its high level of precipitation, there was some sagebrush, the result of rain-shadow variations that play out in yards rather than miles. Manzanita bushes were scattered on the edge of the meadow area. The soft sounds of the Truckee River burbled from just beyond, overwhelmed by the rush of traffic on the highway behind us.

It wasn't a place where someone would carefully hide a body, hoping the discovery of its desiccated remains would be delayed until the following spring or summer. Whoever had left it here was only looking for a place to dump it. They may have been in a hurry and pulled over before they headed up Echo Summit and out of the basin. Or they were driving around, looking for a wide place on the road to pull over. None were wider than the broad apron of the Echo Summit chain-up area, designed to accommodate large semi-trucks. The kidnappers could pull well away from the traffic lanes and it would be unlikely that anyone would notice the door opening up and a body being thrust out onto the dirt.

After a moment, chilled by the cold morning air and the imagined scene playing in our heads, we left.

I drove across the bridge over the Truckee River and started up the long incline that leads to the summit, then quickly turned left on South Upper Truckee Road.

I followed the road as it wound back a short distance, then turned right on the old Meyer's Grade. A block ahead were several parked cars belonging to early-morning walkers and bicyclers. I stopped and we all got out, Spot sprinting around with such enthusiasm it was as if he'd just discovered the joy of running.

We started off at a walk, waiting for our bodies to warm up before we picked up the pace.

Meyer's Grade is the old road up to Echo Summit. Although it is solid and paved, it is steep, and long ago was replaced by the new road which comes down the cliff at a shallower angle. When accidents or avalanches close the new road, Meyer's Grade becomes the detour route. The rest of the time Meyer's Grade has locked gates, top and bottom, which makes it a magnet for those looking to exercise on a paved surface. Hikers and dog-walkers and bicyclists can enjoy the great views down Christmas Valley and across the basin without having to constantly look down to check the trail for roots and animal holes and ankle-twisting rocks.

After we'd walked a half-mile up the road Street said,

"Warmed up, yet?"

"I was worried about this moment," Diamond said, puffing much harder than Street but no harder than me.

"We don't have to run," she said. "Just pick it up a little."

"A little," Diamond muttered. "Scary words coming from you."

Street began jogging, thin thighs bulging, hamstrings taut under the Spandex, calves flexing easily, the separate muscle groups distinct beneath shiny skin. With her angular physique and her acne scars, no one would ever call Street beautiful. But she was striking to a superlative degree, and the sight of her body working in perfect tune always ratchets up my hormone production.

Diamond and I began a slow jog as Street gradually pulled away from us.

"Hate it when a young broad does that," Diamond said in a low voice. "Makes me feel old."

Street turned around and began jogging backward. "I heard that. I'm not very young and I'm not broad." She kept jogging backward, moving up the mountain with more ease than we had moving forward.

Diamond was panting. "Okay. You're narrow. And you're almost as old as me. Makes me feel even worse."

Spot noticed that Street was running backward and he ran over to her, jumping from her left side to her right, bouncing up and down. Wow, it's fun when people run backward.

"The thing I wanted to talk about," Diamond said, panting. "Been wondering about this kidnapping. Ever since the boy was found murdered."

"Me too," I said.

"Something seem off to you?"

"Yeah," I said, conserving words so I could breathe.

"What?" he asked.

I huffed and puffed, storing up oxygen. "Can't see the girl as a random victim," I said.

"My thought, too."

Street had slowed so that we were closer to her. She was still running backward. "Why not?"

"Couple reasons," I said. "She doesn't look the type for bikers to pick up. I've tried to put my mind into those of gang members looking to get into trouble, wanting to grab a girl for some dirty sex or worse. I'm no good at that kind of empathy, but I see them cruising until they find a girl hitchhiking." I stopped talking to breathe. "Or possibly they see a girl at a bar or down the street. If the girl were wearing revealing clothes or looking loose, that would figure in as well." I sucked in some more air.

"But this ain't blame-the-victim reasoning," Diamond said.

"No, not at all. A woman should be able to dress as she pleases, go where she pleases, when she pleases. I'm just recognizing that a gang is more likely to grab someone who is dolled up like a streetwalker than someone who looks like Silence. The streetwalker would look more provocative."

"What's the other reason she doesn't seem like a random victim?" Street asked.

Diamond spoke up. "The other one I can think of is that her house isn't directly on Pioneer Trail. The bikers had to turn down the street and drive more than a block to get to her. They could possibly have seen her from Pioneer if they knew exactly where to look, but it's a stretch."

"Suggesting," Street said, "that they were specifically looking for Silence."

Diamond said, "Yeah. And they wanted her bad enough that they had to fight off Charlie in the process."

I nodded. Both of us were sucking air like vacuum cleaners. Street didn't seem to be breathing at all.

A woman with a Black Lab appeared around a curve up ahead, coming down the mountain toward us. The lab spied Spot and stopped, hesitating. Spot ran toward it. Suddenly, the lab sprinted toward Spot, having decided Spot would be fun, not dangerous. I don't know how it works. Doggie body language. They flew around in circles, intensely interested in each other and then, just as suddenly, they lost interest and went separate ways, the lab rejoining the woman and Spot continuing on up the mountain.

"If what you're saying is true, then that changes everything, doesn't it," Street said.

I nodded again.

I said, "If bikers take just any girl at random, there's not too many clues to follow. But if bikers take a specific girl, it suggests they knew her. Or knew of her. Makes for lots more clue possibilities."

"Clue possibilities being your business," Diamond said.

We were approaching the top of the old grade where it joins the newer highway. I knew that Diamond was as relieved as I was that we could turn around and go downhill.

"Shall we continue on to Echo Lake?" Street said, impossibly cheery and unwinded.

"You're kidding, right?" Diamond said. "Love the way gringas like to kid."

"I looked on the map before we came," she said. "We've only come up one and a half miles and six or seven hundred feet of elevation. Echo Lake would bump that to three miles plus and over a thousand feet of elevation gain."

"Yeah, but that's just one way. Then we gotta go all the way down," Diamond said, his voice weak with effort.

"Something any real man would want before breakfast, right?"

"I like exercise before breakfast. Just a different kind."

Street turned around and ran facing forward. Diamond and I focused on breathing. A little pain in my left calf muscle hinted at an oncoming cramp so I tried to shake it as I ran. Diamond turned to look, no doubt wondering what creature must have crawled up my sweats. But he was too winded to speak.

We went around the locked gate at the intersection of old road and new, waited for a break in traffic and ran across Highway 50. For a short block we turned and ran downhill to the intersection where another old route leaves the uphill side of the highway and climbs in steep zigzags up the mountain. Street, of course, led the way up the switchbacks, not slowing at all despite the major increase in steepness.

After an excruciating sprint we popped out at the top and stopped to rest next to the old Echo Summit Lodge that belongs to the California Alpine Club, a hiking club that dates back decades.

Just as the black dots in my vision began to recede, we started again and followed Echo Road up a gentle climb and out a mile to Echo Lake.

There are few places on the planet that are as picturesque as the glacier-forged cleft in the mountain where the ice cold waters of Echo Lake lay at 7400 feet. Talking Mountain rises to the left, Flagpole Peak is on the right, and the narrow water stretches back several miles with Pyramid Peak in the distance. Even at this late date, there were patches of snow left over from the previous winter.

It is the water from Echo Lake that flows out the Tahoe side of the granite ridge and tumbles down Echo Falls, a rushing cascade that distracts drivers coming into the basin from Echo Summit. There is an old hidden tunnel that dates back to when the early water engineers made their imprint all over the basin. The Echo Lake tunnel diverts water away from its natural flow toward Tahoe and adds it to the American River. From there it all cascades down toward Sacramento and the hydropower plants that help keep the city's air conditioners humming.

We stopped at the crest of Echo Road where the view of Echo Lake is straight ahead and the view of Lake Tahoe is off to the right and 1200 feet below. Street jogged in place. Diamond and I leaned over, hands to knees, and tried to catch our breaths. Spot was tired, too, and realizing we might be there for several seconds or more, he seized the opportunity to lie down in the dirt to the side of the road and rolled over onto his side. His pink tongue lolled out, flopping with each breath like a fresh-caught salmon.

Running a route on pavement obeys the same equation as hiking on a dirt trail. With little variation, it only takes one-third to one-half as much time to go down as it does up.

We were already halfway down when Diamond and I had recovered from our oxygen deficits and were once again able to carry on a conversation.

Street said, "If Silence was targeted, that would mean the kidnapping was planned in advance."

"They would've checked out the roads around her house," Diamond said, "staked out the place to find out who was home and when were they home, and they would have noted the most common times she was outside."

Street jumped in again, "They also would have mapped out their getaway for the fastest route and the route least likely to attract attention. Right?"

"Marlette should have hired you two," I said.

Street ignored me, her mind obviously racing. "If Silence was the target, then perhaps they had no intention of killing Charlie. Maybe he just got in the way when she was abducted. He posed too much risk, so they had to kill him."

"The question is why?" Diamond said. "Why would someone kidnap Silence?"

Nobody spoke for a minute.

I said, "The fact that there hasn't been a ransom demand suggests several reasons. The most prominent ones would be that she heard something or saw something significant."

"But if she learned something that could incriminate someone, wouldn't they just kill her to keep her from revealing it?" Street said.

"Not if what she learned wasn't incriminating," I said.

"I don't understand," Street said.

"If she learned something significant, maybe the kidnappers want it."

Both Diamond and Street stopped jogging, so I stopped, too. They looked at me.

"You mean," Diamond said, "if she learned something like the location of buried treasure?"

"Yeah. Maybe not a chest full of gold doubloons. A different kind of treasure. Buried inside the quiet of her mind."

NINETEEN

After we'd dropped Street off at her condo and Diamond headed home, I started putting together some lunch, a ham and cheese and tomato and lettuce sandwich with mayo on twelve-grain bread, potato chips, apple, cookies and milk. For Spot, I poured some more of the sawdust chunks into his bowl and gave him some gourmet faucet water on the side. If he was envious, he didn't show it. He devoured his large bowl in seconds. When he was done nosing the bowl across the kitchen and licking it dry, he turned and looked at me expectantly.

"But you ate all of yours," I said. "If you weren't willing to share with me, why should I share with you?"

I'm not certain he agreed with my logic, but after watching me eat for awhile, he went and lay down in the corner. He hung his head in the potent poor-little-me posture that I should photograph and have trademarked and turned into the theme for a chain of dog-treat stores. He held the pose for so long I finally gave in.

"Your largeness," I said.

Spot looked up just a degree or two, his eyes drooping.

"Catch," I said and frisbeed a potato chip his direction.

Michael Jordon could have learned something from the way Spot launched, twisted in mid-air, swung his head around as the chip arced, and snapped it out of the air.

The phone rang and I picked it up.

"Mr. McKenna?"

"Speaking."

"This is Deputy Randy Rasmussen of Humboldt County. Got a message to contact you and see if I can give you some information on the Granite Mountain Boys. A pet project of mine. Heard you got a snatch down in Tahoe, might be one of Antonio Gomez's transactions."

"He doesn't kidnap, he transacts?"

"Tony Go? Bet your ass. It's always a deal of some kind. Usually the currency is greenbacks or white powder. Sometimes it's young girls. What can I help you with?"

I explained what I'd learned to date about Silence's kidnapping and Charlie's murder. I went long on the details of the killing and disposing of the body and the reports of motorcycles in the neighborhood at the time and stayed short on the details of Silence's autism. No particular reason other than a little respect for Silence's privacy. When I'd finished the report I said, "Does it sound like a Gomez transaction?"

"Yeah, if you can find a reason why the girl would be currency," Rasmussen said.

"I'm working on that. If it doesn't turn out she's currency, if she was taken for kinky stuff, would that make it less likely Gomez was behind it?"

"I think so, yeah. The problem, though, would be explaining the Aztec word on the boy's forehead. Although, if one of his rank and file did it on the side, keeping it from Gomez, that could accommodate both a kinky motive and an Aztec God. Gomez's gofers know about the Aztec thing, and they might try to play with it themselves."

"If Gomez did do this, how would you imagine it going down, where they'd hold her, how they'd treat her."

"Gomez is a planner. Most of the goons who follow him are idiots, but his inner circle are guys like him. Not much different than your average corporate board of directors. Gomez would have every detail figured out in advance, and he wouldn't set the transaction in motion until he was sure he could bring it to a full and satisfying conclusion."

"The murder of the brother," I said. "Does that sound like

part of a sound plan?"

"The way you describe it, no. Gomez wouldn't plan a body dump like that. He'd want to take the girl clean. No muss, no fuss. If he planned to kill the boy, he'd do that clean, too. He certainly wouldn't drive around with a dead person and then throw him out someplace. So either Gomez isn't involved, or it was one of those glitches that intrudes on even the most careful plan.

"As for how he'd handle the details," Rasmussen continued, "it's hard to say. Gomez is a neatnik. Everything in its place. He'd probably keep the girl in a decent place, not out in the dirt. A trailer or a basement where people couldn't hear her. I heard she's mute. But she could still scream, right?"

"I don't know."

"I think Gomez would treat her reasonably well, feed her, get her a coat if she's cold, stuff like that. As for his minions, I can't say. They'd know they weren't supposed to touch the money, so to speak. They'd keep it in good shape until the payoff. But you never know."

"Commander Mallory at the South Lake Tahoe PD mentioned that he'd heard Gomez was into sacrifice. Can you add anything to that?"

"Not much. It's a persistent rumor that won't go away. There's a lot of stories about this guy, some verified, some rumors to be verified later. Verified includes the girl who was kidnapped from Sonoma several years ago. She was raped, then murdered, and later found in a ditch. Her forehead was inscribed with Aztec words. The two bikers who confessed to it rode with Tony Go. Then there was the meth lab bust in the El Dorado foothills. Five men, all bikers who rode with Tony Go.

"In the unverified department are the religious sacrifices. There's some anecdotal evidence to the effect that Tony Go personally performs a sacrifice at the rise of the full moon. Drinks the blood, the whole nine yards.

"I wouldn't be surprised if that turns out to be true as well, but for now it's all just stories from guys who rode with him for a time and then ended up getting three squares from the state. Incidentally, I looked it up."

"What?"

"The ancient Aztecs really did that. They made sacrificial offerings. Had blood rituals and stuff. It was a way to make room for new life."

"Can I call you with questions as they come up?"

"Certainly. Let me give you my cell, skip the phone tag in the department."

We hung up and I saw that it was time to try the doctor again.

TWENTY

I dialed Dr. Power's office and he took my call.

"Any chance you could run over here now?" he said. "I've got a cancellation."

"Be there in a few minutes," I told him.

When I was back in his office I said, "As I mentioned when I was here before, I'm considering the possibility that the girl was not a random victim."

Power nodded. "Kidnapped by someone who knows her?"

"One possibility," I said.

"Perhaps the kidnapper became fixated on her."

I nodded. "Another possibility would be that maybe she saw someone commit a crime."

"Interesting," Power said. "A witness who can't say what she witnessed. Even so, why kidnap her? If she presents a danger as a witness, why not just kill her?" Then Power's eyes widened. "Sorry to be so crass about it."

"You're just thinking like an investigator."

"Maybe Charlie was the witness, so they took him and killed him and wound up with her as baggage. But then that wouldn't make sense either, would it? If they had no compunctions about killing him, they'd kill her to get her out of the way."

I said, "A third type of non-random kidnapping would be if a kidnapper thought she was the key to something important and is trying to use her to get the important thing."

Power paced back and forth in front of his desk. "I wouldn't want your job, Owen. Too difficult and too disturbing."

"Let's go back to the first scenario," I said. "Suppose someone was fixated on Silence and kidnapped her. What can you surmise about such a situation?"

"It's a possibility with lots of antecedents and a thousand psychological explanations," Power said. "The literature is full of examples. But I won't bore you with the verbiage. The main point is that mental pathology knows no limits. Once you've been in this business for awhile, you realize you could never have a body of research exhaustive enough to cover every scenario. Every day in this country a new event triggers a reconsideration of the psychiatric canon." Power seemed to think about what he'd said. "By my reckoning, anyway. But back to your question. What kind of person is likely to do that? Frankly, it could be anyone. For anyone you can pick, I could construct a reason."

"How about a teacher?" I said.

"Sure. I'll try to keep to layman's terms. Let's say a teacher once had a student, or more to the point, an autistic student. The teacher loved that child dearly and was making good progress with her. One day the child died a tragic death. It left a gaping hole in the teacher's psyche. The passage of time only made the longing worse. One day the teacher saw the opportunity to replace the missing child with a similar child. Only, this time the teacher decides to keep the child to herself, hiding the child away where no harm could come to it."

"What about a neighbor?" I said.

"Certainly. The neighbor gets to know the child through daily contact. Or maybe the neighbor only sees the child from a distance. The neighbor seems normal to everyone else in the neighborhood, but in fact has serious problems and doesn't have appropriate coping skills. The neighbor develops fantasies about the child, and the child is perceived as the missing link to the neighbor's happiness. The neighbor believes his constant hunger will finally be sated once he has the child in his possession. The fantasies may have nothing to do with the specific child but everything to do with the neighbor's pathology. Perhaps the neighbor observes the child's schedule and routine and figures out the perfect time to take the child so that the police will think a motorcycle gang took her. And like the teacher, the neighbor could care less about ransom and is only interested in possession."

I spoke up. "You make it sound like anyone in or near Silence's life could be the kidnapper, regardless of how unlikely it would appear."

"That is exactly my point. We've all heard the stories after a kidnapper or killer is caught. The sister says it couldn't be her brother. He's a pillar of the community and he paid for the new church and he's been a super uncle to her kids. Or the son says it couldn't be his dad who was the little league coach and the town's favorite barber and grew orchids for a hobby."

Power stopped pacing and sat on the edge of his desk. "No, I'm afraid that you can't easily pursue a kidnapper by searching for a particular mental health profile. There's two main reasons. First, the profile is too general. You'll notice that in most of these cases where there is no specific evidence, the profile is always the same. The kidnapper is likely to be male with low intelligence, little education and poor social skills. Further, the kidnapper usually has a low income from a menial job. While this may describe the man who is eventually caught, it won't help you find him. There are simply too many men who fit the description to make it a worthwhile sorting mechanism."

Power continued. "The second reason such a psychological profile won't help you is that the profile isn't causal. The vast, vast majority of men with below average intelligence and income and education and social skills are not kidnappers."

"You make it sound hopeless," I said.

"No, I just want to dispel the notion we get from TV and movies, that without much in the way of clues, we can nevertheless use psychology to find a killer."

"From what you know of the girl, can you form an opinion about the kind of person who may be drawn to kidnap her?"

"Not beyond the scenarios I already described. The only

additional possibility that comes to mind is that this particular kid-napper may have had some exposure to children with autism dis-order or some other communication disability. But it is a small likelihood."

I thought about what he said. "What can you tell me about autism?"

He paused, took a breath and made a slow shake of his head. His unruly eyebrows caught the light. "As I mentioned ear-lier, I'm not an autism expert. But I can give you a little sense of what is involved.

"Perhaps the single most salient feature of autism is that the individual has trouble communicating. They usually have dif-ficulty forming clear speech and difficulty in understanding what other people mean with the jumble of words that make up speech. They also have difficulty understanding how other people receive communication. This last thing is probably a problem with empathy. For example, an autistic child knows when they are hungry. But they may have trouble realizing that you could be hungry at different times than they are. If they think of it at all, they will often assume that you share their feelings, that if they are hungry, you must be hungry. In a sense, they cannot distinguish between different senses of self, theirs or yours or mine.

"When you think about it, the problem of differentiating between themselves and others creates almost as many communi-cation problems as not being able to use language. Communica-tion functions because the speaker has some kind of understanding of how the listener is receiving the words. An empathy for the listener. Without it, the speaker just drones on, never knowing what is appropriate to say or when and how to say it. Autistic people also have difficulty writing. The complexi-ties of language, spoken or written, seem to elude them.

"I should probably interject that we refer to autism prob-lems as a spectrum because there are many, many manifestations of autism. For those of us in the business, it is possible to see an autistic child who is unlike any other autistic child we've ever seen."

Power paused, thinking.

"I've heard of Asperger's Syndrome," I said. "How does that differ?"

"Kids with Asperger's Syndrome are often very verbal and much closer to you and me. They have certain autistic characteristics, but we refer to them as high-functioning kids. These kids can be bright and good with words. Their problems are more about social awkwardness, not picking up the subtle social and emotional cues that people telegraph. They may not be able to look you in the eye. They won't pick up on the meaning behind certain facial expressions or body language. They may exhibit unusual or repetitive body movements. Sometimes they will say things that are inappropriate for a situation."

"Is there any good treatment for autism?"

"Yes, for some kids. Some of the most successful intensive intervention techniques are focused on working with the child's language skills. Many autistic kids get better with behavior modification that has language improvement as its goal."

"What about Silence? Could she get better?"

"I don't think so. I'm sure the Special Education teachers in the schools have done their best, but the problem with the Ramirez girl as I see it, is that she is too retarded. There may also be brain damage that is specific to those parts of the brain that control verbal development. Language is a very complex process, and she probably doesn't have the brain power to use even the most rudimentary language."

"Sad," I said.

"Yes. This business of autism is one of the saddest and most disappointing afflictions that we come across. Whenever I see a child with autism disorder, I see in the parents a level of hope and fear almost unmatched with other disorders. The result is that everything about autism is loaded, and doctors quickly learn to tread lightly."

"You mean that you're afraid to say or do anything that might give people a false sense of possibility regarding their child?"

"Yes, we don't want to give false hopes, but of course

almost worse would be to give parents a sense that their child's limitations are greater than they really are.

"Naturally, parents are desperately eager to hear anything that suggests that their child is not so impaired as it seems," he continued. "They want to know that things can get better. Much better. And sometimes, with some children, they can.

"But with other children, if you tell the parents the truth, some of those parents will keep going to other doctors until someone tells them what they want to hear. There is a large emerging community that looks aghast at the doctor who is realistic about the future life of the autistic child. That doctor is now considered by many to be trapped in the intellectual ghetto of Western Medicine, hopelessly shut off from all of the alternative and holistic and Eastern concepts that might improve the child."

"Like the search for new cancer treatments outside the realm of Western Medicine," I said.

"Yes, exactly. And I should add that we all, Western doctors included, would be ecstatic if cures could come from a shamanic tradition using unfamiliar techniques or herbs or Eastern spiritual practices or something else that Western Medicine is ignoring. Most of us educated in Western medical schools freely admit the limitations imposed on us by our scientific method. But we also recognize that our double-blind-study approach to medical science has produced an improvement in human life span and alleviated misery in a manner unmatched by all of the other approaches combined a hundred times over."

Power said the last line like it was something he wrote and memorized for a speech.

I stood up. "Thank you very much for your time."

"Welcome."

"May I call again if I have any questions?"

"Of course. Any time, day or night."

TWENTY-ONE

"Do you think it's too yellow?" Street said. She was putting a coat of high-gloss paint on my new Adirondack deck chairs. It was an obvious yet effective way to find a good mood during a rough ordeal. The previous night Street had stayed over at my cabin. She'd brushed off my thoughts that the broken beer bottle had been a warning. But she agreed to sleep over to keep me comfortable. She changed the subject to Silence and I told her about Dr. Power and his assessment that Silence was quite retarded. It rendered unlikely the idea that Silence could know something that would precipitate her kidnapping. With the arrival of morning, we were avoiding the subject of Silence altogether, trying to find a little fun.

"You're wondering if hot lemon yellow is too yellow?" I said. "Not a chance. You will, however, attach a pair of sunglasses to each chair, right? Hang them on cords?" Near the chairs was the table she'd just painted electric blue. In the distance across the lake the mountains around Emerald Bay glistened with white from a surprise snowfall during the night. With the colored furniture in the foreground, the picture would make a good postcard.

Street was celebrating the hot sun of late-fall by wearing very little, but with very bright colors. She had on short shorts, bright pink, with little notches at the side seams. Her tank top was magenta, no notches. Her sandals were woven leather, lime green, no notches but lots of openings. I couldn't decide whether to stare at the curves of her neck and shoulders, her waist, her knees, or her ankles. Despite her excessively lean physique, all her curves were perfect, and all illustrated the artist's axiom that the negative space of any object was just as important, or even more important, than the positive space. Which was another way of saying that where a woman went in mattered just as much or more as where a woman went out.

"What are the notches in your shorts for?" I said.

Street leaned sideways in a graceful magenta-pink arc, holding the yellow brush away from her body, looking down at her shorts. Strong as the explosion of color was, it was trumped by essence of female.

"Oh, these notches," she said. Her knee canted inward as she looked. "I think they're supposed to help the fabric give when I bend. Like this." She bent. The fabric gave. My pulse jumped thirty or forty points.

"Ah," I said.

Street pretended I was still breathing normally, and she went back to her painting.

I went back to experimenting with my new cordless phone. I had assumed the position, slouched back on the old plastic deck chair, feet stretched out and resting on Spot-The-Footrest.

Having just inhaled another bowl of tasteless fiber-chunk-cardboard and washed it down this time with gourmet garden-hose agua, Spot was napping on the deck, splayed in a giant curve, elbows wide, chin down on the deck boards. His lips were flopped out to either side, curving down from the flat nose like the eaves of a Japanese temple roof.

The phone had digital this and that, came with an eighty-nine-page instruction booklet and had maybe eighty-nine buttons. All I wanted to do with it was make a phone call. So far, that task had eluded me.

My cell phone was mercifully ancient, and over the years I'd been able to learn how to use it. But cell reception is spotty in Tahoe, so a landline is useful.

I'd navigated six or eight layers of menu on the new portable when it rang.

"It works," Street said as she stroked a luscious liquid

swath of yellow along the arm of the chair.

"Yes, but I don't know how to answer it." I was trying to back out of the menu and came up with a weather report. The temperature and barometric pressure pulsed at me. I started pushing buttons blindly.

It rang two more times.

"Better run inside," Street said.

"You are an endless fountain of good ideas," I said as it rang again.

"Or hand it to me," she said.

I handed it over.

Another ring. She reached for it with her left hand while she held the yellow brush in the air with her right. Her thumb found a single magic button out of the crowd.

She pressed the button and handed it back.

"Hello," I said.

"Owen, it's Henrietta. I'm so glad you're there!"

"On the deck, watching the artist paint Ode To Yellow."

"Do you have a minute? Marlette and I are looking at something amazing. A drawing from Silence! Are you going to be there? We have to show you."

"What is it about?"

"I'm not sure. It shows a room and a view out a window."

"I don't understand."

"I'm sorry, I've confused you. This isn't a drawing I've had around. This is brand new. It got delivered to the high school last night. Someone slid it under the door. The janitor found it and dropped it off in the office. One of the secretaries called me because she thought it was similar to another drawing by Silence that I'd shown her."

I said, "I'm still missing something. Are you suggesting that Silence did the drawing and her kidnapper delivered it to prove something?"

"Maybe. I don't know. Can we come and show you?"

"Yes, of course. Marlette knows how to get here."

"Oh, I should also say that Commander Mallory wants

us to keep quiet about the drawing, no one is to know. He says it will make it easier to catch the kidnappers if they don't hear about it. That is, if they don't already know about it. Like you just said, maybe they're the ones who delivered it."

"Got it," I said.

TWENTY-TWO

"Apparently Silence drew something and someone delivered it to the high school," I told Street after I hung up the phone.

"Could it be that one of the kidnappers is taking a liking to her and helping her by sneaking out a drawing?" she said.

"Maybe," I said. "Unless it's an old drawing and someone found it and turned it in to the school."

"Perhaps the kidnappers have been trying all along to convince her to write something that would prove she's alive."

"Yeah. And being mute, she responded with a drawing."

"Or," Street said, "maybe she did the drawing when no one was looking. Maybe it contains information on her whereabouts."

"But how would it find its way to the high school from where she's being held?"

"I can't imagine, unless one of her captors is helping her."

We were quiet awhile, thinking.

Spot groaned, perhaps uncomfortable at being my footrest. He pushed himself up, front legs first. My ankles slid down his back, heels hitting the deck with a thump. Spot stood up, turned and sniffed at my feet as if they were distasteful burdens that only an olfactory-challenged pack mule should have to carry.

"What, now you're an alter boy, too pure to be a footrest?" I said.

He glanced at me, then walked over to Street. She was painting the backboards of the chair. Before she could stop him, he stuck the end of his nose onto a fresh stroke of lemon yellow.

He turned, his nose brighter than a stoplight on the way from green to red.

"Spot! You'll get paint poisoning!" Street said.

I grabbed a newspaper, took his snout in my hand and pushed paper and nose together. Four times. Then I lightly scrubbed my palm across his nose and wiped it on my jeans.

Street stared at her paint job. "I have a perfect nose print in my paint. I'll never get it smooth again."

"A loss offset by opportunity," I said. "I have four limited-edition prints." I held up the newspaper with the blotchy yellow nose prints. "We could sell them at the Great Dane Art Show."

"Never heard of it."

"Me neither."

A horn honked, accompanied by the sound of a car turning into the drive. Spot was lowering himself back to the deck boards. He gave a single subdued woof, then trotted down the short deck stairs and out toward the drive.

I heard a car door shut as I followed him down the side of my cabin. Henrietta and Marlette were getting out of an old brown Subaru with rusted fenders. Marlette was clearly trying to put a pleasant smile on her face, but it didn't hide the rough redness that days of grief had caused.

I grabbed Spot by his collar and said hi.

"Did you get a chance to watch my video?" Marlette asked.

"Yes. Your kids are great performers. And the video is very professional. You could film movies."

"Oh, stop it. But thank you."

Henrietta was staring at Spot. "And who is this?" she asked, excited.

"This is my dog Spot."

"Hello, Spot. What happened to your nose? It's all smudgy yellow."

"He's been making art prints," I said. "A nose doesn't give as much control as a brush, but a true artist makes do with the resources available."

Henrietta raised an eyebrow. "Well, he's awfully big," she said. "He looks sleepy. Is he a good watchdog?"

"Not during post-prandial afternoon lethargy," I said.

"I bet he gets all focused if he hears a noise at night, huh?"

"Yes, if the noise is the microwave beeping that a Danish is hot."

I held Spot behind them as I showed them up onto the deck and introduced them to Street. Street switched her brush from right hand to the left and shook hands with Henrietta who was pleasant though not warm. I saw Marlette studying Street with the pejorative frown of a virginal nun who'd never seen a woman in short shorts. As Street turned to Marlette, the roles reversed, with Marlette smiling sweetly and Henrietta frowning a little, a lifetime accumulation of what-ifs playing across her face. It is the curse that all attractive women know well and something I've noticed a thousand times as other women look at Street's thinness with a mixture of envy and judgement.

Street spoke to Marlette as she held her hand. "Marlette, Owen has told me about both your kids. They sound wonderful. I'm so very sorry about Charlie. Owen said he thinks there's a good chance that Silence is okay. I told Owen, if there is anything I can do, anything at all..."

I didn't think Marlette knew about Street's forensic role or that she had seen the body. I hoped it would never be revealed.

Marlette said, "Thank you."

"Did you bring the drawing?" I said.

She nodded like an eager kid.

"I have it right here," Marlette said as she reached into a manila folder and pulled a piece of paper out of it. It was folded in thirds.

Henrietta said, "As soon as I saw it, I knew it was from Silence. So I called Marlette and then the police department. Commander Mallory came and took it. But he let me make a copy before he left. This is the copy."

I took the piece of paper from Marlette, unfolded it and looked it over.

The drawing was in pencil, a little smudged, but spectacular in how it rendered a room and a view out a window. The number of tiny pencil strokes was astounding. The detail was more like a photograph than a drawing, and the perspective was photographic as well.

The room looked like an upstairs bedroom in a house. There was a window, and it had four boards mounted across it horizontally. The drawing showed each of the screws that held the boards to the sides of the window. The boards looked smaller than 2x4s, possibly 1x3s, but still strong enough to prevent Silence from breaking them. The spaces between the boards were narrow enough that no one could crawl out. The window framed a view of a tree and the backyard down below. At the edge of the yard was a solid wooden fence. To the side of the window was a bed, neatly made, and a dresser with a mirror above. In the mirror was reflected part of the room.

"This drawing is amazing," I said. Street had set down her brush and come over. I angled it so she could see. "You're convinced this was done by Silence," I said.

Marlette nodded eagerly. "No question about it."

"Henrietta?" I said.

"Well," Henrietta said, "convinced is a strong word. I suppose I couldn't swear to it in court because I didn't see her draw it. But aside from that, yes, it absolutely looks like her style."

"So you are convinced."

"Yes, I'm certain. I..." Henrietta stopped talking. She stared at the drawing, pointed her finger at something and began counting.

"Oh, my God." Her voice raised up in a cry. "Oh, my God!" Her jaw quivered. Tears welled up in her eyes.

"What is it?" I said. "What are you seeing?"

"Henrietta!" Marlette said. "What's wrong?"

Henrietta pointed to the part of the drawing that showed the view out the window. "See the tree? Look at the branches! Oh, Lord, it is Silence! Do you see?! It has to be!"

"What are you referring to?" I said.

"The branches! Fibonacci numbers!"

I held the drawing close.

Street got next to me. "Fibonacci numbers," she said. "The number sequence you were talking about, right?"

I nodded.

There was a tree depicted in the window view. Not a typical Tahoe pine or fir, but something like a maple, perhaps an ornamental not native to the area.

The marks on the drawing were very small. Street used the nail of her baby finger as a pointer and moved it as we both counted.

First was the single trunk. Then came a split making another trunk. One plus one makes two. Then one of the trunks split again. One plus two makes three. Then two forks. Two plus three makes five. Then three more splits. Three plus five makes eight.

Incredibly, the next level was thirteen. And penciled in up at the top of the window view were many finer branches. I counted them carefully. Twenty-one.

"Look at the back, Owen," Marlette said.

I turned it over. In the center panel between the two folds, there were two smaller drawings, one in the center and one in the upper left corner.

"Notice the folds?" Marlette asked. "The original that the policeman took had two folds. So before he left I folded the copy the same way." She glanced toward Henrietta. "It was Henrietta's idea." Marlette took the paper from me and folded it. "Now look at the two smaller drawings. They're both on the center section between the folds. See? It's a letter. The center picture is the address. It's a picture of the high school. And the upper left drawing is a miniature picture of a house. It's the return address."

"Incredible," Street whispered.

I turned the paper back over to the main drawing. "If she is in this room, drawing it as she looks at it, then how could she draw the outside of the house for the return address?"

"From memory," Marlette said. "The same way she

knew how to draw the high school."

"But she's looked at the school hundreds of times. She probably only saw the outside of the house for a few moments as she was brought inside."

Henrietta said, "She has a photographic memory. She only has to look at something for a second or two and she can remember it exactly."

"She doesn't write," I said, "but she can draw. So she figured out how to send a letter using drawings in place of words."

Henrietta was nodding vigorously. "This is the first time Silence has ever done anything like this." Henrietta's excitement was palpable.

"By that you mean, accomplishing a specific task with drawings."

"Yes!"

"Marlette," I said, "I don't mean to be tedious, but is there any chance that this could be an older drawing that just got turned into the high school now?"

"I wondered that as we drove over here, and I don't think so. Maybe I'm just being hopeful, but I don't remember Silence ever drawing on letter paper. Wouldn't you say that's what the original was on, Henrietta?"

"Definitely. Plain old copy paper. Just like what we made the copy on. Only not quite such a bright white."

Marlette said, "Silence always draws on lined notebook paper or in her sketchbook. She's had lots of sketchbooks. Remember those ones I showed you in her room? The paper varies in some of them, but it's always a little rougher than copy paper, and if you ever tear out a sheet it shows on the edge. And I don't think any of her sketchbooks are the same size as copy paper. Some are a little bigger, but most are quite a bit smaller."

Both women looked at me. "So it looks like Silence got hold of a pencil and a regular piece of paper," I said. "Maybe the kidnappers gave it to her so that she could demonstrate that she is still alive. They tell her to draw something she knows, so she does a picture of the high school from memory. She puts the other drawings on it to give it the sense that it is a message, like that of a letter. Then the kidnapper slips it under the door of the high school. The result is that we now know she's alive, so they can make their demands with assurance that everyone will do whatever is necessary to save her."

"Tell them about the other marks," Henrietta said.

Marlette said, "The paper had those two folds to make it shaped like a letter, right? But it looked like there were other folds that had been smoothed out. I didn't know how to make them on this piece of paper, but I memorized the pattern. I can sketch it if you have a pencil."

"I'll get one," Street said. She went inside and came back out with a pencil and another sheet. "You can sketch on this so we don't mar the drawing."

Marlette walked over to the old plastic table that was about to be replaced by the new, electric blue wooden table. She set the paper down and sketched several lines, which all converged on a single point at the short edge of the paper. She held it up to Henrietta. "Isn't that about right, Henrietta?"

"Yes. I think so. There may have been one or two more, but that does a pretty good job of showing where the paper had once been folded before it got smoothed out again."

I picked up the sheet with the converging lines and the letter drawing and held them side by side. As I stared at it I had one of those deja-vu moments, a glimmer of a memory from my youth. I kept looking at it, but couldn't make sense of it. I could only recall a sense of familiarity. I set them down on the table and walked away, letting it simmer in my brain.

"The main thing is, this is strong evidence that she's alive," I said.

"Yes!" Marlette said.

I reached again for the paper with the lines that Marlette had drawn. "Like a map," I said, folding it on one of the lines, then another. "But it doesn't make sense that the folds all converge." I tried it a different way, starting with the center line, then attempting a second and third fold that created the convergence Marlette had sketched. Then the childhood memory came back, and I figured it out. A paper airplane. I finished the folds and held it up.

"Why would Silence write a letter on a paper that had been used as a paper airplane?" Marlette asked.

"Maybe it was the only piece available to her," Street said. "Maybe she had no paper and she found an errant paper airplane under her bed."

"That would be a long shot," I said. "I'm guessing that she found a paper and pencil, wrote the letter, then folded the paper into an airplane to send it."

Marlette looked a little sick as if thinking about the details made the kidnapping more vicious. "Do you mean," she said, "that if she is being held in a room, she would fly the letter out the window? To where?"

I raised my eyebrows. "I don't know." I continued the thought. "But let's assume someone found it and saw that when the airplane is unfolded and smoothed out and then refolded on the two parallel folds to make the three panels lie next to each other, then it looks like a letter. So this person recognized the picture of the high school and delivered it there. A postal Good Samaritan."

"But why?" Marlette said. "If the rest of us found a paper airplane that unfolded to reveal these drawings, we'd be unlikely to think it was a letter. And we'd be even less likely to deliver it."

"I agree," Street said. "Even if I thought it was a letter, I'd think of it as a pretend letter. Something an artist did as a party joke. It would never occur to me that it was a sincere attempt at a real letter and that I should deliver it myself."

"Another puzzle," I said, "is why the person who delivered it did so before the school opened. Most people would want to go during school hours, see what the reaction was among the school personnel. All of which points to the kidnapper as the person who delivered the drawing. But if it was the kidnapper, that wouldn't explain the airplane folds. Also, if the drawing that is in the return address position is accurate, then it goes a long way toward revealing where she is being held. The kidnapper would never allow it."

Henrietta spoke up, "I can visualize Silence in a room. She finds a piece of paper, makes the drawings, folds it into a letter format and creases it well so that whoever finds it will see how it can be used as a letter. Then she refolds it into a paper airplane. She flies it out the window and it goes all the way over the fence into the neighbor's yard. The neighbor picks it up and decides to deliver it anonymously."

"Why remain anonymous," Marlette said.

"There could be several reasons why," Henrietta said. "Maybe the person is really shy, a shut-in who doesn't want to see or talk to people. Or maybe the person is mentally ill and doesn't understand that the letter might be significant in some way and that they could help by identifying themselves to the school. It could even be that they think that if the school wants to get back to the letter-writer, they would just go to the return address. Of course, that is just a drawing, too, but if a mentally ill person thinks the high school drawing is a reasonable address, so would be the house drawing in the return address position."

"What would be the motivation for the neighbor to even deliver it?" Street said.

"I've an idea," I said. "Maybe the neighbor suspects that something is strange in the house next door. Maybe they even suspect that Silence is being held there. But they don't want to get involved. The neighbor could be wanted by the police or they're afraid of retribution from the kidnapper. Either would be a powerful motivation to just deliver the letter in the night. No additional notes about what the neighbor suspects because handwriting could lead the police and the kidnapper to the neighbor."

I turned to Marlette. "Did Silence ever make paper airplanes?"

"Oh, yes, of course. Don't all kids? In fact, a few years ago she and Charlie went through quite a phase where they made different kinds of airplanes and they flew them for hours."

TWENTY-THREE

I asked Marlette if I could borrow the drawing. She hesitated, then agreed. After she and Henrietta left, Street and I drove to Street's lab where she has a good scanner. We ran the drawing through, then Street used her computer to greatly expand the drawing that served as the return address on the center panel. She printed it out. Then I left her to her bugs and Spot and I went across Kingsbury Grade to my office.

Spot poked around, checking my office corners for bad guys while I put the expanded drawing of the house on my copier. I ran off a hundred copies.

I called Mallory and he said he had to leave in a couple minutes, but he would wait if I were quick.

Spot and I drove across town and turned on Johnson, the back way into the police department. I pulled into the lot just as a police department-emblazoned SUV was exiting. The vehicle honked and pulled to a stop. Mallory jumped out and walked over to my Jeep.

"You talked to the mother about the drawing?" Mallory said as Spot stuck his neck out the rear window, inspecting.

"Yeah. I made more copies of the drawing."

"Crime lab couldn't get any good prints off the original," Mallory said. "Which is what to expect with paper like that. Same for skin cells and hair. Nothing but a few graphite smudges."

I lifted one of the copies of the expanded return address drawing off the passenger seat and held it out to Mallory. "An uncanny rendering of the high school suggested that the drawing of the house in the return address position was equally accurate. Any ideas about the house? Do you think this is the place where she's being held?"

"I don't know anything about autism," Mallory said. "How it works, and all. But it makes sense, right? Girl gets taken by some goons, first thing she's gonna want is to get out. Girl can't talk or write. But she can draw like hell. So in her own way she draws a little letter. It says, 'Help me. I'm being kept in this house.' Then she addresses it to the high school where people will recognize who sent it and know what to do. How she got her outgoing mail delivered is another story."

"We're thinking she folded it into a paper airplane and flew it over the fence into the neighbor's yard. The neighbor delivered it."

"That would explain the other folds," Mallory said. "But why wouldn't the neighbor speak up? Why hide?"

"Afraid of you guys?" I said.

"Oh, that." He looked at the drawing of the house. "You're thinking this is the house where she is held. Could be something there. Can I keep this?"

"Made it just for you," I said. "I've got others I'm going to show some realtors. See if anyone recognizes it."

"Good idea. Gotta go, pal." Mallory knocked twice on the roof of my Jeep. He turned and got in his SUV.

I called Geoff Lambdon at his office.

"I didn't get you out of bed?" I said when he answered.

"McKenna, my man, a party boy like me? Hell, I'm often up at two in the afternoon. Incidentally, my wife and I have been pouring over maps. We're planning the ultimate mountain ride. Every road hand-picked for its curves, its gain and loss of elevation, its distance from civilization. It will be awesome. You want to come? I can help set you up with the machine of your dreams."

"I'll pass on the road trip, but I'll take your advice on the machine. Where do you recommend I go for a custom bike?"

"There are lots of good venues. What kind of wheels do you want? A cruiser? Something for speed? Travel?"

"Something that will blend in. Probably a cruiser," I said.

"New or used?" Geoff said.

"Preferably used. Problem is, I'll need some custom work and I'll need it fast."

"What kind of work and how fast?"

I thought about it. "The custom work could probably be done in several hours by a very good team of mechanics. As for when, sooner the better. Tomorrow would be good."

"Oh, so time is not a problem. Christ, McKenna, you don't make it easy. Tell you what. I'm thinking I should call up Slider in Carson. He's got a small shop off the highway. Just him and Farley, the guy who works for him. They could probably do it. But they're busy. Whenever I have him do any little thing he makes an appointment three weeks out. However, Slider is a businessman. If he sees enough profit in it, he can make adjustments to take the business. The way I see it, if you bring a credit card with enough room on it, maybe he takes one of those nice used rides out front and brings it into the shop for some emergency work, huh?"

"I'll be there in forty-five minutes. Where do I go?"

Geoff told me, then added, "But you gotta give me an update, make it so I can justify this interruption in my afternoon trip planning."

"I found a place I want to investigate. Because of the local biker population I thought I'd blend in a little better if I had the same wheels as the rest of them."

"I'll call Slider. Let me know how things turn out?"

"Will do."

At four in the afternoon, Spot and I pulled into the gravel lot in front of the unpainted concrete block garage in Carson City where Slider held forth under a sign that said, "Slider's Rides – We Make'em Growl."

There were six bikes parked out front, all threatening to

tip over as their kickstands sank into the gravel. They were different models, but they were all Harleys, and they all sparkled in the desert sun.

I walked over and looked at them.

Eventually, a big man with long hair and a big gut came out of the building and said, "What all can I do for ya." He didn't sound eager.

"Are you Slider?"

"He's on the phone." He looked toward the building.

"Got a question for him when he's done," I said.

The man nodded, spit in the dirt and went back inside.

A few minutes later, a small man came out. He had short hair and no gut. He looked up at me as he chewed on a toothpick. "You McKenna?"

"Yeah. Lambdon call?"

"Uh huh. Said you needed some quick work."

I nodded. "I need a bike. Maybe one of these would do. Got a gig going down soon. I need some wiring done so I can run without lights or, depending on my circumstances, run with the low beam but still no brake lights."

"Not a problem."

"I didn't think so. The real work is I'd need a muffler. Something serious. Make it sound like a Goldwing."

Slider inclined his head a few degrees. "Goldwings don't make no sound."

"That's the point," I said.

"You robbing a bank?" he said. The toothpick moved from the left side of his mouth to the right.

It occurred to me that I might get better service if Slider thought I was less than pure and honest. "There's an outfit that's got something that doesn't belong to them. I intend to make an unannounced withdrawal."

Slider didn't speak. The toothpick went back to the left side.

"You got a problem with that?" I said.

"Pro'bly not."

"I may spend some time on some backwoods trails, not real rough, but not asphalt either. So I need some clearance."

He took his time. "I could send out. Get some kind of Japanese muffler. Jack it in, I don't know. Pro'bly work."

"But it's got to have a valve. So I can turn it on or off. Depending."

"Wait. See if I understand. You want quiet sometime but not all the time. Like you reach down and turn a valve and the exhaust gets routed through a muffler."

"Right. A quiet muffler. Make it so you can't tell it's there."

"Shit. Lemme see what Farley thinks." He went in and brought the big guy back out.

They talked awhile. Some of it I understood. Some I didn't.

Slider came back over. He pointed to one of the used bikes. "This Sportster twelve hundred. We're thinking we could weld in a valve, hide a pipe underneath and put the muffler there. The valve would be a ninety-degree crank. The crank would show. But maybe it could be put down low and oriented so it doesn't catch a lot of light."

"Sounds good," I said.

"I don't know. Be a lotta work and it would mess up the exhaust back pressure. Maybe I could modify the muffler and adjust it. Still pro'bly cause backfires and foul your plugs and other shit. And it would take away some clearance. I couldn't guarantee nothing about it."

"I don't want a guarantee. I just want to blend in with some other bikers and then go silent at the right time."

"Goldwing muffler sure as hell will make you silent."

"Perfect. What will it cost to have it all ready by tomorrow? I'm on a budget. Right price, you make some good money. Too expensive, I figure a different way."

Slider stared at me. He turned and walked over to Farley who leaned against the building. They talked for a couple of minutes. Then Slider went inside. Through the window I could see him flip through some catalogs. He picked up the phone and talked and looked in some more catalogs, then came back out with a note pad. He wrote as he walked toward me. He stopped and studied the Sportster, then wrote some more.

Eventually, he came over and showed me the pad. I couldn't make out any of the writing except the columns of numbers and the total at the bottom. I figured it was far more than Marlette could afford.

I pulled out my wallet, fished out a credit card and said, "Put half on this card as a deposit. I'll be back when you're done and you can charge the rest then."

I called Street at her lab as I drove away. I had to swerve as a guy talking on a cell phone drifted into my lane. I honked. People who make phone calls while they drive.

Street answered.

"Hello?"

"It's cocktail hour. Want a glass of wine on my deck?"

"Of course," she said. "In fact, I was going to leave soon. I have to stop at my place. Then I'll head up the mountain."

"Take your time. I'm coming up from Carson."

"Will an hour work?" she asked.

"Perfect. Will you still be wearing those shorts with the notches in them?" I said.

"The ones that are suitable for bending?"

"Those ones," I said.

"It's cloudy, breezy and fifty-two degrees."

"Right. We'd have to be quick with our wine and then retire to a warmer, cozier place."

"In front of the woodstove," Street said.

"You want me to drag the bed in front of the woodstove?"

She started laughing and hung up. Which I took for a yes.

When I got home, I looked at the bedroom doorway and compared it to the size of the bed. Maybe twenty years ago.

Ten minutes later Street showed up wearing a long red

coat. Earrings with little pearls set in gold. Strapless spiked heels. I handed her a glass of wine I'd had airing. We went out on the deck, sat in the cold wind and drank the wine. She opened the coat to show me she was wearing the notched shorts and nothing else.

"I'm cold," she said.

So we went in and practiced bending activities until we were warm.

After a long nap we sat in front of the fire, Street barefoot in her coat, me barefoot in my jeans, and talked about Silence's drawing.

"You think, if we find a house that looks just like Silence's drawing, that we'll have found her?" Street asked.

"Yes," I said. "But I can't think of a good way to find the house. I made a bunch of copies. I thought I could hand them out to realtors. But realtors aren't usually in their offices. And I don't want to leave the drawings lying around. I need to be careful about who sees the drawing. I have to be sure they will stay quiet about it. If any of the agents spilled the beans and it got back to the kidnappers, they would move her. Or decide the risk was too great and kill her."

Street picked up the fireplace poker, stuck it in through the open stove doors and shifted a log. It sent a little explosion of sparks up the pipe. "House tours," she said.

"House tours?"

"A lot of realtors do house tours every week. All the agents from an office go out and meet at the new listings. They go through the houses to get familiar with them. We could contact the realtors, meet them at the house tours and explain what we are looking for."

"And hand out copies of Silence's drawing," I said. "We can call realtors tomorrow."

"I saw in the paper that Charlie's funeral is tomorrow," Street said.

"After the funeral," I said.

TWENTY-FOUR

Early the next day, Street and I called realtors we know and asked them about house tours. One of the local companies had a tour originally scheduled for 9:00 a.m. that day, but they had rescheduled it for noon to accommodate several realtors who planned to go to Charlie's funeral. They said I was welcome to come to the tour. Another company had an office meeting at 1:00 p.m., and I was welcome to come to that as well.

Street said, "These are all South Shore realtors. What do you think the chance is that Silence is being held on the north side of the lake, or Carson City, or Reno, or Miami?"

"Smallish," I said. "Her letter was delivered to the high school by someone who knew where it was based on the drawing. Or at least, that's how it appears. If she were being held somewhere else, the person who found her drawing wouldn't be likely to recognize the South Lake Tahoe High School, and we'd never have gotten the drawing."

I left Spot at home because I didn't think it was a good idea to have him in the church parking lot during a funeral. Just in case my bike was ready later, I grabbed my old helmet. Street and I drove in her VW bug to the church where standing-room-only services for Charlie were held at 9:00 a.m. Although it was a Thursday, hundreds of people attended, including half the student body from the high school, which had closed for the day.

In addition to paying my respects, I wanted to attend for the same reason that investigators go and study the crowd that gathers to watch a fire. As the arsonist often attends his own fire, so too a murderer will sometimes attend the funeral of his victim. I watched the crowd for anyone whose presence would surprise me as well as for anyone whose reaction to the funeral was unusual.

It was a standard service with opening remarks by the pastor, followed by the eulogy given by one of Charlie's teachers. After that came two student speakers who lavishly praised Charlie's virtues. At the end the pastor remarked that Charlie no doubt went to his death trying to save his sister, and the pastor added a prayer for her safety and speedy release.

I stayed to the side and back during the service so I could scan the crowd. Among the hundreds of people were all the ones I expected. Many local business leaders attended, as well as the mayor, a couple of councilmen and a councilwoman. Mallory was there along with two uniformed policemen. Diamond sat nearby. His uniform indicated that he was on duty. There was an entire section of teachers, including Henrietta.

The back of the church was largely filled with students. Prominent among a group of athletic-looking young men was Callif King. He was the center of a knot of boys and he commanded their attention. Before the ceremony began, he was jocular, cracking jokes with fellow students, bending his head forward and saying things in low tones that made the others start laughing. After the ceremony began he tried to put on a somber attitude, but he kept glancing sideways at the other students as if he didn't like having their attention leave him in favor of the speaker at the front of the church.

In the front row on the left was Marlette. To one side sat her neighbor Rachael and on the other was a man I recognized from the photos as Shane.

Shane was well-dressed and attentive to Marlette. Unlike in the photo Marlette gave me, Shane was now shaving his head, his light brown skin gleaming. He had a tightly trimmed black beard just around his mouth and chin, making him look like the sophisticated rapper he wanted to be. He had an almost regal bearing, sitting up tall and straight, his shoulder the perfect height for Marlette to lean against. If you didn't know they were divorced, you'd think they were a close couple.

After the church service was over, about a hundred people drove en masse over to the cemetery, where Street and I stood with everyone else at the graveside in a cold October wind. We all listened to a few more words from the pastor and then watched as Charlie's casket was lowered into the ground.

Several people encircled Marlette as she cried. Shane seemed to float free from the group, a look on his face that made me think he was going to make his escape the moment it wouldn't look too bad.

He wandered over toward the fence where the neighboring golf course stretched off. I told Street I'd be back in a couple of minutes, then followed and caught up with him at the fence.

"Hi Shane. Owen McKenna. Good to meet you."

He turned and saw my outstretched hand. He hesitated, then shook. "Do I know you?"

"No. I'm helping on the case. Trying to find Silence."

"McKenna," he said, "You're the PI Marlette told me about. Any progress?"

"We have a few leads we're checking out. Nothing substantial. Wonder if I can ask you a couple of questions?"

"You mean, as if I kidnapped her?" His defensiveness was exactly like what cops hear all the time from people who've spent time dealing with the criminal justice system.

"No. You're not a suspect. Although your defensiveness makes me wonder."

"Look man," he said, "I didn't do it. Why would I do it? She's my own daughter for chrissakes. I can visit her anytime I want."

"That's what Marlette told me."

"Why would I want to see my daughter, anyway?" he said, shaking his head. "Don't get me wrong, it's a terrible thing what's happened. She must be frightened to death, and that's a horrible thing for any kid to go through. If I could get my hands on the guy who did this I'd snap his neck in a second. Even if Silence is rescued, I'd do it. If they don't fry him, then there's no justice.

"But separate from that, it's no secret that the kid is impossible. We have no connection, she and I. Nothing. I try to talk to her, try to get her attention, but there's nothing there. She only has time for Charlie and her sketchbook. Now Charlie's gone."

Shane stared off toward Heavenly Mountain. "There was a kid who could light up the world. Charlie was a dream."

"Why'd you move down to San Diego if Charlie was a dream?"

"The two aren't related, man. I moved for my career. Nothing was happening in Tahoe. I gave it fifteen years. I busted my ass. Ask Marlette. She'll tell you how hard I worked at my job, always putting my rap in second place. But now I'm getting an audience. It's not huge, but those people are waiting on my next rap. I made a CD and it's on Amazon and in some stores down there. I could get my break any time. It could happen tomorrow. I get on the right show, open a concert for the right band, the sky could open. And there would be nothing better for Charlie than having a dad who is creating a niche, making a space that a kid can move into.

"Marlette cleans houses. That's hard work, I'll give her that. But what kind of dream does that present to Charlie? I'm riding the dream, man. I'm finally saying, 'no, I won't let life go by without following my star.'" Shane grabbed my elbow. "You know what I mean? Doing what you were put on this earth to do?"

"Let's assume we find Silence," I said. "Marlette is going to have an extra difficult time working and taking care of Silence without Charlie to help. What about your obligation to Silence? Shouldn't she have a dad right there, helping, solving the problems?"

"I told you, man, that kid is impossible. She and I, we're like fire and ice. Either one can destroy the other. It's not like I don't care about her. She didn't deserve to catch the autism thing. No one does. But there is nothing that passes between us except frustration."

We stood for a time at the fence, looking out at a few aspen leaves blowing across the fairway in front of us.

"Marlette said you ride a Harley," I said.

"Sure. A Road King Custom. Sweet ride, but I might sell it. I could use the change."

"You still pay your child support and alimony?"

"Yeah. I'm a real man, which means I'm a provider. Married or divorced. I guess I've been late here and there. But you don't walk away from your obligations."

"Do you have friends who ride?" I asked.

"'Course. Every biker has some friends who ride. That's the point, right?"

"Any of your friends ever take an interest in Silence?"

"I don't think that... wait a second. You mean like one of my friends would kidnap Silence? Whoa, you're way out on a limb, fella. Way out."

"Does that mean the answer is no?" I said.

"What it means is, you push hard, huh? Well, I can push hard, too." Shane seemed to puff out his chest a bit.

"Anybody you know ever talk about the Aztec language?"

Shane frowned. "You mean, Aztec like in Mexico?"

"Yeah. Or have you heard about any bikers who know Aztec?"

Shane was shaking his head. "No," he finally said. "Man, you're after some strange shit, aren't you?"

"Yeah," I said.

When Street parked near the realtor's house tour at noon, there were already a dozen or more cars and SUVs parked near the house in the Al Tahoe neighborhood where the first tour was taking place. I walked in the open front door to see a small crowd of well-dressed salespeople milling about, looking in bathrooms, sighting down hardwood floors, opening closets. I found Susan, the woman who'd arranged the meeting, and I introduced myself and Street. Susan was a severe-looking woman with a neck like a stork and a hooked nose not unlike an eagle's beak. But she spoke well, and her smile was warm and sweet. I instantly liked her.

"Okay, everyone, listen up," she called out to the crowd. She raised her voice to a strident shout. "All come into the living room, please!"

Incredibly, everyone assembled in half a minute.

"Quiet down, please. I want to introduce someone. This is Detective Owen McKenna. Some of you no doubt know of him. He needs your attention."

"Thank you," I said. "I'll make this quick. As all of you know, a local high school student was recently kidnapped in South Lake Tahoe. I'm going to tell you something about the case that puts each of you in a difficult situation. The responsibility will be great, but this young woman's life is of course a higher priority than the burden I'm giving you. If any of you feel you cannot take on a large responsibility, please leave for the next couple of minutes."

I waited. No one left.

I continued. "There is a house that we believe is connected to the kidnappers. We don't know where it is, but we have a drawing of the house. I would like to ask all of you to look for this house."

I handed out copies of Silence's drawing. People took them and started murmuring. I had to raise my voice to continue.

"There is a great risk to the girl's life if the kidnapper should hear of what we're doing. So please do not tell anyone about this. Not your friends or spouses or fellow realtors. The only people who will know are those I personally tell. None of us wants a young woman's death on our conscience."

I paused to let the point soak in. The crowd was utterly quiet, all staring at me.

"Keep the drawing for reference. But keep it in a place where no one will find it. Someplace really boring where no one will look. Buried in among some closing documents."

A little chuckle rippled through the group.

"If you see this house, please call one of the numbers at the bottom. The first one is mine, the second is Commander Mallory of the South Lake Tahoe Police Department, and the third is Sergeant Diamond Martinez from the Douglas County Sheriff's Department. You can call anonymously if you like. We just want the address. Any questions?"

After a moment, a young man spoke up in a nervous voice. "Does participating in this effort put us at risk from the kidnapper?"

"Not if none of you says a word to anyone about it. If no one speaks, the kidnapper will never know about this and there will be no risk to any of you."

"When will we be able to talk about it?" a woman said. "Or do we have to keep it a secret forever?"

"We can talk about it only after you read in the Herald that the young woman has been found and the kidnapper caught."

TWENTY-FIVE

Street drove us out to Meyers and the other realtor's office meeting, where I repeated my little speech. They all agreed to help look for the house.

Back in the car I turned to Street. "Cold and windy here in Tahoe. Want to drive down to the desert and soak up some warm sunshine?"

"And see if your motorcycle is ready?"

"That, too."

Because we were already out in Meyers, we decided to go to Carson from the south. We turned south on 89 and headed out Christmas Valley. Street drove up and over Luther Pass and down to Hope Valley. She took a left at Pickett's Junction and headed past Sorensen's down the canyon to Woodfords and the desert beyond. At the Carson Valley floor the road turns north, and it's a straight shot to Carson City. It's a longer route than going through South Lake Tahoe and over Spooner Summit or Kingsbury Grade, but it has ninety percent fewer stoplights and traffic. We got to Slider's bike shop an hour later.

I jumped out of Street's bug and walked inside. Slider and Farley were on either side of my Sportster which was up on a rack so that the exhaust system was at chest level. Farley had a section of exhaust pipe locked into an articulated vice. He steadied it while Slider positioned an arc welder. They both flipped down the dark face guards on their masks. I looked away as the sparks flew and white strobe light lit up the shop.

When Slider was done he flipped up his face guard and

turned to me. "It was just like I thought. The first pipe I put on screwed up the back pressure. Nothing but misfires and backfires. These engines, they're designed to tight specs. You put on a heavy muffler, valve and diverter and you destroy the balance. I can pro'bly make it quiet, but I don't know you can have it both ways. Quiet or loud at the flip of the switch, it's a tall order."

"Appreciate it if you could keep trying."

"I already put in a baffle that I thought would solve the problem, but it dint work. Now I gotta come up with a different pressure regulator." He looked up at the wall clock. On its face was a picture of a naked woman in spiked heels sitting astride a motorcycle. "Be at least another hour," he said.

"I'll be back then," I said.

Street and I drove down the block and found a cup of coffee. We were back an hour later.

Slider saw me coming. He waved me over to the side of the shop. The bike was on its center stand.

"First, these are the switches we put into the light circuits." He pointed to two toggle switches mounted under the handlebars in a place where few people would notice. "Leave them both pulled back, everything is normal. Push the first one forward, running lights, brake light and headlight all stay off no matter what. Pull that one back and push the second one forward, just the headlight works. No running lights, no brake light." Slider turned and looked up at me. "What you wanted, right? Run with the low beam but no one can see you from behind?"

"Perfect," I said.

Slider reached over and hit the starter button as he gave the throttle a twist.

The Sportster roared, coughed, then roared again. Slider had to shout to be heard. "The muffler was the hard part. But I pretty much got it. I modified the quiet muffler so its back pressure ain't much different than the stock muffler. That makes the quiet muffler a little more noisy. And it still hiccups a little. But not bad."

He reached down and turned the valve lever ninety

degrees. The roar disappeared as if the bike had been turned off. When my ears adjusted I heard it still running.

"Very impressive," I said. I thought I should high-five him or use the secret biker handshake, but I didn't know what it was.

Slider got off the bike. "Try it," he said.

I got on and revved the engine. The sound was a soft putter that rose and then fell when I released the handgrip. I reached down and turned the valve. The thunderous clatter was back. I throttled up. The engine coughed, then roared, hammering at my ears. Slider grinned like a 13-year-old kid.

"Mind if I take it 'round the block?" I yelled over the roar.

Slider nodded, pointed toward the road and walked to the shop.

I left the bike running and walked back to Street's bug. "Be another minute," I said to her as I fetched my old helmet that I'd brought. I pulled it on and tightened the chinstrap as I walked back to the Harley which was still idling. I swung my leg over the seat and pushed the bike forward off the center stand. The stand popped up and the bike dropped down onto soft suspension. I pulled the clutch with my left hand, kicked it into first and pulled out of the lot.

I went down the back roads, ran it up to 60 a couple of times, never getting it out of third. Then I slowed and pulled the valve. It was unreal, as if I were switching from Harley to Honda. The engine coughed, then revved like before, only without the racket.

The machine drove well. It had punch off the line and good torque, especially at low RPM. It wasn't as nimble as a smaller bike, and it didn't shoot to a brain-tingling redline like the Japanese and Italian rockets. Instead, it was exactly what its advertising sell-line promised: Big Gut, Low Butt. It ran well, was powerful and solid and it carried a big load with an undeniable style.

I came around the block, pushed the valve back into the loud position and pulled back into Slider's. I walked over to where Street still waited in her car.

"What do you think?" she asked.

"I think Slider and company are miracle workers. If Harley could silence their machines like Slider can, I'd probably buy one myself."

Street gave me a reappraising look.

I said, "Don't worry, I won't start serving you wine in paper cups."

With Street following in the distance, I took the bike through Carson City and turned up Highway 50 toward Spooner Summit. I left the valve in the noisy position. While a quiet Harley could hide in the woods, it would draw too much attention on the road. In the beginning I wished I had brought earplugs. But after several miles I became lost in the place that all bikers go to when they take a powerful motorcycle out on a curvy mountain road.

It is a kind of spirit place where experience is all and memories of the past and worries about the future fade away. It's a type of self-hypnosis. Later, you can't really say where exactly you rode and whether there was traffic and if there were stoplights and whether you stopped at them. For a few moments I forgot about Silence and Charlie and Marlette and everything else and just felt the wind and the vibration of the machine and the grand, sweeping, leaning turns, left and right, as I cruised up the mountain.

Halfway to the top I had the thought that it might be like Silence's spinning. The wind and the motion and the speed pushed away at the world, smoothed the edges, softened the bright spots, tweaked some kind of pleasure center in the reptilian part of my brain and made me feel a pure joy, unencumbered by cognition and awareness of process. I just went fast and then went a little faster and fell away into the pleasure.

At the top I slowed and cruised at the speed limit down to the lake, then south to the private drive, and powered up to my cabin. I pulled into the drive and parked, setting it down on the kickstand, figuring it was cold enough that 500 pounds of bike leaning on a narrow point still wouldn't sink down into the asphalt.

TWENTY-SIX

That night Street insisted on staying at her place. Nothing frightening had happened in the last three days, so I relented. I ate an early dinner and watched Marlette's home movies again.

The first time I had played it, the strangeness was front and center. Even if I hadn't known about Silence's autism, her unusual behavior would have been obvious. Unlike Charlie, she showed no connection to the person with the camera. No telltale glance, no self-consciousness, no careful acting performance. It was like a video of a dog chasing its tail, round and round in panic or glee or something else. I couldn't tell.

I sat in the dark at my kitchen table, moonlight throwing a cold, white parallelogram across the kitchen countertop, DVD in the laptop on the table.

The video was the same the second time through. The only difference was my growing sadness at how profoundly distressing it must be for the parents of an autistic child. While Silence was physically coordinated, and she didn't do any of the head banging or other traumatic things that some kids do, she did have one of the most troubling autistic characteristics, which was a nearly complete lack of communication.

When the video was over I went to bed.

But Silence went round and round in my mind. I couldn't stop wondering about what went on inside her mind. She didn't talk or write or type or do sign language or gesture. She wasn't warm, she didn't cuddle, and, as Marlette had explained with great sadness, every time she ever touched Silence, even when she was a baby, the child pulled away.

Yet she draws, and she made a drawing about her predicament, and she figured out how to get it to us.

I lay in bed and wondered about the nature of human communication and how we tend to be blind to anything that isn't speech or touch or certain visual signals that we've learned, like the "thumbs up" sign or making an "okay" sign by forming a circle with the thumb and forefinger.

I'd read that physicists say that the reason we think there are only four dimensions is because that's all we have an awareness of. Height, width, depth and time. But just because we can't perceive more dimensions doesn't mean they're not there. A fly walking across a computer screen can't understand how a computer works, but that doesn't mean there isn't communication in the email beneath his feet.

Are we like flies when it comes to communication?

What about Dr. Power? Was he correct in thinking that Silence is too retarded to have much mental activity? Or is he only able to see those same four dimensions?

Despite his professional expertise, I thought that Silence's drawings suggested a more active mind.

Assuming the letter drawing was really what it appeared to be, Silence's response to the incredible stress of being kidnapped didn't cause her to fall apart or implode into a wreck. Instead, she figured out how to communicate. Her way. With her tools. Using drawing skills that most of us couldn't acquire no matter how much training and education we had. Then she got the drawing delivered to the high school. Either she bested her kidnapper's efforts to keep her hidden, or she cajoled or shamed one of them into doing her will. How? With more drawings? Did she get them to feel sympathy? Or did she simply figure out a way to sneak a drawing out from where she was being held, and do it in a manner that someone would find it and deliver it to the high school?

Either way, I thought it proved she was clever and resourceful. She could scheme and plan. These were all things that people had missed about Silence. The rest of us are locked into our perceptions. We are so ego-centric, so confident that other people are just like us, that we can't see a different way even when it's right in front of us.

I got out of bed and put the DVD of Charlie and Silence into my computer to view it a third time.

The scenes now looked familiar. Because I anticipated the focus of each scene, I could for the first time see other things. It was like looking at an oil portrait over and over and finally noticing whether the person's smile curves up or not.

I'd gotten to the first scene where Silence was spinning. She went round and round, doing a little stamp with her right foot, keeping time like a musician. First, I watched the foot, then her right arm, which also bobbed with the same rhythm. I hit reverse and played it again, this time watching her face.

It was then that I saw the little smile.

At first I thought it was just the light catching on her front teeth as she twirled. But I stopped the DVD, then advanced it frame by frame.

I pulled up close to the computer screen, and played the scene again in slow motion.

Her face was directed down toward the ground so that it was difficult to see her mouth. But on close viewing the smile seemed more distinct. I advanced the video forward then backward and then froze the frame on what seemed the best moment. I zoomed in closer until her head filled the computer screen. The shot was grainy, but her smile was clear. Unmistakable, in fact.

It was a lopsided grin, more to the left than the right.

I leaned back in my chair, staring at the frozen image, and smiled back at Silence.

Here was a communication that the rest of us use all the time. A simple smile. One of the richest nonverbal communications we have. But it was a communication that everyone had missed in Silence. Her mother, her teachers, her neighbors. I'd asked about her moods. Did she laugh? Did she ever giggle? Did she smile when something amused her? Everyone said no. Yet here it was.

I raced forward and back in the video, looking for other such moments. Times when Silence wasn't spinning but simply was looking down, times when she faced away from people.

In a way, it was heart-breaking. Eight or nine times in the video I caught her with her surreptitious smile. It was always when she was facing mostly away and looking down. She smiled to herself. Small, half-smiles, reflecting inward pleasures, private joys.

I went back to the second scene with Silence spinning, the last and most recent shot of Silence in the video. I found the most obvious smile of all. I stopped the video and zoomed in on the frame. Like the other spinning shot, you'd never see this smile unless you were looking for it. And it needed to be substantially magnified to be obvious. But once I zoomed in close, it was quite obvious.

This one wasn't even just a smile. It was a mischievous grin. A giddy, giggling, lip-stretching happy-face.

Was she purposely smiling in a way that no one would see it? Was she consciously denying her mother the joy of her smile? Almost certainly, the answer was no. Silence just had her smile circuits wired differently from the rest of us. Like so many of her emotions, her joys were kept private, so her smile was private, too. The doctor said that autism was a lack of communication ability. It also seemed to be a type of excessive personal privacy. Whatever autistic people felt was not shared, not communicated, hence private.

I wanted to call Marlette right then in the middle of the night. Your daughter is more there than you think. She smiles, she grins, she has private amusements and they're not infrequent. You've seen them and filmed them. You just never noticed.

I didn't call. It would be appropriate even at 3:00 a.m., if the news were entirely joyful. And Marlette needed to be told. She needed to see the video again. It would be joyful, but it would also be very upsetting. Frightening, even. Marlette had the right and duty to know that her daughter was not so removed as she thought. But it should wait until morning.

I finally got some sleep, and in the morning I called Marlette and said I had something to show her.

I brought the DVD and my laptop over to her house. I wanted to play it on the computer so I could zoom in on parts of the frames.

Although I'd already had my breakfast, I took another cup of coffee from Marlette. "What is it you have?" she said as I set the laptop down on the dining table.

"Remember when I asked you about Silence's emotions?"

Marlette nodded. "Yes."

"Everything you said was also echoed by Henrietta. You both said that Silence was always totally removed and unresponsive. That even when she should have been very happy, she didn't laugh or smile."

"That's true," Marlette said. She shook her head as if she still didn't believe it. "It's like she doesn't have emotions, doesn't care about people. That has always been the hardest part. No communication at all."

"I want to show you something. I think that Silence does have emotions. But because she doesn't communicate the way you and I do, she doesn't communicate her emotions, either." I turned on the laptop and put in the DVD. When the screen control box came up I clicked on the skip button until the scene with Silence spinning came up. Then I hit play.

The scene unfolded as before. When the part where she smiled got close I put it on slow-motion. At the right moment I froze the frame.

"What is it?" Marlette said. "I've watched this scene a hundred times. I love the way she twirls. Of course, it is always kind of robot-like. She stares at the ground as she spins like a top. Like a machine. But I think she somehow enjoys it."

"You were right, Marlette. She does enjoy it. In fact, she loves it."

"Why do you say that?"

I positioned the pointer and zoomed in on Silence's face. "She was smiling, Marlette. Look. She was grinning madly. But because she faced the ground you didn't see it. Henrietta didn't see it, either. No one saw it."

Marlette stared at the screen for long seconds. She frowned and scrunched her brow. One hand slowly reached out toward the screen. The other hand seemed to levitate up, fingertips to her lips. "What does this..." she muttered. "I don't understand." Her jaw began to shake violently and tears flowed. "She never smiled. I can't... I can't believe it."

"She smiles, Marlette. But it's private. She doesn't mean to shut you out. It's just like her other emotions. Her autism makes her unable to communicate regardless of the kind of communication. We're just now learning how much she can communicate with drawings. In fact, she may only be learning that now herself. But the ability to draw has always been there. Maybe it's the same for smiling. Maybe she's always been able to smile and will someday learn to smile at other people. Smiling to communicate instead of smiling out of private amusement."

Marlette was shaking her head. "I don't believe it. A one-time fluke doesn't mean anything. I can't let that get my hopes up."

"It wasn't a fluke. Let me show you." I used the computer to move through the video and stop at the other smiles, all of which were hard to see, and all of which mostly faced the ground. Marlette stared at each scene.

After I'd zoomed in on the fourth or fifth, Marlette fell apart. She collapsed off her chair and melted to the floor. I moved quickly and was able to get my hand under her head before it hit. She lay there in a fetal position crying uncontrollably. "I never knew," she sobbed over and over. "I never knew. All this time my daughter has been there in a way I never knew."

TWENTY-SEVEN

I stayed with Marlette until she calmed.

I was driving away on Pioneer Trail when two bikers appeared behind me. As I went around some curves, I could better see the bikers in my rearview mirror. They rode Harleys, one with lots of chrome and a red gas tank and customized extended front forks, what bikers call a chopper. The other bike was chrome and green and looked to be a stock Fat Boy.

Even in the mirror I could see these were out-sized men. They stayed in close and telegraphed intimidation. I turned off on a back street and went around the block to verify that I was their target. They stayed with me.

I turned back onto Pioneer Trail.

I went through the options as I drove. I could call Mallory and have him send out some officers to pull in behind the bikers. But unless the bikers did something wrong, nothing would be gained. I could drive to the police station, but they would just ride away and find me later. I could stop, send Spot to attack one while I tried the other. But the vision of them using chains and knives and guns on my dog ruled that out. Instead, I worked my way over to the road that runs behind the casino hotels. I pulled into one of the parking lots, stopped and got out.

The two bikers pulled in and stopped a short distance away. They turned off their engines and got off their Harleys. One was large. One was a giant. The suspension on the giant's bike groaned, and the bike rose dramatically, as the man stepped upright.

He was the height of a basketball player with the girth of a small horse. He probably weighed 400 pounds. An ugly monstrosity, the height and breadth of which I'd never encountered up close.

The merely large man swung his leg over his seat, pulled an automatic out from under his leather vest and held it at his side as he spoke.

"We got a message for you, Mr. Owen McKenna. You stop looking for the girl. She belongs to the gang. We got a new toy. You leave us alone to enjoy her. That simple. We got to make you feel how important this is." His words seemed rehearsed. But it didn't lessen the impact.

The man spoke to his giant playmate. "Okay, Tiptoe, let's get this job done."

"Right, Marky," Tiptoe said as he walked toward me. Then he giggled. "Remember what happened the last time I said that? 'Right, Marky?' Down in Sac?" He giggled again. "Six guys who thought they could take me." The giant had a dribble of saliva pooling at the corner of his grin.

I didn't know if it was real or a performance. Either way, it was an effective intimidation trick. I put it out of my mind and concentrated on what to do next.

There are lots of cop tricks that stay with ex-cops for life. They aren't flashy like in the movies. Just basic moves and holds that probably come down from dirty street fighting over the centuries. What police trainers have done is collect the most effective techniques and perfect how they are taught. The result is that a young punk fighter often doesn't stand a chance against an overweight, middle-aged cop.

Not only do I practice the moves, I'm not overweight, and I stay in shape. At 215, I'm lean for my six-six height, but my height gives advantages of reach and leverage. Nevertheless, the size and heft of Tiptoe was astonishing, and the deadly earnestness of Marky had me doing a quick nervous pant. I forced a deep breath as we circled. I let it out and took a deeper breath. It was a way of centering myself and forcing all extraneous thoughts to the edges of my consciousness. As in every other area of life, the person with extreme focus will outperform people with far more talent and skill if those abilities are diluted by wandering attention.

Marky had the gun, but I figured his boss told him not to use it. I was not supposed to be killed, just beaten. As such, I sensed the greatest danger lay with Tiptoe.

He was built like a Sumo wrestler, a great hulk of muscle and fat that perched on legs that were huge and misshapen like ancient Whitebark pine trees. Tiptoe looked strong enough to lift a car and toss it on its back. He had long stringy hair on a head the size of a prize Halloween pumpkin. And like a Halloween face, his nose and upper lip were deformed to the left in a permanent sneer the shape of the arcing slash of a knife.

I let out my breath and quickened my circling. By their positions I could tell that Marky was the safety, hanging back, ready to dive in if things went wrong. Tiptoe was supposed to be the heavy. I figured the orders were simple, grab me, punch me up and break a bone or two. And if I were difficult, they'd kick in one of my knees as well.

The three of us circled. I periodically moved as if I were most worried about Marky and his gun. A glance here and there, a shift of shoulders. But they were stage-actor looks, head and eyes turned just enough to make the impression that I was looking toward Marky, but not actually enough to lose sight of Tiptoe. When I glanced Marky's way, I also dropped my arms, tempting a move from Tiptoe.

We three went around several times. I wondered why it took Tiptoe so long to make his move. Maybe they'd been told I used to be a cop and they should be extra careful.

I got bolder, moving closer to Tiptoe, glancing toward Marky, dropping my arms more. We went around again. Tiptoe got in close enough that I could smell his body odor competing with his breath. Either would wilt plastic flowers.

Finally, Tiptoe made his move. He lunged and grabbed my left arm. His movements were awkward. But it would matter little if he could get me in a bear hug.

When a man is the size of Tiptoe, many of the standard moves don't work. Like putting a headlock or an elbow twist on a hippo, they just shake you off. So I tried a pull-and-drop move that had its roots in judo. I took his grab, rotated and added my weight to his momentum. The move was a little improvised, but when the opponent is the size of Tiptoe, the plan needs to have flexibility.

I held hard to his right arm as I made the drop, remembering a mantra from the academy so many years before. Drop an ant from an airplane, it hits the ground and runs away. Drop a hippo from six feet and it dies from internal injuries.

I tightened every muscle as I hit the dirt. I still held Tiptoe's arm, bending him over as I rolled toward his charging legs. His shin bones felt like boards as they crashed into my ribs.

I tried to roll through the impact. Tiptoe made an effort to lift a leg over me as he tripped. I let go of his arm and grabbed the ankle.

Tiptoe went down. The impact was substantial. He made a whoomphing sound as air gusted from his mouth. He didn't move.

I kept rolling and jumped to my feet.

Marky was coming toward me at a run, holding his gun at hip level. I feinted left. He reached to grab my head. I went back to the right and landed a hard kick on his back as he went by. He grunted and stumbled to the ground. It took him a second to push himself up to his knees, reaching around to where I'd kicked him.

I had my knee against his upper back before he could stand. I put one arm around his neck, braced it with my other arm, and gave a quick jerk.

"Drop the gun or I'll break your neck."

Marky didn't move. He tried to suck air through his compressed trachea. He was on his hands and knees, gun in his right hand. He released his grip on it.

"Push it away."

He gave it a shove and it slid five or six feet to the side.

"Who do you work for?"

He hesitated, trying to breathe. "Tony Go."

"Convince me."

Marky wheezed. His right arm started to come up. I jerked on his neck and he gasped. "His real name is Antonio Gomez. Did two years in Granite Mountain Super Max for murder. Runs the Granite Mountain Boys biker gang."

He said the words as if they were memorized.

"How'd he get out of a Super Max?"

"He won't talk about it. Word is he got some expensive lawyering. Then a judge did some stuff. I don't know the details. All I know is they let him out."

"Why'd they take the girl?" I said.

"Usual stuff."

"What is the usual stuff?"

"Fun. Stuff like that."

"Why that girl?"

"I don't know. Skinny. I heard Tony Go likes skinny."

"Tell me about the Granite Mountain Boys."

"What's to tell? Some of them go back to the Super Max. Some like the code."

"Code?"

"The Aztec shit. The ancient language they use. It's called..."

I didn't hear the rest of his words because Tiptoe had gotten up and was staggering toward me, his face red with rage. I stood up and put a mild kick to Marky's head in the region of the right mastoid bone behind his ear. He dropped flat to the pavement. I tried to kick at his gun, but Tiptoe's lunge was sudden. I spun away to the side, my toe just tapping the gun barrel and it skittered a short distance. Tiptoe swung his open hand in a big roundhouse and grazed my shoulder, clutching at the fabric of my shirt. I turned and his hand slipped off, ripping the cloth. His momentum turned him away from me.

I took a quick step in behind him and stomped the back of his knee. He howled and collapsed to the asphalt.

I walked over to their bikes and saw that they'd both left

their keys in the ignition. I was reaching for them when Marky said, "Don't touch it, McKenna."

I turned to see him lumbering toward me, his left hand massaging the side of his head where I'd put my shoe, his right hand holding the gun. It wavered, but Marky's resolve seemed too firm for me to take a chance. I held my arms at my sides, palms out, and backed away.

"Get up, Tiptoe," Marky said without looking over his shoulder. He kept the gun on me as Tiptoe struggled up onto one knee, wincing with pain. Tiptoe grunted as he rose to his feet, then wobbled, limping, over to his bike. They each were in too much pain to try to hurt me for the time being.

Marky kept the gun on me as they got on their bikes, fired up the loud rumbling engines and rode away.

TWENTY-EIGHT

When Spot and I walked in the door of my cabin, the phone was ringing. I was still mad and frustrated after getting warned by Marky and Tiptoe. And I felt like an idiot for letting the situation distract my focus so much that I didn't get the license numbers off their motorcycles. I also wanted to call Street, but she had already left for her flight to San Francisco.

The phone rang again. I jerked the receiver up.

"Yeah," I nearly shouted.

"McKenna?" The voice sounded thick like what can happen to fighters who suffer punches to the throat.

"Who's calling?"

"José. I'm calling for Tony Go. He wants a sit-down with you."

"I just got your message. Tell Tony it didn't turn out the way he planned. In fact, it'll probably be awhile before Marky and Tiptoe report back."

"I don't know Marky and Tiptoe."

"Right. The boys Gomez sent after me."

"Tony didn't send no one after you."

"Tony doesn't tell you everything."

"Maybe not, but I'm the one coordinates errands. Anyone does an errand for Tony, I tell them where and when. You got confused."

Maybe I did get confused. Maybe Marky and Tiptoe were told to say they worked for Tony when they were actually working for someone else. Or Marky and Tiptoe could be working for themselves and trying to obscure it. But they didn't strike me as entrepreneurial wizards.

"You tell Tony, he wants a sit-down with me, he asks me himself."

"Tony doesn't ask. Tony tells. I'm his go-between."

I hung up. The man on the phone was a clichéd jerk, but he didn't sound insincere. When he said he didn't know Marky and Tiptoe, he sounded confused, too. Spot stood and looked at me, confusion on his face. Why was I sounding angry on the phone. Why wasn't I letting him out to run. How come I wasn't barbecuing a big steak for him to eat. Or at least dishing him up a bowl of ice cream.

The phone rang again. I was still mad. I jerked it up a second time.

"Yeah."

"This is Tony Go calling for Owen McKenna."

"You mean, Antonio Gomez?" I said.

"Nobody calls me Antonio Gomez."

"You anglicize it so dirtballs like Marky and Tiptoe can remember it better?"

"I don't know Marky and Tiptoe."

"They run with your Granite Mountain Boys."

"I'm not so sure." Tony Go's voice was soft and almost polite. "Either way, I want to talk to you."

"What about?" I imagined that the man on the other end of the phone had ordered people less irritating than me killed. But I didn't feel like acquiescing to his desires.

His breathing was audible. "You're looking for a girl. You think I have her, but I don't. We should talk about it. I may be able to help you."

There are times in my business when you have to make a quick decision that could maybe get you killed or maybe save your ass. Here was a known murderer who was possibly setting me up. Or he didn't like that somebody was setting him up to take the blame for Silence Ramirez's kidnapping.

"Where do you want to meet?" I said.

"Drive to Regan Beach. Park and walk down to the water. I'll meet you there. Oh, leave your dog at home."

"What makes you think I have a dog?"

"I know everything about you, McKenna. What you eat, where your girlfriend lives, why you quit the SFPD. Have to, in my business."

I was waiting by the water when a small man walked up. He didn't appear armed, but he could have had any number of weapons underneath the leather jacket, leather chaps, high boots, jangly chains, leather gloves with fringe. It was the bad-boy uniform that had been adopted by a quarter of all bikers. It meant either that you were bad or that you were enamored with the bad image. I knew that even doctors and lawyers sometimes wore the costume, but I couldn't see advanced degrees in this raggedy excuse for a human. I'd have bet good money he never made it past fourth grade.

"Tony Go?" I said.

He shook his head. "Come with me. I'll take you there." He turned and walked away.

I followed him up the stairs from the beach and back to the parking lot. "Which vehicle is yours?" I said, reaching for the door of my Jeep. "I'll follow."

He shook his head again. "You ride with me on my Fat Boy." He stepped over to a Harley, reached into a saddlebag and pulled out a little half-helmet, the kind that barely satisfies the law but wouldn't protect a pimple on your scalp, never mind your brain. He held it out to me.

I walked over to him, stood too close for his comfort and looked down at him. "Gomez requested this meeting, not me. He said he'd meet me here. You are a very poor substitute for Gomez, and I'm going to give you five seconds to get your skinny ass on your big mean machine and lead me to him. Otherwise I pick you up and throw you in the lake. The water is like ice this time of the year. Your choice. Four seconds. Three, two..."

The man turned, swung his leg over his bike and fired it

up. I got in the Jeep, backed out and followed as he cruised out of the parking lot. He turned left onto Lake Tahoe Blvd, quickly shifted up into third gear, then used his left hand to pull out a cell phone.

I knew he was dialing Gomez, calling for instructions, trying to make excuses for why I wasn't arriving as instructed, helpless on someone else's bike. I also knew that in the world of bad-ass bikers, he was the real thing, and the only reason he didn't pull out a knife and attempt to slice and dice me after I insulted him was that he was afraid of what Gomez would do to him. I could have flattered myself and thought that Gomez had told the man I might not be easily sliced and diced, but I knew this guy wasn't smart enough to be afraid of anyone but Gomez.

As we drove up the east side of the lake, I expected bikers to appear and box me in, front, back and sides, escorting me to a forced meeting with Gomez. But nothing happened. Either Gomez didn't care to try to force me, or he realized that I wouldn't be intimidated.

Although most people would feel a loss of control should a gang of bikers surround their car on the highway, the truth is that bikers can't force a car to go anywhere. They can shoot you dead or shoot out your tires and ruin your ears with their un-muffled engines, but they can't force you to drive where you don't want to go.

I followed the Fat Boy up past Spooner Lake toward the North Shore. He turned off at Sand Harbor, and I followed him into the parking area. It was empty except for five bikers, all on their bikes, all arranged in an arc. Gomez would be the one in the middle. It was a silly attempt at Brando in the Wild Bunch, but we all have our rituals. They'd think my candlelit dinners with Street were silly, too.

I came to a stop, got out, walked over and stood directly in front of Gomez's motorcycle. The other men tensed, but Gomez stayed relaxed. He made no move to have me searched, no doubt confident that his boys could overwhelm me no matter what weapon I might pull out.

"Good to meet you, McKenna."

"We're such good buds, Tony-G, why don't you call me Owen."

"I'm offering my services at no charge, and you are being disrespectful."

"Sending skinnyass here, in your place is disrespectful. Expecting that I'd ride behind him, sucking the miasma off his unwashed body in place of breathing oxygen, is an insult. Putting Marky and Tiptoe onto me was worse. I'm waiting for you to make it up to me."

Gomez didn't frown and didn't smile. To his credit, he made a small nod. "Like I said on the phone, this Marky and Tiptoe don't work for me." He turned toward the other men. "Any of you know a Marky and Tiptoe?"

They all shook their heads.

Gomez looked at me. "I didn't kidnap the girl, either." he said.

"You got to vacation at the Super Max for murder. Two of your boys kidnapped a Sonoma girl, then murdered her. Her forehead had an Aztec word on it. Several of your boys were caught in a meth lab in the El Dorado foothills, and they told of religious sacrifices you perform during full moons. When you're done, you pass around a vessel of blood for all to drink from. They said you cut up the body and burn it on a funeral pyre. And you want me to believe that even though you were here in Tahoe when the girl was taken, you had nothing to do with it."

Gomez turned his head and spit onto the pavement.

"I was convicted of murder on false testimony and later released. The girl who was kidnapped from Sonoma was a real tragedy. The men who did it were never known to me. They may have tagged along on one of our rides, but they were not part of my church. Perhaps they learned some Nahuatl, the Aztec language, from my men. A lot of men join our rides. We have an open invitation. I can't vet them all for moral purity. But I can have an effect once they join my church. The ceremonies during the full moon are our cleansing rituals. We sacrifice one sheep a month. There must be death to make room for new life. Yes, there is blood. Yes, we burn the sheep's body."

"What kind of sick religion is that?" I said.

"It is legitimate. We pray and give thanks to many gods, such as the sun god Huitzlopochtli who gave us the gift of fire, and the rain god Tatloc who gave us the gift of fertile soil. We find transcendence. Our rituals go back to an Aztec sect from seven centuries ago. I learned of it from my grandfather in the southern Mexican state of Oaxaca.

"Through my church I've turned over a hundred men from parasites on society to working, tax-paying citizens." Gomez turned and glanced at the men to his side. "They may not be pretty to look at, they may frighten people, but they have jobs. Most of them, anyway. They are mechanics and janitors and trash collectors and construction workers. Three of them formed a business selling motorcycle parts on eBay, and those three employ four others. Are they saints? Of course, not. But we are making progress. Other churches turn down our kind. Other church-goers shun my men. My church remains open to all who are willing to give themselves over to the gods of nature."

"If you want me to think you're an altar boy, then you brought me up here for nothing. Your debt to me is climbing."

"Listen, tall boy, I never said I'm pure. I've done some serious shit, shit that runs all over the rules that lawmakers and most church types focus on. But I've got a code. A man isn't anything, he doesn't have a code. My code precludes many kinds of behavior. One of them is murdering young boys and another is kidnapping young girls. Do I make myself clear?"

"A slick speech," I said, "but all I care about is the missing girl. How would you help me?"

"You want to find her. Maybe we can help. Or, when you find her, maybe we can help rescue her."

"Why would you want to help?"

"The Aztec religion is based on making peace with nature. Our church finds the violence done to the kidnapped girl and her brother an affront to all we believe in. It is like tearing the fabric of the cosmos. If we can help with the girl, we can heal the tear."

"You and your men never resort to violence."

"Only in pursuit of a greater peace. It is rare when I endorse a violent act. But I do it when it is the justified violence of repressed people fighting back."

"I think you are more concerned with getting me and the police off your back. Convincing them you didn't kidnap the girl is the ultimate goal."

"Not the ultimate goal. But our church could be more effective if the police realized that peace is our only desire."

I considered what he said against his clear megalomania. Gomez was a persuasive cult leader, possibly convincing even me that his motives were not those of a simple thug. Like all successful leaders, he exuded a compelling charisma, and the men at his side seemed loyal by desire, not by threat.

I said, "How do you want to proceed?"

Gomez reached out and handed me a card. It had a phone number printed on it. Nothing more. "That is my private cell number. When you need help, reinforcements, men for a stake-out or even, possibly, some intimidation services, give me a call. There are no strings attached. My men wish to serve. I wish to serve."

"And you want me to put in a good word about you to the authorities."

"You have the ear of Commander Mallory. Also Sergeant Martinez. I understand they are both tenacious police officers whose talents would be best put to use by not wasting time investigating us."

I put the card in my pocket, got into my Jeep and left.

TWENTY-NINE

Saturday morning I fed Spot and jumped in the shower. I pulled out some clothes that would be appropriate for both a talk by a noted entomologist as well as a night out in The City.

I'd made reservations at a four-star restaurant just off Union Square. We'd have just enough time to have a leisurely dinner, then head to our play, Chekov's *Uncle Vanya*, at the grand remodeled theater on Geary. Afterward we could walk up Nob Hill and grab a single malt scotch at the Top of the Mark, listen to the jazz band, then retire to our hotel on Post. It would be the kind of night a woman like Street should expect far more often than she gets.

The phone rang. It was Diamond.

"If you're calling about helping with dog chores, I appreciate your eagerness," I said.

"Wasn't calling for that, and I'm not eager to tell you this on your big day in San Fran. Jim Giniesch, my realtor friend, just called. Found your house. Over in Sierra Tract."

"Mallory know yet?"

"No. Figured you should have a look first. See what you think. But Jimmy thinks it's perfect match with the drawing. Even has two motorcycles parked outside."

"Address?"

Diamond gave me the number and street. "Jimmy says it's two blocks from Sierra Boulevard."

"Thanks. I'll drive by before I call Mallory."

I left Spot, took one of the copies of Silence's drawing

with me, and headed out. If it didn't look right, I could still make it to Street's talk. If it was a ringer for the house in the drawing, well, I'd better turn up with the girl alive and well.

I had no way of knowing whether the kidnappers knew I was looking for them, and if so, if they had gotten a description of me or of my Jeep. My default presumption was that it was still Tony Go's kidnapping and that the boys in the house not only knew all about me but were waiting for me to show up. Even so, I figured that if I drove by at a steady speed and didn't slow down, then it was unlikely that anyone in the house would notice me. Tahoe is filled with Jeeps just like mine.

I looked at the number pattern on the street two blocks over and planned it so the house would be on my right, out the passenger window. That way a spotter would have less of a chance of getting a good look at me. I still had my summer straw hat in back, and I put it on at an angle to obscure my features.

When I turned onto the street, I drove at a steady 20 miles per hour. As I approached, I took a last scan of the area to look for kids or dogs. Seeing none, I concentrated on the house as I cruised by without slowing.

It was identical to the drawing. Same door and window placements, and the same roof layout with the gable dormer on the front and the shed dormer on the side. I tried to see if there were boards screwed across the upstairs window, but the reflection of the sky in the glass was too bright.

In front of the house, perched on kickstands and leaning over at precarious angles, were two Harleys. The one with the red metallic gas tank was custom chopped, and the one with the green tank was not. They looked identical to the bikes Marky and Tiptoe rode.

As I went past, I turned to see if I could get a glimpse toward the back of the house. Just like the drawing, there was a gable dormer on the back. And the yard was enclosed by a wooden fence.

Only one more thing to find out.

I parked one block down and one block over. I switched

the straw hat for a baseball cap with a Yosemite logo and got out.

I approached on the street behind the house. Kept the baseball cap canted to shade my face. Walked at a steady pace, not fast, not slow. Didn't slow down or hesitate or turn my head.

I watched for the tree. I didn't move my head, but I turned my eyeballs as if to twist them out of their sockets.

There it was. Then it disappeared behind a neighbor's shed. There it was again. I memorized those branches. Burned them into retinal memory.

I got two more glimpses of the tree and then I was past.

Think. Concentrate. Focus. Pick a level and count them from memory. Eight. I was sure there were eight branches visible just above the neighbor's shed. Now count one level higher.

I closed my eyes as I walked. Scrunched them tight, trying to see something already gone. It was confusing. Branches in front of branches. Count them!

Maybe I was dreaming, but I could visualize thirteen branches. Maybe twelve, maybe fourteen. But I was fairly certain the number was thirteen.

Now came the hard part. The next level.

Concentrate. Count them. Left to right. Count them again, right to left.

It was too difficult. I tried to count them from memory four different times, suddenly realizing I was walking down the middle of the road three, maybe four blocks down from the house. I turned the corner and went perpendicular. In another block I'd double back to the Jeep.

I tried again. Shut my eyes, visualized the pattern and counted. My best guess was it had seemed like eighteen or nineteen. Considering how easily one branch obscures another, especially from a distance, it could have been twenty.

Or twenty-one.

Eight, thirteen, twenty-one. Fibonacci numbers.

Silence's prison.

Back in the Jeep, I watched the house as I called Diamond. "Sergeant Martinez," he answered.

"Diamond, I think it is the house."

"Matches the return-address drawing on Silence's letter?"

"Yeah. Two Harleys out front, just like your realtor friend said. Same bikes as belong to a couple bikers who tried to warn me off. Tree in back matches, too, same branch pattern."

"That number series?"

"Yeah."

"Any sign of the girl?"

"Not yet," I said. "I'm going to run to my office, look up the owner. Are you still on duty?"

"Just got off. You want a stakeout?"

"Pay your moonlighting fee in Carta Blanca if you want."

"When do you need me?"

"Now," I said.

There was a short wait while he thought about it. "I'm down in Carson Valley. Take me some time to get up there. Where will you be?"

I told Diamond where I was parked and he showed up twenty minutes later. "That was fast," I said as I got out of the Jeep.

"Sounded urgent," Diamond looked around the neighborhood.

I gestured down the street. "Through the trees over there. A block over, a block up. You can just see a blue-gray house, two-story, just to the left of the green rambler. The front door is visible under the fir tree. The backdoor faces the fenced yard. You can see the gate in the fence. You should be able to see if anyone goes in or out."

Diamond nodded. "What's your plan?"

"After I find out who the homeowner is, I'll call you and check in."

I did an online search and found the property owner, a Manford Poltacci who lived in Contra Costa County in the Bay Area. I called the number listed for him, got a machine and left a message asking for a return phone call. Then I called the City Hall in the town where Poltacci lived. They were closed on Saturday, but the message gave an emergency number. I dialed it, got an operator and eventually got routed through to a woman who could access the city's database.

"This is Detective Owen McKenna calling from Lake Tahoe. I need to get in touch with a Tahoe property owner, a Mr. Manford Poltacci who lives in your town. We have an urgent situation that requires his attention. The number we have is the nine-five-nine-eight number, but all we get is his machine. I'm calling to see if you have an alternative or emergency phone number in your records."

"Oh, dear, I hope everything is all right," she said, exuding worry. "You said you were a detective?"

"Yes. Working on a case that may impact one of Poltacci's properties. Of course, this is all very confidential until the case is sorted out. But I'm sure we can count on you to keep this to yourself."

"Oh, yes, sir. We have the utmost respect for our citizen's privacy rights. Here, I found the record. There is a cell listed. Would that help?"

"Yes, thank you."

She read the number, I thanked her again and dialed it.

"Yello," a high male voice answered.

"Mr. Poltacci?"

"Yessir."

"Detective Owen McKenna in Lake Tahoe calling. Sorry to intrude on your private number. We've got a situation that may involve your tenants in your house in Sierra Tract."

"Damn! I knew I shouldn't have rented it to them. They were clean-cut, gave good references, you know the routine. But afterward I thought the references were probably relatives. And those kids are young. Never rent to kids, I always say. But landlords all face the same dilemma, you know what I mean? The people who'd make the best renters already own their own homes. So what did they do? Burglary? I wouldn't think they were bold enough for robbery. Then again, they're not smart enough for anything complex. Things like embezzlement, tax fraud, identity theft, people who do those things probably own their homes. Am I right?"

I was thinking about Marky and Tiptoe. They weren't clean cut, and they weren't kids. But the bikes matched. It could be a coincidence. Or it could be that one pair of men borrowed bikes that belonged to the other pair. Or maybe Marky and Tiptoe lived with the renters.

I said, "Mr. Poltacci, what I need is their names and some identifying information. Whatever you've got. Birth date and Social Security number are the most helpful."

"Right. Hold on, I'm just pulling up to my office. It's in the file inside."

I waited and listened to car sounds and doors being opened and shut and the heavy breathing of an out-of-shape man negotiating a hallway and an elevator and another hallway. Finally, I heard a file drawer being opened. "Okay, lemme see, I organize these by street number. That one is a five hundred number, right? I can never remember. Oh, here we are. Jimmy and Jeremy Carmensen. Brothers. Both single. And get this, under the employment section they put down chefs. Is that something or what? The kids claimed they were both chefs and I believed it. Well, maybe I didn't, but they had the deposit and the first and last month's rent. Money talks, right?"

"Does your form have their Social Security numbers?"

"Of course. I'm thorough. You have to be thorough in this business. You ready?"

"Ready," I said.

He read off both numbers, which were one digit apart.

"Twins?" I said.

"Identical. Can't tell'em apart." He also gave me their birth date and their California Driver's License numbers. "Tell me again what they're wanted for?" he said.

"We're still in the preliminary stages of our investigation so I can't reveal details. But once a warrant is issued it is official. You will be informed when that happens. Until that point, we'd appreciate it if you respect the confidentiality of our investigation."

"Of course. I never talk out of line. Discretion is my middle name. Just one thing. Tell me my house is still okay. Tell me they haven't trashed it."

"It looks fine. This isn't about the house," I assured him.

"Good, good. That is good to hear."

"Thanks. I'll be in touch."

"Lemme know when that warrant goes out," he said. "And take my advice, never rent to kids." The resignation in his voice was heavy as he hung up.

Armed with names and identifying numbers I was able to quickly pull up criminal records and found that Jimmy and Jeremy Carmensen were from Long Beach. They had both been arrested two years ago after speeding on their motorcycles and leading police on a long high-speed chase up Highway 1 from L.A. to Malibu and points north. They had an affiliation with a skinhead biker gang called the Hotzis.

A little more research revealed that the Hotzis were actually run by an East German immigrant and art student at UCLA named Boris Hotauski. Hotauski gave soapbox speeches in parks and on street corners claiming that the Holocaust never happened, and that it was a Jewish invention as part of a Jewish conspiracy to take over the U.S. Government. I found nothing that indicated what, if anything, the Carmensen brothers had done with the gang besides getting the gang logo tatooed on the base of their heads where it would only show if they shaved their heads, which, back then, they did.

I dialed Mallory.

"Commander, it's Owen," I said when he barked his hello. "I've got a report on some bikers who tried to scare me off Silence's case. They claim to work for Antonio Gomez. I later met with Gomez and will also run that by you. But that can wait. We may have the house where the girl is being held."

"How do you know?"

I explained about the match with the drawing, the tree in back with branches matching Fibonacci numbers and the house's tenants, the Harley-riding, neo-nazi Carmensen brothers who'd been arrested after an attempt to evade police. "Also, their motorcycles match those of the men who tried to scare me off. Those men went by the nicknames Marky and Tiptoe. They can't be the same as the tenants, who are described as young twins. But the matching bikes are suggestive. All four men could be using the same two motorcycles."

"We'd still need more specific evidence for probable cause," Mallory said. "There are no words on the drawing indicating that the picture is where she is being held. We're just inferring that bit of information. Hell, we ain't even got proof the drawing was done by the Ramirez girl. And how many houses look like that drawing, anyway?"

"Previous arrests and affiliation with a neo-Nazi biker gang is suggestive," I said.

"Absolutely. And when Antonio Gomez came along, they probably switched to the Granite Mountain Boys because Gomez's halo was bigger and brighter than the Nazi's halo. I understand why you're antsy, McKenna. But you know I'm looking at Fourth Amendment hell if I convince a judge to sign paper on that. Not that I could."

"Let me see what else I can find," I said. I realized that Mallory was right and I shouldn't have called until I had something more. I was overeager and it was affecting my judgement.

We hung up.

I got up and paced around my little office. I stared out the window at the huge, blue, second-highest large lake in the world. My phone rang and I picked it up.

"There's a girl at the downstairs window," Diamond said. "Looks like some guy is holding her arm. But I can't see him. He's in the shadow."

"You can see clearly from that distance?"

"These glasses are eight-power. You think I'd go to a

stakeout without some refractive help?"

"What color is her hair?"

"Brown. Hangs straight down. Can't see the length behind her back. Oh, wait. He's turning her sideways. There we are. Comes to maybe six inches below her shoulder."

"Her build?" I said.

"Hard to say. Looks thin. Skinny, almost."

"Can you make her from the picture I showed you?"

"Hard to say. This girl's got cheekbones, I'll give you that much. And Silence has cheekbones, too."

"Her face is half cheekbones. I'll call you back."

I got Mallory back on the phone.

"Diamond's looking at the girl through the window as we speak."

"The girl or a girl?" Mallory said.

"A girl. Probably the girl. Same hair, same build, same cheekbones."

"Can I tell the judge it's a solid ID?" he asked.

"It's a likely ID. Probable cause for me," I said. "My concern is what happens to the girl. If you knock and announce, that will put the girl at supreme risk. The Supreme Court exceptions to a Knock-and-Announce warrant include Apprehension of Peril. Knowing the kidnap victim is in there, you could make an unannounced forced entry predicated on saving her life."

"Look McKenna, I know you want the guys that did this. Having them try to scare you off cranks up that desire. I've been there, felt the taste in my mouth, too. But I won't do it. If you're convinced a no-knock entry is justified on Diamond's ID, then you do it. You don't even need the police or a warrant. You know how it works. You get a large friend or two. You happen to be walking the neighborhood. Maybe you even have some legal armament. You hear something and see something that indicates the girl's life is in peril. It calls to your duty to save her from being victimized in a violent crime. You go in as private citizens and get her out. If she's really there and in mortal danger, then that kind of intrusion is legal. If you're right and you rescue a kidnap victim, they'll give you a medal.

"But if you're wrong, you'll be convicted in the criminal prosecution and lose everything else in the follow-up civil lawsuit.

"What's your decision?" he continued.

I thought about it, tried to calm myself. Maybe Mallory was right. I was too eager. "Okay. Play it conservative."

"Judges are hard to reach on Saturday morning," Mallory said. "Iffy, finding one. Iffier convincing the judge that this is where a kidnap victim is being held prisoner. But maybe I can do it. He or she signs the warrant, we put together a team. Because the girl may be in there and she'll be in danger, we'll squeeze the Knock-and-Announce rule. Instead of twenty seconds, we give them about a five-count, then go in front and back."

"Let me know as soon as you find out anything," I said.

I was pacing my small office, back and forth, when Mallory called half an hour later.

"I caught the judge on the third green at Edgewood. Briefed him by phone. Says he'll sign. He maybe thinks the ID on the girl is firmer than you described."

"But I said it was a likely ID, not a firm one."

"We'll have a team ready in a couple hours," he interrupted. "Meanwhile, I've got two men in the neighborhood, a block the other side of where Diamond is watching. We want to see everybody stays put."

I took some deep breaths.

After I hung up, I called Street's cell and got her voicemail. "Sweetheart, I'm very sorry, but I won't be able to make your talk. We found the house where Silence is being held. The police are going in this afternoon. I'll check in with you after your talk. Good luck."

They went in at 3:00 p.m. just when Street would be finishing her paper in San Francisco. I watched from a few houses down.

Eight officers rushed the house. The first one to reach the front door pounded on it three times and yelled, "Police! We have a warrant to search your house! Open the door!"

Five seconds later they kicked in the front and the back doors at once.

The two 20-year-old Carmensen brothers were watching TV in the living room. They were put on the floor at gunpoint and frisked. Their 19-year-old sister was taken from the upstairs bedroom where she'd been napping and brought downstairs in her sleep shirt and underwear. The officers were efficient, professional and understandably rough. As a result, one of the boys broke his wrist as he hit the living room floor during the frisk. The other hit his nose on the floor and it bled profusely. The girl's shirt was torn, and she sustained a substantial bruise on the side of her ribcage.

All three siblings were taken to the hospital for treatment.

The search revealed that none of the rooms, up or down, showed any signs of any other human presence aside from the three siblings. There was no indication of any contact with the Granite Mountain Boys, no evidence of any connection to a kidnapping. There were no boards across the upstairs window.

An interview with two neighbors confirmed that the two kids were good kids, employed full time as chefs at Perry's Perfect Pizza shop, well-behaved, and never had visitors other than their sister. Their boss was reached by phone and said the two brothers were the best employees he'd ever had. The boys had short haircuts, yet sufficiently long to conceal the tattoos they'd gotten when they were younger, and they both stated their intention to one day have the tattoos removed.

On careful count, the tree out the back turned out to have one trunk followed by two branches, followed by four branches, then seven, then fourteen, then nineteen before branching into uncountable twigs. It was a reasonable deviation from the natural Fibonacci sequence, but nothing like the exact sequence, and nothing like the tree in Silence's drawing.

THIRTY

It was 10:00 p.m. when Mallory sent me home from his office. Street would be leaving the theater and heading back to her hotel. I'd had my cell off during the afternoon raid and during the evening's frantic efforts at sorting out what happened and who was responsible and what could be done about it. Street would be worried, but I had to think a moment before I called her.

I paused in Mallory's office doorway before I left. "It was a big mistake," I said, "and it was all my fault. I'm really sorry."

Mallory stared at me, his lips pressed tightly together. "I'll call you in the morning."

I drove home, my stomach writhing. The highway was empty and desolate. Heavy gray clouds, weakly lit with lunar light, flew across the sky, gathered together in a huge dark cluster and blotted out the moon completely.

I tried to tell myself that it hadn't been that bad. There were no severe injuries and no weapons had been discharged. But what mattered was that I created the problem and Mallory was enduring the judgment for it.

In every respect Mallory was in a worse position than I was. He'd been the official in charge. The warrant had come at his request. The police involved in the raid had assembled at his orders. The young men who lived in the house knew that their castle had been breached by Mallory and his men. The landlord who would have to coordinate repairs to the broken doors would have Mallory's name on his lips and in his thoughts as he considered his expenses. And the lawyers who earn a living turning mistakes and bad judgement into large monetary rewards would be talking about Mallory at every step of legal planning.

And Mallory did it all for me.

I let Spot out, picked up the new portable, found the right button to get a dial tone, and called Street's cell.

She must have looked at the readout before she answered. "First, tell me you are okay," she said. "I'm worried sick." Her words were caring, but her tone was flat.

"I'm okay. And I'm very sorry I didn't come today. I've made a bad mistake."

"The raid was on the news. But they kept talking about it as Mallory's raid."

"That makes it worse. He took me at my word, and my word was wrong."

Street paused. "I suppose the powers that be will say that even though you suggested the raid, Mallory should have exercised better judgement and held off until he had more evidence."

"Yes, that's what they will say. He is no doubt kicking himself as we speak. He listened to me, former big-city homicide inspector, thinking I knew what I was talking about. It's hard to get someone into more trouble than what I've created for him."

Street said, "The news reported some injuries?"

"A bruise, a broken wrist, a bloody nose. The girl's shirt was torn."

Street didn't say anything. I took it as her recognition of the seriousness of the situation.

I continued, "There will be people calling for Mallory's resignation. There could be lawsuits. But let's change the subject to my other screw-up. How did your talk go?"

"It went well." Street's voice had the flat sound that revealed her disappointment and anger.

"I apologize for missing it. I'll try again to make it to your next talk," I said, realizing afterward how lame it sounded.

"I'm sure you will," she said. Her delivery was monotone, but I'd put her in a difficult situation where anything she said would either sound hollow or falsely cheerful or resentful of my actions, which, regardless of how well-intentioned, still rankled.

"How was the play?" I said.

"I didn't go," she said. "I was worried about you and sad and disappointed that you didn't come. Lonely, too."

I winced. "Dare I ask if your dinner was okay?"

"I didn't eat. I had no appetite."

I shut my eyes and took a deep breath. "You flew down. So now you're trapped in San Francisco without a way home. And you're starving. Is there a way I can make this better?"

"You could drive down tomorrow and get me."

I apologized again and told her I'd be there in the afternoon.

After I got off the phone with Street I called Glenda Gorman at her home.

"Hi Glennie. It's Owen," I said when she answered. I was pacing about my cabin.

"I heard about the raid," she said. "I was driving up from some errands in Sac, but Nathan over in sports keeps his scanner on. He kept calling to fill me in. Can you comment?"

"Yes. It was my fault. I'm hoping you can get that in the first sentence or two of Monday's paper. Mallory took a big risk listening to me and it blew up in his face. Maybe I can redirect some of the community's anger toward me."

"Can you tell me how it evolved? If I can get the right flavor in my story, readers might understand why it happened."

"Let's hope." I went over it from the beginning.

"How did you initially come to think that the girl was being held in that house?" Glennie asked when I was done.

This was the most difficult question of all. I stalled.

If I answered it truthfully and told her about the drawing Silence had sent, then her kidnappers would find out. They might punish her severely for sneaking a drawing of the house out to the outside world. Also, the kidnappers would immediately move her. That would destroy our only chance of finding her.

Instead of leaving her alive, they might decide to kill her.

On the other hand, if I lied and gave Glennie a false story about how we found the house, then she would be obligated to reveal the lie once she discovered the truth. That would almost certainly happen at some point, and when it came out it would make the situation even more difficult for Mallory.

And if I simply withheld the information from Glennie, she would be extra eager to learn about it.

"Owen?" she said, still waiting. "Are you still there? I was wondering why you thought the girl was held in that house?"

"Glennie, this is a hard one. So I'm going to give you my best explanation and hope you can go with it for now. Suffice to say that we had a reason we were looking at that house. But if that reason is made public it could cause the kidnappers to panic and kill Silence Ramirez. And it will certainly cause them to move her from her current location. We don't want that to happen because it would eliminate our only current chance of finding her."

"Which implies," Glennie muttered, "that the reason you were looking at the house comes from a tip. The tipster thinks he knows where Silence is he and told you. Am I right? You can tell me off the record."

"Yes. We got a tip we believe is credible. We don't want the kidnappers to know that anyone is passing us information."

I thought about another way she could help with her story. I said, "On the record, there were two motorcycles at the house. They were the same as others that belong to possible suspects. Further," I said, hesitating, choosing my words carefully, "a witness saw the girl in a window of the house, a house that was known to only have two men as occupants. The girl's description matched that of Silence Ramirez. Of course, the girl turned out to be the sister of the tenants."

"Your mistake was in erring toward any possibility of saving the kidnapped girl's life," Glennie said. "Better than if it were the other way around."

"True," I said. "But I should have handled it much differently."

"I'll tell it straight. The readers will see the sense of the action."

"One more favor?" I said.

"What?"

"Some words of praise for the kids who got roughed up? Something about how well they handled the stress of the raid?"

"You mean," Glennie mumbled, "something about how character is revealed by how someone reacts under adverse circumstances?"

"Yeah, something like that. I'll owe you."

"When this is all over," Glennie said, "will you give me a full interview? The inside story?"

"Yes."

The line went quiet and I had the sense that Glennie was taking notes.

"And how is Street?" Glennie said after a minute.

I hesitated, thinking about Street alone in a hotel room. "She's well," I said. "Thanks for asking."

"You two are still close," Glennie said.

"Yes," I said. "Very."

"That's this reporter's bad dream, you know. I want conflict. I need conflict."

"Yes, Glennie," I said.

After Glennie and I said goodbye, I got a beer out of the fridge, made a small fire and sat in front of it. I dangled one hand down from the rocker and stroked Spot as he tried to become one with the floorboards in front of the woodstove.

In a ruthless reporter's hands, the story could be presented in a way that would invite lawsuits and destroy careers and ruin reputations. But I hoped that Glennie would take it a different direction and attempt to heal the wounds. Monday morning would tell.

THIRTY-ONE

I found myself looking at the clock all night long, aware that the moon coming in the window was getting fuller each night. I finally got up at 5:00 a.m. I let Spot out to prowl the dark for night creatures while I drank my coffee standing at the window that overlooks the view of Tahoe below.

The lake often has an eery flat blackness at night, interrupted by the occasional boat light and, this particular morning, the three-quarter moon, which was about to set behind Rubicon Peak on the western shore. The moon was reflected in a long silver swath that split the dark water into halves. My mood was as dark as the water but with no bright spots to distract me.

I felt a powerful frustration at a situation that had no potential for improvement save the passage of time. I wanted to call Mallory and somehow make it better, but it was a magic-wand fantasy. He was going to be squeezed by his colleagues as well as by the community, and nothing I could say would reduce his misery or his resentment toward me.

Although Mallory and I don't socialize as friends, we went back to when I was on the San Francisco PD. He was a sergeant working on an attempted murder of a fellow South Lake Tahoe PD officer. A witness had written down the suspect's plate as the suspect fled. At the time, I was working on an assault case wrapped in a drug smuggling operation, and my suspect turned out to be the owner of the car. So Mallory and I spent some hours sharing information and doing a little strategizing at the same time. The suspect was eventually caught and convicted.

When Mallory was next in San Francisco, he and I got together for a celebratory beer at an Irish pub in the North Beach neighborhood. We found common ground in our family backgrounds filled with Irish and Scottish law officers, our antipathy toward politicians, and our growing cynicism about the trend toward incarcerating minor drug offenders with hard-core violent criminals, thus filling up prisons at great cost to the state while immersing pot-smokers in the world of serious crime.

The next time I was up skiing in Tahoe, I talked Mallory into joining me on the slopes, and we maintained a solid, mutually respectful relationship ever since.

Mallory was gracious about my decision to move to Tahoe and go private, a decision that some other law enforcement personnel see in a pejorative light. If Mallory thought that private cops were quitters who were more interested in money than in keeping our communities safe, he kept it to himself.

When it got light, I took Spot out for the trek down the mountain to the highway and back up, only this time I didn't jog. I was too weary, psychologically as well as physically.

Although it was Sunday, I tried Mallory's office number at 8:00 a.m., thinking I could at least leave a message on his voicemail.

But he answered. "Mallory," he barked.

"Checking in," I said. "Anything I can do to help? Personally or officially?"

"Naw. The review process is already underway. Ain't much I can do to prevent them from burning my ass with a branding iron. I'll explain to them what happened, best as I'm able. After that, if they call you in, you can explain best as you're able."

"Will do," I said.

"Someone's calling now. Gotta go." He hung up.

The phone rang.

"It's me," Marlette said when I answered. "Silence sent another letter. This one shows the kidnappers."

THIRTY-TWO

Marlette and Henrietta and I met at Marlette's house.

"It was delivered the same way?" I said as Marlette handed me the drawing.

Henrietta nodded. "Slipped under the high school door sometime in the night. The weekend janitor had heard about the first drawing, so he knew what this was. He called me as soon as he found it. Then I called Commander Mallory, but apparently he's unavailable ever since, well, you know. The police department sent down an officer to meet me at the school." Henrietta pointed at the drawing. "This is a copy, just like before. I made two of them so you can keep one. I gave the officer the original."

Marlette spoke up. "Open it. She drew the kidnappers."

I unfolded the paper. Like the first letter, this drawing had lots of detail in the room and out the window. But the main difference was the two men in the room. They stood at the window, their backs to Silence as she drew, or more likely, as she looked at them with her photographic memory. They were looking out the window, one of them pointing at something.

Stomach acid rose in my throat as I realized that one was large and the other was a giant who had to bend over and lower his head just to see out the window.

Marky and Tiptoe.

"Turn it over, Owen," Marlette said. "Look at the back side. She put on a stamp."

I looked at the other side and saw that in addition to a drawing of the high school and the house where the address and return address normally would be, there was a drawing of a stamp in the upper right corner. It was as remarkable as the other drawings. Miniature in size, and to perfect scale, the flag and the Statue of Liberty were rendered in amazingly fine detail. The waves in the flag made it look like actual fabric.

I turned it again to check that the rendering showed the same room as before, although the perspective was shifted a bit to the left. The window with the view of tree and fence outside was now on the right edge of the drawing, while more of the room showed on the left.

"Did this one have the same folds?" I asked.

"Yes," Marlette said. "It was folded in thirds so it could make a letter, and it had more of those faint fold lines like it was once folded into a paper airplane and then straightened out."

"Either of you see anything else unusual in this drawing?"

Henrietta shook her head. "We were talking about that before you got here. Obviously, Silence wanted to show us the men. But was there some additional information in this letter that wasn't in the first?" Henrietta waited a second as if Marlette or I might comment. Then she said, "I know what the doctors would say. They'd think that the drawing is just another rendering of her environment. But I think there's something else here."

"You mean, a message of sorts?" I said.

"Yes. I don't know what it would be. I keep looking at this to find some meaning. But I haven't seen it yet."

"What about a hidden image within the drawing?"

"You mean, like in a Bev Doolittle painting where you can see Indian faces in the rocks? No, I don't think so. I'm talking about some detail that is easy for all of us to see when we look at the drawing, but has a significance that is obvious to Silence and not to the rest of us."

"Like the tree branch pattern that demonstrates Fibonacci numbers," I said.

"Right."

We all stared a minute longer at the drawing.

"Let me know if anything comes to you," I said. "I have

to drive into San Francisco to pick up Street. I'll be in touch."

We said goodbye, and I walked out to the Jeep.

Spot was standing on the rear seat, bending his legs so his back would fit up against the ceiling. He had his head lowered to stick out the window. I heard him wagging as I approached, his hard tail banging between the front and rear seat backs.

"You think I'm bringing food or something?" I said.

He wagged harder. Probably could tell we were going to get Street.

As I drove through intermittent rain showers, up and out of the basin and then down the West Slope of the Sierra, I thought about the drawing sitting next to me on the passenger seat. Silence had done an exemplary job of detailing the room and the men. She revealed the essence of the men so well that I was certain of their identities even though it showed them from behind.

Nevertheless, I kept the information about the men to myself. I didn't want to tell Marlette and Henrietta about Marky and Tiptoe because I sensed that knowing something of their sick personalities might make Marlette and Henrietta even more afraid for Silence.

Perhaps that was the same reason I didn't point out the other unusual thing I spotted in the drawing, something neither of them seemed to notice.

On the wall of the room hung a calendar. One of the squares in the calendar had a tiny drawing in it. Not until I was in the Jeep and driving away did I take a closer look.

It was of a fire, like a campfire, but with a large crooked log stuck vertically into the fire. By holding the drawing in the bright light of day I saw that the log had something attached to it. The pencil strokes were so fine that it was difficult to tell what it was. Difficult, that is, unless you were looking for a girl tied to a stake. Then the funeral pyre became obvious.

The drawing was on the square denoting next Thursday. In the upper right corner of the square, printed as part of the calendar, was the circle that designates the full moon.

THIRTY-THREE

I called Mallory and got his voicemail. I left a short message, then called dispatch and asked if Mallory could be contacted. The woman said she'd try. Eventually someone else answered.

"Sergeant O'Conner," a voice said.

"Sergeant, this is Owen McKenna. I have some urgent news for Mallory. Is there any way I can get in touch with him?"

"Sorry, sir. He's busy. I can pass on a message."

"Okay. A second letter drawing from the kidnapped girl was delivered to the high school this morning."

"Right, sir. I'm the one who picked it up."

"Then you know it depicts two men."

"Yes," he said.

"Those men go by the names Marky and Tiptoe. They were the men who tried to scare me off. They claim to ride with the Granite Mountain Boys, but I'm not convinced of it." I gave the sergeant thorough descriptions of them and their motorcycles.

"I'll pass that on to the commander, sir."

"There is something else in the drawing." I told him about the drawing on the calendar the day of the full moon.

"Thank you. I'll pass that on as well."

"When is the best time for me to get hold of Mallory?" I asked. "Or can you ask him to call me back?"

There was a small delay before the sergeant answered. "Sir, I should probably let you know that word in the department is that you need to make yourself scarce on this kidnapping. That would include not talking to the commander. The commander has held the chief and others off of you. But it sounds like the tiniest mistake on your part will have them looking to see what kind of charges they can bring against you. Just thought you should know."

"I appreciate that," I said.

I hung up and drove. Once I got to the Central Valley floor, the highway was busy with cars and trucks all rushing their cargoes to destinations across northern California. I had a dog in the backseat and a girlfriend waiting for me in San Francisco, but I felt as if I were on a lonely highway without any destination at all.

Spot was sprawled on his side on the backseat, lulled to sleep by a heavy downpour, when I pulled up in front of Street's hotel on Post. I'd called as we'd gotten near, so she was waiting. She came out of the hotel, running through the rain. I jumped out, grabbed her bag and opened the passenger door. She climbed in and Spot finally woke up, groggy but happy to put his head over her shoulder from behind, his cheek next to her cheek, his head dwarfing hers, his pointy right ear flickering at the tickle of the wispy hairs on Street's left temple. As I pulled out into the traffic, he lay his chin down on her chest and closed his eyes and she pet him. He looked unconscious, but we could both hear his tail thumping behind us.

While Spot pretended sleep, I gave Street a more thorough replay of the events of the previous day, my mistakes, regrets, apologies to both her and Mallory.

"Don't beat yourself up," she said. "You made your best judgment."

"Best misjudgment," I said.

We were silent as we drove over to the Bay Bridge, the rain like a dirty veil pulled over the once sparkling arches. Instead of people strolling, laughing, and enjoying the world's most charming city, they scurried from vehicles to doorways, bent and furtive as small animals, as if they knew that something much worse than rain could swoop down from the sky and carry them away.

Much later, as we reached the eastern suburbs of Sacramento and began the climb up into the foothills, I handed Street the copy of Silence's second letter drawing. I explained about Marky and Tiptoe and pointed out the drawing of the funeral pyre.

Street held the drawing close to examine it and was silent a long time. Finally, she said, "I suppose it's possible that one of the men drew the fire on the calendar as a threat and she just replicated it in this letter. If so, we could doubt how much message she intends. This drawing could be just another rendition of her environment. But the fire is so well drawn that I doubt a kidnapper could do it unless he was a very good artist. So it looks like Silence put it in to illustrate a threat she heard. Either way, what a horrible thing for her to face! I can't imagine her fear."

When we got back to Tahoe, Street had me drop her at her condo. I gave her a kiss and headed on up the mountain to my cabin.

I called Doc Lee. I didn't know his Sunday schedule, so I tried the hospital first. He was not in or on-call, so I dialed his home number.

He answered, "'lo?"

"Hey, Doc, it's Owen. Hope I'm not interrupting anything important."

"Just this El Dorado County Zin. The foothill wineries won't put Napa out of business any time soon, but they're getting damn good. And with all those new studies on red wine, I take it instead of vitamins. How is your case going? What do you do, get a motorcycle and try to infiltrate the biker gang?"

"Actually, I did get a Harley."

"You even know how to ride?" Doc Lee asked.

"Had a bike for years before I moved to snow country."

"Everyone knows you're tough enough, you don't have to get a Harley to prove it."

"Not trying to prove it, trying to blend in. Maybe you

haven't noticed, but Harley has a brand lock on certain activities. If you're racing, then other bikes are king. But cruising in packs is a Harley specialty. Gotta have the approved gear to fit in with the group."

"Please tell me you're not going to get one of those donor helmets?"

"Donor helmet?" I said.

"Those little bowl jobs that sit on the top of your head. By some incredible act of legislative stupidity they satisfy the letter of the law. But they don't do shit for your brains. That's why we call them donor helmets. Bikers who wear them are the best source of organs. Something happens, they bounce their heads and their brains turn to mush. Leaving an entire body to be harvested. Which, come to think of it, may be intentional on the part of the legislature. Maybe those representatives aren't so stupid after all. There is a chronic shortage of donor organs."

"Don't worry. I have a real helmet. Even has padding on the inside. Full face guard and chin guard, too."

"Thank you," Doc Lee said, his relief audible over the phone. "Sorry, I've forgotten why you called."

"I've spoken with Dr. Power, the psychiatrist who treated the Ramirez girl a few times. But I'd like to talk to someone who is more of a specialist on autism. Power said a pediatric psychiatrist or neurologist would be good. I wonder if you know of anyone."

Doc Lee was silent for moment. "An autism expert, huh? There's a pediatric neurologist I've met, specializes in Pervasive Developmental Disorders. She's probably worked with autistic kids much more than your average shrink. The lady practices in Reno. Let me look in my little book. I think it is something Netman. If I don't have her number, you can probably reach her through the university in Reno." I heard Doc Lee flipping pages as he talked. "I recall she does some adjunct teaching at UNR. Here we are. Rhonda Netman. Got a pencil handy?"

"Yeah." I wrote as Doc Lee recited it.

"Tell you what," Doc Lee said. "It's Sunday night, so I'll

give her a call first thing in the morning. Make a little introduction and let her know you'll be in touch."

"Thanks," I said.

"By the way, how's the good sergeant coming along?" he asked, referring to my case of a couple of months earlier.

"Diamond is doing well. No more sucking sounds through bullet holes. You'd never know he'd been through anything unless he took his shirt off."

"Glad to hear it."

Before I went to bed I stepped out onto the deck. The moon coming through the pines was bright enough to read by. I looked up at it, squinting. It was large enough to clearly see the Sea of Tranquility.

I was anything but tranquil. The moon would be full in four days.

THIRTY-FOUR

The next morning when I heard the Monday morning Herald get tossed into my drive, I didn't let go of Spot's collar until I had it in my hands. Glennie's story topped the paper. The headline was huge.

LOCAL INVESTIGATOR TAKES BLAME FOR BOTCHED RAID

Well-known Private Investigator Owen McKenna spoke to this paper in an exclusive interview following Saturday's mistaken raid on a rental house in the Sierra Tract. The house that was raided was believed to be the place where kidnappers were holding SalAnne Ramirez captive.

McKenna said that all roads of blame in the forced entry lead to him. He added that every police officer involved from Commander Mallory on down operated on evidence and conclusions that McKenna had misinterpreted. McKenna said that he deeply regrets Saturday's actions, and he expects that the eventual safe recovery of SalAnne Ramirez will demonstrate that the efforts of the police were not in vain.

McKenna had been retained by Marlette Remmick, mother of Charlie and SalAnne Ramirez, the two children who were kidnapped from their front yard a week ago last Friday. Charlie, a rising star on the high school football team, was later found murdered.

When asked about the status of his investigation, McKenna said that he was making progress until a series of bad judgements and faulty evidence led to the mistaken raid on the house.

The house was occupied by Jimmy and Jeremy Carmensen, two brothers who work as chefs at Perry's Prize Pizza shop. Their sister Cheryl was visiting them at the time of the police entry. Cheryl and Jeremy were bruised in the event and Jimmy sustained a broken wrist. All three were treated at the hospital and released. Commander Mallory was unavailable for comment.

There was a smaller article, also on the front page with a smaller headline.

CARMENSEN KIDS STRONG AND BRAVE

The three Carmensen siblings who were injured in Saturday's mistaken raid on their home exhibited unusual bravery during the forced entry. Despite the sudden intrusion of many police officers into their peaceful Saturday afternoon, all three Carmensens remained remarkably calm and under control.

As could be expected in such a raid, there was some confusion and enough physical movement that all three Carmensen siblings sustained injuries. Yet none of the siblings raised a voice or a hand to the officers, and all three cooperated even though they knew that they'd done nothing wrong.

Owen McKenna, the private investigator who provided the information that led to the raid, said he'd rarely witnessed a situation where young adults acted with such maturity. He said that he is recommending that all three Carmensen siblings receive a special commendation from one of the civic organizations on the

South Shore and that he is coordinating the effort.

McKenna added that he will be contacting the Carmensens to discuss how they can further serve as role models to young people in the community.

I dialed Glennie.

"Perfect," I said when she answered.

"A little thick," she said. "But I felt inspired to read between your lines, so to speak, and help assuage their collective hurt. I figured you wouldn't mind."

"No. I will do as you say I will. If we can get them to see the raid as an honest mistake instead of an opportunity to call up a lawyer, everyone will be better off."

We talked a little more, then hung up.

I waited until 9:15 to give Doc Lee time to call the doctor he'd recommended, then I dialed Netman's office. The secretary put me through.

"Dr. Netman, thank you for taking my call," I said when she answered.

"Pleased to. Dr. Lee said you were working on the kidnapping of the autistic girl and her brother who was murdered. What a terrible thing that is for her. Do you think she's still alive?"

"Yes. We're hopeful."

"Good. How can I help?"

"Did you ever treat her?"

"No, I've only read about her since the kidnapping. I wonder if I can be of much help."

"I still have questions about autism," I said. "I'm hoping you can fill in some blanks for me. It would be best if we could talk in person."

"Certainly. My last appointment today is at one o'clock, then I head home to review paperwork. Can you come to my home in Glenbrook? Let's say, three o'clock this afternoon?"

"I'll be there."

Netman gave me directions.

THIRTY-FIVE

Diamond called and said that he'd seen the paper and would I like to have lunch. I suggested he stop by my cabin.

We grilled brats on the barbecue.

After we ate, the wind came up and we moved inside. Diamond sat in the rocker. Spot immediately walked over and lowered his chin to Diamond's lap. Diamond rubbed Spot's head. Because of Spot's height he has to slouch forward if he wants to rest his head the way a smaller dog would.

Spot slowly rocked forward on his front legs, forcing the chair and Diamond to slide back until Spot's front legs projected back at an angle. His butt stayed up high and his back angled down so that the full weight of his chest and head was on Diamond's lap.

Diamond scratched Spot's ears. "You remember when the lady set me up with the false story when I discharged my weapon a couple months ago?"

"Of course," I said. "But you didn't make a mistake. I did. And Mallory made the mistake of listening to me."

"We learn from our mistakes. Anyway, in my country somebody would have been looking for a serious bribe to clear me. But here, the shooting review board was fair. The system works well. Mallory will be okay."

"Technically. I appreciate your confidence."

Diamond nodded, then picked up the small photo of the Ramirez family off the end table. He angled it in the light and squinted his eyes.

"Back when they were happier," he said.

"Yeah. Scary how quickly life can fall apart."

"Who's the father?" he asked.

"Shane Ramirez. He lives in San Diego trying to make it as a rapper. His stage name is NSNG – No Shane No Gain."

"I mean, who's the real father. Of the girl."

I looked at Diamond. "You mean..."

He was staring at the photo. "'What is your substance, whereof are you made,'" he said.

I raised my eyebrow.

"Was looking at Shakespeare's sonnets the other day." Diamond said it the way the rest of us might say we'd read the sports section the other day. "Anyway, you're the cop went private. I'm just a simple public servant. I'd've thought you'd immediately notice the salient features. So why is it obvious to me?"

I reached for the photo. Diamond strained against Spot and handed it to me.

I held it in the bright light coming in the window. It looked the same as before. Charlie and Silence standing in front of Shane and Marlette. "I don't see it," I said. "Maybe Silence is lighter than the others. That's what you're referring to? I thought it was just a normal variation."

Diamond was shaking his head. "Call the mom and ask her. You make it clear you know, she'll capitulate."

"You mean, 'fess up."

"Yeah."

"You're confident about this." I held up the picture. "Because I don't see it."

"'Course," he said. "The girl's father is white. Could be a special radar Mexicans got. Pick up white DNA at a distance."

"I should probably ask her in person," I said. "Easier for her to stonewall over the phone."

After Diamond left, Spot and I got in the Jeep and drove to Marlette's house.

As soon as she opened the door, I held up the photo and

sounded as if the facts were clear.

"Marlette, why didn't you tell me that Shane isn't Silence's real father?"

Marlette paled and stammered, "Of course he is."

"I can't help you if you don't tell me the truth."

"I...I thought that...I mean, Shane has always been her father. Even he thinks he's her father. If he knew otherwise, he'd never have helped raise her. Not that he's been that helpful." She looked over my shoulder, staring into the past.

I said, "We have to examine every possible reason for why someone would want to kidnap her. The fact that her biological father isn't Shane is the most promising bit of information yet. And you decided it wasn't relevant."

Marlette was crying the soft tears of someone who is lost and confused. She turned in the doorway and walked inside.

We sat at her dining table. She had her elbows on the table, her face buried in her hands. Her muffled voice was hard to understand.

"I didn't know it at the time, but I was pregnant when I met Shane. When I figured it out after Silence was born, I didn't see that any good could come of telling him. We'd all thought he was her father, me included."

"Back up. Who is Silence's biological father?"

"Before I met Shane, the cleaning service I worked for sent me out on a job cleaning in the physics department of UC Berkeley. It was two days a week. I liked it better than cleaning houses. Working around scientific equipment was more interesting than working around litter boxes. Anyway, I met a graduate student named Michael Warner. We were not in love. But we eventually began an affair of sorts. It was a relationship of convenience more than anything else. Someone to go have pizza with. It sounds unusual, a physics grad student dating a cleaning girl. The thing is, Michael was very shy. He probably thought it was easier to go out on a date with a maid than with another student. He often said how remarkable it was that he could talk to me about physics."

"Not many people interested in physics," I said.

"Oh, I don't get it at all. It's a strange science. Michael would tell me things and I couldn't remember any of it even five minutes later. Except some of the names for things. The physic jocks – that's what Michael called them - they have a very unusual sense of humor. I still remember the names of quarks, not that I have a clue what quarks are. I remember that Michael said they are the building blocks of nature. Really tiny, I guess. Anyway, the different quarks are called Up, Down, Top, Bottom, Strange and Charmed. Is that strange or what?"

"I think those physicists have fun," I said.

"It was no big deal for Michael when I met Shane and left town with him. Shane and I were married in a ceremony at Emerald Bay just a month later. When it later became clear that I was pregnant, we both assumed that he was the father. I'd always used birth control when I was with Michael and in the beginning with Shane there were a couple of times when I wasn't prepared. So it just made sense. It was only after Silence was born that I began to think otherwise. Yes, she had some of Michael's skin tones, but mostly it was her personality. Even with her autism I could see something of Michael in her and I could not see any of Shane.

"I didn't tell Shane. Maybe that was wrong. But at the time it seemed best for Silence that I keep my mouth shut. And it wasn't like I had betrayed Shane in any way other than not telling him my doubts about his paternity. He knew that I was involved with Michael before I met him.

"All these years later I've wondered many times if that was a mistake. Not that it matters, but there's probably been millions of women throughout history who've been in the same position and faced the same questions, right? I have lots of company."

"Marlette," I said. "I don't judge you for any of those decisions. All I want is all pertinent information about Silence. I'll keep it to myself as much as possible."

She nodded. "What else can I tell you?"

"Tell me about Michael. Everything you can remember."

"Michael was quiet. Other people thought he was shy.

But I realized he was simply not social. I suppose he was a little off in some way. Or maybe I should say he was different. Real different. I just figured that's the way physics students are. But he was a very thoughtful man. Not attractive in any standard way. The opposite of Shane who has a big personality and is very exciting. But Michael seemed to consider the qualities of every little thing, things that the rest of us take for granted. This would be a dumb example, but the rest of us just accept that gravity pulls you toward earth, but Michael would wonder how it grabs hold of you to pull you down. Stuff like that. He has that kind of curiosity about everything."

"You met him in the physics building?"

"Yes. I first met him in one of the labs. I came in to clean. He was doing some kind of electronic measurement or something on a machine. Like something in a science fiction movie. He watched graphs on a screen. He wrote in a notebook, typed on a keyboard, made some more notes. Like I said, I wasn't terribly drawn to him, but I was struck by his quiet self-sufficiency. He was self-contained, very interested in things and processes, but not so interested in people. It was that, more than anything else, that I noticed in Silence from just after she was born. Of course, you could say that I was just equating autistic characteristics with Michael. But it was more than that.

"Michael and I saw each other a lot in that physics room. One day I was leaving and he said he was about to lock up. We walked down the hallway together, him carrying a thick briefcase, me pushing my cart. When I got to my closet I asked him if he would like to have coffee or something. I thought he'd be embarrassed to be seen with a cleaning girl. But he said yes.

"We ended up having coffee once or twice a week. He'd talk about his experiments. I'd talk about my dreams of owning a home someday." Marlette looked around the rental house.

"Did you ever stay in touch with Michael? Did he ever know your suspicions that Silence was his daughter?"

"Yes to both. After I married Shane, I sent Michael Christmas cards for a few years. Shane knew he was an old friend and he was okay with that. That's one of the great things about Shane. He is very trusting.

"One day around the time Silence had her first birthday, Michael called me and said he'd gotten a teaching job. He was going to be an Associate Professor in Physics at Sacramento State University. He said he called because he knew I'd be pleased. And I was.

"We got to talking for a long time and I ended up telling him about Silence. I said I thought he might be her biological father."

"How did he react?"

"In a classic Michael kind of way. He was quiet and thoughtful. He said that the news was quite a surprise. He wanted to know what Silence was like. I told him about her personality, that she reminded me of him. I also told him about her autism. He expressed concern. He said he realized that he was out of the picture, but that if he could help in any way, financial or emotional, he would do so. He didn't want to intrude, but he didn't want to be distant, either. He said that he respected that Shane was Silence's father in every important way. But he also thought that being Silence's biological father gave him certain responsibilities." There was a wistful look in Marlette's eyes as she said it.

"Do you wish you had married him instead of Shane?"

"I don't think so. Michael is very kind. I think he is the essence of a good man. But he doesn't make your heart beat like Shane does. Yet, here I am, divorced from Shane, alone in most ways."

Marlette paused. "You know that Shane is back in Tahoe, right? Oh, of course, I saw you talking to him at the funeral. I don't know where he's staying. Somewhere nearby, I think. Of course, he's thrashing over what's happened. Even though Shane hasn't been real involved with the children in the last few years, it was still very difficult for him when I called and told him the news. I don't think he really likes Silence in a meaningful way, but he's like anyone when it comes to having a daughter kidnapped. You just want to explode. You want to find the man who did it and rip his heart out!" Marlette was suddenly breathing hard.

I waited while she calmed.

"Sorry," she said. "Hearing that Charlie was killed was so difficult for him. I think Shane is suddenly wondering what life is about that this kind of thing can happen to his own kids. But Shane goes to friends to sort things out, not to me."

"When was the last time you had contact with Michael?"

Marlette swallowed. "As soon as you ask that, I realize I made a big mistake not telling you about Michael from the beginning. I called him just two months ago. But ever since I've been afraid of the world finding out. I thought it would be best for all if Shane and everyone else still thought that Shane was the father. I knew that Silence couldn't tell, and I was certain that Michael wouldn't tell. So I haven't told anyone except Silence."

"Why did you call Michael?"

"Silence had been having problems with Shane whenever he came to visit. It started a year ago, and got worse and worse. She was stubborn and difficult around him. She wouldn't do anything he wanted. He ended up yelling at her. That is the worst thing you can do to Silence. Her ears are so sensitive. If you yell at her she falls apart and won't come out of her room for days. She won't eat or even drink. The few times it's happened I worried she was going to starve to death.

"Anyway, Silenced started complaining about Shane. I suppose I'm to blame. A divorce is always hardest on the kids. But I thought it would just be Charlie who'd get upset. I didn't see it coming with Silence."

"How does she complain?"

"She makes her sounds. Sounds and certain movements. At first, I thought it was probably just normal teenager stuff. But it kept getting worse and she'd get very upset whenever she knew he was coming to visit."

"How often does Shane come by?"

"About once every couple months. He stops by our house, then goes off to stay with friends. So with Silence getting very difficult around Shane, I began to wonder if she should know about her biological father. I knew it would be like opening a can of worms. But as soon as I had the thought, I started to think it might help. I knew Michael would be nice to her and maybe give her a better focus on life. Or at least, a different perspective.

"I went round and round thinking about whether it would be a good thing. After another couple of visits from Shane, I could see that Silence and Shane were ready to explode. I kept worrying that Silence would run away again. Her behavior was so impossible I thought I'd lose her completely. She was out of control. The last time Shane visited, Silence made a terrible drawing of him looking like a devil. She threw it at him. Shane was real mad. He said he didn't know when he'd be back or even if he'd be back. I was about to crack. Charlie needed his father's attention even if it was only a little here and there.

"I decided to introduce Silence to Michael. Things couldn't get any worse. I thought that any possibility of improvement was worth taking a chance.

"I called Michael. He's still teaching at Sac State. I explained that I was losing control of Silence and that I wondered if he could meet her. I told him I didn't want to bring stress into his life, but that I didn't know what else to do."

"He agreed to see her?" I said.

"Yeah. He was real nice and said he'd do whatever he could to help."

"You told Silence about him?"

"I didn't know if I could do it right. In a lot of ways I'm not a good mother to her. But it went pretty well. I took her out to lunch. When I could see that she was in a good mood, I told her the story from beginning to end. The truth, with nothing held back. Of course, I never know what gets through. When she doesn't look at you and doesn't seem to pay any attention, you always wonder." Marlette gave me a look that seemed to be embarrassment. "In some ways, it's like a truth serum, the way Silence is. You end up saying much more than you planned just because she seems to not be paying attention. My inner-most thoughts end up in words." Marlette made a nervous laugh. "I should watch myself. Charlie always said that Silence hears and understands every little thing. I don't know if that's true, but I suppose it could be."

"Did you give her a reason for why you had decided to tell her the story?"

Marlette nodded. "I explained that the first reason I wanted her to meet Michael after all these years was that I thought it might help her with Shane. I also said that the more I'd thought about it, the more it occurred to me that she might like her biological father."

"How did she take it?"

"She took it very well. For Silence, that is. She stayed calm. Kind of intrigued. Although saying that Silence is ever intrigued is a stretch. But in her way she seemed interested. I think the main thing she wondered was if he was nice."

"How did she ask that? Is that something she does with sounds?"

"She makes a high-pitched grunting sound and she has certain gestures. I'm not sure how to explain it. Whenever she's worried about being around someone, she rubs her left arm. It's her way of showing her anxiety. When I told her that her biological father was very nice she didn't rub at all. If you watched you might not notice much. Like I said when I first talked to you, Silence's utterances mostly sound like gibberish to anyone except Charlie. I get the gist of most of what she does. But Charlie – it's amazing – you'd think she talks to him in words."

Marlette's eyes welled with tears. "I'm talking about him like he's still alive." She wiped her eyes with the back of her hand. Reached for a tissue and blew her nose.

"Sorry," she said. "Anyway, between Silence's movements and sounds, I usually get the meaning. I knew I could call Henrietta for help, but I wanted to keep the news about Michael as private as possible, out of respect for Silence and Shane. And Michael, too, for that matter."

"You told her he was kind," I reminded her.

"Yes. She seemed reassured to hear that. But she was most

interested when I said he was a physics professor."

"Why do you think that was?"

"I had no idea. I don't think she knows anything about physics. But she does have a general interest in science. She'd rather collect rocks or leaves than watch TV. So I thought she was just intrigued that Michael taught science. Or it could be that the word professor made her interested. But I don't know if she even knows what a professor is. The only times you can really tell if Silence knows something are when you see her do something concrete. Like loading the dishwasher. Then you know she understands what a dishwasher is. But with other concepts – I don't know what it's called – abstract ideas, maybe? Anyway, you can't tell if she gets it."

"Did they meet?"

"Yes. A month ago. We drove down on a Sunday afternoon. Michael wanted to show her his lab, and he said Sunday was when it would be least busy. I found where he said to park, and he was standing there waiting. I introduced the two of them and we talked for about ten minutes. Actually, Michael and I talked and Silence just watched. But she wasn't as withdrawn as normal. Of course, I'd spoken with Michael at length before we drove down, so he knew something of how Silence acts. He shook her hand and said it was a pleasure to learn that he had a daughter and that he was pleased to meet her. Then he said that he didn't have any other kids, so he didn't really know what to talk about with a seventeen-year-old girl. But he said he'd like to show her his lab if she was interested."

"And she was."

"Yes, it was wonderful to see. It was like she became lit from within. She kind of glowed. So I said I had a book to read and I'd wait in the car and they should take as much time as they wanted."

Marlette smiled at the thought. "I tried to read, but I could only wonder what they would be talking about. I mean, what Michael would be saying to her. Then they came back out and Silence seemed more comfortable with him than most any adult.

She actually walked next to him. Except for looking down to the side, she almost looked like a normal kid."

"I'll need Michael's phone number."

Worry flashed across Marlette's face. "Yes, I suppose you do. Although I can't imagine what he can tell you that will help. Should I call him to let him know you'll be calling?"

"No. Don't call. I want to get a fresh perspective, not one that has been carefully prepared."

"Of course," she said. "I'll get the number."

THIRTY-SIX

I had just enough time to get up to Glenbrook for my appointment with the pediatric neurologist. I wanted to ride the Harley, so I dropped Spot at home. I fired up the bike in the loud mode, made the short ride up Highway 50 and turned into the Glenbrook. The guard at the gate leaned out the window of the guardhouse, staring at my motorcycle, her displeasure obvious.

"Good afternoon," I said, smiling. "Owen McKenna here to see Dr. Rhonda Netman. She's expecting me."

The guard came out and walked around behind me to write down my license plate. She waved me through.

Although Dr. Netman's house was modest by Glenbrook standards, it was immaculate and well-designed with maple floors, four-foot-wide doorways and a view of the lake from most of the rooms.

A housekeeper took me through the living room, past an antique harpsichord that stood in front of floor-to-ceiling windows. We went into a large wood-paneled study where a woman sat behind a desk.

"Hello. I'm Rhonda Netman," the doctor said, standing up and coming around from behind her desk. She reached out to shake my hand.

"Owen McKenna. Thank you for seeing me on such short notice."

"Certainly. May I pour you a cup of coffee?" She walked over to a sideboard with a coffee maker and cups and a little tray of pastries.

"Please," I said. "Black is fine."

The doctor poured two cups, set them on the pastry tray and brought them over. She set the tray on a small table and we sat down on Queen Anne chairs upholstered in a fabric that looked like it was from an art tapestry.

Dr. Netman was a large woman in her late sixties who could barely fit between the chair arms, yet she moved softly. She dressed like a professional woman from decades earlier. There were ripples in her nylons where her plump feet pushed into thin brown pumps. Her brown wool skirt rose up almost to her knees when she sat, thick knees held primly together. She wore a matching wool blazer over a high-necked white blouse. Her gray hair was pulled back into a perfect bun, held in place with a golden hair clip. She was a lesson in how style and attitude trump physique. Her size not withstanding, she radiated grace and femininity, warmth and comfort.

"You are investigating the kidnapping?" she asked.

"Yes. The girl's mother, Marlette Remmick, hired me. There are few clues. It's been a frustrating case."

"I read the childrens' names in the paper, but I forget."

"SalAnne and Charlie Ramirez. They have their father's last name. The mother went back to her maiden name after their divorce. Everyone who knows the girl calls her Silence."

Dr. Netman raised her eyebrows.

"She is non-verbal," I explained.

"Quite common with autism."

"So I understand," I said. "Which is why I want to talk to you. I've never met Silence. I've spoken to her teacher and a psychiatrist who treated her and a friend of hers. Her mother gave me a disk with video clips of the girl and her brother over the years. The picture that emerges is confusing at best." I sipped my coffee, which was rich and strong.

"Tell me, do you or the police have any idea why the children were kidnapped?"

"Nothing concrete. My approach is perhaps a bit unorthodox, shaped by the knowledge that random kidnappings are

difficult at best to solve. Of course, Silence may in fact be a random victim, picked for sexual slavery or something worse. In spite
of that possibility, I'm proceeding with the presumption that she
was instead specifically targeted, not randomly targeted. I take this
approach because that is the only scenario where – if it is true –
I'm likely to have a small chance of finding her."

"If you're hungry," Dr. Netman said, "you climb the type
of tree that you think is most likely to bear fruit."

I nodded.

Netman's hands were resting on the chair arms. She
raised an index finger an inch. "How do you think her autism figures into this?"

"I don't know. But because her autism is such a prominent facet of her personality, the better I understand autism, the
better I will understand how she will respond to her current situation, how she will react if we can make a rescue attempt. It may
even suggest why she was targeted in the first place."

Netman nodded slowly. "Let me give you an overview of
autism. Although you must keep in mind that having never
treated the girl, I won't be of much help."

"I understand, Doctor."

"Please call me Rhonda." She took a dainty bite off a croissant and sipped some coffee. "Let me begin by saying that a portion of what we think we know about autism will eventually be
proven wrong. And we don't know how big that portion is."

"As it has been throughout all of medical history, right?"

The doctor smiled. "Yes. All areas of science have their
components that are later shown to be false. Having said that, I
think all the scientists who study autism – and I'm one of them –
agree that autism is a word we use for a wide range of disorders
that revolve around a person's ability, or rather, inability to communicate with other people. One person with autism can be quite
retarded and another can be quite brilliant. One can be verbal
albeit with certain abnormalities, another completely non-verbal.
One can have normal physical movements while another can
exhibit awkward and repetitive movements.

"Because of this range of characteristics, the DSM refers to autism as Autistic Spectrum Disorders."

"Excuse me. DSM?"

"I'm sorry. The Bible of the American Psychiatric Association is the DSM. It stands for Diagnostic and Statistical Manual of Mental Disorders. It is where these disorders are defined."

"Do we know what causes autism?" I asked her.

"We have some ideas. But nothing definitive. There are several genes that may have something to do with autism. At this time we don't know how genetics are involved, but a genetic predisposition seems a factor. For example, if a child has ASD, the..."

"Excuse me?"

"Forgive me, there I go again. Autism Spectrum Disorder. Every child with autistic characteristics seems to have a different manifestation of autism. There are countless variations, so we refer to the problem as a spectrum of disorders."

"Ah. You were talking about genetics."

"Yes. If one child has ASD, the chances of their siblings having ASD is increased because of similar genetic makeup. If the child with ASD has an identical twin, the chances that the twin also will have ASD is huge, ranging up to ninety percent."

"If the genes predispose a kid to ASD, what is the trigger?"

"I dearly wish we knew. But it appears that there may be many triggers. There's been some speculation that environmental factors may contribute. Certain industrial chemicals and such that have increasingly found their way into the environment. If that is the case, it might explain the dramatic increase in recent autism diagnosis across the country and throughout Europe. On the other hand, the increase may just be attributable to more accurate diagnosis. It could also be that autism is like cancer in that it can be caused in several different ways. Bacterial pathogens, irritants, even viruses. Brain studies have found physical and functional differences in the brains of children with autism. So it could be that something about early brain development is the trigger."

I said, "Differences a person can see, or differences in how the brain operates?"

"Both. Certain parts of the brain appear less developed in people with autism, whereas the overall brain is larger than normal and there is an excess of white matter. There are also differences in brain function. For example, when we do brain scans we can see which areas of the brain are involved in certain activities. If we scan the brains of normal children and show them pictures of people they know, a certain part of their brain lights up, so to speak. But if you do the same observation with autistic kids, that part of their brain often remains inactive."

"Facial recognition is absent in autistic children?"

"Impaired, anyway. But it's important to remember that while we often see children – and adults - who exhibit so-called classic autistic characteristics, we also commonly see unique combinations of behavior and cognition disorders. There is no single pattern. But regardless of whether these characteristics are common or uncommon, the bottom line is that if a person has characteristics that interfere with communication, we often categorize them as having Autistic Spectrum Disorder."

"You are being very careful with the nomenclature."

"Because there is so much room for confusion. And because one person we say is autistic can be so very different from another person we say is autistic."

"May I describe what I've learned about Silence Ramirez, and perhaps you could give me your thoughts?"

"Please do." Rhonda Netman took another bite of croissant, then waited expectantly.

"When Silence was born, her mother Marlette noticed unusual behavior from the beginning. As a baby Silence wouldn't turn to look at sounds, wouldn't focus on her mother's face, and didn't move her hands and arms like other babies. As she grew, she didn't learn to speak or read. Or at least, if she did learn to read, she didn't reveal the ability."

"She looked at books?"

"She paged through them as a child and still does now. Marlette says it looks like she might be reading, but there is no way to verify it. It could be she just likes looking at the printed words. Marlette says that Silence always noticed symbols. And words and letters are merely symbols, correct?"

"Yes. Abstract symbols that we arrange in meaningful order."

I continued. "Silence never looked anyone in the eye, didn't try to communicate with anyone, didn't play with toys. She likes to be squeezed. She actually climbs under her mattress to let the weight of it push down on her. Apparently, it gives her comfort and calms her when she's agitated. And she is a spinner. According to Marlette, she spins more the older she gets."

"Does she do things in a ritualistic way?"

"Things like brushing her teeth, yes. The videos her mother took over the years periodically captured Silence doing some basic things like brushing her teeth or spinning or how she gets into a car. She does things exactly the same this year as ten years earlier. If her routines are interrupted, she gets very upset."

"What kind of medical intervention did she get?"

"The Special Ed teachers at the school have been good at getting her regular psychiatric evaluations, and they've been focused on designing appropriate lesson plans. But outside of the school, she's gotten almost no specialized treatment."

Rhonda Netman closed her eyes and took a deep breath.

I continued. "The family was poor and was not adept at using social services. Through the school, Silence has seen a psychiatrist every year for some time, a Dr. Raymond Power."

"I know Raymond," Rhonda said. "A good man."

"He thinks the girl is quite retarded and from the first time he saw her he didn't think much could be done. The most significant help came from a Special Ed teacher who has worked as Silence's advocate for many years."

"This sounds like many cases I've been acquainted with over the years. Does the child have any special abilities?"

"Yes. She is a fairly amazing artist," I said. "Although she may just be a great draftsman. Either way, she can draw anything, quickly, and with photo-realism. Her perspective is perfect, and her attention to detail is astonishing."

"Tell me, Owen, what do you mean when you refer to the difference between an artist and a draftsman?"

"I'm not sure. I suppose an artist puts something more into a drawing than just depicting what they see in an accurate way. Art interprets life, rather than just rendering a scene from life. I don't know if that distinction is germane, but it occurred to me that artistic expression or lack thereof may be important in understanding how a person's brain works."

"I think it is relevant," Rhonda said. "It could be that Silence is a savant."

"You mean, like the Dustin Hoffman character in the movie Rain Man."

"Yes," Rhonda said. "A person with a special talent unaccompanied by normal related behaviors. The Hoffman character could see patterns and instantly quantify aspects of those patterns. Like how many coins are scattered across the floor. A musical savant may be able to listen to a piano piece just once, then sit down and play it perfectly and even transpose it into other keys. But they might not be able to compose such a piece themselves or rearrange the movements in a logical fashion. A savant may be able to recite a speech from Hamlet, but have no understanding of the speech's meaning. Think of it as performance without understanding." The doctor paused, as if waiting to see if I understood.

"Let me tell you about Silence's Special Ed teacher," I said. "Henrietta Johanssen works for the school district and first encountered Silence when the girl got to junior high school. Henrietta had read through Silence's file. She'd worked with a few other autistic children over the years, and after reading Silence's file, expected more of the same. But from the first time she met Silence, she thought the girl had been misdiagnosed."

"She thinks the girl is high-functioning?" Rhonda said.

"Yes. Those were exactly her words. She believes that Silence is not only high-functioning, but actually brilliant."

"But you said the girl is non-verbal."

I nodded. "She's never said a word in her life. She apparently makes sounds, little grunts and squeaks. And she hums. She also points and gestures."

"There are cases of autistic people who don't speak, yet who write very well. Does Silence write anything?"

"According to her mother, no."

"Not even her name?"

"Not that I've heard of."

"These drawings you mentioned. What do you think? Do they seem to you a kind of communication? Or are they just renditions of the things around her?"

I thought about it. "Mostly renditions, I think. Here, have a look." I was holding a folder of drawings that Marlette had given me. I kept the two recent letter drawings and handed the rest to the doctor.

Netman opened the folder and picked up the first drawing, a picture of the kitchen in the house where Marlette and her kids live. The doctor studied it for awhile, then slipped it under the pile and looked at the next drawing in the stack. This one depicted Silence's backpack leaning against her bedroom doorway. The third drawing was a birthday cake that had several slices cut out of it. The fourth drawing was of her high school classroom.

The doctor flipped through the rest of the drawings. "These are very good, indeed. But it appears they are of the things and places that are important to her. It doesn't seem that these drawings are much in the way of communication."

"You mean, a substitute for speech," I said.

"Correct."

"Her mother says that Silence draws her Valentine cards. Is that a kind of communication?"

"Yes. As are all of these drawings in some way. But I wouldn't want anyone, especially the girl's mother, to read too much into it."

I finished my coffee and got up to return my cup to the sideboard as well as to stretch my legs. I came back to Rhonda, reached for the folder and pulled three of the drawings out of the stack. "Have a look at these," I said. "Silence's teacher Henrietta is particularly taken with the way Silence notices Fibonacci numbers in nature."

Dr. Netman smiled. "I'm sorry, I don't know that term."

"Henrietta didn't either, at first. But she looked it up after Silence pointed it out." I spread out the drawings and pointed to a tree in one, a flower in another, a pinecone in a third. "It is a number sequence, common in nature, first identified by a Thirteenth-Century Italian mathematician."

"That would be Fibonacci?" Netman said.

"Leonardo, yes." I nodded and explained how the numbers work. "What do you think of the girl's observation of the sequence?"

"Well, of course it is fascinating. I'd love to meet Silence and explore this area."

"But you don't think it is indicative of high-function?"

Netman gave me a polite smile and then frowned. "Hard to say. The drawings and the Fibonacci observation are impressive, of course. But I'm not convinced it means much. There is a regular occurrence of such abilities in autistic people. Not a frequent occurrence by any measure, but regular. The usual question is whether the person has a gift for arithmetic or a gift for math, the latter being indicative of a larger understanding." Rhonda thought a moment and then said, "Perhaps the more important question is how any of this may factor into her kidnapping. What difference does it make if she is high-functioning?"

"That's why I came to you," I said. "I may be completely misguided, but I'm hoping that something about her is connected to why she was kidnapped. If she is smarter than it appears, then perhaps that is a factor in why the kidnapper targeted her."

The doctor's eyes widened. "You think Silence heard or saw something that led to her kidnapping?" Rhonda said.

"Like?" I prompted, curious about where a doctor would go with the reasoning.

"All I come up with are clichés," Rhonda said. "Again, a metaphor applies. The location of something very valuable."

THIRTY-SEVEN

Rhonda Netman continued, "You're wondering if the girl has the intelligence of verbal people, but is simply missing the communication link that allows the rest of us to use words. A kidnapper could be thinking the same thing, that Silence has a different communication ability, and that she could possibly use her drawings to reveal whatever valuable knowledge she has. But I'm out of line speculating on such a thing. And as I said, I think it unlikely. A high-functioning child with no verbal ability whatsoever would be very rare."

"But is it possible?"

Rhonda took another deep breath. I could tell that she was concerned that I was pursuing a dream instead of reality. "I think it would be possible under only a couple of conditions."

I waited.

She continued, "Let me explain about the brain hemispheres. In most people, the left side of the brain controls the verbal center. If a stroke or a blow to the head in a car accident or some other damage to the left side of the brain eliminates the verbal center, the person is left without any speech. This is true even if the right side of their brain continues to function very well. One of the ways we know this is from studies of epilepsy. In some cases, doctors have cut the connections between the hemispheres of the brain in order to stop life-threatening seizures. While the operations are often successful, the side effect is that the right side of the brain can no longer communicate with the left side."

"What does that do?"

"It does something quite extraordinary. A simple experiment will show that the right brain is active but unable to communicate. You may recall that the nerves from the body cross to the opposite side of the brain. The right brain controls the left half of the body, and the left brain controls the right side of the body.

"I should add that above the neck it is a little different. Each eye is connected to both sides of the brain so that each hemisphere of the brain controls half the vision in both of the eyes rather than all the vision from one eye.

"Here's where it gets interesting. Imagine a person who has had the connections between the two halves of their brains severed. You show them a picture and place it to the side of their visual field so that it is only perceived by the left brain. Let's say it is a picture of peanuts. You ask them what they see and of course they answer, 'I see a picture of peanuts.' They can answer because the left brain sees the picture and the left brain controls speech.

"Next, you take a picture of a train and place it to the other side of their visual field so that it is only perceived by the right side of their brain. You ask them what they see and this time they say they see nothing because again the left brain controls speech and the left brain can't see the train. Only the right brain can see the train and it can't tell the left brain because those connecting nerves were severed."

"Yet, you know that they saw the picture," I said.

"Right. But the knowledge of what they saw is trapped in the right side of their brain. So you get an idea. On a blackboard you write down several words: peanuts, house, dog, ocean and train. You ask them again what they see and tell them to use their left hand to point to the appropriate word. Their left hand rises and points to the word train. Why? Because the left side of the body is controlled by the right brain, the side of the brain that saw the image of the train. The right brain can't tell you what it saw, but it can use the left hand to point to what it saw."

"Just to make sure I understand," I said, "in normal people this isn't a problem because the right brain can tell the left brain it saw a train and then the left brain's verbal center can say so."

"Exactly," Rhonda said. "What all this means is that in the event that the right brain cannot talk to the left brain, the right brain is completely isolated. The right side of your brain can be very smart, but it can't communicate. Your right brain cannot talk and cannot even write or do sign language because that is all controlled by the verbal center in the left brain."

I said, "But Silence hasn't had an operation to sever the connections between the two sides of the brain."

"No, she hasn't. But if Silence is in fact high-functioning – meaning that somewhere in there is a bright, engaged girl, curious and self-aware – then only one or two explanations would explain her complete lack of speech. One would be that she has no functioning verbal center in her left brain. The other would be that while the right side of her brain may have high capacity, it cannot communicate with the left side. Tell me, is she left-handed?"

"Yes."

"I thought so. That would fit because the left hand is controlled by the right brain. It would also fit with her drawing ability because the right brain is the creative center. When artists draw or paint, it is the right brain that is most active."

She continued, "I should add that there have been a few autistic people who appear completely non-verbal – they never speak a word – yet they are able to write and express themselves very well. Some of them test out with genius IQs. Some of those people have told, or I should say, have written of being verbal as young children and they found that the act of talking was too intense, too painful. Similar to the way some autistic kids can't take anything louder than soft sounds, anything brighter than soft light. Every input must be attenuated and reduced to a low level or they undergo stress beyond what the rest of us can imagine. Normal sights and sounds and smells make them panic, make them withdraw. For these few bright kids who once had speech and went mute, we imagine their systems are simply too sensitive for normal human communication. It is as if they discovered they were allergic to human interaction. So they communicate in other ways, mostly by writing. But it is very rare."

I said, "Because Silence doesn't write and has never spoken, she isn't like that."

"Correct. But she may have the super-sensitivity to inputs. Like kids who are more or less allergic to speech, Silence is probably allergic to much of human interaction in addition to enduring the burden of not having a functional verbal center."

I said, "If some autistic kids are allergic to normal human interaction, how do they respond to the allergy? Do they get a rash? Do they have trouble breathing?"

"Actually, there are cases of rashes and difficulty breathing. But the most common reaction is they shut down, turn away, and, quite often, they engage in repetitive physical activity."

"Like," I said.

"Like pounding on the floor. Or moaning over and over. Or rocking. Or banging their head against the wall."

"Or spinning?"

"Yes. Spinning is quite common."

I thought about it. "The central question I have in asking you about all of this is if her drawings are a kind of substitute for words."

"It may be possible."

I pulled the letter drawings out of my pocket and handed them to her. "We think these drawings show the place where she is being held. They were slipped under the door of the high school. We don't know how they got there. We think that Silence folded them as airplanes and flew them out her window. Someone found them and anonymously delivered them to the high school. Notice how they are addressed, with drawings in place of words. The first drawing shows a room by itself. The second one shows two men we believe to be her captors. The second drawing also has a tiny picture of a funeral pyre on the calendar. It shows a girl being burned at the stake during the full moon. It would seem an outrageous idea but for the fact that there is a motorcycle gang in the basin with a reputation for making religious sacrifices and burning the body at the rise of the full moon. What do you make of it?"

Rhonda turned them over several times. "It is fascinating," she said with the detachment of a scientist. "If your assessment is correct, then of course this is much more in the realm of a direct communication. But I must say I find it very far-fetched."

"Far-fetched that she could put it in a drawing? Or far-fetched that she could have something a kidnapper wanted so badly that he would threaten her with death?"

"Both."

I said, "Another factor is the death of Silence's brother Charlie. Apparently, he was very good at understanding her desires. In many ways, he served as her communication link. Now that she has found herself in this situation where she has a powerful motivation to communicate to the outside world, yet she no longer has Charlie to do it for her, isn't this kind of letter drawing something she might conjure up in an effort at communication?"

Rhonda held my eyes. "Yes, I should think so."

"Let me ask another question that may seem ridiculous. Considering what I've told you about Silence, is there anything about her or her situation that gives you an idea of how I might best proceed?"

"Do you mean, how to catch the kidnapper?"

I nodded.

"I'm sorry, Owen. I'm a neurologist. What you're suggesting is so far from my area of expertise that it's nearly ludicrous to ask me."

"Try," I said. I walked over to the windows that looked out at the lake. I stayed there for a minute, studying the boulders on the shore, giving the doctor a chance to think.

"Well," Rhonda eventually said, "all you have to go on is the supposition that the kidnapper wants something that Silence has. What does Silence have or know? Figure that out and perhaps it would lead you to the kidnapper."

THIRTY-EIGHT

I was disappointed as I rode away from Dr. Netman's. She'd told me much about autism, but I still had no good idea about how to proceed. I focused on thinking about what Silence could know that would attract a kidnapper.

My most promising lead was Marlette's revelation about Silence's biological father. If he had told her or shown her something valuable, that would give me a direction to search.

Marlette had given me his work number, but it was past six. I knew there would be very little chance to catch him that evening, so I decided to do a little cruising for biker gangs.

When I climbed back up the Glenbrook road to the highway, I turned left at the guardhouse and headed up Spooner Summit. I took the left where Highway 28 turns off and headed up through the twilight toward Sand Harbor. I had no idea where the Granite Mountain Boys would be on a cold Tuesday evening, but Sand Harbor was where I last saw any of them. I opened the bike up here and there on empty sections of the dark twisting road, the rush of cold air draining heat from my bare fingers. I left the muffler valve in the loud position, and the bike ran well, the engine never skipping.

As expected, Sand Harbor turned out to be empty, the parking lot vacant except for a Nevada Division of Parks pickup sitting empty in one corner.

I continued on toward Incline Village and saw my first group of bikers turning up the Mt. Rose Highway. I turned after them and roared up toward the rear of the group as they charged up the steep road toward the pass. There were eight of them, dressed in the bad-boy uniform, but as I watched their various headlights flickering in the dark, I realized that the two riders in front had on full helmets.

I knew that no Granite Mountain Boy would be caught dead in an emasculating full helmet, so I slowed, turned around and coasted back down to town. I turned right on 28 and continued counter-clockwise around the lake.

Another group of bikers came toward me near Kings Beach. I studied them as they went by, six groups of two, all in donor helmets. I spun around and came up behind them. One of the rear riders turned, watching me as I drew near. We all cruised the curves around the lake, a long noisy parade through the quiet North Shore neighborhoods. On the curves my headlight periodically washed over the four closet bikers in front of me. They too had the bad-boy uniform. All but one, anyway. He had the big leather jacket, but his pants didn't fit. Instead of the standard leather or jeans, his pants were some kind of light gray, probably corduroy, definitely indicating his bad-boy quotient was wannabe status instead of the real thing.

Again, I turned around and continued to Tahoe City. I came across several other biker groups, but each time decided that they were unlikely to have any affiliation with the Granite Mountain Boys.

It was now very dark and cold, so I turned and rode home.

The next morning I called Silence's biological father Michael Warner and reached his voicemail. I left my name and number and a vague message saying that I'd been referred to him by Marlette Remmick.

After a quick breakfast-for-two, Spot and I drove to Marlette's house. I left Spot in the Jeep and talked to Marlette at her kitchen table.

She seemed in a sour mood as I asked for the physical addresses of both Michael Warner and her ex-husband Shane. I thought it might help her to hear of my conversation with Dr. Netman, so I summarized what I'd learned from the pediatric neurologist.

Marlette became upset as I recounted the doctor's thoughts, mostly, I think, because she thought that I was spending too much time analyzing Silence's predicament and not enough time shaking down bikers and gang members.

"Let's go for a walk," I said. "Get some fresh air."

She hesitated, then stood up without saying anything. As she straightened her legs, she used the back of her knees to aggressively push her chair back from the table. The legs caught, and the chair tipped over backward. The crash on the linoleum was loud. Marlette leaned forward as if to fall, caught herself by placing her outstretched hands on the table. She hung her head, shut her eyes and was motionless.

I stepped over and picked up the chair.

In a moment, she walked to the door, pulled a sweater and scarf off a hook and went outside.

I followed her out and said, "Do you want me to lock the door?"

"No," she mumbled as she walked to the street. "You don't need to lock your doors around here." I pulled the door closed behind me.

Suddenly she stopped and turned around. "Jesus, what am I saying?"

I turned around, opened the door, twisted the lock button and shut it again. I joined her where her gravel drive met the asphalt. We turned right and walked the neighborhood.

"Let me ask you something," I said. "What if the kidnapper isn't Antonio Gomez."

"You mean the Aztec biker guy."

"Right. What if it is somebody else, somebody who has nothing to do with the bikers. Somebody Silence knows."

Marlette stopped walking and turned to face me. "There is no way somebody who knew Silence would kidnap her." There was palpable tension in her voice as if her frustrations with my lack of progress were about to erupt in a full boil.

"Why couldn't her kidnapper be someone who knew her?"

"It's obvious. She's sweet and kind. Well, maybe kind isn't the right word. But she's inoffensive, and she never did anything bad to anybody. And there's no money to ransom. Not even from distant relatives. You said yourself that the fact that there isn't a ransom note shows that the kidnapping isn't that kind. The only explanation is something really sicko." Marlette's eyes flooded. She quickly turned away and resumed walking, faster than before.

I caught up with her. "I want to consider all the possibilities. I'd like you to think about all the people who know Silence."

"But it couldn't be someone she knows because there aren't that many people who know her. Except for the kids at school, I probably know all of them myself. I've met all of her teachers, her doctors, the few people from church who talk to her. Everybody. None of them would do such a sick thing."

"Maybe not. But if you talk to a psychologist about what seemingly ordinary people are capable of, it is surprising. We need to be open-minded."

"No. You're talking psycho-babble. We're talking about people I've known for years. Some of them are my best friends. Common sense is how this will be solved. Silence was kidnapped by those bikers. I heard the motorcycles! I saw her spinning. She obviously saw them coming toward her and she reacted by withdrawing into her spin. And the Aztec word was on Charlie! What more do you want! You can't afford to waste time going in stupid directions. You're also wasting my time and my money. And every moment wasted brings Silence one step closer to ending up like Charlie!"

"Marlette, you may be right. But I've talked to you enough to know that you want to see the world in good terms. You want to see the good in people. But we need to consider everybody, even the people you think would never do such a thing."

"What's this, the cynic speech?" Her voice had a sneer in it. "You sound like the cop I heard on TV the other day after they caught the Basement Killer in St. Louis." She lowered her voice to mimic him. "'Even his mother didn't have a clue and she lived in the same house.' Well, I do have a clue. This terrible thing was done by those bikers. They're probably torturing her as we speak and you're doing nothing about it except giving me lectures on the evil in ordinary God-fearing people. You try to sound like the cops on TV, but you're just a PI trying to make a buck off other people's misery! If you were a real cop, you would have made progress by now!"

She said it with such force and disgust I thought she would sprint away. But she didn't. She walked faster, her entire body tense and stiff. She swung her arms like a wooden soldier. I stayed with her. "I was a cop. Homicide. In San Francisco."

"Sure!" she said. "Next thing you'll tell me you were in gun battles like Dirty Harry, and you killed people and you saw the underbelly of the scum in the swamp." She walked faster. "You don't even carry a gun. Don't try to protest. I've noticed. All ex-cops carry a gun. Even if you were a cop, you were probably fired. How did Commander Mallory have the audacity to put me onto a two-bit, pretend detective like you!"

I stopped and took a deep breath. When we're suddenly attacked in a personal way, the impulse to lash out is in our genes. You see it from corporate boardrooms to kiddie playgrounds. I was no better. I grabbed her shoulder and forced her to stop.

"So this is where I trot out the history? Roll back the sleeves and parade the scars? When I bring out the citations and hospital files, you should pay special attention to the diagnoses of the shrinks who all agreed that the mental trauma caused by a single dead child was out of proportion to the incident. Who all agreed that the symptoms were more like those of a soldier in combat than those of a decorated cop responding to a bank holdup with an armed kiddie robber. Clearly, the cop had questionable mental stability in the first place. And when the cop voluntarily became an ex-cop and decided to give up guns for good, it only proved their suspicions that he was not all there. He was a wimp, no better than a meter maid, a self-emasculated prima donna."

Marlette was making motions with her mouth, but no words came out. She stared up at me as if I were an alien, a man talking about himself in the third person, voluntarily revealing the warts and pimples and ulcerated wounds of the psyche.

I was angry now, spit on my lips, too late to stop myself before I got in deep. "And you should add to the pile of character indictments the missing persons report from the unannounced solo trek into the rain forest wilderness of British Columbia where the weary excuse for a man exorcised the demons by hiking twenty miles a day. Where he starved the nightmares by fasting for two weeks. And at the very bottom, when he crawled out of his tent in the middle of the night and walked to the edge of the bluff to look at the moon setting over the Hecate Strait, he startled a prowling mama Grizzly with a single cub. Mama charged, all 700 or 800 pounds of her snarling and roaring, and he sat down on the rock, shivering and sweating at the same time, watching the moon and waiting for her to grab him from behind. He dared that ursine monster to find some stringy flesh from the starved, wasted 180-pound carcass on the six-six frame. Chew away, if you please, and when you're done throw the remains into the ocean.

"But mama Grizz turned away, and he thought maybe, just maybe, he could try life one more time. So, awash in adrenaline and hallucinating from starvation, he went and climbed up the creaky ladder into the mental attic, dimly lit by that moon over the waters just south of Alaska, dusted off the old mainframe, and started sorting the old disks. Memory triage. Those to burn, those to consider revisiting and those to save.

"Life reduced to three departments, one of which to destroy. When completed, the bonfire consumed most of the past.

"The few memories that weren't special but were not so bleak to torch comprised a very small bundle, but at least now there was more space to store them.

"And the precious good stuff, the few really great times,

the wisecracking, tear-jerking moments that make all the hard effort worth it, were brought into the moonlight and savored anew. They were arranged in the center of the big dusty table, where the moon came in like a spotlight. They became the rare moonbeam memories that resurrected the life."

I continued, "The person who helped with the mental house-cleaning and subsequent garage sale and trash bonfire and then planted flowers in planters all over the attic was a girl with the funny name of Street Casey, a girl who studied bugs and got a Ph.D. in Entomology from Berkeley, a girl entirely too thin with small acne scars on her face and bigger scars embedded on her own memory circuits, the ugly scars of an uglier childhood. Of course I know that hers and my struggles and wounds and pain are nothing against yours, Ms. Remmick, but at least I found a way to let someone help me get through."

I was breathing fast, eyes narrowed at Marlette. "But while I'm pushing my brand of help your way, trying to help you find your daughter, you're free to find my shallow no-account efforts fatuous and fraudulent, and you are welcome to find a macho gun-slinging lawman to put together a posse and bust up a gang of bikers. There'll be a lot of flash and noise, and it'll look like your hired hand is getting a lot done and maybe that'll make you feel better.

"Meanwhile, I'm going to keep on pushing and poking and looking under the rocks and seeing what slithers out. It's not glamorous, and you will no doubt think that it won't help you save anything meaningful from your past life, but it's the only thing I know how to do."

I took a couple of steps back, ready to turn and leave. I paused and looked at the mess of a woman who stood, still doubtful, before me. "And if I find your lovely daughter Silence, I'm going to take her out on Nevada beach to a place where the few remaining tourists never go and the sand stretches on for a mile, just Silence and me, and I'm going to ask her to show me how to spin and how to make the ugly parts of the world go away a little and how to look down at the ground and make that mischievous grin and I'm going to put that experience on the very top of the moonbeam memories."

Marlette's face stiffened and quivered and contorted itself into a sadness I didn't recognize. Her body lost its rigidity. Her wide square shoulders softened and caved. Her spine swayed and began to melt. When her knees gave way I stepped over and grabbed her from the side, holding her up by her far shoulder and her close elbow.

I walked her that way, propelling her forward and holding her up. She was a good-sized woman and it took some effort, but it was like clutch-starting a car that doesn't want to go. You can keep pushing it until it fires and moves under its own power, or you can leave it in the road.

After half a block Marlette stiffened a little and began her own listing walk. Then came the torrent. It began as a gush of tears and sobs and grew to a series of violent explosive tremors more like a seizure than a serious cry. She tripped as she howled and I caught her and turned her to me and held her as she jerked and spasmed. Her head beneath my chin made me worry that she would buck and I'd bite my tongue, so I held the head and put my nose to her scalp and smelled the scents of skin and stress and worry, and I squeezed her like I'd learned that autistic kids like to be squeezed.

It was a long time before she got her breathing calmed down to a series of regular gasps, much longer still before she tried to speak. She didn't look up at me. I was still holding her close when her arm raised up.

The only words she managed were "I... I didn't mean..." She began sobbing anew, calmer, without the jerking, but still serious tears.

"Don't," I said. I turned her, and, holding her shoulder and elbow, once again propelled her forward, tiny steps at first, then gradually more like a walk.

THIRTY-NINE

It occurred to me that Spot could serve as a distraction, so I propelled Marlette over to the Jeep, let Spot out and told him to stay. I showed Marlette how to hold his collar – no leash necessary because of his height – and how he would walk nicely at her side.

She held his collar as instructed and seemed a little calmed by the focus.

We walked down the street toward the corner. Marlette's breathing had subsided from convulsive jerks to a heavy inhalation with small periodic hiccups. After a few minutes she was able to speak with a semblance of calm.

"I'm sorry, Owen. What can I do to help? I'm kind of on brain scramble right now."

"Understood. We are revisiting everyone who knows Silence."

"Friends, neighbors, people at church," she said.

"Right. Let's start with neighbors. Anyone in any of these houses who knows Silence?"

Marlette slowly shook her head as she glanced up and down both sides of the street. "Not really." She pointed in front of us to the left. "The gray house there, with the shutters with the little pine tree cutouts, that's where Michelle and her sister Tracy live. Michelle is Charlie's age. And Tracy is a couple years younger still. They liked Charlie and are okay with Silence. Not friendly, but not weird about her the way so many other kids are."

"Their parents?"

"I've only just met the mom. Her name is Nancy, but I

don't know their last name. She works at the day-care center down off Pioneer Trail. The dad I've seen, but I don't know his name. He drives an old pickup with ladders up on the overhead rack and boards and stuff in back. I guess he works construction."

"They ever pay any attention to Silence?"

"None that I've ever noticed."

We kept walking, came to the corner and turned left.

"Did Silence know anyone else on the block?"

Marlette shook her head. "Nobody until the next street over. I'll show you when we get there."

"Tell me about her teachers while we walk."

"Well, Silence goes to most of the normal classes except for physical education. I think they usually keep kids like Silence out of most all regular classes. Too much stress for autistic kids. But Henrietta really feels that Silence should be mainstreamed as much as possible. Not PhyEd because the physical interaction isn't something Silence can handle. But the other classes."

"Any of those teachers ever pay any attention to Silence?"

Marlette shook her head. "Not to speak of. Of course, at the parent teacher conferences they say the usual things I've come to expect. Like how they don't think she is getting anything from class, that she doesn't pay attention. But then they always agree that she doesn't cause any trouble, so why not? Plus, there's some kind of Federal law that requires that kids like Silence be schooled in the least restrictive setting possible. So if she can be in regular classes without causing a problem, then they have to put her in those classes."

"Henrietta thought Silence was smart from the first time they met," I said.

"Something she's told me many times," Marlette said with an edge to her voice. "Silence is kind of a mission with her. I think it is partly because Henrietta never had a family. She told me once how she always wanted a daughter. The truth is, Henrietta's been a very good advocate for Silence. Every year, she asks the other teachers to include her in things even though she can't talk."

"Meaning?"

"Just that when they're teaching and use the children's names, Silence should be part of that. Of course, Silence doesn't act like she knows what's going on. But she is quiet and doesn't disrupt. Henrietta says Silence understands the classroom lessons just like the other kids, even though she doesn't show it."

Marlette paused, thinking.

"Henrietta told me I should include her in things, too, talk to her a lot and use her name whenever I can. It's hard because Silence has never really been there in so many ways. Henrietta says she's totally there – and I appreciate her enthusiasm for Silence's potential – but Henrietta sometimes doesn't face reality. I mean, from the day that girl was born she wasn't there. She never even noticed me, her own mother. She never squeezed my finger, never held onto me. I'd pick her up and try to be a good mother, but it was like picking up a doll. No response at all." Marlette was shaking her head as she walked.

"For years now, I've been doing what Henrietta says. When I cook or clean or take Silence grocery shopping, I talk to her just as if she is responding. It's not easy, let me tell you. And after she comes home from school I ask her how her day was. I say, 'Did you have a good day in school? I bet you did. I heard from Ms. Johanssen just last week. She said the school band was going to perform today out on the field and that all the classes were going to watch. Did you like that? I bet it was fun, huh.'" Marlette turned to me. "That's what I do. I suppose the way I do it isn't really, what's the word, inspired. But I try. I really try."

"It sounds like a good approach to me, Marlette."

"Really? Does it? Oh, thank you."

She said it with such earnestness that I got a glimpse of what a lonely, difficult struggle it must be to go on day after day attempting a communication and love with a child who seems to be absent in the most critical ways.

We turned another corner and Marlette spoke.

"Up here on the right is where Salina Cortez and her kids live. Three of them. Cutest little guys. Three boys all under the age of five. Cesar, the dad, works at Heavenly in food and beverage. Salina does phone work from home. They know of Silence. Say hi to her and stuff. But that's all. Maybe that's not enough to make it worth even mentioning them."

"No, I want to hear about everybody."

"Anyway, Salina and Cesar are the hardest working couple you'd ever hope to meet. I guess that's common with immigrants, isn't it? Someday they'll own their own home, unlike most of us in this neighborhood. Someday they'll get good promotions and make a lot of money. You can just tell."

Marlette scanned the street. "No one else on this street knows Silence. But the next street over goes up the hill toward Mr. Baylor. I think I mentioned him. I'll show you in a minute."

We turned at the next corner.

"Do you think Henrietta is right?" Marlette suddenly said. "That Silence is totally there, that she just can't talk and respond normally? I mean, I'm the one who should know. I'm her mother. But I'm so confused. I love that girl. My heart aches for her. But because I don't see the response, I have a hard time imagining what Henrietta thinks. What do you think?"

"Having never met Silence, I can only go by what you and Henrietta say. Henrietta is a highly experienced teacher, so I have to give some credence to her ideas. But she also strikes me as someone who gets very enthusiastic about certain things, so there might be some extra enthusiasm when it comes to Silence."

"That's exactly the case," Marlette said. "It's like Silence is Henrietta's pet project. I don't doubt Henrietta's intentions, but I often feel like I'm not good enough, like because I'm not so sure of Silence's abilities, I'm holding her back. It's hard. I do the everyday work of taking care of Silence, and then Henrietta swoops in and becomes Silence's cheerleader. It makes me feel like I'm just the dumb mom who doesn't know the score and doesn't care enough." Marlette stared off through the trees. "And maybe that's just what I am," she said.

"I recall you pounding on my door in the middle of the night, demanding that I find your kids. Seems like caring to me."

We walked down the block without speaking, then turned up the next street, which rose steeply up toward the mountain. Out of sight from where we stood, 3600 feet above us, was the top of the Sky chair at Heavenly, from which the vast network of runs spilled down into both California and Nevada.

"This is where the money begins," Marlette said, gesturing at the fancy houses that occupied the higher part of the neighborhood. "We don't come up here a lot. Too much work to hike." She was already breathing hard. "But sometimes we do it for the view. When Shane was here he would carry a little lunch for us in his pack, and we'd all climb up toward the Baylor's house." Marlette pointed at a sprawling house near the top of the street. "You can sit there on those boulders and see the lake and all the way to the North Shore. Mostly, we'd do it to watch the fireworks over the lake on the Fourth and on Labor Day. The fireworks are far away, but it's a good view. Do you want to go up?"

"Sure. Does Silence like the fireworks?"

"It's like everything else, you can't tell. But the nice thing about this place is the sound isn't too loud. She hates all loud noises. We could never take her to the beach, down close to them. One boom and she'd completely freak out. But from up here the fireworks just make little popping sounds."

"You mentioned the Baylors."

"Yeah. Nice people." Marlette was panting and put space between each of her words. "Only, Claudette died last year. Some kind of terrible cancer. Stage four when they found it. Now Emerson lives alone in that big house. He acts normal. Smiles at you and says hi. But you can tell he's pretty broken up inside. It's in his eyes. You can always tell by the eyes."

"What's Emerson do for a living?"

"Oh, don't you know Baylor Ford? Those funny commercials on TV where the farmer keeps pulling the last pig out of the Ford pickup, but the pig keeps climbing back in because he wants nothing more than to ride in a Baylor Ford?"

I shook my head. "I don't have a TV."

Marlette looked at me, frowning. I was a little bit of an

alien again. "He's retired now, but I suppose he still owns them. There's something like eight or ten Baylor Fords across Northern California and up into Oregon and Washington."

We got to the top of the street and Marlette sat down on one of the boulders, hands leaning on her knees. She gasped for air like a runner after a race. She let go of Spot and he sat next to her boulder, his head facing out toward the view like a sentry on watch. I took another boulder. There was a bit of haze in the air, and thirty miles in the distance the North Shore mountains had a shimmery softness about them. The recent snow had melted off the lower elevations, but Mt. Rose and the high massif above Incline Village shined a blazing white and made a blurred white reflection that stretched all the way down the lake toward us.

"Does Emerson Baylor ever take an interest in Silence?"

Marlette nodded, still breathing hard. "Oh, yes. He's so sweet. Even when she was a toddler and we'd walk up here to these boulders, he was always kind to her and acted as if she were completely normal. When she was really little, he'd pick her up and bounce her on his knee."

"Did she ever respond to that? Smile? Or look at him?"

Marlette shook her head. "No. It was so sad. This man trying so hard and my little girl not even noticing." Marlette chewed on her lip. "But that's what's so great about Mr. Baylor, he just always acts like everything is fine. Nothing fazes him."

"When Silence got older, was it the same? The way Baylor treated her?"

"Yes. He's always consistent. I can always count on him to be just right with Silence. Even since Claudette died. He still comes out to say hi."

There was a sound from behind us. We turned and saw a man walking down the curved brick drive. He moved gently and with grace, a man who looked trim and fit beyond what his white hair would suggest. As he got closer I saw that he had impeccable grooming, hair swept carefully straight back, glasses freshly washed and shining, canvas shoes bleached a bright white, trousers creased and unwrinkled. He had a small pencil moustache, white as his shoes, trimmed very close like those of film stars from the thirties.

"Hello, Marlette," he called out as he got closer.

"Hi, Mr. Baylor," Marlette said in a soft voice.

He reached out both hands as he approached, took her hand and held it firmly. "I want to say how terribly sorry I am about Charlie and Silence. Terribly sorry." His pale blue eyes crinkled with emotion. "If there is anything I can do."

"Thank you, sir. This man is helping me. Mr. Baylor, meet Owen McKenna. And this is his dog Spot."

"Hey, beautiful dog." He gave Spot a single soft touch on the top of his head like the pope blessing a parishioner. Then Baylor turned to me. "McKenna. I've heard of you, haven't I? Private Investigator?"

I nodded as we shook, with Baylor reaching up with his left hand and clamping me on the shoulder. "Good to meet you, Owen. Like I said, if I can help in any way."

He seemed very sincere. I could probably send him the bill for my services to Marlette. "I'll let you know if I think of anything," I said. "Perhaps I could ask you a couple of questions?"

"Certainly."

"Were you around on the day Silence and Charlie were kidnapped?"

"Yes. I didn't know it was happening at the time, of course. But when I heard about it the next day, I thought about the time they reported in the paper, and I realized I was at home."

"Were you alone?"

Baylor took a moment before he spoke. "I'm alone most of the time, these days."

"Did you hear anything unusual? Voices? Motorcycles?"

He shook his head. "I thought about that, too. Nothing came to mind."

"We're considering the possibility that Silence and Charlie were kidnapped by motorcyclists. We've also wondered about a van being involved."

"It would make sense," Baylor said, "much easier to pack someone off into a van than any other vehicle, correct?"

"That's our line of thinking. I'm wondering if you recall seeing a van in the neighborhood before the kidnapping. Especially a panel van."

Baylor shook his head. "Nothing comes to mind. At least, not any strange van."

"Vans you recognized?"

"Just the vans in the neighborhood. The Monroy's, of course." He flicked his finger down toward the houses below on the left. "And Bobby Riley's van, the one that says Robert and Sons Plumbing and Heating. That's even a panel van. But of course, no way could Bobby be involved. He's worked for me. I can tell he has good character."

"Any others?"

"Well, of course I have a van. Left over from my dealer days." He waved his arm up toward his four-car garage. "Once you have a van, it's hard to ever go without one. Too useful. In my case, it's not so much me as my two nephews. They're always borrowing it for something."

"A panel van?"

"Why, yes, actually."

"Has anyone borrowed it lately?"

"Oh, come now, Mr. McKenna. I see where you're going. No. No one has used my van in a couple months. For all I know, the battery's run down again and I'll have to charge it before I can get it running. I got rear-ended a year ago, right after Claudette passed on, and it caused some kind of a short. A trickle short, the mechanic said. But he couldn't find it. So every few months the battery runs out. And me, an ex-car dealer. Embarrassing to say the least."

"Are you out of the car business completely?"

"Almost. I still have a minority position in a dealership by Redding and another one up in Oregon, but I sold the rest."

"Enjoying retirement?" I said.

"Yes. Although I'm quite active in our investment group.

We've moved into some VC work. Much more interesting than stocks and bonds."

"VC?"

"Venture Capital. Private Equity. It's quite exciting searching out the next big thing. But instead of just investing in a company after it begins to market a hot idea, we get in on it from the beginning. You get a much bigger stake that way. Bigger risk, too, of course. So far, we've helped create two startups." Emerson eased himself down and sat on the boulder next to Marlette. This was clearly a favorite subject. "High tech stuff," he continued. "One of them is in Reno, started by two young kids who were with Hewlett Packard. A new type of hand-held device. I can't really say much about it except that people won't be quite so connected to their laptops once this hits the market. The other company we've helped start is an outfit that makes computer peripherals, hard drives, disk burners, all wireless of course. Idea came from a fellow out of Stanford. That company is based in Mountain View."

"How are they doing?"

"Well, as I said, the one in Reno is just getting going, but advance orders are very strong. We'll do very well on it. The company in Mountain View has stumbled, truth be told. It may go huge. Or we may lose a bundle. That's the thing about VC. You don't want to get into it unless you've got some extra room in your pocket book. Most of us in the group are in good enough shape that it doesn't really matter. Anyway, it's exciting. Thrill of the hunt and all."

I pulled out a card and handed it to him. "You said you'd like to help."

"Yes, definitely."

"Please keep your eyes open. Call me if anything comes up. Anything unusual or out of place."

"You can count on it." He turned to Marlette and took her hand again. "And you call me, Marlette if you need anything. Again, you have my deepest sympathies. And I'm sure that Mr. McKenna will find your daughter."

FORTY

When I got home there were no messages. I fished out the piece of paper Marlette had given me. She'd written down Michael Warner's office address at Sac State and his home address in El Dorado Hills. Directory Assistance had his home listing. I called his office number just in case he was working late, got his voicemail again and left another message. Then I dialed his home number and got a machine. Maybe he went to bed early and let the machine pick up. I left another message and went to bed.

I was sleeping and there was the strangest sounding bird outside in the dark and it wouldn't let me sleep and then the bird got inside the bedroom and chirped louder and louder and then it morphed into the phone and I dropped it on the floor and then got it to my face. But it was turned around and I said hello into the earpiece.

"Owen McKenna? Is this Owen McKenna?" a small tinny voice was buzzing near my lips.

"Speaking," I said when I finally had the phone re-oriented. The clock next to the bed said 6:00 a.m.

"Sorry to call so early. I don't know if you remember me, but I was at the meeting at Geoff Lambdon's house? Pierson Giovanovich. You told us to look for anything that could possibly be connected to the kidnapped girl?"

"Yes."

"Well, I don't know if this is what you meant but we were out riding yesterday and overheard something rather strange. One thing led to another and, well, our dog found a large bone. My wife thinks it's from a deer, but I was in Viet Nam and I saw some action and I'm not so sure."

"You think it's human?"

"I can't say positively, but it looks enough like an arm bone that I am going to call the police. But because of the circumstances of how we found it, I thought I should alert you."

"Thank you. Where did you find it?"

"You know where Kingsbury Grade drops down toward the lake from Daggett Pass? There's a road that winds off the grade toward Castle Rock. Up in there."

"That's in Douglas County," I said. "I'll call Sergeant Martinez of the Douglas County Sheriff's Department, save you the trouble. Okay if we meet at your house?"

I drove south on Highway 50 and met Pierson and his wife Myra at their house in Skyland, just a few blocks over from Geoff Lambdon's house. It was still only 7:00 a.m. I knocked and Pierson came to the door and let me in.

"Sorry again for getting you out so early, but I've got to take a deposition at nine o'clock and I thought you'd want to know about it as soon as possible. Is Sergeant Martinez coming as well?"

"Yes. He lives down in Carson Valley. He'll be here in another ten minutes or so."

"Shall we wait to explain until then? Have some coffee while we wait?"

"Thank you. Black, please."

"Come with me," Pierson said as he walked through the large great room that opened to a modern kitchen. He set a Lake Tahoe mug under a high-tech stainless steel brewer and pushed a button. "Grinds the beans and brews it all at the same time. One cup at a time."

The machine whirred and hissed and a thin stream of steaming foamy coffee filled the mug in thirty seconds. He handed it to me as his wife came in, carrying a tiny dog in her arms.

"Owen, you remember Myra, and this is Peanut."

"Good to see you again, Myra. Hello, Peanut."

Myra said, "Peanut's a Pekinese-Shih Tzu mix and she dragged that big bone out of the woods all by herself. Isn't that right, little munchkin?" She kissed the dog and then rubbed its scalp so vigorously its head wobbled like a bobble-head toy.

"The bone probably weighed more than she does," Pierson said. He reached over toward his wife and duplicated her doggie head-rub, and I thought the dog must live with a constant migraine.

We chatted a few minutes and drank our coffee and then Diamond arrived. After introductions we sat on leather chairs in the great room, and Pierson explained what happened.

"You met our little group of riders at Geoff's house. Only, yesterday none of them could go, so we went with our other friends, Bob and Judy Gannon. We like to do the loop where you go up the East Shore to Incline, over the Mt. Rose Highway and down to Reno, south to Carson City, then south on Jack's Valley Road through Genoa and back up over Kingsbury Grade. We got up to the top of grade in the early afternoon and stopped for a refresher beer at that place on Tramway Drive." Pierson turned to Diamond and grinned. "Don't worry, sergeant, we always cut it off at an even half dozen when we're riding."

Diamond nodded, a serious look on his face.

"Anyway, there was a group at the bar talking about a big campout in Temple Gulch some time back. When did they say it was, Myra?"

"I just remember that they were talking about going hiking during the full moon," Myra said. "They said they went before the tourist season, but it had to be after the snow melted. The snow didn't melt this year on upper Kingsbury until well into June, I think. And the heavy tourist season starts July Fourth, so it would probably have been during the full moon in June."

"Right," Pierson said. "So they said they were out hiking and saw thirty or forty bikers in there and they had a huge campfire and the smoke was drifting through the trees. They joked about what the bikers must have been cooking. Said it really stank. Anyway, I was curious about where Temple Gulch was because you can't ride on most of the trails back in there. Not unless you have a dirtbike, anyway. I asked about it and they explained how you go up toward Castle Rock and watch for this trail that turns off up the mountain slope. It's narrow and easy to miss, but it's quite easy to drive it with a road bike, even though I think it's supposed to be off-limits to motorized traffic." He glanced at Diamond.

"So we all thought, let's give it a try. It took us a few wrong turns before we found the trail. But just like they said, it was easy to ride single file, and it wound way back along the side of the mountain. Then we came to what must be Temple Gulch. The rocks rise up on three sides and it's a perfect large camping spot, sheltered from the wind and big enough for a huge party.

"There's a big firepit in the center and a smaller one off to one side. Somebody had left behind a lot of trash, beer cans and such. Maybe it had been there since June, who's to know? Myra and I always carry extra plastic bags – isn't that right, honey? – so we thought we'd do our good turn and we began to pick up the leftover trash. Meanwhile, Peanut here was running around exploring. Myra always wears this backpack that Peanut rides in. Peanut got away from us and we heard her barking off in the forest."

Myra added, "We were so worried about coyotes. Weren't we, Peanut?" She rubbed the dog's head again.

Pierson said, "So we called her over and over, but she just kept barking. First it was far off, then she got closer. Eventually she came into the camp area dragging a large bone that was charred nearly black. To me it looks like a human arm bone. Poor little Peanut could barely carry it."

"Did you leave it there?" Diamond said.

"No, I put it in one of our plastic bags and brought it home. It's in the garage. Would you like to see it?"

We said yes, and Pierson took us out to a garage that was much bigger than my cabin and picked up a bag that was lying on a workbench. He opened the bag and peeled it back so he could show us the bone without touching it. It was large and blackened with charcoal and looked to me like a humerus. The ball end looked intact while the elbow end was shattered off.

Diamond said, "I'll take it in. I'll also need you to show me where your dog found it."

"Okay, but I'll have to call my secretary and check my schedule. Give me a minute."

Pierson got on the phone while Myra took the dog outside.

"What do you think?" Diamond said to me.

I shrugged. "Who knows? Not too smart to leave a human bone lying in the woods. Will you let me know what you find?" I wanted to drive down to Sacramento and see if I could find Michael Warner.

"Will do," Diamond said.

Pierson got off the phone. "I'm free after three. Does that work for you?"

Diamond said that it did and they made plans to meet near the top of Kingsbury.

"Do you have a bike?" Pierson said. "Because it's too narrow for your cruiser and too far to easily walk."

"Ride on the back of yours?" Diamond said.

"Works for me," Pierson said.

FORTY-ONE

I went home and dialed the number of the Humboldt County deputy who'd given me some background on Antonio Gomez and his gang.

"Deputy Randy Rasmussen," a man said.

"Hello. Owen McKenna calling from Lake Tahoe. We spoke a few days ago about..."

"Sure, sure, Gomez and his gang. Anything happening on that?"

"I've spoken with him and a couple of his boys, but we haven't linked him to the kidnapping. However, I have a question about him. Any idea if he and his boys have been through Tahoe before?"

"Of course. I told you about it the other day, didn't I?"

"Not that I recall," I said.

"No kidding? Christ, I just turned forty and I'm already losing it. Short-term memory is shot, long-term memory will be next. Yes, he and his crew were in Tahoe earlier this summer. I don't have my notes, but I think it was June. Mitchell, my informant, told me that they planned to go back to Tahoe before they'd even left the first time."

"A repeat tourist is a good tourist," I said.

"What? Oh, right. Anyway, Mitchell is a fake name. Protect his identity."

"Got it. Does the gang do that often? Go back to the same places?"

"Not too, from what I gather. Mitchell mentioned one

other place. Up by Ashland, Oregon. And get this, he claimed that Gomez went to one of the plays at the Shakespeare Festival. How do you like that? A gang leader sitting through cultural stuff."

"Yeah, that's something," I said.

I fed Spot some lunch, loaded him into the Jeep and headed out of the basin on Highway 50. Two hours later I was at Sacramento State University. I found a place to park half a mile away from the science building. Sacramento was cloaked in a heavy blanket of October clouds so I didn't need to worry about Spot overheating. I cracked the windows and told him to be good.

The building where Michael Warner had his office smelled like concrete and wooden pencils. There were four students shuffling down the hallway. None of them had pencils behind their ears, just the wires going to the iPods on their belts. No doubt listening to Quarks-On-Tape. Warner's office door was shut. There was a piece of paper on the wall next to his door. It showed Warner's regular office hours. According to the schedule, he was in. I tried the doorknob. Locked. I knocked. No answer.

I went to the nearby offices. Three doors down a woman was in, her door open.

"Excuse me. I was looking for Michael. He is supposed to have office hours now, but he seems to be out. Any idea where I might find him?"

She shook her head and raised one eyebrow. "I'm sorry, we're all wondering the same thing. Before he left he made it clear he'd be back last Monday. We put it on the schedule. But he didn't show up and he hasn't called. The dean told me she left a message and emailed him. But no response. Are you one of the parents?"

"No, Michael and I are working on an extracurricular project together. I hope he's okay."

"All we know is that something came up with some family member, and he said he'd be gone two weeks. Samantha Scola was able to take his classes the last two weeks, but she has another commitment this week so we had to cancel his classes yesterday and today. Hate to do that. I checked his horoscope. He's a Gemini, you know. And do you know what it said? It said big changes are coming, not all of them good."

"Really," I said. "Anyone else here who knows him well?"

"The dean probably knows him best. Her name is Catherine Timmeron. They sometimes have lunch together. But she's a Leo. So you can just imagine the implications. She's left for the day. She'll be back at eight tomorrow morning."

"May I have her number?"

"Sure." She opened a little plastic box, took out a card and handed it to me. "Maybe he's at the emergency room as we speak," she said. "You know how the stars work. Even for Geminis. For that matter, he could call the second you leave."

"No doubt," I said. I thanked her and left.

It took forty minutes to get back across town to where the freeway rose up into El Dorado Hills. I got out my map and figured out how to get to Warner's house. Much of El Dorado Hills is comprised of recent subdivisions filled with large expensive homes. I couldn't imagine an associate professor being able to afford to own even a fraction of one. Then my road took me into an older part of the area and I found Warner's number on a dented mailbox that leaned at an angle next to a short dirt drive. It was a lonely setting in the country, with the closest house a couple hundred feet down and across the road.

Out front sat a 1970 Volvo wagon, rusted enough that I couldn't tell if the original color was brown or dark red. Behind the car was a detached single car garage. Most of the paint had peeled off long ago. Like the mailbox, the garage also leaned and its roof was swaybacked. Behind the garage was a matching house, two bedrooms at most. It stood straight but had the same bare siding and swaybacked roof.

I knocked on the door. No one answered. I knocked again, louder. No sound of movement from inside. I walked around the house and found just one window without drapes.

Cupping my hands next to my face revealed only a bare linoleum floor in an old kitchen.

On one side of the house rose a steep wooded embankment. There was a field behind and to the other side of the house, and it stretched back to one of the new subdivisions. I could see why the owner of this rundown house didn't fix it up. The lot was so valuable that whenever the house sold it would almost certainly be torn down to make way for a new palace.

When I came back around the house, I knocked again, then tried the doorknob. It was locked.

I walked across the road and down to the next closest driveway. It led to another old house, this one a Victorian in perfect repair. The filigree on the deck railings and along the eaves and under the gable trim had been painted in blues and turquoises.

There was a Studebaker in the drive, its front wheels up on ramps, a mechanic's legs protruding from under the engine.

"Hello?" I called as I approached.

The mechanic slid out on a dolly and sat up. She stood up, her baggy greasy jeans hanging loose on her slim frame. She had short hair lacquered up into a shiny flat-top. The short sleeves of her T-shirt were rolled up to her shoulders. In her right hand was a ratchet and socket. "What d'ya need?" she said.

"I stopped by to see your neighbor Michael Warner, but he's out. Car's in the drive, but no answer at the door. He's gone missing at school, too. I wonder if you've talked to him recently?"

"Not since a week or two ago."

"Was he okay? The school is wondering if something happened. He was supposed to be back from his break yesterday, but he didn't show."

"Seemed well enough to me when he left," she said. She looked at me with suspicion. "He a friend of yours?"

"We're business colleagues. One of my collaborators is close to him. We're all working on the same project. I stopped by to go over some details. Any idea where he went?"

"When I saw him he was loading up his van for a camping trip to Tahoe."

"That was a couple weeks ago?"

"More or less. Not like I keep track. I was out walking and he was in the drive. I saw him checking out his tire chains, so I said that I didn't think he'd need 'em for two more months if at all. We're only at twelve hundred feet. We don't get snow but a couple inches once every year or so. But he said he was heading up to the lake, and the weather report was predicting snow at the higher elevations."

I wasn't sure of the exact days, but she was talking about the time that Silence and Charlie were kidnapped. "He's been here since then, hasn't he?"

She shook her head. "Not that I've noticed. But I don't watch for him out the window."

"His van, is that the panel van my colleague mentioned?"

"Sure. Old Dodge. Michael bought it used."

I thought about that a moment. "If you see him, could you please ask him to call Marlette?"

"That your business colleague?"

"Yes." I took a step back as if to go. "Quite the wheels," I said, gesturing at the Studebaker.

"Yeah. A forty-nine. Needs a valve job and some other work. But the tranny and drive train are still good. Hope to have it running soon."

"Good luck."

She gave me a small nod, got down onto the dolly and slid back under the car.

FORTY-TWO

I leaned against my Jeep in Michael Warner's driveway and called information for Sacramento while Spot leaned out the window and used his snout to push at my arm.

"You want a pet?" I said. "How needy can you be? I just pet you last week."

He grabbed my wrist with his teeth, just as a voice with a Southeast Asian accent said, "What city, please."

"Spot, that hurts," I said.

"I'm sorry, I don't understand what city, please."

"Sacramento," I said as I pulled out the Catherine Timmeron card and spelled the name.

They had a listing for a C. Timmeron and I dialed it as Spot chewed on my arm again. I pulled my hand out of my pocket and wrapped my arm around his neck. "You'll never escape the Hulk Hogan Headlock," I said to him as a small cultured voice said hello in my ear.

"This is Detective Owen McKenna from Lake Tahoe calling for Catherine Timmeron. Is this Catherine?"

"Yes."

"I'd like to ask you about a professor who teaches at your school. Michael Warner."

There was a pause. "How do I know you are who you say you are? And why should I talk to you?"

Something in her tone made me suddenly think that she was in love with Michael and that she would be very protective of him even if he was a suspected kidnapper. She was also one of the generally careful ones, responding to all unknown people with skepticism. Although I respected her caution, I could tell it was going to be a pain and slow me down.

"Okay," I said, trying to stifle my heavy sigh and render it less noticeable. "I'm going to tell you a story about a kidnapping. If you think I'm insincere or of questionable character or working some kind of scam, hang up. If not, perhaps you could please answer a question or two that might help save a child's life."

Catherine said nothing, an impressive control.

I continued. "Michael Warner is an old friend of a woman named Marlette Remmick. Marlette's two children were kidnapped two weeks ago. The boy was murdered. The girl is still missing and presumed alive. I'm an ex-homicide inspector from the San Francisco Police Department now working as a private investigator in Tahoe. Marlette Remmick hired me to help find her daughter." I paused, thinking that if I explained Michael's paternity it would make him look like a suspect and Catherine would be less inclined to help me.

Instead, I said, "The kidnapped girl has demonstrated an interest in math and science. So her mother called Michael a few weeks ago and he agreed to meet the girl. Marlette drove her daughter down to Sac State. Michael showed her his lab and office. Call it a one-child, one-visit outreach program."

I continued, "Marlette knows how brilliant and perceptive Michael is. Now that Michael and the girl have met, Marlette thinks that Michael could help figure out this kidnapping case.

"Of course, it is a reach to think so, and I for one am not confident that the brilliant professor can extend his insights into a kidnapping up in Tahoe. But the police and I haven't been successful. We need every scrap of information and every useful thought that any intelligent person can provide. It would be a shame not to talk to Michael and see if he can help. So this is a long way of getting around to my request that you help me find him. I went down to the school and found out he took two weeks off. And he didn't report back to work Monday as planned. His neighbor said he was going camping in Tahoe. I'm hoping you can tell me where exactly he was going or how to reach him."

Finally, Catherine spoke. "If Michael only met the girl once how could he possibly be of any help?"

"Something I haven't told you yet is that the girl is autistic. She won't have anything to do with adults other than her mother and one teacher. Michael was the first exception in years. That puts him in the unique position of being the only other adult to have spent any time conversing with the child."

"I still don't understand," Catherine said. "How could he illuminate any aspect of her kidnapping?"

"We have reason to believe that she wasn't a random victim. There is no ransom note. We think she was chosen for a specific reason. Michael was one of the last people to spend time with her. I'm wondering if he noticed anything unusual, or if she gave him any indication about any recent changes in her life. A stranger approaching. Someone she knows who began acting differently. Something she recently learned that made her a threat to someone. Her mother and her teacher haven't been able to help. Any input from Michael could make the difference."

I waited a long time. "Catherine? Are you still there?"

After another long wait, Catherine said, "Michael had a friend, a fellow grad student from back in his days at Berkeley. For many years they used to go camping together at an old cabin in Tahoe that belongs to the friend's uncle. The friend died from cancer a few years ago. The friend's uncle works in the American Embassy in Paris. He rarely gets back to the states. Michael said that the uncle not only allows him to use the cabin, but he appreciates that Michael checks on it from time to time. Michael has a key. I think that is where he was going."

"Did Michael plan his break from school in advance?"

"No. It was quite sudden. He came to me a few weeks ago and said something had come up, and he needed to get away to work on it. We went over the schedule and figured out that Ms. Scola, one of our other professors, could take his classes. So we let him take two weeks off. With the weekends on either side, that would give him a long break. But of course he didn't come back to classes Monday, so it has been longer than he planned. Frankly, I'm worried about him."

"Any idea what he was working on?"

"No. Just some kind of project, I imagine. Knowing Michael, I'd say it was almost certainly something in his professional field."

"Why would he go to a cabin in Tahoe to work on a project?"

"You have to understand that Michael is a brilliant scientist. He's probably on the verge of a new theory. He's the kind of man who could potentially come up with breakthrough insights into physics. A man like that, well, he needs to simply think uninterrupted. For scientists like Michael, it's only the prosaic work that is done in the lab. The real work is done in the brain. I've seen it. He walks and thinks. He sits and thinks. He's not even aware of the details of life. He's completely distracted. He loses track of the hours, even of the days. Of course, I don't know that he went to the Tahoe cabin. But I surmise that he did because it would fit with his needs."

"Where is the cabin?" I asked.

"It is at Fallen Leaf Lake. But I've never been there."

"Do you know the address?"

"No."

"Have you a picture? Did Michael ever give you a description?"

"I've never seen a picture of it, but I remember him talking about it. He said it is an old log cabin, quite primitive. He said it sits way back from the road and that it is up on a slope."

"Did he mention which road?"

"No. He only said that he likes to go out on the front steps at night when the moon is out because Mt. Tallac reflects in the water of Fallen Leaf Lake. Does that help?"

"Yes, that helps a lot."

"If you see him, please have him call me?" She sounded frightened.

"I will, Catherine."

FORTY-THREE

I thought about Michael Warner as I drove back up to Tahoe.

Warner learned he had a daughter, met her and then she and he spent some time in private. A short time later she was kidnapped. No ransom demand was sent. Warner also had a panel van. He lived alone. He packed his van for a camping trip, presumably at his friend's uncle's cabin on Fallen Leaf Lake.

Around the time Warner met Silence, he made a request at the university for two weeks off. His last day of class before his week off was a Friday. Charlie and Silence were kidnapped five days later on Wednesday.

I knew that a large percentage of kidnapped children are taken by parents who don't have custody. Marlette had said he was unusual, a little bit off.

Normally, I would call Mallory at the SLTPD as well as the El Dorado Sheriff's Department and fill them in on my likely kidnapping and murder suspect. But given that I'd made myself unwelcome in the local law enforcement community, I'd have to pursue it alone. If I found direct evidence of Michael Warner's involvement in the kidnapping and murder, I'd call them in.

The highway up Echo Summit was remarkably void of traffic, a benefit of the shoulder season. The tourists who are the economic lifeblood of the basin and who fill the highways wouldn't return in force until the ski resorts opened come Thanksgiving. I made good time until I hit snow flurries at 7000 feet.

Coming down from the summit, I drove back out of the snow. I made a left turn onto North Upper Truckee Road. North Upper Truckee winds through a large middle class neighborhood. One third of the houses are owner-occupied. The other two-thirds sit vacant except for when the vacation homeowners come to town.

Several miles to the north I made a left turn onto Tahoe Mountain Road and climbed up into the Angora Heights neighborhood, a small area of million-dollar homes, some of which had the ten million-dollar view over Fallen Leaf Lake. With Mt. Tallac looming over the opposite shore and reflecting in the sparkling waters, it is one of the grandest views in all of the Sierra, and the area has been used in many Hollywood films.

I made several turns through the neighborhood to access the one-lane road that crawls down to Fallen Leaf Lake. At the intersection with Fallen Leaf Road I turned left and drove along the lake, grateful that Spot was lying down in back, less likely to attract attention.

I watched up to the left, looking for any cabin that could fit the description the university's dean had given. Eventually, I came to the end of the lake where the entrance to Stanford Camp angles to the right and the trail to Glen Alpine Falls goes to the left.

I turned around in the parking lot and headed back the way I'd come. Most of the cabins and houses on the lake were deserted this time of year because the snows could come at any time and Fallen Leaf Road is not plowed. Nevertheless, I didn't want to take a chance on being seen, so I continued until I found a stretch without cabins where I could pull well into the woods and park unnoticed.

Spot was now awake and curious about the lack of car movement. I let him out and let him wander the woods for a minute. Then I called him, took hold of his collar and put my finger across his nose, the signal for quiet.

I bent my head down for emphasis. "No sound, Spot. Nothing."

He ignored me, suddenly watching the woods on high alert because he realized I was up to something.

We started into the forest, choosing a high line where we'd be far from the lake road and above all the cabins. Although the sky was still a bright blue, the sun had set behind the peak of Mt. Tallac, 3400 feet directly above us. The forest is thick and the pine and fir trees tall, so that even though their highest branches were enjoying the late afternoon daylight, the forest floor was already moving into twilight. Most of the birds of summer were long gone, trading the cold Tahoe evenings for the warm humid sunsets of Guatemala and other points south. The few remaining birds, the Steller's jays, the Mountain chickadees, the crows and ravens had gone quiet.

A little red Douglas squirrel, quivering with angry energy, advanced down the trunk of a Sugar pine, screaming at Spot and me for our thoughtless intrusion into his landscape. Spot tensed, but did not pull away from me as the first of the two cabins I wanted to investigate came into view through the trees.

We stayed well back and above and walked an arc around it. It was made of logs, darkened over the decades. Each wall had two small windows. The door was in the center of the front wall. In one corner rose a crooked metal stove pipe. The roof was low and built at a shallow angle, its shingles covered with green mossy nap. There was no vehicle in front of the cabin, and there were no lights on inside. But it didn't mean much as I saw no power lines either. Someone could be living by candlelight, not easily seen from the outside.

Because Spot's coloring is the opposite of camouflage, I stopped at a place where we were hidden from the cabin and said, "Sit-Stay."

He reluctantly sat and looked up at me, wondering what craziness I was about to engage in at a time when I should be home preparing his supper.

I took a step away and turned to him. "Stay," I said again.

I walked away, staying largely in Spot's view to lessen his temptation to run and give our location away. There were many large trees and I kept them between me and the cabin as I approached.

My path took me to the pine needle-covered drive where I stopped and looked at the ground. Many of the needles were unbroken and had not been disturbed. My guess was that no one had pulled into the drive in many weeks.

Spot was still sitting when I came back. I praised him lavishly and he jumped up and put his front paws on my shoulders, his nose to my nose, to celebrate his grad-school-level skills. Then we continued on into the woods.

I'd barely gotten a glimpse of the second cabin, a dark shape through the trees, when Spot whined. It was a high plaintive cry, unlike what you'd expect from a 170-pound animal whose growl can break windowpanes.

The second cabin was just as old and dark as the first, but it was much bigger and appeared to have a second floor loft under a steep roof. As we approached, I could see that there was no vehicle in front, yet even in the dim light it was clear by tire tracks that a vehicle had been in and out recently. Perhaps someone was inside, watching, but I doubted it. Spot's whine had changed my perception of what I was dealing with, so I kept him with me this time, walked up the front steps to the front door and knocked.

I turned around and looked through the trees at the jaw-drop view. Mt. Tallac and Cathedral Peak filled the sky through the trees, and the waves on the lake below scintillated in the waning light like the lights of Atlantis.

I let go of Spot. "You can run, boy. Go ahead, it's okay." I gave him a little pat on his rear and he walked down the steps, out from the cabin, and lowered his nose to sniff the needles. Then he lay down next to a Manzanita bush, looking enervated instead of energetic after being stuck in the Jeep for hours. I knocked again, wondering about Spot, hoping he was okay.

When no one answered, I walked around the cabin. The windows were all double hung. None of them slid up as I pushed on them. When I peered inside nothing was visible in the dark other than a glimpse of wooden floorboards here and there. The second floor had one window on each end, tucked under the roof gable. But I saw no easy way to get up and look inside. I went back around to the front.

Spot still lay on the ground, watching me.

On the front side of the house the ground sloped away enough that three feet of the foundation wall showed. There was a cellar window on either side of the front steps. They each had two hinges on the top edge so they could swing out at the bottom. Peering through the dusty, spider web-covered glass I could see the little rod that could be set in different notches on a metal track to prop the window open at various angles. I dug my fingernails into the edges of the window and pulled, but the window held fast, its prop rod firmly lodged in the track.

I moved to the second basement window. It too was locked. I looked around at the forest and distant houses down on the lake and saw no one as I eased my toe against the glass. It made a soft ting and cracked diagonally across one corner. I moved my toe to the broken triangle of glass and applied more pressure. Another ting and the triangle split. It was easy to push the two little panes in. A fly buzzed out as the broken glass fell inside to the basement floor. I bent down to take another look, and it smelled like someone had put up a freezer full of steak and unplugged it a couple of weeks ago. I whistled for Spot and he came at a slow walk, stopped and looked at me.

"Come here, Spot. Tell me what you think." I tapped my foot near the broken window. He walked over, reluctantly, snout reaching toward the window. But he stopped five feet away, pulled back his ears and moved his head from side to side as he backed up. Another high-pitched whine issued from the back of his throat. Now I was certain why he'd cried from far back in the woods.

"It's okay, boy," I said. I walked over, put my hand on the side of his neck. "I just wanted to check. Didn't mean to make you sad."

I couldn't get reception on my cell, so we walked up the mountain toward Angora Ridge above us while I checked the cell's readout. When a reception bar appeared, I dialed 9-1-1. Spot sat down with a large boulder between him and the cabin, trying to distance himself from the smell of death.

When the dispatcher answered I gave her my name and the address of the cabin and asked her to contact the El Dorado Sheriff's Department. Then I walked down the road with Spot as I waited. I talked to him in reassuring tones, petting him, telling him he did a good job. We came back to the drive as the first two Ford Explorer cruisers showed up five minutes later. In another ten minutes three more vehicles arrived. Two men went into the house, handkerchiefs over their noses. They came back out gagging and reported that the victim was in the basement, but that decomposition of the body had progressed too far to make an immediate identification possible or to establish how the victim died.

There were seven men and one woman and all were young and only one of them had any knowledge of me. I've learned that with other cops it is best to first tell them that I'm an ex-homicide inspector from the SFPD. Then I showed them ID and mentioned the name of the El Dorado lieutenant who knew me.

Only after I'd established my qualifications and bona fides did I explain that I was now working as a private investigator on the Tahoe kidnapping and murder case and that Commander Mallory of the SLTPD was in charge and would field their inquiries. They all had varying degrees of familiarity with the case.

Two crime lab boys arrived and went to work while one of the officers, a Sergeant Kelly, kept firing questions at me, so eager in his interrogation that he interrupted my answers. Finally, his partner intervened and suggested they just let me tell it from start to finish. I ran through the story twice.

I was thorough, eventually covering how I ended up at the cabin and Michael Warner's likely paternity of the kidnapped girl. I explained that I hadn't been in the cabin and had not had any suspicion about his death until my dog whined. I added how I was peering into the basement window and accidentally cracked the glass and smelled the odor myself.

"So you're coming through the woods and your dog gets one whiff of something from some distance away and he whines and that made you think there was a body inside the cabin?" one of the men said, his voice incredulous.

"It made me wonder. After I cracked the glass and had Spot sniff it again and I saw the way he pulled back, then I knew for sure." I turned and gestured at Spot who was still lying down a good distance away, watching but not wanting to come any closer.

"Is he a trained police dog?" the officer asked.

"No, but he's had some training on suspect apprehension and search and rescue. Not enough to be a professional dog. But he knows the smell of death and he shows it."

They all turned and looked at Spot who lay there and hung his head.

"Looks major league bummed out," one of the men said.

"Dogs with search and rescue training feel that they've failed in some way if they find a dead body. They like to find live people."

I wanted to get home, so I got out one of my cards and handed it to the sergeant in charge. "Anything else you need, give me a call. Remember to check in with Mallory. I need to get back to work."

The men nodded, and Spot and I headed home.

FORTY-FOUR

I stopped at Street's before I headed up the mountain. Her VW bug was in the drive so I knocked rather than use the key she'd given me. Spot and I stood like gentlemen callers when she answered the door.

"Hi, what a nice surprise. I was just thinking that... Spot, what's wrong?" She grabbed his head and rubbed his ears. "Why so glum?"

I gave Street a short explanation of my activities. "He's sad about the body. Can I leave him here a bit? A change of scene will cheer him up."

"Of course. C'mere, you big canine creature." Street took his collar. "Spot and I will drink champagne and roast hot dogs in the fire," Street said to me over her shoulder as she walked him into her condo. "You make your calls. When you're done, come back for a nightcap in front of the fire?"

"Will do," I said, shutting the door behind me.

As I drove up the mountain in the dark, I could sense the moonlight hitting the mountains of the opposite shore even as it hadn't yet risen over the mountain behind my cabin. The moon glow was bright. It would be full in two more nights.

As I picked up the phone to dial the dean, Catherine Timmeron, I thought about what had transpired in the last couple hours. Michael Warner had gone from being my best suspect to a likely murder victim. Marlette had said he was a sweet, kind, somewhat strange person who'd been helpful and gracious in meeting his biological daughter. He'd disappeared from school about the time that she was kidnapped. Now that the body in the cabin was probably his, it was likely that he too had been killed around the time that Silence and Charlie had been kidnapped. Maybe even before. Maybe Warner's van had been stolen and was used to kidnap the kids.

From there it was a connect-the-dots conclusion that Michael Warner had been the original source of the information that the kidnapper wanted.

Perhaps Michael and the kidnapper had been friends. Michael could have been eager to talk about the amazing experience of discovering he had a daughter he'd never known.

Maybe Michael ruminated on the nature of talking to a mute person, a person who didn't respond in any normal way. Perhaps he'd had the same experience that Marlette had described, that talking to Silence was like taking a truth serum. Because it didn't seem that she understood what you were saying, it loosened your inhibitions and you found yourself saying things that you would never reveal to anyone else.

So the kidnapper figured it out. He realized that Michael had revealed to Silence the secret that was so valuable. The kidnapper met Michael at the cabin and tried to get the information out of him, but Michael wasn't forthcoming. The kidnapper killed Michael and took his van, using it to kidnap the kids. He killed the son Charlie and ever since has been trying to get the information out of the mute girl.

I punched in Catherine's number. It rang and I debated whether to tell her about Michael's death. I decided that it was appropriate to withhold the information for two reasons. The first was that we didn't technically know that the body in the cabin was Michael's. The other reason was that once Catherine was told of his death, it would be difficult to get useful information out of her. The possibility of saving Silence trumped any concerns about when she learned of his death.

"Hello," she answered again in the same small cultured-sounding voice.

"Hi Catherine. Owen McKenna calling again. Sorry to

bother you, but I have another question."

"Yes?"

"I'm back in Tahoe. I found the cabin that fits your description. Michael's van is not there. I'll check back tomorrow. But in the event I don't find him, I'm wondering if you can tell me whether anyone else at the university worked with him. Are there any professors who might be familiar with the projects that Michael worked on?"

Catherine was clearly someone who didn't speak until she was ready. I was about to ask if she were still there when she spoke.

"The only person I can think of is Ruben Olivera. He is an associate professor of chemistry. They seemed to get along well and sometimes had lunch together. Michael never said anything about sharing projects, but I've sometimes noticed a kind of cross-discipline talk that you don't often see within a discipline."

"I'm sorry?"

"It's just that physicists will sometimes go slow when talking to other physicists about their ideas. Especially, if the idea is kind of out-there, so to speak. I think it's just human nature to avoid possible ridicule. Same with chemists and astronomers et cetera. But physicists would feel more open to talk to chemists and vice versa."

"Any chance you have Ruben's home number? It could be very important."

Another pause while she considered.

"Let me get my book." She put down the phone, came back after a minute and read off a number.

"Thank you very much," I said.

I called Ruben's home number and got voicemail with a complicated menu. I chose the pager option, punched in my number and hung up. He called back in one minute.

"I'm returning a page. You called me," a voice said. The man's perfect diction and enunciation were clear despite his Mexican accent and a lot of background noise.

"Thank you for returning my call. My name is Owen McKenna. I'm calling about..."

"Wait a second, please." Someone was shouting in the background. Something about tacos and cheese and cerveza. The noise went away and Ruben was back. "Sorry. I'm in a restaurant. You were saying?"

"Dean Catherine Timmeron gave me your home number. I'm calling about a colleague of yours. Michael Warner." I gave Ruben the gist of the situation, including the hope that Warner could provide information that might help in solving a kidnapping. "We've checked his home in El Dorado Hills and the cabin where he often stays in Tahoe and we haven't been able to talk to him. I'm wondering if you've heard from him?"

"No. Not since he went on his camping trip."

"Any idea about the purpose of his trip? Dean Timmeron said that he was working on a project and that she thought he needed to get away to think. Can you give me any sense of what this project was? It may be linked to the reason the girl was kidnapped."

"First of all, I would never violate a confidence. Second, I don't know any specifics. I only have a conceptual idea of what he was working on. Having said that, let me see if I can answer you without violating his trust. In general terms I can say his project was an invention of sorts. Not an object, but a process. A kind of new mathematics applied to a technical procedure." He paused. "Does that help?"

"Is this the kind of thing that could make money?"

Ruben laughed. "Oh, you have no idea. From what Michael said, it would revolutionize part of an industry."

"Did he ever say whether he'd spoken to anyone about this?"

"He never spoke about it. It was a secret."

"Just you, then?" I asked.

"Like I said, he spoke about it only in conceptual terms. I don't know what it is. I don't think anyone knows what it is."

"How about the conceptual terms, then. Do you think

you were the only one he told? Or would he have given other people a conceptual sense of his project?"

"Michael was private. He didn't need outside approval."

"So no one else even knew that he was working on something big. Just you and, to a lesser extent, Dean Timmeron."

"Right," Ruben said. Then, after a moment, he added, "And the money guys."

"What money guys?"

"Michael talked to some venture capital firms about his idea. Again, conceptually. He knew it was worth money. He wanted to have an idea about how to proceed when it became time to launch."

"Any names of the venture capital firms come to mind?"

"No. There was an outfit in Palo Alto. Another in San Jose. There was even a group in Tahoe, come to think of it."

"Do you remember him mentioning any names?"

"Not that I recall. He just called them venture capitalists. Sometimes he abbreviated and referred to them as the VC. I remember that because my dad was American and he was in Viet Nam. He talked about VC, too, but of course that was an abbreviation of a different term. Even so, it stuck in my mind."

"Okay, thanks," I said. "I appreciate your help. Let me give you my other numbers in case anything else comes to mind." I started to recite my phone numbers when he interrupted.

"One thing I do remember," he said.

"What's that."

"About the Tahoe VC. Michael said some name that I don't remember. But I recall that he referred to the name as like the writer."

"Emerson?" I said, thinking of Marlette's neighbor who said he invested in businesses.

"That's it. The American writer Emerson. The Tahoe firm was named Emerson, or Emerson was the name of one of the principals. Something like that."

FORTY-FIVE

I thanked Ruben, hung up the phone and went out to the Jeep. I was at Emerson Baylor's house fifteen minutes later.

I parked in his drive. There were no other cars in the drive, but the garage doors were closed and light shown from several of the windows. The doorbell chimed like a four-note chord on a church organ when I pushed the glowing button and I had to wait only a few seconds before Emerson opened the door.

"Hello?" he said, then, "Oh, you are the detective. I'm sorry, I forget your name." He was dressed in off-white trousers with crisp creases and tan leather slippers and a white dress shirt open at the neck and a tan V-neck sweater of exactly the same shade as the slippers. He held a snifter of brandy in his left hand.

"Owen McKenna," I said.

"Yes, of course. McKenna." He shook my hand and gestured with the snifter. "Please come in." He turned and walked into the house. "I'm just watching one of those crime shows. You know, unbelievable situations with no purpose other than to show off the tall femme fatale and her long hair and long legs and the taller lawman who makes a point of not leering even though the woman is wearing an outfit that should only be allowed in a bedroom and even then only with a permit from the county supervisors." He picked up a remote and turned off the big flat-screen TV on the far wall.

We were in a huge room suitable for a large spread in a magazine. There was a marble gas fireplace with large faux logs caressed with flame. Out in the room were multiple sitting areas and leather furniture with Native American throws artfully arranged across the chair arms. In one corner was a grouping of Washoe Indian woven baskets, poised as if for a still-life drawing class. At one end of the room was a brick wall painted white. On it, framed in a wide gold moulding, hung four small paintings of grand pianos, each from a different perspective and each highlighted by an ellipse of light from recessed ceiling lights. In front of the paintings was a large couch upholstered in a rough white fabric. The couch sat at right angles to a matching loveseat. At their intersection was a marble table on which sat a tall purple vase and from which sprouted a burst of red-orange gladiolus, again lit by a recessed light fixture.

Emerson waved his hand toward the furniture and said, "Have a seat. Anywhere you like."

I walked through a pattern of circles where ceiling cans threw light onto a thick white Berber carpet and sat on one of the couches. Emerson sat across from me. He held his snifter out and swirled his brandy, but I still hadn't seen him take a sip. "Can I get you a Remy Martin? I have the V.S.O.P.," he said.

"No thanks."

"You've made a breakthrough, have you?" Emerson said. "Or so I infer from your unannounced visit in the evening."

Up close, I could see a network of tiny veins across his nose and the balls of his cheeks. The thick white hair that I'd remembered looked a little less white and a little less thick. His speech, still warm and friendly, had gotten a little more thick.

"I've come to ask you about Michael Warner."

"Who?" Emerson frowned.

"Michael Warner is a physics professor at Sacramento State University."

"Warner? Michael Warner? I'm trying to remember."

"He's developed some kind of new idea and he's spoken to several venture capital firms including yours. I'm wondering what you can tell me about him."

Emerson stared at his glass and swirled his brandy. Light from the fireplace refracted through the liquid and threw amber kaleidoscope patterns over his face. He frowned. "I don't remember many of the details. There was a young man who made an appointment to see me a few months ago. We met at my new office over near the gondola that goes up to Heavenly. Was that Warner? Let me think." Emerson stood up, walked over to an open area of carpet and stood under the wash of one of the recessed lights. He looked like a performer in a play, in the spotlight, about to begin a soliloquy. I couldn't tell if he was trying to jog his memory or trying to buy time. He finally took a sip of brandy and then spoke. "Okay, it's coming back to me now. Michael Warner is a slim fellow, brown hair, brown eyes, about five-nine or ten? Late thirties or early forties? Real geeky as they say? Quite nervous?"

I realized I'd never gotten a mug-shot description of him, but it fit the way Marlette described her former lover. "I haven't met him. It sounds right."

Emerson was turning in the light. He shut his eyes and listed toward his left side as he spoke. "He came in and began talking about his invention. No hello or how are you. Just the focused talk of the scientist. I've heard it before. I think it's called Geek Speak. I've sometimes thought that the less someone has of the social niceties, the greater the chance they have a valuable invention. What do you think?" He looked at me.

"Could be," I said. "What was the result of the meeting?"

"He didn't go with us."

"Does that mean you offered to invest in his invention?"

"No, no. It's not like that. What I did was outline how it could work, not how it would work. I explained that if he had a marketable invention or concept, and if we felt there was a chance of substantial profit in it, we would undertake a feasibility study."

"Did he tell you what his invention was?"

"No. Not a chance. That young man is smart. He wanted to see how much information he could get out of me without playing any of his own cards. I also recall that he told me he was talking to several firms. He obviously wanted to play us against each other. See where he could get the best deal."

"How do you evaluate a proposal if you don't know what the focus of the proposal is?"

"You don't. All he told me was that he'd developed something new that could revolutionize a high-tech industry. He said it could greatly increase the efficiency of all high-tech industries. There would even be spillovers into consumer goods. Of course, those are grandiose concepts. And ninety-nine percent of them go nowhere. But hell, good ones do come along now and then. Apple Computer, Microsoft, eBay, Amazon. Wish I had put some VC into one of those. I wouldn't have had to work so hard in the auto and truck business."

"If you didn't know the invention, what could you tell him?"

"I just explained that many areas of inquiry are involved and it depends on what the invention or product category is. As a potential investment partner, we'd seek to identify the current market for the concept as well as potential future markets. What will this thing sell for and what are the potential profits? If it is a new kind of long distance service, for example, it has the advantage of being used by everyone, but the profits are measured in pennies per customer. On the other hand, if it is a new kind of luxury boat, the market is very small, but the profit per customer can be quite large. An iPod is somewhere in between.

"I explained about target demographics and the critical aspect of whether or not they are upward trending or downward trending. I talked about production costs. What kind of human resources will we need and can we find the talent? What will be the costs of the physical plants necessary to build the item, if in fact it is an item?

"Equally important is the marketing. How will we bring this to market? How long a run will it have? How easily can we lock it up with patents and such? How little time will pass before competitors jump on the idea and out-perform us?"

"How did he respond to these concepts?" I asked.

"As I said, despite his nervousness, young Mr. Warner is focused and direct. He asked me how much I needed to know before I could float him some numbers. I explained I had to know what he had before I could give him specifics. He asked me to make it hypothetical. So I got out a calculator and did a little figuring and gave him a hypothetical."

"What was it?"

Emerson shook his head. "I work with numbers all day long. I can't remember specifics unless I'm consulting my notes. Suffice to say that a hypothetical would be based on what our return on investment would be. Some ideas aren't worth taking a chance on. Some are worth throwing a million or two into. Less than that and it isn't really worth the time. The ideal for our group would be a ten million-dollar investment in return for fifty-one percent ownership and a company that had the potential of sky-high returns." Emerson smiled at me. "We don't expect to find the next Dell Computer. But it would be nice."

"Is that the scenario you floated by Michael Warner?"

"Something like that."

"Why do you think he went elsewhere?"

"He said he thought his idea might take several million or more to launch and had enormous potential. But he said he'd want to run the company and own fifty-one percent. I told him that was a smart idea, but that serious investors want control. If he worked with us, we'd insist on majority ownership, and one of our firm would be chairman and we'd pick the CEO. That fellow would naturally want to work closely with Michael, but our CEO would be in charge. I think that is what sent Michael Warner on his way."

"I'm curious," I said. "Why didn't you work with him a little more? If his idea is great, wouldn't it be worth it to let him be boss? You could still own fifty-one percent."

"It's a good question," Emerson said, nodding. "It does happen where the creator ends up being the boss. Bill Gates, Steve Jobs, Bezos at Amazon, Page and Brin at Google. Sometimes that works well. But it's uncommon. Business skills are completely different than invention skills. You almost always have to bring in a grayhair with a lot of experience running a corporation if you want any chance of success. But the main reason I wouldn't do it with Michael Warner is that despite his smarts he isn't good boss material. I've been in business a long time and I can read people.

"For example, one of our outfits is just starting production of a new innovative handheld device. We're doing it all in Reno, sales and marketing, product development and manufacturing. I don't understand the details of how this thing works, but it does nearly everything your laptop does, plus it talks to everything you own. Your office computer network, your home coffee maker, your DVD player, your garage door opener. The two guys who came up with it are wizards, but they could never manage people and run a business. So we brought in a guy from Intel to be CEO. The initial orders look like we've got a hit. If so, the minority ownership stake of those two young men will bring them millions. A good deal for all."

"And you serve as chairman," I guessed.

Emerson grinned. "Yes. But it is a figurehead position. All of us have equal shares in our group so we split the profits or losses of the group equally."

"How many in your investment group?"

"There are seven of us. Because our original buy-in was the same for all, we each get one vote. With seven votes there is always a majority. Easy to make decisions. Our eventual goal is seven companies. Bill Reed is chairman of the second company in Mountain View. They are another manufacturer of computer peripherals. You probably know Bill? He owns a bunch of restaurants around the lake. Active in the Chamber of Commerce and such."

My phone rang. "Sorry," I interrupted. "I should answer this."

"Of course. No problem at all."

I fished my cell out of my pocket. "Owen McKenna," I said.

"Mr. McKenna, I'm Shirley Letmeyer with Century 21. I was at the meeting where you showed all of us realtors the drawing of that house you were looking for? Well, I found it."

FORTY-SIX

I asked Shirley to hold, covered the phone, thanked Emerson, told him I had to go.

"Yes, of course." He swirled the still-full snifter. "Come back any time. It was good to talk to you."

Once outside, I got in my car before I resumed talking on the phone.

"The house matches the drawing?" I said to Shirley.

"Yes. I went to a listing call and I spotted it just down the street. I looked for a long time. Of course, I was very careful. No one could see me holding the drawing under my steering wheel."

"You got the address?"

"Yes. It's over in the North Upper Truckee neighborhood. It's on one of those loops. There's a fence around it and there's another house right next door. But they're the only two houses on that part of the street. The other nearby lots are vacant. They're probably unbuildable because they are steep and one of them has what looks like some seasonal seepage. And you know how the Tahoe Regional Planning Agency is about water flow..."

I interrupted her and asked for the address. She read it off as I backed out of Emerson's driveway.

It was quite dark and the moon was just rising over Heavenly, looking very full even though it wasn't technically full for two more nights. I drove across town out to North Upper Truckee and began to watch the street signs closely. I drove past the road with the target house, continued two more blocks and turned off to the west. I came to the end of a loop, parked and shut off the engine.

I had a flashlight in the car, but I wanted more privacy than that, so I waited a couple of minutes for my eyes to adjust to the moonlit night.

It was easy to find a way around the neighboring houses. I came through the woods and approached the target house, eager to see if it matched the drawing that Silence had presumably sent on a paper airplane flight to the neighbor. Even though I approached from the back and side, the match was obvious. Roof layout, gable dormers, shed dormer and window positions. I eased my way closer to the backyard fence and studied the tree that was just outside of the upstairs window.

The branches were clear in the neighbor's yard light. I counted each section from the first split above the trunk. Two, three, five, eight, thirteen, twenty-one. I moved around to one of the nearby vacant lots, staying in the shadows, peering out from behind the large trunks of mature Jeffrey pines.

In front of the house were three motorcycles glistening in the dark, the chrome reflecting every tiny bit of light from distant houses. I didn't recognize the Low Rider painted blue with yellow pinstripes. But the Fat Boy had a green gas tank and the chopper a red tank. Marky and Tiptoe.

Inside the house was the blue light of a TV in the living room. There were no other lights on down or up.

I gradually traced most of a circle around the house and ended up near the neighbor's house. I made note of the number, then worked my way back through the woods to my Jeep.

Back on the East Shore, I stopped at Street's. We sipped wine in front of her fire while I gave her a summary of what I learned. An hour later, we said goodnight and Spot and I headed up the mountain to my cabin.

Spot, drunk on hotdogs and hugs from Street, lay down and went to sleep while I got to work on the computer.

The house where Marky and Tiptoe possibly held Silence

was owned by a woman in Modesto. There was no way to tell if Marky and Tiptoe were connected to her or had her permission to use her house as their base camp.

The neighbor's house was owned by Mathew and Tillie Bilkenstein. They had lived there for thirty-two years. A little more research revealed that Mathew had been deceased eight of those thirty-two years and Tillie, 88, had lived there alone ever since. Then I found a reference to another Bilkenstein in a law enforcement journal. The article, dated two years earlier, related the case of a San Jose-area woman who was shot and killed in her house by a robber dressed in a police uniform. The victim was Mandy Bilkenstein. She was single, 59, with no children or siblings. Her only surviving relative was her mother in Tahoe, Tillie Bilkenstein.

Was Tillie the police-phobic letter carrier, confused and frightened by the bikers next door? Did she find the paper airplanes in her yard and deliver them to the high school? I wanted to bring her some flowers and knock on her door and drink her tea and ask her if she'd seen the girl in the upstairs window next door. But I didn't dare risk the attention of Marky and Tiptoe.

Knowing where Silence might be, where she'd been imprisoned for two weeks, burned a hot hole in my gut and I could barely keep myself from going back there now, this time with Spot, and drive my Jeep through the front wall of the house and send Spot in with the attack command. I was enough cranked up about it that I actually thought I would have half a chance. Twenty years ago I wouldn't have hesitated. A one-man blitz against three dirtballs.

Now I was more restrained. I wanted to think my restraint was mature judgement rather than lack of courage.

I turned off my computer and sat in my rocker in the dark and rested my legs on his largeness and drank a couple beers.

With nothing else to do but churn, I went to bed.

Hours of sleepless fatigue later, I still lay in bed, unable to sleep, heart pounding with adrenaline-powered anger as I thought about Silence.

I thought of her mother's video and remembered the way Silence looked away from inquiring eyes, moved in her strange repetitive fashion, performing her daily chores in the ritualistic way that gave her comfort knowing that each part of life had its predictable rhythm and its proper place.

I saw her retreat from the celebrations of others, confusion and worry on her face, uncomprehending how other people had the easy speech that allowed them to say what they think, tell what they want, give voice to their dreams.

I saw her crushing the poor unknowing dog in the powerful grip of desperation and desire. I saw her crawling under her mattress for the squeeze that helped her shut out a harsh world where noise and visual commotion and the overwhelming jumble of life rose to a crescendo and threatened her sanity. I saw her unable to communicate, speak or write, living in a place where her thoughts and worries and hopes were locked in a brain with no ordinary outlet.

Mostly, I saw her spinning round and round, shutting out the inputs, smoothing away the roughness of life, bowing her head to face the earth as if it held in its elemental purity some kind of safety zone.

And I saw the smile. Her gleeful response to spinning that had escaped notice by the rest of the world.

The silent grin.

I looked at the clock. 5:00 a.m.

I got out of bed and pulled on my jeans and sweatshirt and running shoes. Spot always senses a break in pattern and he stood at my side, looking up at me, ears focused, brow furrowed, nose pushing at my hip, wondering what I was up to.

We walked outside under a cold night sky lit by a moon so bright that only the most brilliant stars could be seen. Across the lake the snow-covered mountains stood in stark white relief against the black sky. In the far distance was the tiny flash of the anti-collision strobes on a jet, one or two hundred people cruising south, six or seven miles above the Central Valley or maybe above the coastal range or maybe even out over the Pacific, on course to land in L.A. or San Diego or Acapulco.

I stood alone in my frozen driveway and bowed my head like Silence did. Then I slowly turned around one full rotation, then did it again fast. My cabin wavered and tilted and I felt a touch light-headed. In a moment the world steadied. Spot was wagging, giving me the look that means he is considering jumping on me. I turned twice again and the same little dizziness crept up, then evaporated away. I remembered turning as a child and feeling the giddy dizziness that it brought on. I liked it then.

I rotated three more times in a row and stopped as the uncomfortable feeling returned. I didn't like it now.

Spot liked it. He bounced on his front feet, ready to leap. I held out my palm.

Maybe the trick was found in constancy. When Silence began spinning she kept going, speeding up, becoming more stable not less.

So I took a couple of deep breaths and counted one, two, three, go.

I pushed off into a fast spin and kept it going, pushing it harder as the world streaked and blurred and Spot elongated into a moonlit rush of black and white and his barks roared from one ear to the other and I went faster and faster still.

And then the ground went vertical and slammed my knee and hip and elbow, and my head suddenly felt as though it had twisted a few degrees too far on my neck, and my sinuses made that prickly sensation that comes from a shock to the skull.

I lay my head down on the dirt while Spot bounded around my prostrate form, and I thought about Silence trapped in the upstairs room in that house with three big stinking men standing guard. Silence's only ally was an old lady next door, a woman with no family, who lived alone, whose friends had probably all died, a woman frightened to death of anyone in a police uniform. I wanted to rush in and save the child, but I felt the powerlessness that comes from being a pariah, from being alone at night, from not having a sound plan.

I couldn't even spin.

FORTY-SEVEN

The next day I explained my plan to Street. She was predictably concerned, not just for my safety, but also about whether she would do her part perfectly, for everything depended on her acting ability.

I assured her she would do fine and added that she'd have Spot with her for protection, and that Diamond would cover her as well. Then I called Diamond and explained my request.

"A lot could go wrong," he said.

"I know. But the potential problems are small against a girl's life. One more day until the full moon."

"If the full moon thing is real."

"Can't take the chance it isn't," I said.

Diamond was silent. Then he said, "This will be unofficial?"

"I did it the official way before."

"And it blew up in your face," he said. "I'll see what I can do."

I left Spot with Street and asked her to wait for my call in approximately two hours. Then I drove through town to the house where I believed Silence was held prisoner. I parked three blocks away. The Jeep would be my safety vehicle. I chose a place that would be easy to get to in the dark in case my plan didn't work.

At the end of the road I found one of the many entrance trails that lead to the large network of trails in the forest between the North Upper Truckee neighborhood and the ridge from Angora Peak to Echo Peak to Flagpole Peak. I followed the trail back toward the street with the target house. There was another trail that led to that street as well, but I stayed in the forest and found a small rise with a group of fir trees. It took a bit of shifting to get comfortable, but I was able to lie under them and have a clear view through their branches. My binoculars are eight-power, have a small field and are lightweight. So it is hard to get a steady view. After arranging small piles of needles to make hollows for my elbows, I settled down to watch, my body and arms holding the glasses steady as if they were on a tripod.

The same three bikes were out front. Marky's and Tiptoe's and a third. Except for two Steller's jays playing tag in the fir in the front yard, there was no movement. Nothing moved in any of the windows, upstairs or down.

I studied the house again, revisiting the question of how much it matched Silence's drawing. It seemed perfect in every way.

But so did the one in the Sierra Tract neighborhood. And in that one Diamond even saw a girl who looked like Silence.

Here, I had no indication of a girl. I watched the upstairs window. There was no light, no movement, nothing to reinforce my thinking that she was there. All I had was three motorcycles, and I couldn't be positive that any of them were Marky's and Tiptoe's. I hadn't gotten the license numbers. I couldn't see the license plates now, either. How many other bikes in the basin looked just like these? There could be many. And while the house looked just like the drawing, how many other houses were there like that, built to the same design, perhaps built by the same builder?

Doubts began to permeate my thinking. Was I planning another folly? Would I burst in on more innocent kids? Without the benefit of a search warrant executed by the El Dorado Sheriff's Department, I was taking a huge risk. Like before, the house might be the wrong one. If so, I would be convicted of Breaking and Entering and if someone got hurt, Assault and Battery. With Spot involved, it could escalate to Assault with a Deadly Weapon.

I could spend the rest of my years in prison.

The alternative would be to try again what I did with Mallory. Because I was out of the city limits of South Lake Tahoe, I'd need to contact the county sheriff and try to convince him that I had a case.

But I had no real evidence. Two of the three motorcycles looked like two other bikes I'd seen. The house looked like a drawing. In a court of law it was nothing. The sheriff would never even ask a judge for a warrant. He'd think it a joke.

I had no other options. Play it safe for me and others and leave Silence at serious risk. Or go in myself and risk my future. And not only mine. I was asking both Street and Diamond to help me. If Silence wasn't in the house, they'd be accessories to my mistake and be charged with crimes along with me.

I took several deep breaths to try and clear my head. I was nuts. I couldn't put my lover and my best friend at risk. I was too close to the situation to see it clearly. The video of Silence spinning, trying to cope with a frightening world, had played too many times in my head.

I decided to call it off.

I put the binoculars in my pocket, and I started to slide out of my hiding place when something caught my eye.

Movement at the house. The front door opening. I put the glasses back on the house.

A man stepped out of the door. He walked over to the blue Low Rider. He set his half-helmet on his thick pile of long brown hair and pulled the chin strap through a bushy beard. He turned back to the house and said something. I watched the door as Marky and Tiptoe came out. Marky spoke, then both of them watched as the first man started up his machine, made a big sweeping turn into the street and roared away, the intense rat-tat-tat of his engine noise shaking every window for a mile.

FORTY-EIGHT

I was walking down North Upper Truckee, several blocks away from the house, when Street pulled up as planned. I jumped in and she drove away.

"How did it go?" she said.

"I saw Marky and Tiptoe." Spot was sniffing me from the little backseat of the VW bug.

"Any sign of Silence?"

"No."

"But you're still convinced this is the house and you should go in."

"Yes."

Street drove home while I turned on my cell to check for Diamond's message. He'd called around the time Street picked me up. The message was short. He was able to acquire a tranquilizer gun from Solomon Reed, the large animal vet down in Carson Valley.

I dialed Diamond.

When he answered I said, "Doc Reed ask you why you wanted a tranquilizer gun?"

"I told him we might have another mountain lion to capture."

"Were you able to get off work?"

"Yeah. I'll be there in fifteen minutes or so. Got a sandwich and a thermos of coffee. Come evening, I'll move into the woods, stretch my legs and such. So don't worry if you see my truck empty. At the appropriate time, I'll get into position in the trees across the street."

"Thanks."

Street dropped me off at home and kept Spot with her.

Diamond called just as I walked inside.

"I'm in position and I saw the old neighbor lady," Diamond said.

"Tillie Bilkenstein?"

"Yeah. She's kind of cute. Walks real straight up and stiff. Takes little steps. Real little. She went to her mail box and then, get this, she walked over to her side yard and looked around at the grass like she was looking for something. Then she looked up over the fence and stared at the upstairs window of the neighbor's house."

"Where we think Silence is," I said.

"Right."

"She's our letter carrier."

"Looks like it," Diamond said.

"I'm glad you saw that," I said. "Remember to put your phone on vibrate."

"Already did."

I ate a large enough meal to cover both lunch and dinner, then went over my plans in my head. I sat on the deck chair, staring at the lake, and visualized each step of the next few hours.

Late in the evening I rode the Harley through South Lake Tahoe, headed out past the airport and on out to the little community called Meyers that lies just before the long climb up to Echo Summit. I kept the exhaust valve on the loud setting as I went through the Meyers commercial district, which is little more than a couple of gas stations and a small gourmet grocery store.

The fall evening was bitter cold to a motorcyclist, and the hard moist wind blowing up from the Central Valley formed lenticular clouds that hovered over the mountaintops and caught a mystery glow from the stars and the rising moon.

I cruised past the chain-up area where Charlie's body had been found, crossed the Truckee River and began the incline up to the summit. Once again, I came to North Upper Truckee. This time I drove past the turnoff. Although my destination was the house just a couple blocks off North Upper Truckee, I wanted to sneak in from the woods behind.

So I continued on up the summit. The next road was Chiapa, which led into a small closed neighborhood of expensive homes. I cruised on by, then slowed as I approached the first big curve in the highway that turns to the left and crawls up the side of the cliff. I backed the throttle to idle, leaned hard into a right turn and coasted into the small parking area where Caltrans has their avalanche control tower.

It is shaped something like a modern lighthouse. Tonight it was dark, awaiting future snowfalls on the mountain above the road up to the summit. When the danger of avalanche is imminent, Highway 50 is temporarily closed, the big doors are opened, and the explosive artillery is fired up onto the huge granite slope above. The explosive charges release the snow in small controlled avalanches preventing an unplanned catastrophic slide that could bury all traffic on the highway.

I braked to a stop at the edge of the small parking area, checked to make sure that no one was in view, then reached down and turned the valve that rerouted my exhaust through the hidden muffler.

The result was as dramatic this time as before. The deep, throaty blat-blat of the Harley went silent, replaced by a soft, airy whish-whish. I still looked like a bad-ass biker, but I was a phantom.

I hit the first switch that Slider had put on the handlebars. My headlight and running lights went dark as I toggled it off. When I braked, no red light would come on. Using only moonglow from the mountains and clouds to see, I went around the locked gate and onto a trail that is used by hikers and mountain bikers in the summer and snowmobilers in the winter. I followed the dark twisting trail a short distance down into the forest.

As soon as I was away from the highway, I stopped where a group of trees hid me from view, then pulled out the roll of duct tape that I'd stashed in the left saddlebag. I ripped off a piece and stuck it over the upper half of my headlight, curved like a visor. Then I used a socket wrench and screwdriver to adjust the headlight so it would shine more to the ground than normal. I wanted to minimize any chance that anyone out enjoying the moonlight would notice me riding through the woods. I flipped the second switch and my new, lower beam headlight came on, while all the other lights stayed off.

The soft muffled putter of my bike along with my truncated headlight beam was reassuring. I felt the strange lonely comfort that comes from being in the mountain woods at night when everyone else is indoors watching TV.

I rode slowly, the suspension providing a cushioning bounce and wallow as I went up and over bumps and humps, in and around trees and giant boulders, following a trail carved through the thick forest.

The trail led to a small meadow directly below Flagpole peak, rugged and frosty in the cold moonlight. Then I was back into thick forest where I joined another trail, well worn from hikers and mountain bikers. I drove at five or ten miles per hour, crawling a mile and then two into the forest. I went up a rise and for a moment saw the slow crawl of a headlight on one of the ski trails at Heavenly twelve miles distant, a snowcat doing a test groom on the heavy snow that fell at 10,000 feet the previous week.

I slowed to nearly a stop, went past a huge fir tree and turned off on a small access trail. Fifty yards ahead I pulled off the trail, drove through a thicket of trees, turned back around and stopped so that my bike was pointed back through an opening that led straight to the trail.

The forest floor was too soft for the kickstand, so I leaned the bike against a tree and turned it off.

Although the newly muffled engine had been relatively quiet, the sudden total silence was thick in my ears. I stood in the dark forest, smelling the cold humid air, heavy with scents of pine and the peppery herbal aroma of a late fall nightshade plant. The bitter wind was softer in the trees than out on the highway, but it still made a hum in the pine needles, rising in pitch, then falling.

I pulled a penlight from my pocket and used it to move through the thicket, trying to figure a plan for how I was going to find the bike. Despite the moon, it would be dark under the tree canopy, and I'd be in a hurry. I'd have the girl with me, and I'd be pursued by angry men with guns.

I decided to make a barricade and put down some kind of marker to precede it. For a barricade, I wedged a broken branch across the trail, bridging it from one tree to another at stomach height. I placed it just after a turn on the path. Watch for it carefully and you could get past it by crashing through the thicket to the right. Be less careful and you'd be likely to run straight into it and knock the wind out of yourself.

For my marker I heaped a pile of needles in the middle of the trail ten yards before the obstructing branch. I could kick it aside as it warned me. Anyone coming behind me would be unaware. But it would require that I had a good feel for the path in the dark.

I walked fifty yards toward the nearby neighborhood and turned off the penlight. I waited for my eyes to adjust to the dark, then gave my marker a test.

Running at medium speed, penlight off, straining my eyes for a sense of the trail in the dark, I watched for the pile of pine needles. The path went left, then straight, then right. A branch slapped my face. I leaned sideways to let it slip off. My left foot hit a small boulder. I spun to the side, hit another boulder and sprawled into the dirt.

My chin bounced on gravel and I rolled to a stop. As I rose on my knees, grabbing a sore elbow, my head bumped the barricade.

I never saw the pile of pine needles.

The solution was to make the pile bigger. Then I'd have a better chance of plowing into the pile and knowing the barricade was soon after.

After another, more successful practice run, I continued on through the woods toward the house where I believed Silence was being held.

I checked my watch. 10:50 p.m. Ten minutes to liftoff. I'd chosen the time because the moon would be high and night vision would be good.

The small knoll where I crouched had a view of the house and the street. To the side was the house where Tillie Bilkenstein lived, the lady who picks up paper airplanes that glide down over the fence into her backyard. Her house was dark. She was gone or she'd gone to bed.

I looked at my watch. Four minutes. Diamond would be in the trees across the street, veterinary dart gun ready and trained on the front door.

Street would have parked off North Upper Truckee, on a side road a block away. She was going to walk through the dark, Spot at her side. I'd reminded her how to lay her finger across his nose and whisper "Quiet" in his ear. At this moment, three minutes before eleven, she and Spot would be waiting near Diamond, in the shadows of the giant firs.

She would tell Spot to "Sit-Stay" in the dark of the trees. Then she would walk across and knock on the door of the house. Whether Marky and Tiptoe peaked out the upstairs window or looked through the peephole in the door, all they would see was a thin woman standing in the dark at the front door, obviously unarmed, obviously no threat at all.

The moment they opened the door, Diamond would draw a bead on them with his dart gun. Street would sob and point toward the dark curb and tell them about the terrible situation she'd come across, the sweet Golden Retriever that lay in the road, the Golden named Honey Bun from three blocks over, the same Honey Bun who was the darling of every neighborhood kid, wounded from a hit-and-run. Could they please come and help! Could they lift the dog into her car? Could they come quickly and maybe save the dog's life?

As soon as either Marky or Tiptoe got more than thirty feet from the house, she'd point at him and yell, "Spot, take down the suspect!" Neither one of them would be quick enough to get back to the safety of the house.

If any comrades came out of the house, Diamond would attempt to hit them with a tranquilizer dart.

While Spot held one of them and Diamond ran to help, I hoped to kick in the boards over the upstairs window, get Silence out onto the garage roof and down into the forest where we could escape on the silent bike with no running lights.

I checked my watch. 10:57 p.m.

There was no light on in the upstairs room where I thought Silence was being held. From my position in the trees, I could see just a glimmer of light shining out into the yard from the living room. I heard a few grunting sounds like muffled laughter coming from big men with deep chests. A poker game, maybe. Or guffaws generated by a porno movie.

I waited, watching, nervous as a kid about to confront a Grizzly bear being let out of its cage.

At two minutes before eleven, I climbed up into the Lodgepole pine at the rear corner of the house and snaked my way out onto the branch over the back of the garage. I found a good set of handholds and swung down. I held there a moment, hanging from my hands, visualizing Street telling Spot to stay and then walking across the street to knock on the door.

I was about to drop to the garage roof, silent as a cat, when the branch I hung from broke, and I fell in a loud crash to the roof.

FORTY-NINE

Before I'd rolled to a stop, a shout roared from the house. I couldn't make out the words. It sounded like a command. What happened next was like a Green Beret unit suddenly going on red alert. The lights that had shined out onto the yard below went dark. The movements of heavy men thudded through the house.

The evacuation was going according to plan.

I could try to interrupt it.

I ran to the upstairs window that opened onto the garage roof. I kicked out at the glass and frame and the boards that went across. Once. Twice. Glass exploded into the dark room. Boards cracked, splintered, then fell away. I swept my foot around the opening once more to knock out protruding shards, then ducked through into the musty darkness.

"Silence," I whispered, "Can you hear me?"

I was too late.

More footsteps pounded below. I turned on my penlight and shined it around the room. Silence was not there. The only sign that she'd been in the room was a small torn sketchbook on the floor by the door. One page faced up at me. It was a self-portrait of Silence. Her eyes were huge and sad in my penlight. One side of her face was on paper that had torn off.

I ran through the bedroom door into the hallway. The stairway went down the center of the house. I ran down the stairs as the back door slammed. I followed them at a run.

Once outside I realized I could call Spot from the trees on the other side of the house. But I thought better of it. Street would need him for protection.

I heard men going over the fence and into the trees away from where I'd left the bike. Not knowing the trail they were on, I followed the sounds, running blind, trying to stay close.

The sounds turned. I took several more steps, then turned the same direction.

I saw movement up ahead. In the faint glow of a distant post light were moving shadows. One of them had a strange shape. A big man carrying a thin girl.

I raced on.

Although it was hard to see through the trees, it looked like the men were angling toward where I parked the Jeep. They stopped and got into a panel van. There was a distant streetlight and I saw at least two men. There might have been a third. I'd expected three or four from the thud of footsteps leaving the house.

The giant man, Tiptoe, held Silence. She was strangely rigid, and as he put her into a van it was more like he was holding a stiff 2x12 than a 17-year-old girl.

I couldn't get to them in time, so I sprinted to the Jeep. I was fumbling my key into the door when I heard footsteps behind me. I jerked the door open and was swinging my body inside as I heard the same sliding snick I'd last heard when Diamond cocked his nine millimeter Glock the night a killer came into his house down in Carson Valley.

"Don't think about it." The man panted from running.

I turned to see Marky standing fifteen feet away, the gun up and pointed at my chest. Marky's heaving lungs made the gun waver. But I didn't think he'd miss at short range.

I started to get out of the Jeep.

"Un, uh. Stay where you are. You're driving." He pulled open the back door and got in behind me. I felt the cold blunt end of the automatic against the back of my neck.

I turned the starter. "How far are we going? I need gas."

Marky leaned to look at the gauge. "You're okay. See that van? Follow it."

I pulled forward and drove up behind an old dark panel van. A Dodge. No doubt, Michael Warner's.

The van pulled away and I followed. I thought about ramming it, trying to rip it open so that I could grab Silence and carry her into the woods. But the gun barrel on the back of my neck was a strong motivator to do as Marky said.

The van headed toward town, went toward the "Y" intersection and turned off into the supermarket parking lot. It stopped in the far corner, facing away from the few other vehicles that belonged to late-shift employees and the odd customer.

The driver door opened and Tiptoe got out, leaving Silence inside. He shut the door, checked to make sure the other doors were locked, then came over to my Jeep. He opened the passenger door and got in, grunting with effort. His bulk filled the passenger seat almost to the dashboard. His head was jammed against the Jeep's headliner. The suspension tipped to the right.

"Watch his hands," Marky called out.

Tiptoe tried to turn his massive body toward me, jerking in his seat with the dexterity of a rhinoceros.

"Okay," Marky said, "turn out of the parking lot over there and head toward Emerald Bay."

I drove down Emerald Bay Road. For a time Marky and Tiptoe were silent, and I kept a watch for an oncoming cop that I could skid in front of. Any unusual maneuver might make Marky blow my brains out, but they intended to kill me anyway.

I thought of Silence, tied up in the back of the van, scared beyond anything she'd ever known.

We cruised by Camp Richardson and headed out the dark highway to Emerald Bay. As I drove up the switchbacks, the nearly full moon was high above Heavenly, shining on the white of the high-altitude snow, casting moon shadows from the giant Ponderosa pines along the highway and splashing a bright white glow on the mountains above Emerald Bay.

"Let's see what shorty here listen to," Tiptoe suddenly said as he grabbed my stack of CDs off the center console. He flipped on the reading light and leafed through the CDs, saying the names haltingly, with excruciating pronunciation. "Count Bah-si-ee, Ss-chewbert, Lou Reed. Hey, I hearda him. London Phil-har-moan-ic, Mozz-art Con-ser-to for Obo-ee. Nothin' I recognize. No Lynard Skynard, no Allman Brothers."

"See if he got Johnny Cash," Marky interrupted. "Johnny played at Folsom Prison. He's my man."

I was climbing the switchbacks, heading down the road toward the point of Emerald Bay.

"No Johnny Cash," Tiptoe said. He tossed all the CDs but one on the floor. Let's see what this stuff sound like. This one is..." he paused, working his lips. "Kelsey Stanton Cho-ire."

He put the Kelsey Stanton CD in the player. One of the choral numbers came on, filling the jeep with a full range of voices, basses, baritones and tenors with the sopranos arching above all.

"Whoa, Marky, listen what it say on the paper. 'Kelsey Stanton is a all male chorus.'" Tiptoe turned toward me in his seat as much as a 400-pound slab of fat can turn in the confines of a Jeep seat. "You tellin' me them high voices is all male? Hey, Marky, shorty like men with high voices." He cocked a grease-darkened middle finger behind his thumb, reached over and flicked it hard across the tip of my nose. "That so, boy?"

The pain was sharp. The ex-cop in me almost exploded. I could have killed him with an elbow chop to the Adam's apple, but I knew the man behind me would splatter my brains across the windshield. Marky sensed my tension. He jammed the gun barrel hard into the back of my skull. After a long silence he said, "What's the answer, McKenna?"

"I like their music," I said. "I've never met the men."

"Jus like I thought, Marky," Tiptoe said. "Shorty like men with girlie voices. Now that I look at him, shorty look kinda soft hisself. You gonna tell us what you do with them high-voice types, shorty?"

I didn't speak.

Tiptoe ordered, "Answer me, boy."

I was watching the road. The Emerald Bay parking lot

was up ahead. If I said the right thing and timed it just so, their reaction might give me an opening... I said, "I can tell you about a scientific study that was reported in the New York Times. Psychologists at a university studied a large group of men. They found that the men who were the most homophobic were the ones who had the biggest response to male stimuli."

"What he mean, Marky?" Tiptoe asked, his voice small.

Maybe Marky didn't understand because he didn't answer.

"What it means," I said, "is when they show pictures of well-muscled men to a group of guys, the ones who couldn't care less what someone does in the privacy of their own bedroom don't have a reaction. But the gay-bashers like you are the ones who get erections. The homophobia is really just self-repulsion."

The reaction took a second. Tiptoe tensed so much I anticipated his assault. He swung his right fist out toward my jaw. I stomped on the brake and jerked my head to the left. His fist rolled off my chin. I cranked the wheel and the Jeep slid sideways into the Emerald Bay parking area. I shoved the shifter into Park, hit the door handle and rolled out my door onto the pavement. I rolled again, saw a downed branch and reached out to grab it. It was thin, but seemed strong.

Marky came out first, gun raised. I swung the branch onto the arm with the gun. The sound of wood on forearm was solid. The gun fell. I did a poor version of a front kick, but he was slow and the edge of my shoe caught his jaw on the outside. He went down. I dove, grabbed the gun, rolled again and came up as Tiptoe came around the Jeep.

"You think I'm afraid of Marky's little Glock, yer dumb as yer queer friends," Tiptoe said.

I took careful aim at his thigh in the darkness and fired. It was the first time I'd even held a gun since I left the SFPD. It didn't feel good, but it did the job.

Tiptoe screamed and fell to the ground grabbing his leg. He rolled over, bawling like a baby. "You killed me! I'm going to die! Oh, God, it hurts! I can't stand it!"

I saw where the bullet went in, and it was a good distance from his femoral artery, which meant he'd live. But the bullet possibly caught the outside of his femur and shattered it, which meant he'd be in serious misery.

I turned to see Marky standing in the darkness, staring at Tiptoe. He was holding his arm where I'd struck him. He bent down and used his good arm to pick up the piece of wood I'd used. He advanced on me, swinging the wood from side to side.

I thought about shooting him, but it would be like one of those hunting ranches where the prey is set up in advance. So I tucked the automatic in my belt and waited, arms out and ready, for him to come at me.

He was a big man, almost as strong as Tiptoe, but not bogged down with 150 extra pounds of fat. He varied the swing so the stick went at my feet, then at my head. I jumped back, then ducked. On the third swing, I bent at the waist as it cut the air by my midsection, then I jumped inside. I made two quick jabs at his jaw, then put all my weight into a belly shot. He bent forward as the air went out of his system. I grabbed his head and pulled it onto my rising knee. I didn't want to kill him or even knock him out. If someone picked up the van with Silence in it, I needed Marky to tell me where to find her.

But my knee may have carried too much force.

He went up and back and fell hard onto his back. I thought he was out. I squatted down in the dark and knelt on him with one knee on his chest and my other foot next to his shoulder. He surprised me.

He turned his head and sunk his teeth into my ankle.

I felt his teeth cut through sinew and into bone.

One of his hands was palm up on the pavement, next to his ear.

I pulled the gun out of my belt, put the barrel on the base of his thumb and fired.

FIFTY

The explosion was loud enough for me, ear shattering for Marky.

He curled like a caterpillar into a tight ball. Unlike Tiptoe, Marky was soundless. His thumbless hand gripped the opposite shoulder. The blood from his thumb artery pulsed like a little geyser, but, like Tiptoe's injury, it was not life-threatening.

I stood and tapped my shoe toe on the back of his skull. "Get up!" He rolled onto his knees and slowly pushed himself up.

"Can't hear," he whispered. He held the bloodied hand to the side of his head. "Gun blew out my ear."

I directed him into the driver's seat, then got in next to him. "Put your hands on the wheel," I said. "Hurry!"

He didn't respond, just held his ear.

I said it again, almost a shout.

He did as I told him. I put the key in the ignition, turned and started the Jeep. The headlights came on and illuminated Tiptoe writhing in the dark parking lot.

"Drive!" I shouted. "Hurry, or I'll put your nose where your thumb is!" I put the gun barrel against his nose.

"Where?" Marky said, shaking.

"Back to the parking lot at the supermarket! Where Tiptoe left the van with the girl in it!"

Marky pulled out of the lot and turned toward town.

"Faster!" I yelled. I pressed the gun into his face.

Marky whimpered as he raced around Emerald Bay and down the switchbacks.

I fished under the passenger seat and found the roll of duct tape I keep there. I tore off a piece and stretched it over the stump of his thumb. Marky winced. The blood still oozed, but the tape slowed it down.

We went through Camp Richardson at 60 or 70, the narrow road unwinding like film in our headlights, the giant Ponderosa pines flying by like nightmare trees.

There were no cops as we came into town, engine racing, speedometer needle hovering around 80. Marky swerved around several cars and pickups. His last obstacle was a semi-truck making the turn on Lake Tahoe Blvd. Marky skidded sideways past him, then spun the other way into the supermarket parking lot.

The van was gone. Marky came to a stop, his chest heaving with fear.

"Where is the girl?" I said.

"I dunno."

"Where were you going to take me?"

"What?"

I repeated myself, louder.

"Bliss State Park."

"Why there?"

"We were supposed to take you in there and question you. See if you knew how to make the girl talk. Then we were supposed to drown you in the lake."

"Rubicon Point," I surmised. "Where the bottom drops off so steep my body might never be found."

Marky said nothing. He sat in the parking lot, hands shaking on the wheel, blood dripping onto the floor mats. It looked like a lot of blood. I didn't think he was going to go into shock, but I couldn't be sure. I wanted to call Street and Diamond, but I needed to get as much information as possible out of Marky while he was still lucid.

"Pull out of the lot and drive south," I said.

Marky did as told.

I wondered if Emerson Baylor was part of the connection between Tony Go and Michael Warner. I said, "Gomez ever mention Emerson Baylor?" I spoke loud enough that it was nearly a shout.

Marky was slow to respond.

"What?"

"Tony Go. He mention a man named Emerson Baylor?"

"No."

"Did Baylor ever call you?"

"No." Marky's voice was weak. He sounded dazed.

"What does Tony Go think Silence knows?"

"I don't know exactly. Something technical. He said it had something to do with storage. It was hard to hear over the phone."

"He tell you everything important over the phone?"

"Yeah. That's how he contacts us."

"What about storage?" I said.

"I don't remember. It sounded like poetry."

"What did?"

Marky thought a moment. "The words," he said. "The words were about poetry. Maybe."

"Try to remember the words."

"What?" he said.

"Try to remember the words," I said again, louder.

"It sounded like he said paired rhyme and storage."

"A paired rhyme about storage," I said.

"Yeah. Only not 'about.' Just the words paired and rhyme and storage.

I tried the words. "Paired rhyme storage?"

"No. Other way around. Storage paired rhyme."

I thought about it while Marky drove. Then I said, "Could Gomez have said, 'storage paradigm?'"

"That's it," Marky said. "Whatever that means."

We were approaching the airport. "Turn in here and stop," I said.

Marky pulled into the airport entrance and drove down to the parking lot. He stopped in the corner. "Now what?"

"Just sit." I held the gun on him.

What was a storage paradigm? Paradigm referred to a model or a format. The implication was that Michael Warner was working on a new storage model. It didn't make sense. There were thousands of kinds of storage from lockers to shelving to rental garages to warehouses. But why would a physicist work on storage models? Physicists study the building blocks of matter, of the universe. They study energy, the flow of light and heat and electrons. They studied the basic forces. I still remembered them from high school. The nuclear forces and gravity and electro-magnetism. What did that have to do with storage?

Unless it was some kind of nuclear or gravitational or electro-magnetic storage.

Electro-magnetism. Computer storage. Hard drives. Computer chips.

What if Michael's invention was devising a new kind of information storage? A new storage paradigm could, what, put more information on a hard drive or on a microchip? Could it change computers?

It fit with what Michael Warner had said to Emerson Baylor. Michael thought his idea could revolutionize a high-tech business and have consumer implications as well. A new computer model could change all of industry, all of personal computing, change the world.

And Michael had told his daughter Silence, safe in the knowledge that she could not pass it on.

Tony Go was trying to get the information out of her. One of his men had picked her up in the supermarket parking lot, bound and gagged in the back of a van. They would make another attempt at getting her to talk. If that didn't work, would they sacrifice her tomorrow night in their full-moon ceremony.

"I want you to call Gomez," I told Marky. I pulled out my cell phone.

"I don't know his number. He always calls us."

"Then we'll use your phone. Hit star sixty-nine."

"Tiptoe has the phone," Marky said. "But star sixty-nine doesn't work. I tried it. Tony Go's number is blocked somehow."

I had the number Tony Go had given me. I was about to dial it when I stopped. "Where do you think they would take the girl?"

"I don't know. He just told us that if you came, we were to tape up the girl and leave her in the van in that parking lot."

"If you can't call him, how does he know she's there?"

"He has a GPS transmitter in the van. It tells him whenever it's moved."

"When was the last time you talked to Tony Go in person?"

"I've never met him. He just calls on the phone."

"What about the kidnapping?" My voice was getting louder. "He just order that up on the phone, too, like goddamn room service?!"

Marky paused. "Yeah. Like room service."

I turned and leaned against the passenger door. Again I lifted the gun and put the barrel against Marky's lip and pressed it into the flesh. "Tell me how it worked. I want you to be very focused on how quickly you can give me the whole story, nothing missing, so that when you're done I have no further questions."

Marky was breathing hard. "I can't talk with that on my lip."

I pulled the gun back a half inch.

"Tiptoe has a friend who lives in Tahoe. We came here three weeks ago for the Tahoe Heaven Biker Festival. We stayed at the friend's house. He rents a condo up in Tahoe City.

"Our second day here we were playing a video game and the phone rang and someone asked for Tiptoe. So Tiptoe went to the phone, and the person said he's Tony Go, and he got Tiptoe's friend's number from a business partner, and he needed some work from two good workers. Tiptoe said, sure, him and his friend Marky are real good workers. So they talked for awhile and pretty soon Tiptoe handed me the phone and said Tony Go wanted to talk to me.

"So I answered and Tony Go asked me a few questions,

like what is my cell number and I said what Tiptoe's cell was 'cause I don't have one. Then Go said maybe I would be a better person to talk to than Tiptoe and didn't I think maybe Tiptoe was a little dumb? So I said I didn't know, but what could I do for him.

"So he gave us a little assignment, kind of a test. We were supposed to ride down to the South Shore and find a panel van in one of the casino parking lots. The key was to be under the mat. We were supposed to leave our bikes there and take the van and drive over to this liquor store and take all their cash. He said we could rob them with a gun or break in at night or whatever. Just so we take all their cash. If we succeeded, we would be paid five thousand cash. Plus we could keep the cash from the store.

"So we figured, what the hell, we'd be in someone else's van, hard to trace to us, and there was money in it, right? So we did it. I used my piece and Tiptoe yelled what we were going to do if they didn't hand over the money, and they did it. It was fast and easy."

"What about the five thousand? How did you get paid?"

"Tony Go said he would put the cash in a storm drain about fifty yards behind the Cruiser Bar. He said he'd put the money in a coffee can and leave it inside the storm drain.

"The next night, we went there and sure enough, there was a coffee can in the storm drain with fifty hundreds in it."

"And," I said, prompting.

"So I guess we passed the test. Then he called and said we were to take the van and one of our bikes over to the girl's house and pick her up. He had a whole lot of specifics about how we'd do it and when we'd do it and that it had to be that day when the big caravan of bikes was going through Tahoe. So I drove the van, and Tiptoe and some other guys rode their bikes."

"And you still never met Tony Go?"

"No. He said he'd pay us each five thousand for the job." Marky turned to me to make certain I understood. "That's ten thousand, total. It was in the storm drain the next day. I've never seen cash money like that. It was awesome."

"But you took the girl and her brother."

"Yeah. We didn't know what to do with the brother. He was a tough little kid. Punching and kicking and yelling. Finally, Tiptoe hit him real hard and the kid hit his head on the corner of the van and then Tiptoe pushed the boy and the girl into the van. I put some tape on the girl like we were told, but I didn't need to with the boy.

"Tiptoe followed me on his bike and I drove out to the chain-up area to dump him. Tony Go hadn't called, so I had to figure out what to do. I learned some Aztec words from one of the guys and I thought it would be smart to write one on the boy's forehead. It was a cool thing to do, like in the TV shows. Makes the cops have to figure it out. But it didn't make the news. I even looked in the paper. Nothin'. I don't get it."

"Where did you take the girl?"

Marky looked at me like I was an idiot. "To the house, of course. You were just there."

"But Tony Go wasn't there?"

"No. He just called and said where to go and where the key was and to put the girl upstairs and tape her up. Then we were to leave. So that's what we did."

"Tony Go came after you left?"

"I guess," Marky said. "I don't know how much he was at the house. We just did what he said. Come when he said, and leave when he said. Same for when he wanted us to scare your girl, throw shit at her condo. And bust you up. Only that didn't work out too good."

"You got paid for all of it."

"Yeah. In the coffee can. In the storm drain."

"And when I came tonight?" I said.

"He'd prepared us for it. We were like trained soldiers. If someone surprises us, comes for the girl, we hustle her out the back door and through the woods to the van. One of us drives the van to the parking lot. The other follows on one of our bikes so we can leave the van and get home. If we succeed in the evasion maneuver – that's what he called it, the evasion maneuver – we get an extra thousand each."

"Which you would have to pick up in the storm drain tomorrow."

"Yeah."

I tried to get my brain around it. It was a perfect cover. Tony Go could get someone to do his deeds, but if it ever got to court no one could testify against him. They'd never seen him in person. They had no direct contact. Everything was disconnected from him. There were the phone calls, and the phone records could be obtained, but they would no doubt connect to a stolen cell phone.

Unless the money could be directly connected to Tony Go, every scrap of evidence would be hearsay. Tony Go would be next to impossible to convict.

Yet something was off. I tried to keep my focus on the gun I held against Marky, but my thoughts kept wandering. I couldn't put my brain on it. Go had planned it perfectly. A kidnapping and a murder. No one would ever prove he did it.

And then I remembered the old cop's axiom. Turn it upside down. Flip it the other way. Assume that black is white and white is black. Which is another way of saying make no assumptions.

The only assumption I'd made was that Tony Go was behind it. But was that true? Did Tony Go order the kidnapping and murders?

The perfect foil that made it impossible to connect the kidnapping and murders to Tony Go also meant that someone else could be responsible. Someone else could have called Marky and Tiptoe and pretended to be Tony Go. The imposter would have paid Marky and Tiptoe money, sent them on missions, and paid them again to build loyalty. They would assume they were working for Tony Go and when caught would do their best to send him back to the Super Max.

Tony Go had told me he didn't know Marky and Tiptoe. Now I wondered again if he'd been telling the truth.

FIFTY-ONE

I said to Marky, "You said Tony Go referred to a new storage paradigm."

"Yeah."

"How'd that come up?"

"I don't know. I guess he was talking about the girl. Like if she talked, we were supposed to pay attention. Especially to anything about the storage para... whatever. We weren't supposed to touch her, just pay attention. Not that anyone would touch her anyway. She's real weird. Retarded. Doesn't talk. Doesn't act normal. More skinny than practically anyone I ever seen."

"Did she ever talk?"

"No. Just draws. Got a little book and draws in it all the time."

I was thinking about the copy paper she'd used for her letter drawings. Nothing like sketchbook paper. "You see any copy paper in the house?"

"We didn't need copies of anything."

"So there was no copy paper in the house?" I said.

Marky shook his head. "There was some printer paper, I guess. I didn't really look."

"Where?"

"Upstairs. Where we kept her. A computer printer. But no computer. Tony Go probably took it out."

"Was she tied up?"

"No. Tony Go screwed some boards over the windows so she couldn't get out. She pretty much had the run of the upstairs. We just locked the padlock on the door at the bottom of the stairs."

"You treat her okay?"

"We treated her good," he said, a kind of pride in his voice. "We brought her pizzas and Cokes. But she didn't really eat much."

"How did Tony Go treat her?"

"I don't know. We weren't there when he was there. But he probably roughed her up some. One day her shirt was torn. Another day, some of her hair was kinda melted. And her shirttail was burned. I don't think he hurt her for real. More just to scare the crap outta her. Probably freaked her out good. But she's so weird, who knows?"

"You ever touch her?"

"No. She's gross-out skinny."

"Tiptoe touch her?"

"No. Why?"

"Deciding if I let you live," I said, truthfully. "What else did Tony Go talk about?"

"I don't know."

"He doesn't talk about the things you and Tiptoe talk about, right? Did he talk about Lynard Skynard? Did he talk about his bike?"

Marky shook his head.

"What about his church or the Aztec stuff? Did he ever talk about the Aztec language?" I said.

"No."

"Think back on when Tony Go called. What were the things he said? What sounded different from normal talk?"

"Everything. He sounds totally different from normal."

"How? What kind of things did he say?"

"I don't know, man. I just listened. He'd say, like, 'I would like to have,' I don't know, 'a beer' or something. Where a normal guy would just say, 'Gimme the beer, dude.'" Marky thought a moment. "Or this come back to me now. I remember once when Tony Go said, 'I'd appreciate it if you boys kept a close eye on her. It's worth money to you.' A regular guy would just say, 'You want some bank, you sit on the bitch.' You know what I mean?"

"He have an accent?" I asked.

"Like Mexican or something? No. He's got that suit-coat accent. Probably went to college."

"You think he was born in this country? Never had an accent to start with?" I said.

"I didn't say that. Just that he got that college talk. Covers up what came before. I've heard it from guys who work for companies. And on TV. Guys who tell the news."

"Didn't it strike you as odd that Tony Go talks like a newscaster?" I said, thinking that when Tony Go talked to me at Sand Harbor he had a slight Mexican accent.

"I don't know. I guess I never thought about it."

I sat there, gun on Marky, parked in the corner of the airport lot, thinking about it. I was looking for a man who was educated and was technically savvy. He knew how to use Global Positioning System transmitters and understood the value of a new storage paradigm. And he had enough money that he could spend thousands of dollars to pursue millions.

I dialed Emerson Baylor's number. It was one in the morning. He'd be asleep. I hoped he didn't turn off his ringer at night.

The phone rang five times and then an answering machine picked up. At the tone I said, "Emerson, this is Owen McKenna. I've got a question I need to ask you. It's important enough that if you don't pick up the phone I'll have to drive over there and get you out of bed. If you..."

"Hello?" he said. His voice rattled with the thickness of sleep and old age and the dehydrating effects of brandy.

"Owen McKenna calling," I said again. "I need to ask a question."

"Yes. Of course. Let me get my glasses. Should I go get..." He coughed several times, then cleared his throat. "Owen McKenna? What did you say?"

"A question. Are you awake?"

"Yes. Yes. Of course. I'm awake. I'm awake."

"Your investment group," I said.

"Yes. Of course. My investment group."

"You said there are seven members."

"Yes. Seven members."

"Did any of them meet Michael Warner? Did any of them get a chance to hear his proposal?"

"Well, let me think. Did any of them meet Mr. Warner. I don't think so. He was... wait. Of course, they didn't meet him. But they heard about his proposal from me. I told them, yes I did. At our monthly meeting. I remember now. We get together up at Harrah's Forest Buffet. Each one of us tells whether we've found anything interesting. I told them about Michael Warner. After all, his proposal was interesting. Of course I also told them about the obstacles. Just like I told you. Warner wanted to be boss. Warner wanted fifty-one percent. It just wasn't going to work. They understood. I can assure you they agreed with me. We didn't do anything wrong in not making an offer to Michael Warner."

"Emerson, please understand that I'm not accusing you of anything."

"Oh. Yes. Of course."

"Were any of them disappointed that your group wasn't going to invest in Warner's idea?"

"No. Not that I recall. Of course, several of them were curious. But I wouldn't say they were disappointed. They all agree that we need majority ownership and we need to appoint the CEOs."

I said, "Who are the members of your group?"

"Our investment group? Well, there's Bill Reed. I think I mentioned him. He's into the restaurant business. And Bob Tripp up in Glenbrook, whom I'm sure you know. The media business has been good to him, hasn't it? Then we have Conrad Menendez the orthodontist. And Joshua Fidlar of the Fidlar Hotels chain. Let's see. Except for Menendez, the business interests of the others are everywhere. But if you can live in Tahoe and still run your business, well, why not?"

"You've listed four. Including you, that makes five. Two left."

"Yes, of course. Sorry, I'm tired and when you get older, you... Oh, right, Raymond. How could I forget Raymond. He has his financial struggles, missed his last capital contribution, but he came up with the buy-in. I'm sure he'll be back on his feet soon. So I shouldn't judge, should I?"

"Raymond's last name?" I said.

"Power. You probably know him. Local psychiatrist. Dr. Power."

I knew him, and I knew he had evaluated Silence for several years, and I knew he had a book on his shelf about GPS systems. And I remembered that Power had told me emphatically that Silence was a low-functioning, retarded, autistic kid, and her drawings didn't add up to much, when all evidence suggested otherwise, when her teacher Henrietta and even her classmates thought she was smart.

"Tell me, Emerson, was Dr. Power at the meeting where you told the others about Michael Warner's proposal?"

"Let me see. I don't recall. We sat at the corner table up there at the top of Harrah's. I was on the outside, Bill and Conrad were next to me. Bob was... Yes, of course, Raymond was in the corner. I remember because I had a hard time seeing his face against the light. Mt. Tallac was behind his head and the sun was on the mountain."

"How did Dr. Power respond when you told them about Warner's proposal?"

"I don't know what you mean," Emerson said.

"Was he bored? Did he get excited?"

"I think he was somewhat excited. Everybody was interested. Raymond asked some questions about it. I remember him wanting to know where Warner taught."

"Did you tell him?"

"Certainly. I said he was a professor at Sacramento State University. I remembered that because my niece went to Sac

State. She's from Colorado and she always wanted to go to school in California. Of course, Sac State isn't what most people think of when they think of California's sunny beaches and snowy mountains and such."

I thought of how Power had claimed Silence didn't have much mental capacity. But his observations may have given him doubts about that conclusion. Especially after he learned of Michael Warner's invention and, perhaps, plied him with drink and attention and learned that he was Silence's father and maybe even learned that Michael had told Silence of his work.

"Where does Power live?" I asked.

"Raymond? I don't see what that has to do with anything. You're still looking for the girl, right?"

"Yes. But I have a question I need to ask him."

Emerson hesitated. Perhaps he was still groggy with sleep. "I don't know the street. He's over on that meadow by the creek that flows out of Heavenly. Off Pioneer Trail up toward the mountain. You'd know which house is his by that barn he has out back, up by that little canyon. Raymond showed me. I'll never forget those cliffs that drop away. They're covered with loose rock. A guy could lose his life in a second if he weren't careful. Say, you're not going to bother him tonight, are you?"

"No, no. I wouldn't do that. I just thought I could catch him in the morning before he goes to work."

FIFTY-TWO

"Drive!" I shouted to Marky.

"Where?"

"Into town. Hurry!"

He started up and sped toward the parking lot exit.

I dialed 9-1-1 as Marky turned out onto the highway and raced toward town.

"Nine, one, one emergency," a woman's voice answered.

"Owen McKenna calling. I have information on the kidnapped girl. I'll give it to Commander Mallory. Have him call this number as soon as possible." I didn't bother to read it off because I knew they'd have it on their caller ID.

I hung up and dialed Street. "Are you okay?" I said when she answered.

"Yes. Diamond thought the men who had Silence must have gone out the back and you would have followed. But we didn't see where you went. So we waited for you to call."

I didn't have time to explain where I'd been, so I told her where I thought Power's house was. "If you can't find it, call back. I should know the house number in a few minutes."

"What should I do when we get there?" she said

"Send Spot after me."

"How?"

"Just open the car door and tell him to find me." Then I said, "Hold on." Marky was coming toward the "Y" intersection at 70 mph. "Turn right," I said to him. "Head through town to Ski Run." I spoke again to Street. "I'm back."

"What should I do after I send Spot out?"

"Wait until I find you. If we save the girl, she will be traumatized. You're the best chance we have tonight of keeping her calm. You may be the only woman there. Can Diamond talk?"

"Yes," she said, then added, "Be safe. I love you."

"Sí?" Diamond said in my ear.

"I told Street roughly where the girl is. I haven't been there. The property backs up to Heavenly. There is a barn on the property. If you don't find us in or around the house, you might look in the barn. And, if it comes to that, I was told there is a cliff area up behind the place. So be careful. Tell Street, too."

"Got it."

I hung up and dialed what Tony Go had told me was his private number.

It rang twice before he answered. "I thought you might call, Mr. McKenna, so I put your number in my phone." He sounded as alert as if he'd just finished his morning coffee.

"You said you'd like to help me."

"Offer still stands."

"I have an idea where the kidnapped girl is. I'm heading there now. I'll know for certain in a few minutes. I could use some backup. It's in South Lake Tahoe. Any chance you've got troops near the south shore?"

"How many men do you need?" he said.

"Eight or ten would help."

"Can you wait on hold? Let me make another call." He put me on hold and was back twenty seconds later. "My men are assembling," he said. "What's your plan?"

"The kidnapper has an old Dodge panel van. I think he's at a house not too far from Pioneer and Ski Run Boulevard. I'll give you the address as soon as I get there."

"What kind of backup do you want?"

"I'd like a perimeter. He may try to escape in the van or on foot or in another vehicle. He may have the girl with him. I obviously don't want him hurt. But it is imperative that any effort to stop him does not harm the girl."

"Understood. Want me to stay on while you go there?"

"Yes. I'm going to put the phone down." I told Marky, "Make a right turn on Ski Run. Hurry!"

Marky skidded around the corner at high speed, tires screeching. The engine roared as he floored it up the street.

I was trying to figure out the numbers, guessing which direction to go. "Turn on Pioneer," I said, pointing. "I think our road will be just a few blocks in. We'll head up toward the mountain."

Marky took it fast. I was glad there was no other traffic. We raced down Pioneer and found the cross street. Marky turned toward the mountain, sped up, then slowed as the street turned in a big S shape. There were three houses early on, then a stretch with nothing but forest on either side.

A house appeared off to the side. It sat on the steep mountain slope. "I think that's the one," I said.

Marky slowed.

"Turn in the drive," I said.

He turned and our headlights washed over a large one-story house that was like two ramblers stuck together at an angle. There was one light on over the door, illuminating the house number. Everything else was dark.

The drive split, one part winding up and across the front of the house. The other went around to the side.

"Go that way," I pointed.

We went around the dark house. The drive climbed up in a big curve, behind the house and up the lot. Our headlights arced through the woods. They washed over a red barn and an old Dodge van. There was a crack of light showing at the edge of the barn door.

"Stop," I said to Marky. Then, into the phone, I told Tony Go the address.

"We'll be there," he said, and hung up.

The barn door slid to the side and Dr. Power stepped out, silhouetted by the light behind him and illuminated by our headlights. He held a pitchfork. His eyes caught the light and glistened in the dark and his hair stuck up in the breeze.

I opened my door. "Let her go, Power," I shouted.

He set the pitchfork down and reached inside the barn door. In one smooth motion he pulled out a rifle and swung it up to his shoulder and fired. There was a crack and the windshield shattered and Marky's head snapped back, a single dark hole between his eyebrows.

I rolled out onto the dirt, over and over across a steep slope. There was a large icy slab of rock. It was steep and slippery. I wanted to get to the cover of the trees on the other side. I reached for a small tree that grew from a crack in the rock. My hand caught it, but I dropped the Glock. It skittered down the rock into an area that was in full view of Power. I considered sliding down after the automatic, but a shot rang out, and Power's round sparked on the rock at my feet and ricocheted off into the dark with a metallic whine. I found better footing at the edge of the rock slab, and I ran into the dark of the forest, aware that I was still clutching my phone and it was ringing. I stopped behind a large Ponderosa trunk and answered.

"McKenna, it's Mallory. What you got?"

"Dr. Raymond Power has the girl in the barn behind his house. Tony Go's men are on their way to set up a perimeter. Diamond and Street will be here in a minute." I gave Mallory the address as I leaned around the tree trunk to take a look. Power was advancing toward me, rifle up at his shoulder, still lit by the headlights of the Jeep.

"Power's coming toward me through the woods. He has a rifle. He's just killed Marky, one of the bikers who did the kidnapping on Power's order. Power caused the murder of Charlie and I think he personally killed Michael Warner, Silence's biological father. Power is trying to kill me next. It would be good if you could come and arrest his ass. Watch for an old Dodge van. If he tries to escape, I wouldn't be surprised if he uses it as a battering ram. And tell your men that the Tony Go's bikers are on our side." I hung up and turned off the phone so it couldn't ring again and give me away.

FIFTY-THREE

Although Marky was dead, he hadn't turned off the Jeep, so the headlights still shined on the van and the barn and spilled light through the woods. I saw a big Jeffrey pinecone near me. I grabbed it and gave it a soft lob toward the barn. When it hit with a loud thump, I ran the other direction, staying low and making a serpentine path through the trees, away from the light and into the darkness. I stopped behind another tree and peered out.

The forest appeared silent and empty except for the idling Jeep. Then Power appeared, racing toward me like a soldier from one tree to another. He was bent, rifle held at an angle in front of him. He looked as experienced and competent and deadly as his shot at Marky demonstrated. I studied the ground, looking for another pinecone, but I was under the tree canopy where the moon couldn't penetrate and it was too dark. Squatting down on one knee, I swept the ground with my hands. There was nothing but pine needles, slick with frost. I shifted forward and tried again. Nothing. Again, I moved. My hands hit a cobble, too big to throw any distance. I reached left and right, groping in the dark. There, a small group of cobbles. I picked out two in the three-inch range and stuffed one in each front pocket, big awkward lumps, but the only weapon I had. A third cobble, a little smaller, was better for throwing a distance. I looked again, but Power was not visible. At the speed he'd run between the trees, he could be anywhere. I wanted him to talk, to reveal his location. But if I called out, he might not respond and I would be compromised.

Twenty feet away was a huge boulder projecting out of

the earth like an egg balanced on one end. I darted behind it. If Power hadn't moved far from his earlier position the boulder would give me some coverage.

I stood up straight, took careful aim at the Jeep and threw the smaller rock. It struck a branch that I hadn't seen as it arced through the air. I thought it would be deflected too much, but it hit the corner of the rear fender and made a very loud bang that resonated for a precious second. Before the sound had stopped echoing off the barn and nearby trees I was running through the forest. I was able to gain some distance without making any loud noise. I slowed to a fast walk, stepping carefully, trying to avoid the branches that littered the forest floor.

I moved in a curve, up and back toward the barn. Light still spilled out the open barn door. There was a large open area in front of the barn. It would take several seconds to sprint across it. Power was probably still in the trees below. If he saw me he would have a good chance of making another well-placed shot.

In the distance came the roar of a motorcycle, then another. As they grew louder I got ready. I waited, watching for the first headlight. Out on the road came a glow, then a bright single headlight appeared around a distant corner. In a second, another appeared. It was my chance.

I sprinted for the barn. If Power glanced in my direction I was out of luck. But I hoped he would be turned toward the bikers.

I got to the side of the barn and ran softly across the front, trying for quiet, and slipped through the open door. I stepped sideways, back to the barn wall so that I'd be out of view from the outside.

The barn was illuminated by two bright bare bulbs that hung down from the roof. To the side of the door was a stairway that went down to a lower level. There was an open area on the left with a wide sliding door on the far wall. Above was a hayloft, open to the center of the barn. Although it looked like the barn hadn't been used for horses in a long time, there were still bales of hay visible in the loft, and the main floor of the barn was covered with a thin layer of scattered hay.

On the right side of the barn were two horse stalls. Pad-locked inside the far stall, lit by stripes of light coming through the boards, was Silence. She sat in the corner, bent with fatigue and hopelessness. Her right arm was tied to a post, lashed with a pain-fully thin cord. Her hair was limp and stringy and hung down over a stained pale pink shirt that had a diagonal scar of wide masking tape running across the front.

I held my finger to my lips as I approached. I spoke in a whisper. "Silence, I'm Owen McKenna. Your mom sent me. I'm going to get you out of here as soon as possible."

She didn't look at me, but looked to the side. There was no sign that she'd heard me. In the distance I heard more motorcy-cles.

"Glad you are so optimistic about getting her out of here, McKenna," Power said. He stood inside the door, rifle in his hands. "But you know she isn't leaving here unless you convince her to talk. I've spent some money on this project, but once I have the new storage paradigm, our little outfit in Mountain View will be the next Intel. No more worrying about my practice dwin-dling away to nothing. No more debts and no more working for a living." Power closed the big door and pointed the rifle at me.

"She doesn't talk," I said. "You know that."

"She will talk. And she knows what the storage paradigm is. I got that much out of her daddy before he shut up. I tried some medical techniques on him, but they didn't work. But I should have more success on the girl."

He continued, "Of course, you have made things more difficult, making us move out of that vacation home. It was a per-fect place. The owner is only there in the summer. Never comes up after October first. She pays me lots of money every summer to listen to her drone on about what meanies her parents were while she was growing up. We could have kept using that house until Silence talked. But you got in the way."

"You're not thinking, Power. Every indication is that Silence will never talk. She's smart, we know that. But not verbal."

"I think she will. After I'd convinced Marky and Tiptoe that I was Tony Go, I thought, why not borrow from Tony Go's plan? So I explained to her that she will burn at the rise of the full moon tomorrow night. From her agitation, I'd say the plan is working."

Power looked past me toward Silence and spoke in a sing-song voice. "Tell me daddy's little secret, quiet girl, and you don't burn. You don't want to burn up in a big hot nasty fire, do you?"

He turned back to me. "Although, now that you're here, McKenna, I may decide to move our big bonfire up to tonight. Of course, if you want to live, you can save me the trouble and spare her death by coaxing the secret out of her."

"She's never met me or even heard of me. How would I get her to talk? Think of it from her point of view. I could just be another of your accomplices. Brought in to fake her out."

"That's easy to prove otherwise," Power said. "If you were in with me, I wouldn't shoot you, would I?" He raised the rifle and took aim.

The roar of motorcycles outside was suddenly like a jet on take-off. Power turned and stared at the closed barn door. His forehead was knotted in cords, and the whites of his eyes glowed. He glanced back at me, no doubt figuring that I was far enough away, then leaned the rifle against the wall and picked up a piece of 2x6 bracing.

He had obviously planned for the possibility that he'd end up using the barn as a bunker. Screwed to both the door and the wall on either side were brackets to fit the brace. The door was made of heavy stock. With the brace it would be extremely diffi-cult to kick in. Power slammed the 2x6 down into the brackets. He pulled his hands away fast and looked down at his hand where a large sliver of wood had drawn blood. I saw my chance.

I hurled a cobble at him and hit him in the knee. He yelled. I took three running steps toward him, lowered my shoul-der and hit him in the gut, powering him up and backward. His back slammed against the wooden wall hard enough that the air went out of him in a gust and he stared at me, wide-eyed, unable to breathe, unable to move. The rifle fell and clattered down the stairway to the lower level. Power slumped to the floor. His eyes rolled up.

Near Power were several tools hanging on the wall. I pulled a wood-splitting maul off the wall and rushed over to the horse stall where Silence cowered.

"Don't worry, Silence. I'll have you out of there in a bit. I need to break the lock on the stall. It's going to make a loud noise, so you should cover your ears."

I swung the maul, blunt end forward, and struck the hasp and padlock. Wood broke and the lock flew. I pulled the door open.

I bent to where Silence was tied. Her palms were over her ears, the cord from her wrist to the post pulled taut with tension. She shook with fear. "I'll have you free in a minute," I said, then quickly realized that the cord that tied her to the post was knotted in several knots, pulled tight enough that she couldn't untie them. I'd need a knife. I looked at the tool wall, but there was no knife.

I could do it with the maul.

I stood up. "Give me some slack in the cord, Silence, so I can cut it with the maul." She was turned away from me, but she held her arm out. It shook violently. I held the cord to the floor with my foot and aimed the maul at the cord. The maul made a hard thunk into the wood floor and a chip of wood flew past my face. The maul was stuck in the floor, but just barely caught the cord and nicked it. I heard a noise behind me and turned to see that Power had come back from the dead.

He lunged toward us.

I pushed Silence sideways.

Power missed us, hitting the floor to my side, knocking the maul out of the wood and across the floor. I pulled up on the cord, but it wouldn't budge. Silence was balled up, knees to chest, paralyzed with fear.

While Power pushed himself up, I dropped to the floor in a sitting position next to Silence, my feet against the post where the cord was attached. I braced one shoe against the post and jerked on the cord. The little rope was tough and I couldn't break it. I shifted to a better position and jerked again and again.

The cord frayed a little at the nick, held fast, then came free.

In my peripheral vision I saw Power swinging the maul at me. I rolled, throwing Silence to the side.

Power slammed the maul into the wood where I had just been. I yelled, "Run, Silence! Run!"

She bolted up and out of the horse stall, trailing a piece of cord from her right wrist. She ran to the back door of the barn, and grabbed at the latch as Power, newly energized, kicked me in the side. I felt a sharp crack in a rib, but my focus was on the sound of the back door sliding sideways and Silence's footsteps running into the night.

Power launched another kick at my side, but I bent and took his foot the way a wide receiver picks the pigskin out of the air. I twisted and his momentum carried him over my body. As he fell, he kicked out with his other foot, grazing my head.

Power scrambled to his feet and I pushed up, a sharp pain ripping through my side. Power took three big steps and grabbed the pitchfork as Spot charged in through the door Silence had run out.

Spot raced over to me and jumped, happy as hell to find me. Then he turned, sensing the danger from Power. He growled. Power raised the pitchfork as if to throw it. I grabbed Spot's collar and held him back. Power glanced again at the braced door as the motorcycles got even louder. Then he turned and ran out the back door into the night.

"Spot, c'mere," I stepped into the horse stall where Silence had been tied. I looked for something of hers to scent him on, hoping for a lost hat or mitten, but there was nothing.

Nothing but the cord she'd been tied with. It wasn't much. I grabbed the cord and balled it up. "Smell this, Spot!" He was confused by the commotion, but he obeyed. I stuck the balled cord on his nose, rubbed it back and forth. "Do you have the scent, Spot? Do you?"

I pulled him over to where Silence had been sitting. I put his nose to the floor. "Do you have the scent? Find Silence! Find her and guard her!"

I directed him toward the open back door. He stuck his nose on the floor, then lifted it high into the air, searching for an air scent. He waved his head up and down and to the side, nostrils flexing. Then he alerted on a scent coming in the door and he ran out, nose held high, and disappeared into the dark forest.

I ran out after him into a forest lit up and throbbing with a bass rumble. An arc of spotlights illuminated the forest. Motorcycle headlights. They were scattered through the woods so that their headlights shined all directions through the trees. The bikes were all up on their center stands, engines running, no riders.

The bikers, twelve or fourteen in all, had come out of the woods around Power and drew together in a closing circle as he dashed this way and that, threatening them with his pitchfork but realizing he couldn't escape.

They pulled the circle in tighter until it was twenty feet across with Power in the center.

Power stabbed his pitchfork toward the bikers. I thought he'd claim another victim before he was subdued, but one of the bikers swung a chain and it wrapped around Power's legs. The biker gave it a jerk and Power went down.

The bikers rushed in around Power. A vicious pack mentality permeated the night.

I shouted at the top of my voice. "Hold him, but don't hurt him!"

I turned to see an SUV cruiser pull into the drive, red lights flashing. Another followed closely behind. I ran toward them, trying to keep my face in the headlight beams, my hands up so they could see I was unarmed.

Mallory jumped out of one SUV and trotted toward me just as Diamond materialized out of the darkness.

Diamond said, "Find the girl?"

A half second later Mallory called, "Where are we at?" He

came rushing up the drive, breathing hard.

"Lost the girl to the forest. I sent Spot after her. We need a search and rescue team. Preferably a chopper. There's a canyon up there with steep cliffs. Best to search from the air."

"What about Dr. Power?!" Mallory demanded.

I pointed toward the circle of bikers. "Tony Go's men have him. With luck they haven't done much more than scare him to death."

Mallory glanced at Diamond as if irritated at seeing a cop from another county and even another state in his jurisdiction.

"Your territory," Diamond said. "Your collar."

Mallory hustled up to the circle of bikers.

Diamond said to me, "I'll see what I can do about a search. I know some of those boys on the El Dorado search and rescue team." He vanished into the night.

"Street!" I called out. "Can you hear me?"

"Right here." She appeared at my side and gave me a quick hug. She'd brought a flashlight and it shined at the ground. "I heard you say that Silence is in the forest."

"Yeah. Brave kid. She saw her chance and ran past Power even though he was armed with a splitting maul. She ran into the woods. Maybe Spot will find her. Maybe not. I had nothing to scent him on but a tiny bit of cord. I'm hoping he picked up a general scent from the horse stall where she'd been tied."

"How can I help?" Her eyes were large and earnest and worried, and they reminded me of the other times when my work had put her up against that darkness that no civilian should ever have to face. I knew the best thing for all of us was to focus on the task at hand.

"We'll start a ground search immediately. If a chopper becomes available we'll switch to that."

Diamond came back with two flashlights. "They've roped off your Jeep, but they let me pull these out of your glove box. I turned your Jeep off. Left the key. I also talked to a sergeant I know in the El Dorado Sheriff's Department. He knows the drill with their search and rescue team." Diamond tapped the radio that was clipped to his belt. "He'll let me know what develops."

We headed up the mountain behind the barn. We stayed about twenty yards from each other, swept our flashlights through the woods and called out for Spot. Periodically, Street called Silence's name even though we knew she wouldn't answer, but we wanted Silence to hear a woman's voice. Periodically, we came to an area where the moon shone through the tree canopy, and it was easy to see how many pitfalls could trip up a person running in the dark. Then we plunged back into the trees, the moonlight switched off, and our visual world shrunk back to the depth that our flashlights could probe the forest.

After twenty minutes of searching, we came to the canyon that cut across the landscape. The canyon wasn't more than thirty or forty feet deep, but the drop-offs were vertical. There was nothing below but rocks. Even with the bright moon it would be very difficult to gauge the depth of the drop-off if you were running through the night. There was nothing to prevent Silence from running until she saw the hole in the ground at the last moment. She wouldn't be able to stop before her feet struck empty air.

The little canyon wrapped in a large arc before it stopped. If by some chance Silence had not fallen off the edge and had gone around the end, she would have headed up the slope that led to Heavenly and the huge wilderness of mountains that stretched toward Freel Peak. Any person lost there would likely succumb to the sub-freezing temperatures that are the norm during fall nights at elevations that range up to and above 10,000 feet. Search dogs and a helicopter would be the only hope.

I heard Diamond's radio squawk. In a moment he called out to Street and me. "The search and rescue team is in the air. They will drop one searcher and dog on the ground and then carry another team on an aerial search. They're hoping there is enough room to land on the intersection at Pioneer Trail. If we hurry, you can go back up with them. Best if you and Street look from the air. Silence is scared and could be running. It wouldn't take long for her to get a mile or two away. They can drop you down once you find her."

The chopper ended up landing in a meadow down below the barn. A woman jumped out, her large Black Lab eager to find a scent and begin the tracking procedure. The chopper reduced its throttle, but still we had to shout to be heard over the roar of the bird. I explained to the search woman where in the barn she could scent her dog. I also told her not to be surprised if she found Spot.

"I'm not confident Spot will find the girl," I continued. "There isn't much to scent a dog on and he's not a professional dog. But I told him to guard the girl. He's friendly to dogs and people, but if he finds the girl he won't let anyone near her until I call him off. If you see him, hold your dog."

"Will do," she assured me. "Anyway, other dogs don't mess with Howler. Do they boy?" she said, patting him on his big chest. She started away, then called back to me.

"Yeah?" I said.

"What kind of dog is Spot?" she said.

"Great Dane."

She made a slow, tiny nod. "Right," she said, turned, and ran toward the barn.

I beckoned to Street. She ran out from the edge of the meadow. We ducked our heads and ran under the spinning rotor up to the chopper.

"Owen McKenna," I shouted as a hand reached out from the open door.

"Sergeant Stafford, El Dorado Sheriff's Department," the man in the front seat shouted back.

I pushed Street ahead of me and we both climbed into the back seat of the chopper. In the seat was another man and a German shepherd.

Stafford leaned back from the front seat. "I'm sorry," he said to Street. "You are?"

"Street Casey."

"She's part of the search," I said.

Stafford said, "We were told McKenna and no one else.

Have to follow rules. She'll have to leave."

I shook my head and shouted back, "The child we're looking for is a young autistic girl. The girl is mute and responds to no man. Dr. Casey is a specialist. She must be the first person to reach the girl."

"But she isn't trained in helicopter rescue. I can't allow it."

"Sergeant, you're going to have to make an exception. There is a canyon up there with vertical cliffs. If the girl is still alive, she will be so traumatized that the slightest shock will cause her to behave even more erratically. We could find her and still lose her to a fall off the cliff. You don't want to be called before the review board with that over your head. Where is the greater danger in this decision?"

I could see the sergeant's jaw muscles bulging in the dim interior light of the chopper cabin. He shook his head, eyes narrowed. He pointed at the door latch. "That latch shuts it. Those are the seatbelts." He reached up to a rack of headsets and pulled two of them off. "Put these on."

The pilot revved up the turbine as we pulled on the headsets. The noise-canceling electronics of the headsets blocked out the tumultuous engine roar and we could all talk into our mikes and hear each other clearly.

I worried that the roar of the chopper would stress Silence so much that she'd run frantically away and fall into the canyon. But without the chopper we'd be unlikely to find her before she froze. It seemed a necessary risk.

They had a large assortment of other gear onboard including radios and devices for lowering both people and dogs from the chopper while it hovered above ground too rough to allow a landing.

The second search dog handler explained the procedure as we flew. The pilot would fly a pattern that allowed his searchlight to do a thorough scan of the nearby territory. At any sign of Silence, the chopper would pause and lower the handler and the dog. With a dog already on the ground and the chopper doing an air search, there was a good chance that they would eventually find Silence. He didn't say how often such searches end with the victim still alive.

I strained to look out a side window, hoping that the pilot had a view many times better than mine. We went back and forth over the landscape, starting at the low-altitude areas and gradually climbing higher.

When the initial search yielded nothing, the pilot flew back to the beginning of the canyon and trained the powerful searchlight on the areas where Silence would have fallen had she plunged off the edge in the darkness.

Again, we saw nothing. But all of us knew that she and Spot could be sprawled at the bottom of any number of rock faces, their broken bodies hidden in the thick fir trees that grew at the canyon's bottom.

When the canyon search also turned up nothing, the pilot began cruising over the granite slope that rose up steeply toward the mountains above. It was obvious that no weak, hungry kidnap victim could make it very far while climbing in the dark. But everyone on a search, dogs included, are unwilling to give up until there seems no possible positive outcome.

We flew for another hour, the turbine behind us roaring as the blade above cut the air. Finally, the pilot spoke in our earphones and said he needed to refuel. He was going to turn and head back to land in the meadow and let us and the remaining dog and handler out to begin the laborious search by land, starting at the barn where the original search dog had begun.

The pilot tipped the stick and we circled around to head back. I still had my face plastered to the side window, staring out at the moonlit night, when I saw something.

Even with my eagerness to see anything at all, it wasn't much, and I almost didn't speak up. But there was a tiny glimmer, a vague sense of something light in color, so brief it vanished as quickly as it first appeared. Nevertheless, I spoke into the mike.

"I possibly saw something catch the light," I said in a low voice. "Two o'clock or two-thirty. Maybe nothing, but something caught my eye."

"That's why we're here," the pilot said. He leaned the stick to the right and we arced around in a steep bank. He straightened out the chopper and shined the searchlight ahead as we flew. Below were trees and rock and more trees. The canyon appeared and the ground fell away and there was blackness below.

The pilot turned the chopper and we retraced our path through the sky. Nothing caught our eye at 2:30 or 9:30 or 6:30. The pilot turned again and we flew the area a second and then a third time. Once more we came up against the quick rise in slope where the mountain rose up. The pilot slowed, came to a hovering stop and then slowly rotated until we were pointing back toward Lake Tahoe in the distance.

"I tried to cover the area you described," he said, his voice low in the headsets. "But I didn't see anything."

"I didn't either," I said.

The other passengers agreed.

The pilot nudged the stick forward. The front of the chopper dropped in a gentle tilt and we started toward the lake. We rode without speaking. The canyon was ahead and we began to cross it when the pilot suddenly pulled back on the stick.

The chopper slowed, stopped and then moved backward. The searchlight shined on rocks and trees, same as before. We went backward fifty or more yards, the pilot carefully holding course so we didn't waver sideways. Then he stopped again.

Below in the searchlight, at the edge of the canyon, under a stand of trees, was a tiny figure in a pink shirt. She sat with her legs hanging over the edge of the drop-off. Next to the figure in pink was another figure, much larger, dressed in white with black spots.

The pilot flew a good distance away and dropped down until we were hovering over a small clearing in the trees. The men on board wanted to send the dog handler first, followed by his dog. I protested, saying that a stranger might startle Silence. She could fall off the precipice where she sat. The men held firm, saying procedure is procedure. I repeated myself, voice raised, and added some strong words. The pilot joined in, agreeing with me.

I reached for the harness, held it out and commanded, "Hook me up. When I'm down, send Dr. Casey next."

Slowly, one of the men complied. "You get hurt and try to sue, we'll make things difficult."

I leaned in so our eyes were ten inches apart. "Dr. Casey and I are not that kind of people."

He helped me into a harness that was attached to a rope that went through a pulley overhead. He opened the side door, and I stepped out into space and was lowered through the trees.

When my feet hit rock, I unhitched myself. They raised the gear and repeated the process with Street. When she was down we turned on our flashlights and started through the trees.

"It's me, Spot," I said.

"Don't worry, Silence," Street called out. "We're here to bring you home."

We walked some distance through the forest and over rocky outcroppings and boulders. It was farther than I had judged based on my view from the helicopter.

We came up behind them. We kept our lights on the ground by our feet as we approached. The less shock of light, the better. Street kept up a soft running patter, her voice reassuring. We stopped when we were thirty feet away.

They were sitting on the very edge of the canyon. Silence had her knees drawn up. Her feet gripped the rock where it dropped away. Spot was sitting to her side, his toes on the same edge. Silence leaned against him, her slight body dwarfed by his mass. Her arms were wrapped around him, one over his shoulders, the other across his chest. Her hands were clasped together at the far side of his neck.

Even from our distance I could see that she was squeezing him with every muscle she had.

Spot sat calmly, his head canted slightly her way, loving every bit of vice-grip, pet-crushing effort that she could muster.

EPILOGUE

The night we found Silence they put her into the hospital for observation. Except for dehydration and malnutrition she was okay. Physically, okay. But she was terrified any time a doctor came near her. After a day, Marlette brought her home and kept her sequestered, except for visits from Henrietta. After ten days, Marlette called and said that Silence wanted to see me. We decided it would be best to meet someplace fun.

Street and I packed a picnic lunch, headed for Nevada Beach and found it mostly empty on a midweek fall morning. We had a mile of perfect sand to ourselves.

Street spread out several blankets while Spot ran down the water's edge. A seagull flew up and Spot gave chase. The gull must have thought it fun for it stayed about eight feet off the sand and just in front of Spot.

I got a large pile of coals going on the barbecue I'd brought. Without husking the corn on the cob, I put it directly on the grill. I pulled the corkscrew from my pocket and went to work on the wine.

"A little Mondavi Private Reserve to start off our festivities?" I said.

"At eleven-thirty in the morning?" Street said. "Of course."

I poured some into my finest wine glasses and handed her one. Street took a sip. She was silhouetted against the backdrop of Mt. Tallac looming over the far shore of Tahoe.

"A pretty picture," I said. "Except you're wearing your

baggy shorts."

"You wanted the tight short ones with the notches? But I wasn't planning on doing much bending."

"Ah," I said.

By noon the corn was cooked. I arranged it on the edges of the grill and added more charcoal so I'd be ready to do burgers when the rest of the party arrived.

Street and I sat in the sand and sipped wine as I filled her in on some of the details.

When I was done, she said, "So Tony Go wasn't a bad guy after all?"

"A bad guy, yes. But not this time."

"How do you explain the bone that Pierson's dog found up by the top of Kingsbury Grade? Wasn't that where the Granite Mountain Boys camped out in June?"

"Yes, and it came from them. But it turned out to be a sheep's leg bone. They'd sacrificed another sheep, just like Tony Go said."

Street looked mortified and started giggling. "A variation on eating leg of lamb."

"Yeah."

"And the giant? The one you shot in the leg out at Emerald Bay?"

"An El Dorado Sheriff's Deputy found him crawling along the highway. With his prior convictions, it looks like his murder of Charlie will send him to prison for the rest of his life, no chance of parole. Same as Dr. Power."

I looked up and saw Henrietta approaching from the parking lot. To her side was an old woman and Diamond. Diamond had his arm bent so that the old woman could hold onto him. Henrietta stopped at the edge of the sand and took off her sandals so she could walk barefoot. She was dressed in her overalls and a heavy sweater to ward off the cool fall breeze, a striking contrast to Street whose high metabolism kept her warm in light clothes when the rest of us bundled up.

The three of them approached slowly, Henrietta and

Diamond matching their pace to the old woman's. The woman had a tight helmet of white hair and crisp azure eyes the color of the Caribbean Sea and a thin face with sharp bones like an exotic bird.

"Owen, Street," Henrietta said. "I'd like you to meet Tillie Bilkenstein, Silence's new best friend."

We nodded and greeted and traded several comments, each of us realizing at different moments that Tillie, like Silence, was alert but also mute.

Diamond had carried a folding chair in his other hand and he set it up near the barbecue and helped Tillie sit down.

Henrietta said, "Have you seen Silence since the night you rescued her?"

"No, how is she doing?"

"As you might expect. Very traumatized. But something extraordinary happened five days ago. I was over at her house, and she communicated to me that she wanted me to get some Computer Science textbooks. Normally, she would have gestured and pointed at books and a computer to get her desire across. But this time was different. She made a drawing of herself and a textbook and a computer. The drawing showed her reaching for the book. It was the first time she's ever made a specific request using a drawing alone."

Henrietta paused, thinking. "Of course, the drawings sent to the high school were similar in that way. But they were more general in nature, a picture of where she was. It didn't show her in the room. It didn't telegraph the self-awareness that makes others empathize and understand her point of view, something the rest of us automatically put into our speech and actions."

"You mean," I said, "that she hadn't figured out how to make a specific request for rescue."

"Right. Whereas this drawing of herself wanting a computer textbook was more focused, more specific. It was like she was talking with her pencil by using drawings in place of words! Do you realize what this means?"

Street spoke up first. "She isn't non-verbal after all. She's just silent."

"Yes!" Henrietta said. "This kidnapping, terrible as it was, somehow focused her on communication. Without Charlie to help her she knew she had to try some way to get a message out to the world about where she was being held. And she realized she had a skill that could substitute for words. It's amazing."

Henrietta continued, "Anyway, I got several textbooks from the computer teacher at school and dropped them off the next day. Just a couple hours later, Marlette called and said Silence wanted to see me again. I went over and Silence opened the books and pointed out some technical things, diagrams and equations that I didn't understand. Then she did some drawings of her father, which I took to mean that she had learned something from him back when she visited him last month. Her biological father, I mean. She knew his discovery was a secret, so she told no one. But now that he is dead, I think the kidnapping experience convinced her it would be safest for her if she brought the information to the world. Her drawing of her father showed him with a computer. The computer was opened up so the inside was exposed. Silence had drawn a picture of a little storage closet inside the computer. Then there was an arrow that went from the storage closet and pointed to a picture of a huge warehouse. That's a simplified explanation, but the intent of the drawing was clear, that a computer could have greatly increased storage."

"Do you think her metaphor refers to the hard drive?" Street said. "Or the memory?"

Henrietta looked embarrassed. "I don't know bits from bytes or whatever they're called. That's all a mystery to me. So I called our computer teacher again, and then he called someone he knows who teaches at UC Berkeley." Henrietta was beaming.

"A computer career awaits?" Street said.

"More than that. Much more. Turns out the professor in Berkeley knew Silence's father and knew he was working on some new storage technique. Or he knew in the general sense, anyway. He also knew that Silence's father had talked to a lawyer who specializes in start-up high-tech businesses." Henrietta bounced a little on her toes.

Henrietta continued, "Marlette told me about her neighbor Emerson Baylor who was in the investment group with Dr. Power. I went and met with him. Mr. Baylor was devastated about what Power had done. He wanted to help in any way he could.

"I made some calls to check on him and everyone repeated what Marlette said, that Emerson is the real thing, a smart businessman who is ethical and who cares deeply about Silence. So I put him in touch with this professor in Berkeley and the lawyer who had worked with Silence's father, the one who specializes in high-tech business startups.

"We all had a meeting. Marlette and Silence and I drove down to the Bay Area and met with the professor and the lawyer and Emerson Baylor and two other venture capitalists from Baylor's group.

"We discussed how Silence's father never actually told anyone but Silence the specifics of his secret. He only referred to it as a new storage paradigm." Henrietta bounced some more. "Silence is the only one who knows what this is. But the Berkeley professor explained to everyone how any kind of digital storage innovation could totally change the capacity of computers. He also explained that he had gotten just enough hints from Silence's father to believe it was real. The only question in his mind was whether Silence actually knew enough to fully explain it and fill in the technical details. Now, here's where it gets exciting!" Henrietta's eyes glowed.

"Silence pulled out her pencil and did a quick little drawing on a piece of paper. It had some computer symbols and some diagrams and some other stuff that made no sense to me. But you should have seen the professor. He stared at it like a kid seeing an elephant for the first time. He has these long fingers and even longer fingernails. He pointed to part of the drawing and spoke to Silence. He said, 'This concept here. You know how it would work?' And Silence did that funny thing where she bends her head down and turns to the side. But everyone could see her reach out and give his arm a little push. So the professor put that long skinny finger of his on another part of her diagram and asked her something about algorithms. And she pushed again. Anyway, this went on a couple more times and she did another drawing and suddenly the professor stopped. He turned to all of us. His face was flushed. I still remember his exact words. He said, 'Ladies and gentlemen, I am convinced this young woman has information that could transform the computer business.'"

Henrietta did a little pirouette in the sand after she said it. "Can you believe it? Then the lawyer and the investors talked about how a basic business plan could work and they signed something called an Agreement-in-Principle.

"Of course, there are uncountable details to work out, and Marlette has asked me to help find some additional financial and legal experts to look after Silence's interests. But the end result looks like a new company will be formed to market and license the technology. And Silence will own a big piece of the stock!"

"A computer career and a lot of money, too," I said.

"Yes! Can you stand it?"

Just then, Marlette and Silence appeared across the beach where the path came from the parking lot. Marlette's grin was visible at a distance. So, too, was Silence's frown.

"I probably don't need to mention it," Henrietta said in a low voice, "but remember that Silence is not, shall we say, fluent in social situations."

"I'm just happy she came," Street said. "She's been through hell. Anyone would have trouble facing the world after that."

"Owen!" Marlette called out as they got within speaking distance. The warrior's countenance was submerged beneath a huge smile. "What can I say?" She dropped Silence's hand, trotted the last few steps and gave me a hug as if to stop my breathing.

Marlette released me, and I turned to her daughter.

"Hello, Silence."

She looked down to my left. Her face showed worry and fear. One hand was clasped over the other wrist, holding it in a white-knuckle grip. Despite her long shirt sleeves, I could see the tightness in her arm muscles and the tension that radiated throughout her body.

Although Silence looked much better than when we found her on the canyon edge a week and a half before, she was very thin and her skin had the reddish color that comes from abrasions. It was probably left over from many nights of thrashing on the rough wool blankets that had been her only bedclothes in captivity.

I considered whether to hold out my hand to shake hers, but decided that would make her even more uncomfortable. Instead I spoke in my most casual voice. "I'm so glad you could come, Silence. You remember Street Casey. And of course you've met Tillie."

Silence stared at the beach and dug her heel into the sand.

I said, "We've got corn on the grill, drinks in the cooler, chips in the basket and burgers on the way."

Silence looked down the beach in both directions. Her frown turned to a scowl.

I said, "Silence, I know Spot will be glad to see you. He's off playing tag with a seagull. Let me call him." I turned and stepped a distance away so I wouldn't hurt anyone's ears, put my thumb and forefinger in my mouth and did the loud whistle that Spot associates with treats. "That might bring him."

We all turned and watched as a speck down the beach grew into charging dog. I stepped in front of Silence to ease any anxiety she might have about whether he would come to a complete stop or charge through like a runaway horse.

He made a quick stop, and sand flew, although most of it hit me and not the others. "Good boy," I said. "Sit, and I'll open the chips."

It's amazing what a dog will do for a potato chip. He sat down, eyes focused on every movement I made, ears quivering. I pulled out the bag, aware of Silence as I did so. She stood off to the side, watching Spot directly as she never did any human.

I took out a big chip and balanced it on Spot's nose. He

went cross-eyed as he tried to focus on it. Twin streams of saliva flowed from his jowls. I waited a long, long ten seconds until I finally said, "Okay!"

It is like a bear trap snapping shut. You can't actually follow the motion. One moment, the chip balanced on Spot's nose. The next moment, there was a loud snapping sound and a string of saliva flying through the air and the chip was gone.

Then Spot saw Silence. He walked over to her, gentle as an old man. She stood rigid, hands and arms stiff at her side. Spot stuck his nose under her right hand and pushed it up. Silence took a step back, fearful, but willing herself to stay calm. Spot nudged her hand again, then again more forcefully. When she still wouldn't pet him, he opened his mouth and lightly nibbled on her fingers.

Finally, she relented, reached out and gave him a tentative pet. He held motionless and half-shut his eyes as if he'd never felt anything so delicious. Silence pet him more vigorously. Spot shifted around to her side and took a step forward. She followed, still petting. He started walking slowly and she stayed with him. In a few moments he was trotting and then running. Silence ran after him.

Spot loped around, ran at Silence and dodged at the last moment. Soon they were both charging around. As they circled and played, Silence's grin was unmistakable.

I turned to look at Marlette. Her grin was unmistakable, too.

Later, after we'd all eaten burgers and corn and Silence was more relaxed, I turned to her.

"Street and I brought something for you," I said.

Silence didn't react.

Street held out a paper bag, a big grin on her face.

Silence hesitated, then took the bag and pulled out the leather sketchbook and the set of pencils in the metal box. She paid particular attention to the metal box, opening the lid and running her hands over the pencils, ten of them arranged in order of hardness.

I gestured at Silence in that universal "come-along" motion. "Silence, I want to ask you a question. Will you please come down the beach a bit?" As I turned and began to walk away I saw a look of doubt on Marlette's face. She was shaking her head as if to say it would never work.

I slowly walked down the sand about five yards. Turning a little, I saw that Silence had stepped a small distance away from the group. Spot charged toward me and flew on past. "Just down here," I called out to her, pointing down the beach in front of me. I turned away and walked another twenty yards until I was well out of earshot of the others. Without glancing back I sat down on the beach. Spot came running by again. "Spot, come here," I said, pointing at the sand next to me. He flew by me at high speed, taunting me, sand flying off his feet and into the air. "Spot, come!" I called out again, aware that he was my secret to attracting kids and adults as well. He looped around, did another quick-stop, and reluctantly lay down in the sand next to me.

I waited without turning my head.

After a minute, I heard a soft rustle of paper. I turned to see Silence standing there, holding the paper bag in front of her with both hands. The sun made her hair glow and lit the sharp angles of her face as it would a chiseled sienna-colored arrowhead. She appeared to be staring across the lake.

"Come sit next to Spot." I gave him a light smack on his back. He rolled away from me, onto his side, moaning a little. He dropped his head to the sand, jowls flopping loose, and straightened his legs, pushing hard against me, his nails digging into my thigh.

After a time, Silence sat down on the other side of Spot. She carefully set the paper bag on the sand and reached out with both arms. Her hands touched Spot, roamed his back and shoulders and then reached around his neck. She leaned forward until she could wriggle her arms under his neck, prying his head a few inches off the sand and gave him a hug that would strangle a smaller dog.

Spot moaned again and began wagging, his tail making sand fly.

Slowly, Silence released him and picked up the bag. She pulled out the sketchbook and pencils. Moving with the care and precision of a surgeon, she flipped open the cover of the sketchbook and set it on her lap. Then, she opened the metal case and selected a pencil.

With her left hand, Silence made a few test strokes on the corner of the paper. She put the pencil back and selected a softer one, then began sketching. With astonishing speed, she blocked in the basics of a scene and then filled in details until it became a clear, almost photographic, picture. Suddenly, she stopped drawing and handed the sketchbook across Spot's prostrate form. She didn't look at me, but kept her eyes turned toward my feet.

I took the sketchbook from her.

It was a picture of Street and me, standing on the beach, holding out the paper bag to Silence. Silence stood before us, her hands clasped together in front of her. Her head was slightly bowed in a gesture of gratitude.

I handed the book back, letting it rest for a moment on Spot's back. "You're very welcome," I said.

Silence turned to the next page and began another drawing. In less than a minute, she handed me the sketchbook. Again, she stared at my feet. As I took the book and studied the drawing, she pet Spot, apparently ignoring me.

The drawing showed the room in the house where she'd been held prisoner. It was similar to the letter drawing she'd sent, but this time, in the background, looking small and frail, was a picture of her sitting cross-legged on the floor, hands tied together, looking terrified.

I said, "Few people ever have to face the situation you were in. But the important thing about fear is how a person responds." I slowly set the sketchbook on top of Spot's chest. "You sent out those letters when the men weren't looking. Those letters made it so we eventually found you."

Silence picked the book up off of Spot, flipped to the next

page, and then set it back down on Spot. She began another drawing, this time using Spot's body as a desk. He wagged his tail twice.

This drawing was much more elaborate, but still took
only a few minutes. When she was done she handed the sketchbook over.

The drawing showed a classroom with a dozen students
at desks. One wall was covered with shelves of books. The students looked to the side or down to the floor. None of them
seemed to pay attention. One had his head down on the desk.
Another was digging a pen into his desktop as if to drill a hole.
One was in the rear corner, spinning in a blur. They all exhibited
some aspect of autism disorder. In front of the classroom stood
Silence, holding a book in her right hand and drawing a picture on
the blackboard with her left hand.

Still looking at the drawing, I said, "Silence, I think you
will succeed at nearly anything you try. And yes, you would be a
very good teacher." I handed the sketchbook back. "In fact, there
is one thing I'd like you to teach me."

She took the book from me and turned a little toward
me, still not looking at my face, but not at my feet, either. Her face
had a strange questioning look. Probably no one had ever asked
her to teach them anything.

"I saw your mother's videos. She wanted me to get to
know something of you and Charlie. I watched the DVD a few
times and each time I got to the part where you were spinning, I
thought, I want to do that. I want to feel what that's like. It looks
fun. But here's what happens."

I got to my feet. Spot jumped up, too, ready for something more exciting than playing easel to an artist.

I started to turn. "I'm okay when I go slow. But when I
speed up, I lose my balance. Like this." I turned around a few
times. Then I sped up, but the world tipped and I began to fall. I
hit the sand, sprawling onto my side. Spot leaped on top of me,
and, as I pushed him off, I saw Silence laughing. Not a laugh like
the rest of us make, but a laugh nonetheless.

I stood up and said, "What am I doing wrong? How do I

keep from losing my balance?"

Silence came over to me. She didn't look at me, but she reached out and grabbed my right knee and made an up-and-down motion with her hands. Then she stepped away and turned in the sand, making an exaggerated stepping motion with her right foot. Each time she came around, she pushed off with her right foot, stepping in the same place. As she sped up a little, her foot began to hit the sand as if slapping it, and I realized that concentrating on hitting the ground with my foot, once every rotation, was the key.

Silence stopped and stood still, facing the lake and the mountains looming above the distant shore. She stood leaning slightly, arms bent like a sprinter about to take off, ready to demonstrate again.

I stood next to her. Silence rotated, putting her right foot down and pushing off. I tried it with her, matching her timing. We moved very slowly at first. After I got a rhythm and sense of movement, Silence sped up a little. I sped up as well. In a minute I was going at a good rate and I hadn't fallen over. In fact, the balance came to me, and the motion made sense.

Spot bounded around us, wagging and barking. In the distance, Marlette and Henrietta and Street and Diamond and Tillie were all in a row, staring at us.

I focused on the beats of our motion, our right feet punching the sand as Silence and I turned faster and faster and then faster still until the world went away a little and there was only the rush of cool fall wind and the blurred sound of distant laughter and the million streaking sparkles of sunlight on the water as we spun like crazed tops. And each time I came around, I saw a quick snapshot of Silence, head bowed, hair flung out like a horse's tail on the final turn, and on her face, hidden from the world, facing the sand, was the grin, giddy and lip-stretching, broad and deep and mischievous. Private and silent.

writ

Mc

ere they

Owen